01/2012

Praise for *The Map Across Time*:

"The novel is fast-paced and tightly plotted, which means that the reader will quickly be drawn into the complex twists and turns of the story and, in fairy tale tradition, led toward a surprising yet satisfying conclusion."

—*Publisher's Weekly*

"*The Map Across Time* is a fairy tale in the classic sense of the term. As J.R.R. Tolkien pointed out, fairy stories serve to draw the reader into a mythical world that conveys the joy of the gospel. Lakin's tale meets this noble task head-on. Her novel is not only interspersed with the Bible (including biblical Hebrew!), it is a retelling of the Bible's overarching narrative. Not many Christian novels manage to blend great storytelling and scriptural truth—but here is a book that does!"

—**Bryan Litfin,** author of *The Sword* and *The Gift*

"[*The Map across Time* and *The Wolf of Tebron*] are set in a mythical world that is permeated with a sense of both good and evil—a world in which the leading protagonists are required to battle not only external forces that seem to be beyond their control, but also their own inner demons of fear, anxiety and self-doubt. The tales are most definitely coming-of-age novels, in which the well-rounded characters come increasingly into their own as they both literally and metaphorically navigate their way across a landscape that is lovingly, though at times fearfully, depicted."

—**Lois Henderson,** Bookpleasures.com

Praise for *The Wolf of Tebron*:

"The Gates of Heaven promises to be one of the best fantasy series to come alc _____ is of this potential is its ability _____ and leave you saying, 'jus _____ ter.' That has happened t _____ ronicles of Narnia,

J.R.R Tolkien's *The Lord of the Rings,* and Susan Cooper's The Dark is Rising sequence. Now C. S. Lakin has done the same with The Gates of Heaven."

—Jonathon Svendsen, Narniafans.com

"Much richer and deeper than traditional tales from fairy-land . . . what Lakin does so well with her fairy tale is to provide images which remind us of what God has done for us."

—Mark Sommer, Examiner.com

"*The Wolf of Tebron* is a grand, sweeping tale of one man's journey to the truth and to rescue his true love. This fanciful, whimsical, wild tale can truly inspire you to perseverance—highly recommended."

—Grace Bridges, Splashdown Reviews

"It's a thoroughly enjoyable adventure story, with exotic settings, unpredictable turns, a terrifying enemy, and unexpected humor. Lakin's work is stylistically beautiful. The exotic locales are vivid, from dark north to burning desert to misty jungle. I found myself looking forward to each leg of Joran's journey just so I could experience another part of her story world."

—Rachel Starr Thomson, Little Dozen Press

"This book is filled with beautiful literary allegory and symbolism. I enjoyed the fairy tale world C. S. Lakin created for her characters to navigate. I love how the story unfolded in the end and look forward to more in The Gates of Heaven series."

—Jill Williamson, author of *To Darkness Fled*

"Lakin has masterful control of the writing craft, developing her characters and drawing the reader to see the world through their eyes."

—Phyllis Wheeler, *The Christian Fantasy Review*

THE LAND OF DARKNESS

A FAIRY TALE BY
C. S. LAKIN

LIVING
INK
BOOKS
Writing Worth Reading

The Land of Darkness
Volume 3 in The Gates of Heaven® series

Copyright © 2011 by C. S. Lakin
Published by Living Ink Books, an imprint of
AMG Publishers, Inc.
6815 Shallowford Rd.
Chattanooga, Tennessee 37421

Print Edition	ISBN 13: 978-0-89957-891-0	ISBN 10: 0-89957-891-8
EPUB Edition	ISBN 13: 978-1-61715-249-8	ISBN 10: 1-61715-249-8
Mobi Edition	ISBN 13: 978-1-61715-250-4	ISBN 10: 1-61715-250-1
E-PDF Edition	ISBN 13: 978-1-61715-251-1	ISBN 10: 1-61715-251-X

First Printing—October 2011

THE GATES OF HEAVEN is a registered trademark of AMG Publishers.

Cover designed by Chris Garborg at Garborg Design, Savage, Minnesota, and Megan Erin Miller.

Cover Illustration by Gary Lippincott
(http://www.garylippincott.com/).

Interior design and typesetting by Reider Publishing Services, West Hollywood, California.

Edited and proofread by Pat Matuszak, Christy Graeber, and Rick Steele.

C. S. Lakin welcomes comments, ideas, and impressions at her Websites:
www.cslakin.com and **www.gatesofheavenseries.com**.

The Bridge across Forever, by Transatlantic (© Morse, Prince, 2001). Reprinted with permission. All rights reserved.

All Scripture quoted in the discussion section in the back of this book, unless otherwise indicated, is taken from the New Revised Standard Version Bible, copyright 1989, Division of Christian Education of the National Council of the Churches of Christ in the United States of America. Used by permission. All rights reserved.

Scripture marked NKJV is taken from the New King James Version. Copyright © 1982 by Thomas Nelson, Inc. Used by permission. All rights reserved.

Please note that Scripture verses quoted by characters in the novel are paraphrased as the author deemed appropriate for the story.

Printed in the United States of America
16 15 14 13 12 11 –V– 7 6 5 4 3 2 1

THE BRIDGE ACROSS FOREVER

There's a bridge made of light
That crosses between death and life
Where shadows walk in the sun
And desperate lovers run

One day a child and an angel
Stood on either side
Of a magic river
That there was no crossing
But as they tried
The water began to rise
Then they raised their eyes

And as the river fell away
They built a bridge across forever
Between tomorrow and today
There is a bridge across forever

We will meet again someday
On the bridge across forever
I know that we will find our way
To the bridge across forever
Between tomorrow and today
There is a bridge across forever

I know that we will find our way
To the bridge across forever

—Transatlantic

PROLOGUE

THE TRAVELER wiped a hand across his weary eyes. He looked down at his dust-laden boots as his feet touched a much harder surface than the dirt path they had trodden upon for the last three days. Stooping, he brushed grit away from the path to reveal ochre stones beneath, and his mind puzzled at the pattern of cobbles spreading out before him. He raised his eyes, straining to define his surroundings in the last tint of twilight. A towering, crumbling edifice of the same ochre stone confronted him but provided no answers. He straightened, weary, achy, and confused.

As he stepped cautiously across what appeared to be an abandoned lane, the cool night breeze dried his damp hair and sent a shiver down his neck. But more than cold wind caused his knees to shake uncontrollably. Uneasiness had plagued him the moment he entered the shambles of what looked like a once-thriving village. He could make out the remains of finely crafted stonework: corniced walls of buildings, corrals for animals, even a nearly intact archway adorning the entrance to a land that must have once boasted a beautiful, wide avenue running the length of its commercial center. In the failing light, he ran his fingers along inlaid scrolling of ebony and oak, polished wood that wrapped doorways in designs of leaf and flower. A sudden breeze from the mountains in the north carried the scent of snow-covered pine forests, and encircled him in a flurry that made him grasp his cloak and wrap it tightly around his neck.

The young man knew he was lost, for this place was not on any map. His jaw clenched in anxiety and his throat felt dry as road gravel; he had hoped to find warm shelter for the night, a hearty meal, and a soft goose-down mattress at an accommodating inn. Instead, he heard eerie, discomfiting sounds carried on the air, flitting around his ears. He stopped, every nerve heightened, and pressed his back against the wooden lintel of a rotted doorway that led to a field of tumbled stones and a tangle of weeds. He closed his eyes and sifted through the sounds, hoping for familiarity: crickets, nocturnal animals, even wolves, whose howling would at least remind him he was still in his world and not some strange aberrant one.

His heart pounded in expectation but was not consoled. A soft voice, high in pitch and achingly sad, drifted on the suffocating night air. His gut wrenched at the anguish underlying indecipherable words, which tugged at him and made his feet move of their own volition. Confused, he found himself running, his boots clacking against the uneven roadway beneath him.

He passed a broken, waterless fountain at the center of a paved square, saw shadows dart through darkened doorways. On a pedestal stood a robed figure carved from dark malachite rock, missing limbs, and parts of its face had been chipped away. A weak voice, deep within his mind, yelled at him to run, but both the words and the urgency fragmented before he could recognize them as his own.

His feet took him down one constricting lane after another. He lost track of time, of his exhaustion, of his fear. More voices, muddled and pressing, swelled around him like a tide, attacking and receding, entangling him like a carp in a fisher's net. Then he stopped abruptly.

Before him hung the remains of a wrought-iron gate that swung loosely from a wooden post. Beyond the gate the cobbled street ended, and perhaps the very world itself came to naught, for the young man trembled at the sight unfolding before him.

An impenetrable darkness, much darker than night, gathered around him, expectantly watching. Shadows like dreams skittered across the ground at his feet. He heard the rustle of branches and took a hesitant step, pushing aside the creaking gate. Wisps of pitch-blackness reached out to him, swirled around him, coaxing, urging. A child's voice startled him by calling his name. He thought he saw a flash of a tiny hand reaching out of the gloom, but the surge of blackness shifting and oozing before him quickly devoured it.

Now, his mind raced with a dozen warnings, but they came too late. For he was a stranger to this part of the world. He had never heard of the tales whispered in dark corners over mugs of ale, or told as harsh threats to badly behaved children. He had set out, as many do, to find his fortune. But now he would find only misfortune, for fate or carelessness or stupidity—it didn't matter which—had led him to the Land of Darkness.

Shepherds from the surrounding hills knew not to venture near the ruins of Antolae, the ancient name given to the once-thriving region. *Shamma* was the common name spoken with bated breath, meaning "city of destruction" in a long-forgotten tongue. If one of their flock strayed near, they surrendered it to a certain fate. They did not worry their herding dogs would follow, for venturing within one league of Antolae, the curs would whine and whimper and slink back to their owners to cower beneath their legs. It was unfortunate that this young traveler had no dog to warn him, and that the sheepherders had only last month moved their flocks farther south to warmer winter climes. The entire week that he had journeyed across a windswept, barren land, following a rutted cart road, he saw no one who could have given him warning. It was too bad indeed, for all the reassuring promises he had given to his aging mother of his safe return would not be kept. She, along with his younger brothers and sisters, would forever wonder in misery what tragedy had befallen him.

All emotion emptied from the traveler's mind and heart, leaving nothing but a dim curiosity that nudged him forward. Now, close, he heard bells jingling and sheep baaing, footsteps clacking briskly across stone, a pail sloshing with water, a giggle, chickens cackling. His heart warmed at the sounds of everyday life, sounds that removed any last vestige of hesitancy.

He stepped into the maw of blackness as if he had been swallowed whole; he left no footprint behind, nor any trace that he had crossed an invisible line. Yet, even if there had remained any sign of his passage, what good would it have done him? No one who entered that bewitched land ever came back out.

• PART ONE •

"A Circle upon a Circle

within a Circle . . ."

ONE

CALLEN FELT Beren's eyes boring into the back of his neck long before he smelled the burly man's pipe tobacco. A tendril of smoke wended upward in front of the block of chestnut wood Callen leaned over, a rich aromatic scent that permeated the huge workroom and often lingered in his clothing and hair for days.

"Go a little lighter with the deep gouge, Callen lad," the master craftsman told him. "Here." He took the tool from Callen's hand and set his pipe in the wooden bowl on the worktable. "You've got to set your wrist so, or it'll get away from you. Especially working with the grain, as in this instance."

Callen watched closely as Beren's thick hand pressed the gouge along the penciled line on the wood. It swam through the grain like a knife through butter, leaving a smooth, even channel. A thin ribbon of dark wood twisted and fell to the planked floor of the shop. He pulled back and gestured to Callen with bright encouraging eyes. "See? Ah, your gouge is nice and sharp too, so the more need to ply with a steady hand."

Callen nodded and took the gouge back. Beren stepped past Callen's stool and studied the sketch pinned to the wall. He played with his thick, short beard, as he often did when thinking deeply. "Ambitious design. But it's coming along nicely."

Beren raised his voice and addressed the other apprentices in the room. His eyes lit on the lanky red-haired youth sitting at a workbench by the front door. "Dariel, this is why I harp on you young'uns about sharpening your tools. Callen here spends a good portion of time with his slip stone and, in the end, saves time and waste." Beren laid a firm hand on Callen's shoulder. "A master apprentice like Callen knows the value of a finely honed tool. You'd best follow his example." Beren winked at Callen and strolled over to another student hunched over a workbench.

Callen examined the scrolled design he'd been tackling for the last few days. He had copied the pattern from a spandrel off the famous bridge in Sherbourne that crossed the river Heresh. With this lull in orders, Beren had him teaching the beginners and, in his spare time, Callen challenged himself with difficult designs he gleaned from the stacks of old parchments on Beren's shelves.

He had spent much of his life carving furniture and small pieces like walking stick handles and ornamental bowls back in his home village of Tebron, but he yearned to craft something grander, more dramatic. Few if any took such an interest in ancient architectural styles, but Callen was enamored with the artful beauty and elegance of line found in the drawings of old buildings and bridges. This triangular piece, nearly two feet across, displayed entwining vines and swirls of interlocking ropes that gathered in the center around a circle of sycamore leaves. The channels ran deep and narrow, challenging Callen's steady hand and skill.

Eliab stood and stretched kinks from his back, and came to Callen's side. "That's unbelievable, Cal." His sawdust-ridden curls shook along with his head. "How are you able to do this?" Eliab picked up a stool and set it next to Callen so he could watch him work.

"Practice, that's how. You'll get there, if you apply yourself," Callen said, "and have the talent." Eliab and the other four students were first order, so Beren had them crafting simple things, like turned legs for chairs and blind mortises for hinged cupboard doors. Callen had been here the longest—four years—and was therefore given the more complicated custom jobs that came into the shop. Because he had spent much of his life in the forests felling trees with his brother, Felas, he had entered his apprenticeship later than most students seeking a trade. To the boys around him, Callen was like an older brother, and they treated him as such—with respect and admiration, laced with practical jokes.

Callen thought how this new student reminded him so much of his brother Joran. He missed his three brothers and hadn't taken a break to see them in over a year. Only Felas had been able to visit last spring, and only for a few days. Living in the Logan Valley, or Loganvale as the locals called it, was so different from Tebron. Instead of towering trees and clinging fog, Callen enjoyed waking each morning to sunshine and warm breezes fragrant with the rich fertile loam that Loganvale was famous for. Farmers in this oak-strewn valley of gently rolling hills grew every kind of crop imaginable—from barley to hay to bogberries—and carted their produce out to distant towns and villages Callen had never heard of. Wine pressed from grapes in this region far excelled that of grapes grown elsewhere. The beer brewed from Loganvale hops tasted brighter and satisfied even the meanest thirst on a hot summer day. Now, spoiled by such year-round warmth and abundance, he wondered if he could ever live in Tebron again.

As Callen picked up his gouge, the front door blew open. Wood shavings flicked up from the floor and tables and danced in the air. Beren swung his head around as his wife, Laera, stepped inside the shop and let her eyes adjust to the dimmer light. A swath of bright sunlight spilled onto the floor, and Callen smelled hay waft in from the newly harvested fields. Through the open door he watched a horse-drawn carriage pass, hooves and wheels kicking up dust that drifted into the shop.

"Laera," Beren yelled, "kindly shut that door behind you before that dirt sticks to every bit of fresh varnish."

Laera, her dark eyes wide and excited, shut the door and rushed over to Beren's side with her full skirts swishing on the floor. A rope of black hair lay over one of her shoulders, braided—Callen noted—much like the pattern carved in the wood block in front of him. Callen thought Laera was the most striking woman he had ever met. With her creamy skin and natural poise, he imagined she had been breathtaking in her younger days. Even at this age—Callen didn't dare guess how old she was—she radiated a youthful energy and inquisitive spirit that caused all the students to grow enamored with her. Never having had children of her own, Laera adopted all who came to apprentice with her husband, spoiling them with mountains of delicious food and fussing over the slightest cut she found on anyone's finger. Many of the younger students, first time away from home, found Laera's comforting words a remedy for homesickness. Even Callen let her baby him from time to time, although at thirty-one he hardly needed coddling. A twinge of guilt poked him as he thought about his own mother back in Tebron in the care of his brother Maylon. Callen was overdue for a visit home, even if his mother now failed to recognize him and most other people.

"Have you heard this latest travesty?" Laera whispered to Beren, the fierce expression in her eyes pinning him in place. Callen turned his attention back to his carving, catching a quick, questioning glance from Eliab. The younger boy followed Callen's hint and pretended he didn't hear the scathing words pouring from Laera's mouth. Beren stood a few feet away, his boots planted and his hands on his hips. Although only a couple of inches taller than his wife, Beren drew himself up like a bear and tucked in his chin.

"Let me guess—more railings about Ka'rel's wife, no doubt. Woman, you just have to leave it alone."

From the corner of his eye, Callen caught a flash of Laera's hand grabbing Beren's sleeve. "Beren, ever since Ka'rel married that witch, the manor has become a madhouse."

Beren sighed. "You've run into Azar at market." It was a statement, gleaned, apparently, from the tone in Laera's voice. "If you're so concerned, you owe it to your brother-in-law to tell him to his face."

Laera snorted and pursed her lips together. "You know he won't see me. He told me never to step foot in his home until I had kind words for Huldah. Can't you see what a spell she's cast over him? He nearly slobbers at her feet!"

"Laera, it's his life. You had no right to criticize his choice for a bride."

"—Whom he married only *weeks* after M'lynn's death. Come now, Beren, even you must think it odd for Ka'rel, who takes months just to choose between rye and wheat for his upper field, to rush into such a marriage." Laera lowered her voice and her face softened. "I'm worried about Jadiel. Azar has seen the way Huldah treats her. He says she beats the poor girl."

Beren pried Laera's fingers from his shirt and took her arm. Callen could tell by the look on Beren's face that he was growing weary of this conversation.

But Beren's intolerant look soon melted into a sweet smile. "Come now, love, you know Ka'rel's a proper father. He dotes on the girl, and he has the richest estate in all the vale. He gives her everything her heart desires. Surely he wouldn't let Jad come to harm, would he?"

He led her to the door and stopped. "I know you love Jadiel, and that you grieve with her over M'lynn's death. Nothing is harder than losing a mother at such a tender age." He brushed a hand across her cheek and wiped away tears. "But, Laera," Beren said softly, "you mustn't begrudge Ka'rel's comfort in a new wife. If she makes him happy—"

"Then why choose a stranger over a local woman? No one knows where Huldah comes from, what life she left behind. She just blew in with the wind one day and swept Ka'rel off his feet. He's either lost his mind or she's enchanted him somehow."

Beren cocked his head. "Woman, you have a wild imagination."

"And Jadiel hasn't visited us once this year. Don't you find that odd? Aren't you the least bit worried over your niece?"

"Enough." Beren let out a heavy sigh. "We'll take a ride to Northfold Manor. Pay a friendly visit. Will that suffice?"

A rush of relief filled Laera's eyes. She cracked open the door and leaned over and kissed his ruddy cheek. "Tomorrow," she said, leaving no room for dispute.

Beren watched the door close behind his wife. Callen let out a breath and turned to Eliab, who appeared afraid to move. "Well," Callen muttered, "back to work."

They both looked over at Beren. Callen noted the scowl on his mentor's face.

Eliab got up from the stool. "I think I'll go practice on my lathe."

Callen nodded, noting the somber mood draped over the room. He turned his attention back to his drawing, then picked up his gouge, and with a slight adjustment of his wrist, dug into the smooth, grainy wood and carved a perfect, deep channel.

TWO

JADIEL THREW herself back onto the soft covers of her bed and let the autumn light bathe her face and neck. The smell of cut hay hung moist and heavy in the air. Fall was usually her favorite time of year, a time of bountiful harvest. But fall also reminded her of the apple tarts she used to make with her mother and the carriage rides they took through the woods where every leaf was ablaze with golden colors. The brisk hint of winter in the breeze coming through her window only sharpened her keen awareness of her mother's absence. She had tried to find solace in a walk along the creek, but it hadn't helped to alleviate her sorrow. Nothing could do that.

She let her eyes drift across the shelf of porcelain dolls her mother had bought her over the years. They stared down at her with glassy, empty eyes—not a one smiling—as if wondering why she neglected them so. How many hours had she spent dressing her dolls in their frilly smocks and untangling their long locks with the tiny brush she kept in her dresser? Not that many months ago she had found happiness in such simple play. And on her dresser lay the small silver flute she used to play in the evenings for her parents. She hadn't touched it since the day her mother died. Now, nothing brought a smile to her face except her treasured moments with Papa, and those were growing rare now that he had remarried.

Just the thought of her stepmother sent a shiver down Jadiel's neck. It was bad enough to lose her mother. Why did Papa have to go and marry someone else? A deep-seated ache returned to her gut. She wanted to share in her father's joy, but the hurt pounded at her. Why couldn't it just be the two of them, comforting each other and grieving together? Marrying Huldah had been a slap in her face. Had Papa forgotten Mama so soon?

Jadiel felt hot tears run down her cheeks. She chastised herself. Her father had always been devoted to her mother, loved her more than the world. Her death had shattered his heart. For the first time in her twelve years she had seen Papa, a man usually confident and capable, completely fall apart and wander the estate like a foundling. Jadiel would watch him at the table picking at his food, staring into space, forgetting where he was. In a few months, he had grown gaunt and feeble, wasting away from grief. Maybe he needed a wife. Jadiel didn't understand that need, but she did understand the pain of loss. No one could ever replace her mother—and certainly not someone as vile as Huldah.

Her mother had been dead now nine months, and the wound still felt as raw as the day Jadiel had heard the news of the accident. A runaway horse in the marketplace had trampled her down. Jadiel cringed, and more tears squeezed from her eyes. She fought to push the image of pounding hooves from her mind, but it battered her, replaying over and over.

Jadiel heard heavy footsteps on the tile floor down the hall. Huldah and her two arrogant daughters—Kinna and Ramah—had returned. Back from shopping, no doubt. Spending as many silvers as humanly possible in one short afternoon. Jadiel grimaced. All those years she had longed for a brother or sister, and now she had inherited the two most unfriendly, mean-spirited sisters possible. Kinna was fifteen and Ramah seventeen. All they did was whine and complain, fussing over their clothing and wild red hair, trying to make themselves look beautiful but failing miserably. With their big hooked noses and pointy chins, they looked more like crows than girls. Jadiel chuckled. But their lack of beauty wasn't the main thing that kept the sisters from attracting husbands. How they clamored for suitors to call on them at the manor. Did they think that with their wily ways and heavy face paint they could hide their petty temperaments and selfish prattling?

Jadiel reached over to her dresser and picked up her ivory hand mirror, a gift from her mother. She looked in the glass at her tear-streaked face, and with the matching ivory comb smoothed out the thick black hair that cascaded down her shoulders. Her mother had always told her she was a beautiful child, but also reminded her that the more important beauty lay beneath the skin. True beauty came from within and radiated outward. Jadiel ran a finger down her pale soft cheek. What did she care if she was beautiful? How could that help her survive this miserable life? How could she go on each day like this—missing her mother so terribly and suffering such harsh treatment at Huldah's hands?

As Jadiel questioned her reflection in the mirror, the silver surface of the glass shimmered. In the background behind her, confined inside the mirror, her mother's face appeared, smiling the warm, loving smile that Jadiel so missed.

Mama! she whispered. *Help me. How am I to go on without you?*

Jadiel watched, enraptured, as the image of her mother drew close behind her and stroked Jadiel's hair with her hand. Jadiel felt the gossamer touch on her head as a ray of warm sunlight. She smelled her mother's rose water, inhaling it greedily. Her mother, so radiant and pale, spoke softly.

"Jadiel, my sweetest, do not fret. Things hidden in darkness will come to light. You are strong and clever; you will find a way. Know I will always love you . . ."

Huldah's voice startled her, causing her to drop the mirror onto her bed.

"Lazy child! Look at you, preening yourself when you should be working. Your father will be home soon. Go set the table." Jadiel cast down her eyes and scurried off the bed. She dared a glance at Huldah's angry face. Her stepmother clenched her teeth and slapped Jadiel on the back of her head as she passed by. Jadiel bit her lip to keep from crying.

As she placed dishes on the large oak dining table, Jadiel heard Kinna and Ramah arguing in their room down the hall. Jadiel rarely heard either of them speak a kind word to the other, or to anyone else for that matter. They snapped disrespectfully at her father's care-taker, Azar, and yelled at the cook whenever their food wasn't per-fectly prepared. The eggs were too salty; the fish too bland. If they were so picky, why didn't they make their own meals?

Jadiel had always worked hard on the estate alongside her father, helping him buy and plant seed, hitch up the plow horses, muck the stables. Even when his fortune grew and he could afford to hire workers and servants, Jadiel still accompanied him to mar-ket and on deliveries. Up until her mother died, she had joined him on all his trips encompassing the entire vale—from Eastfold to Westfold, even as far south as Swiftwater. And he never minded her riding alone to Kettlebro to visit Aunt Laera and Uncle Beren. But Huldah had put a quick end to all that, insisting she stay home and help with the household chores. And her father agreed!

She soon learned that "helping" with the chores meant mostly doing them herself. She never saw her stepsisters lift a finger to clean their own room or carry in firewood, and Huldah only barked orders at everyone in a rude, condescending tone. Just look-ing at the faces of the workers told Jadiel they were as displeased by Papa's marriage as she was. Once, her home had been a joyful, peaceful place. Not anymore.

As she positioned the cutlery beside the plates, she heard the jingle of breeching outside on the circular cobbled driveway. Her father was home! She rushed to the front door and saw him alighting from the carriage buckboard and handing the reins to Azar.

"Papa!" Ka'rel looked up the steps to where Jadiel stood and gave a little wave. Just as she meant to run down to him, she felt a tug on the collar of her dress. Huldah yanked her back into the house and pinned her with a hostile look.

Jadiel, furious, stared back. Then something odd caught her eye.

From a distance Huldah could be called a beauty, with her streaming bronze hair and delicate features. Jadiel guessed Huldah was younger than her mother had been, for she hadn't a wrinkle on her face or neck, not a blemish anywhere. Huldah's hands were smooth and adorned with long fingers and painted nails. Her figure was a slender hourglass. Luxurious eyelashes hovered over deep, alluring eyes. Every tooth white and in perfect alignment. Jadiel often watched Huldah flash her smile and cause men to stutter. Only Azar seemed immune to her charms, but maybe such attractions failed to stir men of advanced years.

She had never been this close to Huldah's face before. Now, Jadiel saw something underneath all that beauty, as if a thin veneer coated Huldah's face, transparent enough to see through. Her stepmother's skin gave off a strange, pungent scent, which made Jadiel grow dizzy. Jadiel recoiled, puzzled. Huldah's eyes widened and then narrowed.

"What are you staring at, you little brat?"

Jadiel could not take her eyes off her stepmother's features. Wavering under the facade of Huldah's perfectly shaped nose was a bulbous, flaring one with little black hairs protruding from her nostrils. Her pale, unblemished cheeks turned to wrinkled, weathered skin, with pockmarks and scars and a big brown wart under the left eye. Her fiery mane looked like a translucent scarf covering hair that was white and stringy, splaying out from her lumpy, misshapen head. Jadiel gasped.

Huldah slapped Jadiel's cheek hard with the palm of her hand, and suddenly all the strange images vanished. The young, beautiful stepmother took a step back and scrutinized Jadiel's disturbed face. Jadiel thought she saw a flash of fear flit in Huldah's eyes, but it passed too quickly to be certain. They both turned their heads as Ka'rel skipped up the steps to the house.

Jadiel's father stomped the dust from his feet on the entry mat, then found her with his open arms. Huldah backed away and smoothed her hair. Odd, Jadiel could almost detect Huldah's hands trembling as she warily watched Jadiel ensconced in her father's embrace.

Jadiel lingered in his warm, strong arms, feeling his love pour through them straight into her heart. "Oh, Papa, how I've missed you!"

Ka'rel brushed a lock of straw-colored hair out of his eyes and grasped Jadiel's shoulders. He squatted down to meet her gaze. "Silly goose, you saw me at breakfast. Was that so long a time to be parted?"

"Even a minute is too long, Papa."

Ka'rel laughed warmly and tousled Jadiel's hair. "My gorgeous princess, you are right—it is agony to be away from you. Come." He straightened and took her hand. "I want to hear all about your day and what mischief you've been getting into."

Jadiel gleamed up at her father and let him pull her into the hallway. Out of the corner of her eye, she saw Huldah leaning against the threshold to the dining room. Her stepmother's voice came out syrupy.

"Ka'rel, my love."

Ka'rel stopped abruptly, as if a hand pressed against his chest. His head turned and he let go of Jadiel's fingers. Jadiel felt her face heat in anger, but she clamped her mouth shut.

Huldah sauntered over to Ka'rel, and with her swinging hip pushed Jadiel out of the way. She draped her arms over Ka'rel's shoulders and lowered her head coyly. "Don't you want to know how much *I've* missed you?"

Jadiel's mouth dropped open as her father's eyes glazed over. From where she stood, she could hear his breath catch in his throat. Jadiel cringed as she watched Huldah run a manicured finger through Ka'rel's neat beard and let it rest on his lips. Her father's bright, eager manner faded, leaving him paralyzed and unflinching, like some hypnotized quarry.

Finally, he opened his mouth. His words came out hoarse and fluttery. "How much—have you missed me?"

Huldah whispered something in Ka'rel's ear, then turned and smiled sweetly at Jadiel. There was no affection in her look.

Ka'rel's attention riveted onto Huldah's face; he forgot Jadiel was in the room. A chuckle echoed off the stone walls. Jadiel jerked her head around and saw her two stepsisters watching, their mouths twisted in amusement.

"Tell the cook we'll be a little late for dinner," Huldah said in a lilting, measured voice.

Jadiel shook her head in disbelief as she watched Huldah escort her father down the hall and up the stairs, as if leading a blind, feeble man. Anger welled up in her heart, mingling with the hurt of rejection. With clenched fists, she let the anger lift and carry her out the front door, down the stairs, and into the herb garden where she collapsed on the grass beside the well.

In the cool breeze of the evening, she cried her heart out, cursing the day her father had brought Huldah into their home.

THREE

"**A**nything I can help you with, lad? Thought all the students had gone to wash for lunch." Beren picked up a rasp from the worktable next to Callen. "This one's seen better days." He tossed the tool in the wastebasket and drummed his fingers on the table.

Callen looked up from the stacks of huge parchments. "Beren, I found these under the drying racks." He pulled three large yellowed sheets out from the stack and set them on the workbench beside him. Callen waited while Beren studied the sketches rendered in gray ink, the edges of the parchments chipped and brittle. In the distance, a church bell clanged, and through the window he saw people traversing the wide lane through the marketplace, jostling carts and horses, off to shop for goods, or to sell their wares.

"Ah, wondered where these had gone." Beren turned and looked at Callen with a spark of interest in his eyes. "Looking for more designs to copy?"

Callen's voice spilled his excitement. "Beren, where did you get these? I've never seen anything so amazing."

The wood master ran a gentle hand over one of the parchments. Callen followed with his eyes—intricate scrollwork surpassing any he'd seen. "What is this—a frieze or molding for a building?" He surprised himself with the anticipation in his voice.

"They're the drawings for a bridge—"

"A bridge?" Callen leaned closer to look. On the right side of the parchment were architectural cross sections and elevations, showing bits and pieces of a structure that Callen had difficulty constructing in his mind.

Beren pointed. "See, that's the arch, and the abutment."

"I don't understand," Callen mumbled. "There's nothing supporting this bridge, no columns, no piers . . ."

Beren smiled. "It supports itself. Called a suspension bridge."

"No," Callen replied. "That's not possible." He furrowed his eyebrows. "Is it?"

"The only one I've ever heard of. Designed so the tower piers support the weight with heavy cables. Nothing underneath."

Callen's voice rose in pitch. "I must go see this—"

Beren put a hand on Callen's chest. "Whoa, lad. What has come over you? Since when have you taken interest in bridges?"

Callen pulled out one of the parchments from underneath the stack. "It's not bridges, it's the woodwork that intrigues me. Look at this!"

Over the last hour Callen had studied the detailed designs drawn across the face of the parchments, mesmerized. Whoever inked these took great care to portray the scrollwork in a realistic style, with cross-hatch shading that made the woodwork appear to recede and protrude from the surface. He ran his fingers over the curves of the illustrations, almost expecting to feel the smoothness of wood under his touch. A shudder ran up his spine. His eyes pleaded with Beren's to learn more.

Beren let out a breath and pulled over a stool. He sat down and turned to Callen.

"I found these sketches at market, ages ago. Some peddler selling drawings out of his wagon, along with some painted canvases. Said he'd found the drawings in a burned-out cottage, in some old ruins far away. Who knows their origin? Like you, I was impressed by the detail. Clearly, this bridge was to be constructed solely out of wood, with every inch of it carved, as you see. But I'm afraid, lad, I have no idea if it was ever built, and if so, where. One day I came upon another strange fellow at market and we got to talking. He seemed quite odd and eccentric, a stranger to these parts, for certain. But he had heard of this bridge; at least he claimed such. Said it was destroyed long ago. No trace of it left."

"Did he say where it had been built?"

Beren shook his head. "You know that bridge in Sherbourne—over the river Heresh? Said that one was patterned after the one you see here. Of course the craftsmanship pales in comparison, but if you go and look at the one in Sherbourne, you'll see some of the same motifs—the sprawling tree branches here—" He pointed at various spots on the parchment. "The leaves in sets of five, like this."

"What about these odd letters—if they are letters?" Callen ran his hand over strange blocked markings that ran along the cornice of one sketch. Each "word" differed from another, but some of the symbols repeated. Callen counted ten, repeated on other balustrades, on all three pages of sketches.

"Have no clue," Beren answered.

Callen sat quietly thinking. He pushed his long wavy hair off his face and sighed. Above him, he heard students walking across the planked hall, in and out of their rooms, tromping downstairs to the dining room. Smells of roast meat and baked bread wafted on the air and set his stomach grumbling. Dishes clattered and an eruption of laughter followed.

"Best be getting in to eat, Cal."

The door to the hall opened. "There you two are." Laera carried a small package in her hand, something enclosed in cloth. She had on her cloak and hat.

Beren took the bundle from her hands and unwrapped it. Laera reached for Beren's coat and hat hanging on the wall pegs. "I have a flask of ale in the carriage and some pears. We should go." She draped the coat over his broad shoulders and plopped the wooly hat atop his head.

Callen saw reticence in Beren's eyes as he took a huge bite of cheese. Laera wasn't one to be kept waiting.

"The boys are all eating. Callen, I've made a good mutton stew. Surely you must be hungry," she said.

"I'm on my way, just had some things to look over."

"Well, those drawings will be there when you return." She pulled Beren toward the door. "Come, love, it's a two-hour ride to Northfold, and I'll need to get back in time to cook supper or there'll be a clamoring from the students."

Beren let his wife drag him toward the door. "Callen, make sure the lads finish their projects no later than four. Then have them do the sweeping and dusting, put everything away for the weekend."

Callen nodded, resisting the smile inching up his cheeks. Not until the front door shut behind the reluctant woodworker did Callen allow a laugh to ring out in the workshop. Laera always kept to a schedule and no one, not even her husband, would derail it. Meals were consistently punctual, and if a student was ten minutes late to table, he risked scrambling for crumbs. Sounds from the dining room reminded him of the hour—and of his opportunity to fill his stomach slipping quickly by.

He let his eyes linger one more minute on the detail of a massive tree etched across one of the bridge spans. An oak, perhaps? Yet different, softer leaves. What was the significance of the tree—if any? Hundreds of small parallel lines delineated the bark of the tree, swirling up into outspread boughs that wrapped around the railings. Similar lines entwined roots around girders, and in the branches nested birds of all shapes and sizes. Whorls of lines wrapped the bridge in a breathtaking elegance. He touched the parchment lovingly.

In that moment, Callen felt a restlessness grab hold of him. He shifted the stack, scanning the tiny notations of numbers and calculations running along the bottom of the parchments. His eyes caught on a word in bolder block print at the bottom right of one page. An odd name. The designer, or the builder, perhaps? In a box alongside the name was a stamp or insignia, a geometric design in darker ink, a three-pointed crown. Callen had no idea what the original color could have been—black, red? Suddenly, questions swept over him, questions that needed answers. His feet wanted to run out the door, chasing those questions before they got away.

Callen exhaled and stood. As he walked toward the dining room, he thought how long it had been since he'd taken leave to travel. He was overdue a furlough. If Beren could spare him a few days, he would take a trip. Where to, he was unsure. He just knew he had to uncover more about this bridge. The image of the bridge in Sherbourne came to him. *Sherbourne!* That would be the place to start—to see that bridge up close and visit the famous library. He'd heard of Sherbourne his whole life, yet had never visited the sprawling city. His whole body tingled in excitement.

With that settled, he entered the dining room and sat between Dariel and Eliab, who were busily spooning stew into their mouths. Callen reached across the table for a heel of bread and slathered it with sweet cream butter. Tomorrow was Saturday. He hoped Beren wouldn't mind him leaving that soon, but leave he must—with or without Beren's permission.

FOUR

IN HER misery, Jadiel failed to feel the cool of evening descend or notice the streaked hues of pink and amber swash across the sky above her, for she had buried her head between her knees. With her back pressed up against the old stone well, she heaved great sobs and let the tears fall. Try as hard as she might, she could not think of a way to reclaim her father from Huldah's ensnaring hands. Her life was a shambles. Could it get any worse? Papa was her only true friend, now that her mother was lost to her. He also served as her teacher, instructing her in her letters and numbers, and in managing all the aspects of the estate—so that one day she could work side by side with him, helping choose which crops to plant, which seeds and saplings to buy. Yet, how long had it been since he had taught her a lesson? Weeks—no—months. And as long as Huldah and her daughters reigned in the manor, Jadiel doubted she would ever be taken under Papa's wing again.

She raised her head and wiped her nose on her sleeve. A chill bit through her thin dress, making her shiver. She may as well return to the sanctuary of her bedroom—and hope she wouldn't get a lashing. Drained of emotion, she fumbled to stand, her knees weak.

As she made to leave, a faint sound caught her ear.

She turned her head and listened, then realized the noise drifted up from the bottom of the well. She called down into the dank stone chute. "Hello?" Surely no one had fallen into the well!

Another plaintive squeak. The voice clearly came from below. "Who is down there?" she called out.

"Pardon me, miss." The rumbly words echoed off the well's cold walls and repeated on the air. "Would you be so kind as to lower the bucket and pull me up?"

What was down there? "Will this small bucket hold you, or should I fetch a rope?"

She heard a little squawk, then a grunt. "No, ugh, miss, the bucket will serve."

Jadiel unwound the rope from the hook and slowly lowered the bucket. The old well hadn't been used in ages, not since Papa had brought water to the manor in pipes running down from the spring on the hilltop. With the lack of rain, she wondered if the bottom of the well was dry or if this poor creature had been treading water to stay alive.

"Here it comes. Is it close?" Jadiel peered in but saw only the rope descending into darkness.

"A few more inches. There! That'll do."

Jadiel held the rope tightly in her hands, expecting a strong tug once the creature grabbed the bucket. She was surprised when the little voice called back up to her.

"All set. Please pull me up."

The bucket hardly felt any heavier. Jadiel watched as it came into the light and strained to see what this passenger could be. She yelped when she set the bucket on the stone ledge and out jumped a hoptoad the size of her hand. Round as it was tall and mottled with warts, the poor thing was gunked with mud, with its beady yellow eyes glowing.

Jadiel reached over, and with the sleeve of her dress wiped the goo from its face.

"Oh, you poor creature. How long have you been trapped down there?"

"Since this afternoon, miss, when your nasty sister pushed me in."

"What!"

He furrowed his brows—if toads could be said to have brows. "The older one, with the sharp nails. Poked me hard with a finger and sent me tumbling." The toad must have noticed the shock on Jadiel's face, for it added, "Well, not to worry, miss. We toads do like a romp in the muck—doesn't bother us a bit. It's just I've worked up an appetite and found the place a bit low on the kind of bugs I eat." He lifted his bumpy chin to the sky. "Ah, the air's much fresher up here." He looked back at her. "Your name is Jadiel, is it not?"

Jadiel's eyes widened. "How did you know?"

"Oh miss, I make it my business to know everything what goes on around me." He narrowed his eyes and shook, flinging bits of mud over the ledge and onto Jadiel's face. "Oops, pardon me."

Jadiel chuckled and wiped the grime from her eye. "No matter. Tell me, are you a girl frog or a boy frog?"

The creature puffed up, making the dark bumps protrude from his olive-green skin. "I'm a male. But not a frog—a hoptoad, *puleeaase* don't insult me."

Jadiel lowered her eyes respectfully. "Forgive me, you're the first hoptoad I've ever met."

"Really?" The toad pursed his lips in puzzlement. "There're plenty of us around. Perhaps you haven't looked hard enough."

Jadiel sensed criticism. "No, I suppose I haven't." She then thought to add, "But you must be so clever at blending in with your surroundings. Makes you easy for a person to miss."

The toad puffed up with pride, then frowned.

"What is it?" Jadiel asked.

"Well, miss . . ." His gravelly voice shuddered. Jadiel leaned in close to hear him. "You must be told the danger you are in."

A cold clamp squeezed her heart. "Whatever do you mean?"

"Your stepmother intends to . . ." He rolled his eyes and, with a dramatic flair, plopped onto his back, wiggled his legs and arms frantically, then fell still, his gummy tongue lolling out the side of his mouth.

Jadiel gasped. "What should I do?"

The hoptoad sat upright and cocked his head. "I spend much of my time in a burrow outside her window. Let me listen to her schemes and I will warn you. Keep your window cracked a bit and heed my whistle."

The toad pursed his lips and a sweet melody trilled from his throat.

Jadiel smiled. "Why, you sing so sweetly."

"All hoptoads are endowed with beautiful voices. It's one of our finest attributes." He cleared his throat. "Now, the hour is late and it grows dark. You should return home before Huldah gets out the strap."

Jadiel exhaled as despair washed over her. What could her wicked stepmother be planning—and how could she save herself? The thought of running away and leaving her father was unbearable. There had to be another way, unless heaven would show mercy and strike Huldah dead. She took a look at the toad's reassuring face and hoped he would keep his word.

"I will do as you suggest." She patted the hoptoad on the head and a flush of red lit up his cheeks. "I am grateful to you, my new little friend. Thank you."

"One good turn deserves another. Listen for my whistle in the morn."

Jadiel nodded and ran up the hill to the driveway and into the house. As she passed through the dining room, with its clutter of dirty plates and glasses still littering the table, she listened for sounds, but the house was quiet. She guessed the rest of the household had gone to bed and left the dishes—as usual—for her to clear and wash. A lump formed in her throat as she entered the kitchen and picked at the remains of a roasted chicken. Her father hadn't even come looking for her. Thanks to Huldah's wiles, he had probably never noticed her absence at the dinner table. She clamped down on the tears pooling in her eyes and finished off a chunk of dark bread.

After washing up and climbing in under her bedcovers, she remembered the toad. Tiptoeing to her window, she unlocked the transom and pushed it open, then listened to the sounds of sheep stirring in the pasture, their collars jingling. Thank heaven she came upon that toad. She hated to think what would befall her if he hadn't offered to help. Hopefully, he would be true to his word and come to her window in the morning. Then, with heaven's help, she would think of a way to thwart her wicked stepmother's plots.

With her father under some compelling enchantment, Jadiel was alone, not a friend in the world. But now, perhaps, she had a new ally, and even though he was a toad, he had nice manners. And a beautiful singing voice. And yet, she had forgotten to ask his name. *Tomorrow,* she told herself as she lay exhausted on her bed and closed her eyes. Tomorrow.

In a wink, tomorrow became today. A sharp tap against the window caused Jadiel to jerk upright in bed. The sun cast an early glow on the horizon, and a chill air seeped in through the crack in the window. A splatter of pebbles rained against the glass, followed by a sweet whistle. *The hoptoad!*

Jadiel grabbed her robe and put it on as she hurried to the window and peered out. A few feet below her, in the dim light of dawn, the toad sat in the flowerbed, kicking pebbles with his hind legs. Jadiel called quietly to him.

"Mr. Toad, I'm here."

The hoptoad spun around in the mulch. "What a sound sleeper you are, miss. I was about to jump up on the ledge, but here you are."

"Yes." She watched him hop over to her window. "Thank you for coming so faithfully. May I reward you somehow for your kind efforts?"

The toad shook his green head. "'Tis no bother at all. But, miss, hearken to my words. Your stepmother has planned your death. You must be careful, for she has only evil in her heart."

Jadiel's hands trembled as they gripped the sill. "What must I do? Is there any hope at all?"

The hoptoad gave a comforting smile. "Take the gifts from your mother—the comb and the mirror. Huldah will send you on an errand, but fear not. Just be clever and cautious and do as she says. You will return safely." He added with a nod of his head, "I give you my word, and toads are known for being true and trustworthy."

Jadiel heard footsteps in the hallway coming toward her. "I must go," she whispered in haste. "I will follow your advice and do as you've instructed. But please, dear toad, would you tell me your name?"

The toad croaked loudly. "My name is too difficult for your gentle throat to pronounce. But you can call me Grork." He hopped across the flower bed, ducking under a camellia bush. "I will return again—tomorrow morning, same as today."

Jadiel was about to thank him when her door blew open. She turned to see Huldah peering suspiciously at her, already fully dressed in her finery and jewels.

"Your room is as cold as ice. Stupid girl, why are you staring out an open window? You should be helping the cook with breakfast. We're waiting, and my patience has grown thin."

"Coming," Jadiel muttered. She searched through her bureau and pulled out a smock, leggings, and socks.

"Hurry up," Huldah snapped. "Or you'll regret it."

Huldah left the bedroom, slamming the door behind her. Jadiel dressed and found a small satchel. She put her mother's comb and mirror in the pouch and went to the kitchen with the satchel slung over her shoulder.

The cook smiled at her as she came up to the big woodstove. "Ah, Jaddie, I trust you slept well." She handed Jadiel a wooden spoon to stir with. The older, heavy-set woman had pity in her eyes, and Jadiel appreciated the way she always tried to cheer her up.

"The oats are nearly done. Just stir 'em a bit while I go fetch some honey and cream. That's a lass."

Jadiel heard her stepsisters clack into the dining room in their fancy heeled shoes and pull out their chairs. When Jadiel helped the cook bring food to the table, she frowned.

She turned to Huldah, who sat at the head of the table, placing her napkin on her lap. "Where is Papa?"

"Oh." Huldah waved her hand in dismissal. "Off on some errand."

Jadiel set the bowl of cooked oats on the table and took her seat.

"And I have an errand for you as well, you little pipsqueak."

Kinna and Ramah giggled and elbowed each other, then fought over the honey.

Jadiel's heart stopped. The toad was right! One look at Huldah's face told her all she needed to know—that her stepmother had something sinister planned.

Jadiel steadied her voice. "And what might that be, dear stepmother?"

Huldah reached across the table and slapped Jadiel hard in the face. "Don't use that tone with me, young lady!" Huldah quickly lowered her voice as the cook reentered the room with a pot of tea. Huldah turned and snapped at the poor woman. "About time. Did you have to swim across the duck pond to fetch the tea this morning?"

Jadiel watched the cook lower her eyes as she mumbled. "No, ma'am. So sorry." She pushed the milk and sugar closer to Huldah, then hurried from the room.

Huldah jerked her head back to face Jadiel. "Now, I have a keen craving for pennyroyal tea, and there was none to be found at market yesterday. So today I want you to go into the woods and fetch me a sackful. And I don't want you to show your face until you have completed your task. Is that understood?"

Jadiel caught Kinna's gloating expression. "By myself? What about Kinna and Ramah?"

Huldah laughed. "Why, dear, they have much more important things to do. Who knows when a suitor will call? They must be ready at any moment." Her eyes grew stern. "Now, the only patch of pennyroyal is down by the creek, alongside the giant boulders beyond the barley fields. Do you know where I mean?"

Jadiel knew. It would be a half-day's walk just to get there. She nodded.

"Well then," Huldah barked, "you better get going, or you won't make it back by dark. And who knows what vicious creatures are lurking in that forest, ready to gobble up a pretty little thing like you."

Jadiel noticed Huldah nearly choked on the word *pretty*.

"Yes, Huldah," Jadiel answered politely.

Jadiel felt all eyes upon her as she returned to the kitchen to fetch her satchel. She stuffed it with fruit, bread, walnuts, and a flask of water. She hurried to her room and put on her sturdy walking shoes and a heavy cloak. As she ran down the manor steps and crossed the driveway, she looked back. Huldah and her daughters stood on the top step, with their arms crossed and a look of utter glee plastered across their features.

Her heart sunk as she hurried down the hill toward the barley field. Oh, that Grork's reassurances would prove true!

FIVE

LAERA LOOKED over at Beren as he sat, unmoving, on the buckboard. The horses snuffled and pawed, hot and sweaty from the dusty ride and thirsting for water.

"Well, I don't see Ka'rel. Do you think he's out in the field, or the orchard?" Beren asked, clearly reluctant to step down and try the door.

Laera nudged him with her elbow. "Just go and knock. I'll find someone to tend the horses." She carefully stepped down onto the cobbles and headed toward the large carriage house. One look inside told her Ka'rel had left, for his carriage was gone. If he was somewhere on the grounds, he'd be on his horse. Funny, they hadn't passed him on the road, but then, Laera mused, he could be off visiting a neighbor.

She came back out and stood in the bright sunlight. The manor seemed quiet, with no one in sight. Where were the workers, the servants—and Ka'rel's wife? Perhaps they were all in the house. A confrontation with Huldah was the last thing Laera wanted. But her need to find Jadiel pressed her. She only hoped she could find her niece and speak with her privately, away from listening ears.

Laera had no doubt Jadiel was in a bad way. How she longed to take her back home her and raise her as her own daughter. The whole ride over she thought how she might broach the subject with Ka'rel, but their last parting had been bitter. How in heaven could she convince Ka'rel to let Jadiel come with her? Would he allow a visit—a long visit? That was all she dared hope, but now it appeared her chance to ask him would have to wait. The question was—could Jadiel endure much more in this harsh environment?

Laera saw the front door open to Beren and hurried to hide behind the carriage. She felt a wave of relief as Azar came hobbling down the steps and took the reins of the two geldings hooked up to the carriage. Then she saw Beren disappear inside the house. *Good, he'll talk to Huldah and see what she is up to.*

"Azar." She greeted the old caretaker, taking his weathered hands in hers and shaking them affectionately. "We won't be staying long; no need to unhitch the horses. Would you just give them water and a light brushing?"

"Of course." His dim eyes met hers. "Ka'rel is gone for the day. Did you wish to leave him a message?"

Laera thought of many things she wanted to say to her brother-in-law but nothing she could pass on so simply. "I'll send a note. But, tell me, where can I find Jadiel? I must speak with her."

Azar's countenance fell. "I wish I could tell you, Laera, but—I'm afraid the woman has sent the girl out on an errand. I saw her this morning running toward the barley fields and haven't seen her since."

When Laera showed obvious distress, Azar added, "I'm sure she'll be fine. She knows her way around the estate. She's safer, anyway, the farther she roams away from Huldah, wouldn't you say?" Azar's mouth turned up in a grin that revealed gaps between his yellowed teeth. Laera sighed but returned the smile.

"Yes, I'm sure you are right. But, Azar, would you do an old friend a favor and please keep an extra eye out for Jadiel. I fear for her."

Azar nodded. "I'll do my best, what with my duties. I'd take her along with me, but that woman always finds some task for

Jadiel to do. She practically keeps her under lock and key in the manor, rarely lets her out of her sight. I don't understand it."

Laera understood. The more Jadiel remained under Huldah's thumb, the less influence she could have on Ka'rel. Oh, there just *had* to be a way to rescue Jadiel from that woman!

Azar led the horses into the cool carriage house, leaving Laera standing in the driveway in the dusty, warm afternoon wondering what to do next. On a whim, she walked briskly along the wall of the manor and around the side, to a back entrance. She entered the house and followed the hallway to Jadiel's bedroom, where the girl's door was open. Laera stepped in and let her eyes travel the room.

Memories of her sister, M'lynn, rushed at her. All Jadiel's belongings—her bed coverlet, her dolls, even her furniture—were things M'lynn had bought, with Laera at her side, as they shopped in Kettlebro, and even once in Sherbourne. Laera remembered the heavy parcels they carried, the stops for afternoon tea and scones, and the many times they had Jadiel along—such a little darling girl, holding tightly to their hands as they crossed streets in the crowded shopping districts.

Even the smell in Jadiel's room—the scent of roses and lavender—awakened pain in her heart, as if M'lynn were in the room. How she missed her only sister, the kindest, most loving woman she'd ever known. Standing there, she let the memories wash over her, memories she had bottled up this last year in a flurry of business, tending to Beren and his apprentices, managing the books for the wood shop. Grief pounded her and caused her knees to buckle. She let herself drop to the floor and cried.

She startled as a hand gripped her shoulder; she hadn't heard anyone come in. Laera quickly stood and found herself staring at Huldah, who scowled at her with intense hatred.

"Just what are you doing in my house?"

Laera stumbled over words that would not piece together. "I'm—I'm looking for Jadiel . . ."

Huldah's grip intensified and Laera winced in pain. "Didn't Ka'rel warn you never to step foot in this house again?"

Laera's stomach clenched. Huldah's evil seeped around her, like a vapor clinging to the ground. Nausea rose in Laera's throat. "I . . . wanted to see my niece."

"She's gone for the day. You missed her." Huldah glared at Laera, making her tremble. She tugged on Laera's coat and escorted her to the back door. As Laera stepped out into the sunlight, she heard Huldah's voice hiss behind her, full of ominous warning.

"I better not see you here again." Her words sent a chill slithering across Laera's back. "Or I'll deal with you in the same manner I dealt with your poor, unfortunate sister."

Laera turned to face Huldah, the implication of her words sending a shock through her heart. What did she just say? Huldah's triumphant expression told all. Far down the hall, Beren's voice bellowed as he called out for Huldah. Laera watched a sinister smile rise on Huldah's face. "Oh, that must be your . . . husband." In a brusque dismissal, Huldah slammed the back door.

Laera did not wait to hear more, but turned and ran as fast as she could to the carriage now stationed back at the front entryway. She willed her heart to stop pounding, but it thumped unmercifully. Laera thought she would collapse in terror. Had Huldah done something to cause her sister's death, or was she merely toying with her emotions? Onlookers said it was an accident. A strong, frightened horse had broken loose in the marketplace and then tore off down Potter's Lane. M'lynn had been standing there at a peddler's booth, choosing a set of platters for the manor. Ka'rel had never met Huldah until weeks later—or had he? Was it possible Huldah had set her goal to capture the richest man in the vale and had orchestrated M'lynn's death to claim him as her own husband? The idea was preposterous.

But, somewhere, deep in Laera's heart, she suspected truth behind the woman's vicious words. Huldah's eyes had shone in victory. Now Laera held no doubt this creature had bewitched Ka'rel. Huldah certainly had no affection for Jadiel. The child was surely in danger and needed rescuing—whether Ka'rel agreed or no.

Laera calmed her breathing as she settled into determination. She would come back for Jadiel and steal her away, if necessary. She would do whatever it took to wrest her niece from Huldah's clutches, despite Beren's or Ka'rel's protests. She had only heaven to answer to, and maybe she was heaven's only hope to save Jadiel.

As she stepped up to sit in the buckboard, she watched Beren come out the front door—with Huldah's arm entwined around his! Laera clenched her teeth and watched as Huldah batted her eyes at Beren and laughed girlishly at something he said. Laera studied her husband's face and saw a vacant, amused look. She could not hear their exchange of words, but anyone could tell Beren was enamored. Huldah slathered him with affection, and Beren drank it in, with a flattered, proud look across his features. Laera almost jumped off the bench when Huldah ran her fingers through Beren's hair, drawing close and giving him a light kiss on his cheek.

Laera kept her eyes pinned on Beren as he skipped merrily over to the carriage like a young boy and leaped up onto the bench beside her. She looked back at Huldah, who waved excitedly, a bright smile on her face and her red hair streaming out behind her. In the afternoon sun, Laera couldn't help but notice how stunning and graceful she appeared, and wondered how such a beautiful woman could harbor such evil.

Even as Beren maneuvered the carriage around, he chuckled quietly to himself, as if revisiting a private moment he had shared with Huldah. Laera stared straight ahead for many minutes until they finally reached the outer gate to Ka'rel's estate. Only then did Beren seem to recall she was there, sitting beside him.

He was more cheerful and animated than she'd seen him in months. "What's with the stern face, love?" He cocked his head as he shook the reins to urge the horses into a trot.

What could she say? Beren would think her mad if she told him of her frightening encounter with Huldah. He would never believe the syrupy-sweet Huldah who had escorted him to the carriage capable of any evil and would only think Laera was jealous. She tried to bury her anger as she forced a smile. "Just tired."

"Well, I feel I could run all the way home." He laughed heartily. "Isn't Ka'rel's wife wonderful? He sure found a charming beauty! Why, I've never met anyone like her." He then added dutifully, "Except you, of course."

He turned and smiled at Laera, but she could tell his smile lacked conviction. She knew Beren too well. He took her hand and gave it a reassuring squeeze, but his eyes told her his thoughts were elsewhere—back a half-league behind her.

SIX

J ADIEL SQUEEZED through narrow rock crevices in the towering sandstone boulders that crowded the creek. Her smock hem caught on a prickly shrub and she felt the fabric rip. Wiping sweat-drenched locks from her brow, she plopped down on the dirt and disengaged the branch from the cloth. She had spent at least a half hour scrambling over these piles of rock, sliding on rough grit and tearing up her nails seeking handholds on the boulders that were too high to clamber over. But she could see where the rocks dwindled and the creek widened. Just a little farther . . .

A few summers ago, she and Papa spent an afternoon fishing and exploring the many caves tucked away in this place. He told her that an earth shake centuries ago had dislodged the boulders from the mountains and caused an avalanche. The caves were pockets created by the boulders piled upon each other, and some ran deep, providing dens for the small animals that foraged along the creek. Jadiel smiled at the memory, wishing her father was with her now. Maybe, if she managed to get him alone, away from Huldah, she could convince him to go with her on an outing—just the two of them. Then she could pour out her heart. Jadiel sighed deeply. But what good would that do? She saw what happened when her aunt Laera had criticized Huldah. Papa banished her from the manor! Somehow, she knew her words would fall on deaf ears.

After eating some plums, Jadiel slid down the last few rocks to the soft grassy forest floor. She longed to take a dip in the creek and wash off the grime, but reminded herself how long it would take to return home. Instead, she knelt along the water's edge and splashed her face with the cool water, and that refreshed her enough to keep on. All day long she startled at every sound, expecting danger. What horrible demise had Huldah planned for her? Her imagination ran wild, frightening her, making a wreck of her nerves. She just wanted to hurry and find the pennyroyal, then hasten home.

For another hour she traveled creek-side, pushing through scratchy willows as she searched for the minty plant. Surely, Huldah had sent her on a wild hog chase. But look! She spotted a clump of pennyroyal up ahead. As she neared, the soft purple flowers gave off a fragrance that lifted her mood. She hurried to gather the slender stalks of mint, and stuffed them into her satchel. As she leaned over to reach for another cluster, she heard a rumbling noise behind her. She spun around, and her breath caught in her throat.

A giant bear, black as night, faced her down. It stood on its massive hind legs, pawing the air with gigantic claws, looming over her with its imposing bulk. Jadiel cowered in fear, not knowing what to do. Was this some monster sent by Huldah to devour her?

The bear opened its mouth and bellowed, exposing thick, sharp teeth. The roar shook the ground, and Jadiel covered her ears, knowing she was doomed. Snarling and snapping its jaw, the bear lowered down and took a step toward Jadiel. Drool slid down one side of its mouth. With wild eyes, it shook its head at her in a fury, and then swiped a paw as large as a skillet in her direction. Jadiel nearly fainted.

Grork's words rushed to her mind in this midst of her panic. He had told her to be clever. What in heaven's name did that mean? She kept one eye on the approaching bear as she fumbled in her satchel, remembering the mirror and the comb. Quickly, she pulled out the small hand mirror and thrust it in the bear's direction. Her heart sank. What was so clever about that? Would a small piece of glass frighten away such a beast? Maybe she could find a branch, or a large rock to hurl. She looked about her feet but found nothing substantial enough to scare away even a mouse.

A streak of sunlight caught in the mirror and flashed into the bear's eyes, causing it to stop and fall back on its haunches. Jadiel froze, then inched the mirror a little closer so the bear could see its reflection. With a soothing voice, Jadiel spoke.

"My, what an impressive coat you have, dear bear. Look how beautifully it gleams."

The bear strained its neck to study the glass, clearly seeing its reflection. Jadiel steadied her hand, then slowly drew the comb from the satchel. She dared approach a little closer, talking in a soft monotone.

"All the other bears must envy such a rich color fur. But look, you have twigs and leaves tangled in your coat. That won't do, will it?"

She knew she was taking a risk, but she leaned closer and let the bear sniff the comb. It seemed mesmerized by the mirror, so Jadiel gently dipped the comb into the bear's thick fur and began pulling out debris. She hummed a tune her mother used to sing to her at bedtime, a sweet little melody that drifted on the quiet forest air. A calm settled over the bear as she continued grooming its fur, so she worked her way around the bulk of the animal, looking over its back in order to see into the mirror alongside it.

In there, she caught the bear's reflection, and behind the beast emerged the hazy outline of a huge cave. Jadiel looked behind her and saw only the creek, with a spattering of cottonwoods on the opposite bank. As she stared more closely at the mirror, Jadiel could smell the cool, dank cave air, and the earthy, musty smell of a den in the recesses of rock. As she continued combing, the bear gave a yawn, with sleep filling its eyes.

"Yes, dear bear, autumn is the time to find a cozy den and curl up for the winter. Do you smell it? It is calling you. So let me finish this last shoulder and then you can go off to your long, untroubled sleep." In the glass, she saw the bear lower its head as it entered one of the caves and trudged to a cool, dark den. She watched the bear paw at the dirt and circle a few times before plopping to the ground with a grunt and a sigh. Snow fell outside the entrance and a winter hush buried the world. The bear snored deeply, twitching from time to time, dreaming of spring.

Slowly, Jadiel put the comb back into her satchel, then the mirror. As if in a daze, the bear raised its head and sniffed the air, and then, without even a glance at Jadiel, turned and lumbered away to the rocks, where, somewhere nearby, a cave beckoned.

A great sigh of relief escaped her lips. As she watched the bear retreat in the distance, she thought what a magnificent creature it was, and how plush its fur. Then she pondered the size of its gigantic claws and how easily it could have ripped her to shreds. A shiver ran from her head to her toes. She turned her eyes to the sky and thanked heaven for the toad's advice—and for her mother's gifts.

With daylight waning, she scrambled back over the piles of rock until she reached the barley field, and skipped through the tan-colored, feathery stalks until finally—exhausted and starving—she arrived at the manor. There, to her delight, she found her father unhitching the carriage in the large barn.

His eyes lit up. "Jadiel! You look as though you have just run across the world." He wiped a swath of black hair from her face and leaned to kiss her cheek.

"Oh, Papa! I'm so glad you're back. Please, can we have a picnic tomorrow—just you and me?" Jadiel's eyes pleaded with Ka'rel's.

"I have a few things to take care of in the morning, but I should be done by noon." He looked lovingly at his daughter and took her hand. "Will that be soon enough?"

Jadiel's heart warmed at his touch. He led her up the manor steps. "No," she answered, "but I suppose it will have to do." She pouted in jest and Ka'rel ruffled her hair.

They laughed as Ka'rel swung open the door. Huldah stood inside the foyer, with her arms crossed. She opened her mouth to speak to Ka'rel as he came inside, but as she caught a glimpse of Jadiel, her jaw dropped. Clearly, the last person she expected to ever see again was Ka'rel's daughter. Her dark eyes simmered with malice and fury. Jadiel saw Huldah's hands clench and shake. Feeling a bit victorious, Jadiel smiled sweetly at her stepmother and reached into her satchel.

"Here." She withdrew the large bundle of pennyroyal and thrust it at Huldah. Her stepmother took the mint from her, as Ka'rel watched this exchange. A forced smile edged up Huldah's face.

"Pennyroyal," her father said. "Jadiel, what a nice gift for your stepmother. How thoughtful."

"There wasn't any at market yesterday, and I know how much Huldah loves her mint tea . . ."

"—Yes, such a thoughtful gift. Now dear . . ." Huldah said gently to Jadiel, "go wash up for supper. You must be so hungry."

Jadiel stood on her tiptoes and threw her arms around her father, giving him a big hug and refusing to let go.

Ka'rel laughed and swung her around in the air. Jadiel alone saw the fury return to Huldah's eyes, and from that look she knew her stepmother would be more determined than ever to get rid of her. But somehow she wasn't afraid anymore. She had Grork to help her, and even though her father was under Huldah's spell, he still loved her. No dark magic could ever destroy that love. With heaven's help she would find a way to win him back. She must.

SEVEN

CALLEN CAREFULLY rolled up the three aged parchments inside a sheath of deerskin. He tucked the parcel inside his pack, along with his small box of carving tools and sketch-book. At dawn, Laera had seen to his provisions, although he could never have fit all that food in the remaining space. He reminded her that the road from Logan Valley to Sherbourne sported plenty of villages that would take his coin. He surely wouldn't starve. But she had insisted.

He stuffed the rest of his things into the pack, cramming in as much food as possible, then tied the flap. As he attached his bed-roll to the top of the pack, he wondered at Laera's strange anxiety. Something bothered her. He guessed it had to do with the visit she and Beren had made yesterday to Northfold Manor.

Northfold. Callen had never been to Northvale. Since he boarded no horse in town, he rarely had opportunity to travel the miles of rolling hills to visit outlying communities. Wolcreek, where his sister-in-law, Charris, hailed from, lay far beyond the woods of Northfold, across two raging rivers, whose bridges often washed out in the winter storms. He rarely heard of anyone travel-ing that far north past harvest season.

But why venture far? Kettlebro had everything he needed and wanted. Within the sprawling marketplace, there were taverns and shops that sold furniture and wares, clothing and tack, seed and machinery. Dozens of cozy inns lured shoppers from far and wide, and almost every corner boasted a teahouse, with racks of chocolates and pastries on display.

He knew Swiftwater Creek outside town flowed through the vale, dissecting it into Eastfold and Westfold. Beren had shown him a map of the road to Sherbourne and the towns it traversed: Mallers Edge, Settlewood, Wheatsheaf. After that, the vale ended and the road linked with the one going east-west. West lay Tebron, his home; east led straight to Sherbourne. On foot, Callen figured it'd take him two days to get to the walled capital of the region—unless he secured lifts from kind carriage drivers along the way. But Callen didn't mind the walk—it would give him time to think, to clear his head, to drink in the scenery. Beren told him to take as much time as he wished, it being the slow season for Callen's kind of woodwork. The other students could keep up with the custom holiday gift orders.

After taking one last look around his sparsely furnished room, he skipped down the stairs and out the front door into the warm sunlight. The early morning carried the usual chill on the air, but that would burn off by midday, as the day turned balmy and fragrant. Few people were on the road heading to market, but by noon the streets would be clogged with shoppers, as on any other market day. Sundays were the only days the shops and vendors closed up, leaving the winding, narrow streets vacant and lonely. He could smell the bakery on the next block, the yeasty aroma of pastries and bread rising. And the butcher smoking meat in the back of his shop; there was no mistaking that mouth-watering smell.

On the weekends, students fended for themselves for meals, foraging in the kitchen, but warned by Laera to keep things neat and clean. Callen imagined the other apprentices were still buried under bedcovers, grateful to sleep in and not have to hurry to work. A tingle of excitement energized him, making him anxious to be underway. As he slung the pack and his water jug over his shoulder, Beren came out the door to the shop, rubbing a tired eye.

"Eh, lad, you're off early." Beren handed Callen a small wooden box.

"What's this?" He lifted the lid and smiled. "How did you know?"

Beren chuckled. "One of the younger lads said you'd been eyeing this pen and ink set at the dry goods. Thought you might want to make sketches of the mysterious bridge—if you find it."

Callen accepted the gift gratefully. "That's a big 'if.' But surely I can sketch other things on my way. No doubt Sherbourne has some fine architecture to capture on paper."

Beren laid a hand on Callen's shoulder. "I hear the palace has a circular council chamber, with arching cornices to the ceiling. May want to take a look at that."

"The palace?" Callen shook his head, amused. "Not likely I'd get invited in there. Think I'll just wander the city streets—and visit the famous bridge over the Heresh." He took Beren's hand and shook it. "Thank you for this gift."

"Well, safe journeys, lad. Take care and keep your head about you. Some places are not as safe as the vale. Best to keep your coin in a deep pocket, where thieving fingers can't reach."

Callen nodded and put his cap on his head. He picked his walking stick up from the cobbles—one he had carved from a burl of Loganvale black oak years ago. The handle was poorly scrolled—in his now-expert opinion—but it had sentimental value, being one of the first projects he had attempted in woodworking. The crafting of it had sparked his love for carving.

"I'll be back before you know it. Somehow I feel this quest to find a mysterious bridge will land at a dead end. But it gives me an excuse to go places I've never been."

Beren nodded. "Well, heaven be with ye."

"And you too," Callen replied.

Callen adjusted the cap on his head and marched a steady pace south, passing small villages much like Kettlebro, stopping occasionally to drink from his jug or rummage through his pack for a snack. He journeyed with purpose and anticipation, passing one farm after another, orchards with their fruit and nut trees in perfect manicured rows, vineyards bursting with clumps of burgundy grapes that field workers picked and gathered into baskets. He greeted those sharing the road; few were travelers like him. Most were busy at some errand for their farm, some leading cows or prodding hogs to their local market.

After many miles, weariness seized him. Callen was accustomed to long days spent leaning over his workbench; this surge of physical exertion had awakened new muscles that now cried out for relief. When the first pale-orange hue of twilight tinted the sky, he spotted the outskirts of Wheatsheaf, the most southern hamlet in South Vale. There he took a room at a small inn, run by gregarious innkeepers who plied him with hearty, steaming food. Sated after a pint of ale and with a full stomach, he gratefully collapsed on a tiny bed in a simply appointed guest room and fell into a hard sleep, knowing that tomorrow he would finally see Sherbourne, "The Crown of the East."

Once more, Jadiel awoke to the sound of pebbles splattering her window. As she stirred in her bed, her legs ached, reminding her of all the running and scrambling she had done yesterday. But today she would picnic with Papa! She leaped out of bed and pulled her robe around her. When she peered out the window, Grork whistled his cheery song.

"Grork! My little friend."

The toad tilted his bumpy head upward to see Jadiel. "Well, good morn, miss. I see you made it back safely to the manor."

"Oh yes, thanks to your advice. I am grateful to you."

Grork hopped closer to the window sill. "Well, don't be so cheery-eyed this morn. Your stepmother has another task for you, and she means you ill."

Jadiel's smile turned sour. What now? Her heart sank, thinking Huldah would do anything to steal her time away from Papa. Yesterday's errand took up the whole day. She recalled the burning hatred in Huldah's eyes last evening, then clenched her teeth. Well, whatever Huldah had planned, Jadiel would *not* let it interfere with her picnic. She was now determined to tell her father everything Huldah was doing—whether he believed her or not. She just *had* to make him see how wicked Huldah was!

"There's little time, miss, for she's coming as we speak."

Jadiel turned and listened. Footsteps, quick and measured, grew louder as they approached her door. "What do I do? Hurry!"

"The flute," he croaked, "take your silver flute and . . ."

Just then, Jadiel's door flew open. This time Huldah stormed directly to the window, to see what in the flower garden interested Jadiel. Huldah stuck her head out, twisting it from side to side, whipping her red hair about her face.

When she brought her head back inside and straightened up, she narrowed her eyes at Jadiel, whose attention wandered the room innocently. "You're up to something, you pesky brat." Jadiel felt like a fly about to be swatted. She cringed under Huldah's recrimination, awaiting the blow to follow. But Huldah only stepped back, her face deep in thought.

"I fancy some mushrooms. After breakfast, I want you to gather a basketful. You'll find them up at the spring box, past the stables."

Jadiel's face relaxed. The spring box was not far from the manor. Surely she would be back by noon. Huldah did not need to tell her to hurry and dress. She drew out a clean smock and leggings from her bureau while Huldah stood at the window, her eyes peering suspiciously into the gardens. As Jadiel splashed her face with water from the basin on her dresser, Huldah slammed the window shut and fastened the latch. Without a word, Huldah stomped out of the room.

When Jadiel entered the dining room, she found her father had left early again. At the table, Kinna and Ramah stuffed their faces with biscuits and gravy, reminding Jadiel of horses with their heads buried in snuffling bags of hay. Ever since her stepsisters had arrived at the manor, they feasted on rich food night and day, as if they had been starved before they moved into her home. Jadiel noticed they wore embroidered blouses that gripped tightly around their bulging waistlines, immodestly low-cut in the front. Their layers of skirts also hugged their hips as if trying to squeeze them into a smaller shape, but without success. At the rate they were eating, they would soon have to let out all the seams in their clothes—or buy new ones.

Huldah sipped at tea and nibbled a piece of cold toast, never letting her piercing eyes stray far from Jadiel. When she had finished her breakfast, Jadiel excused herself and took an armload of dishes to the kitchen.

"I put some goodies in your satchel, Jaddie." The cook handed the soft pack to her. "Don't bother with the dishes; I'll do them."

Jadiel smiled in gratitude, eager to be on her way so she could return before noon. "If Papa comes back before I do, please remind him we have a date!"

Jadiel skipped out the kitchen's back door. As she ran down the hill and through the herb garden, she watched the clouds gather overhead. Today felt cooler, with a hint of winter on the air. She glanced at the copse of beech trees below the garden and saw only a few tenacious leaves clinging to the slender branches. Would there be any snow this year? As she crossed the rolling meadow beyond the garden, she thought of the last time she had played in the snow with her mother. Three years ago, when a strange storm drifted in, dumping almost a foot of snow on the ground and shrouding the land in a white coverlet. She and Mama had built a small castle of snow blocks, and then when Papa came home, they pelted him with snowballs from the secret cache they had prepared for his arrival. And later that evening, while sipping hot pear cider as they cuddled together, Papa took them for a carriage ride through Dapple Wood, under a bright full moon.

Jadiel's heart grew heavy from the memory of that day. If only she could go back and relive it again. But, she chastised herself, it did no good to linger on thoughts like that—they only brought a flood of tears. If she was to rally her wits and strength to outsmart Huldah, she would need to push those memories aside for now. She owed it to her father to find a way to free him from her stepmother's intoxicating spell. But how? Jadiel had no idea how Huldah worked her charms on Papa. She was only twelve years old, surely no match for someone worldly-wise like Huldah.

Jadiel let these thoughts drift from her mind and concentrated on her footsteps. As she ran up over a rise, the stables came into view. A dozen horses grazed in a fenced pasture before her, cropping at the grass, some with spring foals by their sides. Jadiel spotted her favorite mare, a roan she had raised from a weanling. Soon the mare would be old enough to ride, and Jadiel had already started the ground work with her using a lead rope. Jadiel called her Snarl because of the way she lifted one lip when she whinnied. Her father had given the horse a different registered name, one that would sound more attractive to a buyer. But Jadiel hoped Papa would let her keep the mare. Snarl was smart and good-natured, and had a wide, padded girth that would make for comfortable bareback riding.

When Jadiel climbed through the split-rail fence, she nickered at Snarl, who came trotting over, sniffing for treats. Jadiel stopped and opened her satchel. The cook had put two apples in there, among other snacks. Jadiel offered one to Snarl, who crunched at it with her big teeth, devouring it in four bites. She smoothed back the mare's forelock and gave her a kiss on the nose.

"Sorry, no time to play today." Snarl looked disappointed and trotted after Jadiel as she sprinted across the horse pasture. Jadiel passed a stable boy pushing a wheelbarrow laden with straw for stall bedding. He gave a little wave but she hurried on. Down the slope and up the steep hill, she kept a steady pace. Halfway up the hill, she stopped and caught her breath. Her father had found a spring at the top of the highest hill on the estate—one that flowed steadily year-round. Not long ago he dug a pond fed by the spring, and filled it with little gray fish. In summer, Jadiel would bring the fishing pole Papa helped her make and she'd catch fish. Most of them were too little to eat, so she threw them back, but she still enjoyed sitting at the pond, tugging the line and looking out over the green land for miles around.

Now, as she crested the hill, she noted the fields were a ruddy red and brown, most already harvested and lying fallow for winter.

Jadiel took a moment to look around. Mushrooms grew in rich soil, in the shade. She had never seen them up here, but then, she rarely came up to the pond in the fall. Across the water grew a thicket of lanky willows, and behind them were taller trees: cedars and pines. That would be the place to look.

Jadiel stepped slowly, her senses alert. Yesterday, a bear had nearly torn her apart. What would she encounter here? Wolves? The thought brought a fresh terror to her heart. Grork had told her to bring her flute, but then Huldah had rushed into the room. What else had he planned to tell her? What if there was something else she had needed to bring, to get home in one piece?

She reached into her satchel and, with trembling fingers, pulled out the silver flute. Her mother had taught her to play, and she could almost hear Mama's sweet voice singing along with the bright notes spilling from the flute as she blew air through the mouthpiece. The clear, ringing notes carried over the water, filling the hilltop with resonating music and calming her jangled nerves. She let the song die out, put her flute away, and followed the edge of the pond. A few red-crested wood ducks chortled at her, paddling away from shore as she neared. Up overhead, the sun peeked through drifting clouds, nearing the zenith of the sky. Noon would soon be upon her.

Jadiel ran the rest of the way. She ducked under willow branches until she entered the dark wood. There, popping up through the leafy mulch, small white button mushrooms dotted the ground.

Jadiel dropped to her knees and pulled mushrooms from the crumbly soil. When she had filled her satchel to overflowing, she stood and walked toward the pond to wash her hands. Near the edge of the water, her foot caught on something and she tripped—only to find herself on her knees facing a pair of huge vipers, their mouths wide open and hissing.

Jadiel stiffened, afraid to move or flinch. Her heart pounded so hard she thought it would burst. She had never seen a water viper, but her father had warned her often of them. One bite and she would die. Had Huldah somehow summoned these snakes as she had the bear? Jadiel stared at their sleek black skins, their white mouths with perilously sharp teeth dripping with venom. They hovered a foot away, glaring at her with yellow cats-eye pupils. Maybe she could offer them something to eat—if she could reach into her satchel without triggering an attack. But then, she had no idea what they ate—apart from foolish little girls who happened to stumble into their nest!

The flute! Maybe music would soothe them. Music seemed to calm animals of all kinds. Talking in a singsong voice always made

Snarl relax when the horse was in a bad temper. And Jadiel remembered that many evenings as she played her flute, the dogs and cat sauntered into the library, drawn to the music wafting through the house, and settled at her feet to listen with eyes contentedly closed.

Jadiel kept her gaze pinned on the vipers as they hissed and swayed from side to side, primed to lurch at the slightest invitation. Jadiel took a deep breath and said a silent prayer. Then she moved her arm with agonizing slowness, letting the satchel slip off her shoulder to the ground. She wiggled her fingers into the opening and felt for her flute, which, thankfully, sat in the side pocket where she last placed it. Withdrawing it slowly, she brought the flute to her lips as the vipers followed her every motion with their piercing eyes.

Suddenly, one of the snakes lunged, snapping at the flashing silver with its teeth. Jadiel gasped and froze as the viper attacked again. Finding the metal hard and unappetizing, it retreated a few inches, with wariness in its expression.

With trembling fingers, Jadiel positioned the flute under her lip and blew. A tentative, breathy note came out and the vipers stopped their movement. Jadiel shut her eyes, put the snakes out of her mind, and concentrated on the music. Soon, clear rolling notes spilled into the air, the lullaby Mama used to sing to Jadiel at bedtime. Her fingers tapped the holes in a gentle, swaying rhythm, and soon the vipers rocked along with the tune. Slowly, they lowered from their striking position, closed their eyes, and, as Jadiel let the last notes fade out, fell in a heap into their nest of sticks and grass.

Jadiel waited, unsure whether they were asleep or only momentarily mesmerized. Cautiously, she put the flute to her mouth and played again, holding it with one hand while slowly lifting the satchel to her shoulder. In this manner, she stood up and backed away, her eyes glued to the vipers that still hadn't budged. Only when she made clear of the brush and woods did she cram her flute into her satchel and run as fast as her legs could carry her.

By the time she reached the manor, the sun burned above her, but Papa was nowhere outside. Jadiel went up the steps and entered the hallway. The house was quiet. Maybe Huldah and her daughters had gone shopping again. That would suit Jadiel just fine. No doubt her father was running late, but he would come. He promised.

She pushed open the dining room door and found the kitchen empty as well. But as she dumped the mushrooms into a washbasin, she heard the door swing behind her. *Papa!*

Her spirits sank. Huldah, breathless and red-faced, glared at Jadiel with her own venom in her eyes.

As Jadiel pressed her back against the kitchen wall, she noticed a long, sharp carving knife on the chopping block. Suddenly, she had a vision of Huldah grabbing the knife and swinging at her. Jadiel inched her way toward the back door.

"I . . . I brought you the mushrooms, as you asked. See, lots of nice ones . . ."

Huldah marched straight at Jadiel and made to slap her cheek, but Jadiel impulsively brought her hand up to protect her face, tired of being struck. Huldah then grabbed Jadiel's wrist instead.

Jadiel stared at the hand gripping her so firmly. She tried to pull away, and then her mouth dropped open and shock filled her eyes. For what she saw frightened her more than Huldah's attack. A mottled, wrinkled hand, bony and scarred, gripped her wrist. Jadiel's gaze traveled up Huldah's once smooth arm, only to find her stepmother's flesh hanging upon her bones like an old hag's, flaccid and repulsive.

Jadiel gasped and pulled her hand away as if burned by the touch. She raised her eyes in question and met Huldah's fearful expression. That was fear she saw, wasn't it? Her stepmother's unexpected reaction made her breath catch, and somehow she knew that what she had witnessed revealed Huldah's true appearance—like the ugly face she'd detected the other day. This was no mere work of her imagination, but some strange, horrid spell Huldah managed. Now she truly must warn her father, for Huldah had to be some kind of witch, using more than feminine wiles to deceive her father. Perhaps his life was as much in danger as hers!

Jadiel took advantage of Huldah's shock to jerk away and run out the door to the garden. As she hurried around the corner of the manor to the front drive, she collided with Ka'rel, who caught Jadiel in his arms.

"Whoa, what's the hurry, Jad?" Ka'rel lifted her up and kissed her on the forehead.

"Oh, Papa," Jadiel whined, hugging him with all her strength. She ached to spill out everything she had seen, but worried Huldah was close behind her.

"Please," she begged, "let's go have our picnic, before it gets too late."

"That's why I came back. I have a basket already packed in the carriage." He took Jadiel's hand and helped her up onto the buckboard. He looked at her, puzzled. "Do you need to fetch anything? You seem upset."

Jadiel motioned her father to join her. As he sat next to her and picked up the reins, Jadiel said, with one eye watching out for Huldah, "Just drive, Papa. Just drive."

EIGHT

CALLEN EDGED his way through the crowd, surprised at the hordes entering Sherbourne's walls. Was it always so jammed with people? While breakfasting at the inn in Swiftwater, he'd met another guest at the table who offered to give him a lift in his small produce wagon. Midmorning, at the crossroads above Sherbourne, the driver let Callen off, and that's where he encountered all the foot traffic. He noticed many on the road toward the city, and all were heading in, none out.

Another thing he observed was the odd attire. Many were dressed in fine garb, not the usual clothes for an average workday. As he neared the gate, his senses were assaulted with the sounds and smells of a bustling community. Wood smoke drifted by, irritating his eyes. A cacophony of goose honking and goat baaing swelled around him, blending in with the blustery human voices. The aroma of meat turning on a spit, of boiled cabbage, of wet stone mixed in the dusty air. Callen had never been to a city before and was astonished at the masses of people and animals crowding the lanes. He gaped at the imposing stone wall rising up before him. He was finally here, a place he had heard about his whole life and only poorly imagined. He couldn't wait to venture through the city and explore all the wonders contained there.

Upon reaching the open gate with its cylindrical tower, Callen stopped and watched a man in uniform. He guessed the man was a guard of some sort. He wore a brown tunic over green slacks, with a golden firebird stitched on the tunic. Callen wondered at the meaning of the insignia.

"Welcome to Sherbourne," the man called out as he waved the masses in with his arms. A blast of trumpeting pierced the air, causing Callen to look up to see a half-dozen brightly dressed musicians on the wall's parapet blowing through long gold instruments and filling the air with a triumphal sound. Was this something they did in Sherbourne every day? What a strange land, Callen concluded.

After an hour of being swept along by the crowd, Callen found himself in what looked like the center of town. Tired and hot, he ducked into a teahouse, hoping for a cool respite, but found the place packed with people. He found a lone chair and dropped down into it, giving his throbbing feet a rest. As he loosened his bootlaces, a young serving maid with an apron came to his side and set down a pitcher of water and a glass.

"What'll you have, sir?"

"Any meat pies?"

The girl nodded. "We have a few pork and potato left."

"I'll take two. And a pint of dark ale, if you have it."

"Yes, anything else?"

Callen scooted his chair over as a couple pressed in behind the small table next to him. "Is Sherbourne always this crowded?"

The girl smiled. "Oh, no, sir." She cocked her head. "It's Coronation Day, didn't you know?"

"Coronation Day? Is that some sort of annual holiday?"

The girl laughed and blushed. "Oh, no. The only one we've had in ages. Well, at least in my lifetime. Prince Adin's to be crowned today."

So that's why all the fanfare! Callen remembered some talk around a Prince Adin. His brother Joran had met him once, and the prince had actually spent the night at Joran's house in Tebron.

News of Sherbourne rarely made it to Tebron—or Kettlebro, for that matter. Or maybe Callen never spent enough time chatting idly at the tavern to keep up on all the gossip of the outlying areas. Joran had related tales of some strange journey the prince had taken, now many years ago, and how he had lost his sister in a faraway land. And then there were some silly rumors about a curse being lifted. Loose talk. Callen never minded it.

He smiled at the girl. "Well, I hope he'll make a good king for your city."

"Oh, no doubt, he will." She curtseyed, then headed to the kitchen with his order.

Later, with two hefty meat pies and a pint of ale resting heavily in his stomach, Callen's pace slowed as he continued through the city, heading for the library, following the serving girl's directions. His head spun from all the bustle around him, and at one point he could hear a procession of musicians a few streets over, working their way east. The crowd sang and cheered, waving brightly stitched banners sporting the firebird design. He turned and looked up a hill and saw the palace, the sunlight reflecting off the stone, making it shimmer. Callen stopped and marveled at its beauty, impressive in its elegance as it perched like a beacon atop the hill.

By late afternoon, he arrived at the library steps. He gaped at the huge stone building covering two city blocks. Fortunately, the library was open, but, according to the sign posted on the door, would soon close. At least he could get his bearings and start his research. He imagined he would be here two days, mulling through parchments and books. Just the idea of discovery pumped him with excitement. What would he learn about the bridge? Would there be scrolls to tell him where the bridge had been built and if it still remained, even in part? Perhaps it had been dismantled and reassembled elsewhere.

He opened the doors to a cool, somber entry hall. No one seemed to be inside, as all were engaged in the outside festivities. The pale marble floor clicked under his boots as he traversed the spacious room under the canopy of a domed ceiling. Finally, he noticed a wiry, tall man shelving books near the end of the hallway. Callen approached him, and the man lifted his eyes from a cart piled with books to greet him.

"Ah, welcome." The librarian offered his hand. "Is there something I can help you find?"

"I hope so." Callen set his pack down on a nearby table. "I am seeking information on a bridge."

The man's eyebrows lifted in curiosity as Callen pulled the sheaf of parchments from his pack and spread them across the table. "A bridge, you say. Not my specialty, but I can certainly point you to reference books and the like." He studied the sketches and grunted, letting his eyes scan the details on the sheets.

"Hmm, yes, I think I can help."

Callen waited patiently, then had to ask. "Have you seen any other sketches like these? I was told this was called a suspension bridge, the only one ever designed. I am hoping to learn where it was built, and by whom."

The man scrunched his face and tapped his temple with his finger. "Well, we have many places we can begin. But since we'll be closing in a half hour, let me show you the stacks you'll want to peruse. Will you return in the morn?"

Callen nodded.

"Good. Then let's get you oriented." He motioned for Callen to bring his things and follow.

Callen carefully rolled up the parchments and put them back in his pack. He traipsed after the librarian, who led him through twisting corridors that made Callen lose his sense of direction.

Instead of getting oriented, he was getting *dis*oriented. They had taken so many turns that surely he'd never find his way out.

"Don't worry," the man said, as if by rote. "I'll bring you back here tomorrow. I never lose a visitor—unless they wander off without me."

They stopped at one of many towering stacks of books. "This is the architectural section, so anything on bridge construction would be here. But I noticed some interesting motifs on those drawings and it got me to thinking . . ."

The man tapped his temple again and spun around. Callen hurried to keep up with him. The librarian scurried up a lengthy ladder to a row of books ten feet overhead; pulled out a large, leather-bound tome; then came back down, reminding Callen of an agile spider crawling down the rungs. "Here." He dropped with a thud to the floor, then set the book on the table and opened it.

Callen stared at the exquisite drawing in front of him—the very tree detailed on his parchments. Etched in black ink, it spread massive boughs in a semicircle over the trunk, and birds of all sizes and shapes nested in its branches.

"That's it! What can you tell me about this tree? Is there something special about it?"

The librarian set the book on the nearest table. Sunshine filtering in from the glass domed roof bathed the drawing in ethereal light, lending it a sense of mystique.

"It's called the Eternal Tree, or in some ancient writings, The World Tree. It's a terebinth—have you heard of it?"

Callen shook his head. The librarian continued.

"You'll find many references to this tree in ancient writings, in literature and art. The design can be found in friezes of old buildings, enameled floor tile, even in stitchery and embroidered textiles like drapes and tablecloths. The terebinth was highly valued for its balsamic oil, a fragrant scent used in perfumes. It is similar to the oak, or the ancient *elon*."

"Was the tree used in building?"

"As in bridges? I noticed in the corner of each of your parchments something akin to a materials list. May I see them again?"

Callen spread out the parchments again, and the librarian pulled out a small magnifying glass from his tunic pocket. He mumbled over the words, flipping the parchments back and forth.

"Curious. Yes, it appears your bridge was to be made solely of wood—from the terebinth tree. Strange, isn't it, that it calls for no other materials other than some sort of iron cabling to support the bridge. A quite unique design . . ." He pointed a finger at a word at the far bottom right of the parchment. "*This* is interesting."

"What," Callen asked, trying to absorb all the information rattling around in his head.

"This name: *Me'lek Ko'hane.*"

"Is it the designer's name?"

The librarian shook his head. "I'm not certain. It could be a title. *Me'lek* meant king; many ancient kings used the term *in* their name, such as Melek-Abad, and Melek-Berad."

Callen wondered why the word for king would appear on the drawings. Was this a commissioned piece, for an ancient king? "What of the other word?"

"Ko'hane? I'll have to do some checking, but we'll find out."

A ringing of bells outside the building caused the librarian to straighten up. "Closing time, I'm afraid." He offered his hand. "My name is Za'ker."

"I'm called Callen."

"And where do you hail from?"

"I live and work in Kettlebro, but I grew up in Tebron."

"Ah, the forest village at the foot of the Sawtooths. A place I'd love to see." He sighed and rolled up Callen's parchments and handed them to him.

"Well, Callen, come by tomorrow, and we will see what else we can learn about your drawings. Have you been to the Heresh Bridge? There are similarities in the scrollwork."

"No, I've just arrived in the city. Is it far?"

Za'ker shook his head. "A bit east. There are some nice inns there, by the river, if you are looking for lodging."

"I am, thank you. I will see you, then, in the morning. But, tell me please, how does one find a way out of this library?"

Za'ker laughed. "Follow me." They navigated the maze of looming shelves, turning left and right endlessly until, to Callen's surprise, they wound up at the front door. Callen walked out of the cool building into a stuffy evening, facing a mostly empty street littered with food wrappings and bits of colored paper. Following Za'ker's directions, he turned south at the next block and wended his way through the narrow paved lanes, looking for an inn with a vacancy for the night.

Huldah glared out the window of her private dressing room as the carriage clattered along the cobbles away from the manor. She dabbed at her glistening forehead with a lace handkerchief, desperate to calm her pounding heart. She turned swiftly and faced the large standing mirror that usually remained hidden behind ponderous drapes. Today, she would not lie to herself, not any longer. She would face the mirror and let it tell her the unpleasant truth, a truth she already knew but had refused to believe. But now it was too dangerous to kid herself—the brat *saw*! And if she could see, then soon everyone would.

She stared at her reflection, studying the beautiful face, the silky long hair, her gorgeous figure. For decades now, she had kept up this ruse; not even her own daughters knew about the secret potions she brewed, the salves she stirred over hidden fires and applied to her lifeless skin, the nasty formulas she forced herself to drink—awful concoctions made from disgusting things that made her gag. What a price she paid to preserve her beauty—and although these high-priced remedies had done their magic for years, they were failing her now.

She muttered words to the mirror, demanding to see what others saw when they looked at her, steeling her fury and frustration. Soon, the silvery glass wavered and her beautiful features altered. Not much, but enough. A growl grew in her throat, and, grabbing the closest object she could find on her dressing table, she hurled a bottle against the condemning mirror at full force. The bottle shattered in pieces across the tiled floor, leaving the mirror unmarred. A string of evil curses flowed from her mouth as she turned to her table and reached for another bottle. Frantically, she uncorked the top and took a huge swallow of the green, slimy contents. As she forced the liquid down her throat, she encanted a spell, waving her hands over her face and hair. Jadiel's beautiful, soft face haunted her—the tumble of thick black hair, rosy red cheeks, eyes as blue as brilliant sapphires. A roil of hatred filled her throat with bile. She grabbed another bottle and shook it, causing a hissing fizz to spill over the sides of the bottle and onto the table, where it burned a black scar into the wood. This, too, she upended into her mouth, twisting her face into a knot.

She spun back to confront the mirror and narrowed her eyes, studying every bit of her reflection. Finally, an anguished cry tore from her throat. She screamed, shaking the manor to its foundation.

When the cry ebbed from the room, leaving the ornate furnishings in a shambles, she stumbled to her armoire and pulled out the bottom drawer. In her blinding fury, she tripped over a footstool and sent it crashing across the room, then managed to set herself down into her chair with a thick book gripped in her trembling hands. She spoke the releasing spell and the book loosened, allowing her to open it.

Within the pages of this antique book were spells for every evil task—for turning a heart against a lover; for causing slow, painful deaths in dozens of violent ways; for weaving webs of deception and illusions. The section on beauty was so worn that the pages nearly fell from the binding, but Huldah forced herself to read it again. She had followed every spell, every concoction outlined. Over the years she had paid many valuable coins for dark secrets to those she had encountered in distant lands. She alone had outwitted age and time, had preserved beauty for more decades than anyone would think possible. That beauty cost her plenty—but, then, look what it had bought her. Things which only potent beauty could buy.

Seven rich husbands who had doted on her, drenched her with riches and luxury and comfort. Stupid, sappy men she had long outlived. The finest delicacies from the ends of the world; velvet-lined carriages drawn by elegant destriers; servants to wait on her, hand and foot, fulfilling her every command. Beauty meant power, and no power could stand against the demands of a beautiful woman. She had yet to find a man who could resist such intoxicating beauty, who wouldn't jump off a cliff for her if she but asked.

The thought of losing such power was unthinkable and unacceptable! She had this simpleton, Ka'rel, trailing her heels, like a slobbering dog on a leash. Now mistress of the greatest estate in the region, she could live comfortably here for perhaps fifty or more years before garnering too much suspicion, long after her pathetic husband was dead and buried under the rich soil he so loved. And, she scowled, long after that brat of his was also gone.

But Jadiel was an immediate problem, more so now that the child clearly saw through the waning power of her spells with some uncanny gift of sight. However had such a stupid brat managed to survive the traps she had set for her? Huldah seethed as she continued flipping through the pages of her book. Time had run out; she could no longer let the girl live. Tomorrow, she would send the girl off on some errand and follow her. That way she could make sure the child never returned, a victim of some unfortunate accident.

As she pondered how she would do away with Jadiel, she glanced down at the book, puzzled by the page before her. Columns of writing in faded black ink flanked a sketch of a tree with outstretched boughs. Huldah had never paid any attention to the page with its scribbly words. The tree looked like all the others trees in Logan Valley—ugly, boring trees that never bloomed. But the caption printed in tiny letters beneath the tree caught her attention. "The Tree of Eternal Beauty and Youth." What in the world did that mean? And how had she missed that?

Huldah hurriedly read through the lengthy text until her eyes lit upon a paragraph that ignited a spark of hope in her gut. The leaves from this ancient tree, said to have vanished from the world eons ago, contained a unique oil that, when ingested through chewing the leaves, imparted eternal youth and beauty. Ancient writings claimed the leaves, if chewed often, would regenerate a person's natural beauty and reverse effects of aging. Legends stated that when word of this gift of immortality spread, nations warred over the tree, and in the throes of battle, the vanquished armies cut down and burned the tree to prevent their victors from possessing it.

Huldah mumbled through the rest of the pointless history lesson, searching for any hint of where this tree could be found. Surely there hadn't been only one! And even if a single tree had been destroyed, surely there would have been seeds carried by birds and later dropped onto the ground to grow into more of these magical trees.

Huldah leaped up from her chair. This was her saving grace! No more disgusting potions that only masked her true appearance and gave her temporary relief from her aged and creaking bones. True immortality! Eternal beauty! And all from an insignificant, unimpressive tree. No wonder the legend had been lost over the ages. Who would think to look for an elixir from such an ordinary source?

Huldah rubbed her arthritic hands, feeling the weight of her many years eating at her sinews and poisoning her blood. She had no doubt this tree could be found—and she knew just the little brat to send after those leaves. With Jadiel out of her hair, Huldah could keep Ka'rel enchanted without hindrance. And when Jadiel returned with those leaves, why, then she could throw away all her potions and salves and—live forever!

Huldah chortled with glee, dancing around the room and hugging the book to her chest. Tonight she would charm Ka'rel with her ways, keeping her distance from that horrid child. No doubt the girl was presently telling her father all about the strange things she saw this day. But Huldah would make sure Ka'rel forgot his daughter's every word. She had ways of erasing the memory of things recently said and done. By tomorrow, Ka'rel would remember Jadiel's warnings no longer. By that time, the little brat would be on her way, certain to hurry. For Huldah planned to threaten the child with her greatest fear.

Huldah's eyes widened in excitement as a perfect plan formed in her mind. Tonight would rise a full moon. She would give Jadiel until the next full moon to retrieve the leaves and return. Or else, at dawn of the morning following that next full moon, her loving, sweet Papa would be dead.

NINE

Z A'KER'S FACE showed surprise as he unlocked the library doors from the inside and found Callen waiting on the top step.

"My, you're an eager one. I trust you found an inn and had a good rest?"

Callen nodded and stepped inside. "I did. What a spectacular river the Heresh is. And all those cottages and shops built right along the water's edge. Does that river ever flood?"

Za'ker walked briskly down the hall with Callen at his heels. "Oh, my, yes. Almost every spring. Many have to evacuate, and some of the stores close until the flood waters drain from their floors. They have to keep the merchandise high off the ground so their goods aren't damaged." He turned to look at Callen as he wove through the maze of shelves. "Did you have time to see the bridge?"

"Only briefly. I plan to go back this afternoon and sketch."

Za'ker nodded and kept zigzagging. Finally, he stopped at the same place he had brought Callen to yesterday. On the table were a stack of books next to a half-dozen rolled-up scrolls.

"Your drawings piqued my curiosity, so I did some hunting and found a few things I think you'll find intriguing."

Callen felt his heart thump in anticipation as he pulled the parchments from his pack and unrolled them. Za'ker pointed again to one of the bottom corners. "Remember we spoke about this name here, *Me'lek Ko'hane?* Well, it took some digging, but here is what I found."

Za'ker unrolled a yellowed scroll and pinned down the corners with some of the books to flatten it. Callen let his eyes roam over the faded calligraphy. At first he thought it a strange language, then realized he could read it. The letters were embellished with long dashes and swirls, and some of the spellings were odd, but this was his language.

"You see here . . ." Za'ker pointed to a passage halfway down the scroll, "a reference to this Me'lek or King. I cross-referenced this scroll with a number of others of similar dating and origin."

Callen listened intently, soaking up every word. "Please, tell me what you found."

"Ko'hane means 'priest.' In all the references I found, out of the whole march of ancient kings, there is only one with the designation of king-priest. This one, this Me'lek Ko'hane, was an ancient king of a region called Antolae, and as hard as I searched, I could not find a true name for him. The ruins of that great city exist today, northeast of here at the foot of the Antolaian Mountains. It is a land of jackals and wolves—a wasteland, never reinhabited. For what reason, I cannot determine—other than a hint of some terrible event, and a curse that was cast, but not aimed at Antolae. Perhaps of some nearby realm." Za'ker sighed and ran a hand through his short curly hair.

"Now, this Me'lek—this king-priest—is said to have mediated between two great kingdoms that warred against each other for centuries. Because of the great respect both kingdoms had for this man, they buried him in a place of honor among the great kings of history—in the King's Plain."

Za'ker paused; he seemed to expect a reaction from Callen.

Callen pursed his lips. "The King's Plain?"

"You've never heard of it?"

Callen shook his head. "Should I have?"

Za'ker whistled. "I am surprised you haven't. The King's Plain is also called The Valley of Desolation, or sometimes The Valley Perilous." He waited to see if either of those names rang in familiarity to Callen. They didn't.

Za'ker reached over and grabbed another book. "Here, I'll go make us a pot of tea and see if anyone else has come into the library. Read this in the meantime, and when I come back, I'll try to answer any more questions you may have."

"Thank you for your help." Callen sat in a chair and turned the book and opened it.

Za'ker waved him off and hurried down the aisle. Soon Callen heard the librarian's soft footsteps fade, and he was left to ponder the material before him in the quiet, cool room streaked by morning sun filtering through the glass ceiling.

As Callen turned pages, he became enthralled by a tale that spoke of the King's Plain. He learned about the history of these two kingdoms and how vicious battles were fought over borders, an interminable push-pull of boundaries and territories gained and lost. How one group claimed divine right to the land, and that the kings throughout the centuries had been buried in this valley, alongside men and women of noble birth and favor. Yet the valley was regarded with suspicion and fear, as the kings were said not to be dead, but only sleeping. That they were waiting.

Waiting? Callen wondered. *Waiting for what?*

He read through other passages Za'ker had marked with leather strips. He could find nothing to answer that question, but read repeated accounts of bizarre happenings in the valley, warnings to keep away. That because the dead were not really dead, they haunted and terrorized the living, causing travelers to keep a wide berth and avoid entering the valley.

Callen put down the book and rubbed his eyes. He heard Za'ker's steps coming closer, somewhere across the great room.

Why was the name—or title—of this ancient king of Antolae, a king-priest who had been buried in some accursed valley, notated on the bottom of his drawings, drawings of a strange bridge? Again he wondered if this king had designed the bridge, or had it commissioned to be built. Perhaps Antolae was where the bridge had been built.

Callen looked up to see Za'ker setting down a tray. A teapot and two cups sat beside a plate of puffed pastries. Callen's stomach rumbled in response even though he'd eaten a huge breakfast only an hour ago.

Za'ker sat beside him. "Sorry for the delay. I had to help a woman find some gardening books." He took a bite of one of the pastries and then poured Callen a cup of tea. "What have you learned?"

"This King's Plain. Do you know where it is?"

"Of course," Za'ker answered. "It's west of a small village called Rumble, along the road to Ethryn. South, about a couple dozen leagues."

Ethryn. That's where his own heritage traced back—on both his mother's and father's sides. Yet he knew nothing of that land. Callen sipped his tea and bit into the airy pastry. It melted in his mouth with a rush of almond paste. "Have you been there?"

Za'ker drew back, fearful. "Of course not! No one in his right mind would step foot in that valley. It's cursed."

"So I read," Callen said between bites. "Well, what about Antolae? Do you know where that is?"

Za'ker nodded as he chewed. He pulled a scroll out from under some others and unrolled it. Callen held one edge as he looked at the large map sketched on the parchment. "We're here," Za'ker pointed. He ran his finger west along the outline of a road to a crossroads, and then continued northeast toward the jagged lines that appeared to symbolize mountains. "There." He then pointed a finger several inches below that mark. "There's your village—Tebron. Well, where it would be today. This map was drawn long before many of these villages existed." He took a quick sip of his tea. "I don't know anything about that region, but I imagine you could find more writings on it, if you've a hankering to search."

Callen thought for a moment. "I read that the kings in the plain are said to be waiting. For what?"

Za'ker shrugged. "I have no idea. Perhaps if you travel down to Rumble, you'll find more answers to the mystery of the King's Plain. But one thing I do know—there are no rivers of note there, and none at or around Antolae. No call for a bridge to be built, is there, if there's no water to span? Those lands are flat, so you wouldn't even need a bridge to cross from one hill to another. I just don't see the connection between this king of Antolae and your bridge. But then, why is his name on the parchments?"

Callen nodded. "My thoughts exactly."

"Oh." Za'ker pointed at another book. "I did find something else of note about the terebinth tree. That kings were often buried under them, as custom dictated for many of the ancient kingdoms. There are references that call the terebinth 'the King's Tree' for that reason. Some ancient peoples worshiped and set up altars under those trees."

"So maybe," Callen added, "the reason the name Me'lek Ko'hane is on the drawings is because the bridge was meant to be constructed from this terebinth or 'king's tree.'"

"Perhaps. But why not just put 'terebinth' on the legend of the drawings instead?"

"Yes, that would make more sense. There must be some other reason."

The faint tingle of a bell caused Callen to raise his head.

"Someone needs me at the front desk. There are more writings on the tree, but I found absolutely nothing on the bridge. Other bridges, yes, but not yours. Nothing about a suspension bridge."

"Oh, one last question." Callen pointed to a spot on one of the bridge illustrations. "Do those strange letters look familiar to you?"

"Ah, I did take a good look at those. They seem important, running across much of your bridge. But I have never come across writing like that. Perhaps they are numbers, or symbols of creatures or plants. The Ethrynians have a glyph language. Perhaps it is somehow related to theirs."

Another mention of Ethryn. Suddenly, Callen had a desire to see the land his ancestors emigrated from. He knew little of it apart from the fact that the land suffered a hot and inhospitable climate. That was why his ancestors, and many other families, had migrated north years ago in search of more fertile lands to call home. How his family ended up in the cool forest of Tebron.

He smiled at Za'ker. "Thank you, again, for all this help."

Za'ker nodded and rushed off. No wonder he was so trim, Callen mused. The librarian must walk miles each day, and then there were all those ladders he climbed! Since he'd arrived, Callen had seen no others tending the library. Could Za'ker be the only one who shelved and catalogued all these books and scrolls? The task seemed overwhelming for one man, yet, if anyone was up to the challenge, Za'ker would be the one.

Callen spent the next two hours reading texts and jotting notes. He studied a number of drawings of various bridges, but most had little ornamental scrollwork. Most bridges were purely functional, erected for one purpose only—to allow people to cross from one shore to another. The builders gave no thought to aesthetic design or artistic appeal. He looked for references on forgotten languages, but got so turned around in the stacks, he finally gave up.

A weariness settled upon him, from sitting so long and reading more than he had ever read in one day. He had gone through all the materials Za'ker had given him. He had learned all he hoped to learn at the Sherbourne library. The thought of stretching his legs in the warm sun suddenly had great appeal. He still had a few hours of daylight left to examine and sketch the bridge over Heresh.

He stood and stretched, then looked around. How would he find his way out of the library? As he searched, he noticed the little silver bell sitting on the tray beside the teapot. He picked it up and jingled it, and in no time heard Za'ker's footsteps coming toward him. The librarian led him to the front door, where they said their good-byes. Once more Callen thanked the man for his help, then pushed open the door to the bright, sparkling fall day. He drew in a deep breath of air that smelled so different from the vale's fertile air. This smelled like a jumble of food and dust and river.

Callen adjusted the pack on his back and headed down the lane with the sun westering behind him. His mind rattled with all the things he had learned—and all the questions still puzzling him. But he let them simmer in the back of his mind and focused his thoughts on the bridge ahead. His hand itched to pull out a pencil and sketch. He was unused to going days without carving or drawing something. Now, he would sit beside the wide, slow-moving river and let his mind clear. And after that, he had no idea where he would go.

TEN

JADIEL SAT at her dresser, combing out her tangled tresses. She and Papa had enjoyed a wonderful picnic high on a ridge overlooking the miles of estate spreading out in all directions. Papa talked on about the crops he would plant next year, and the new markets for his produce. Jadiel let him ramble, happy to listen to his warm, cheerful voice. As the sun baked them and a mild breeze twirled the fall leaves around them, Jadiel waited for the right opportunity to speak to her father about Huldah. But somehow the right moment had never presented itself. Jadiel sighed. She would just have to make another opportunity, get him alone where Huldah and her daughters could not overhear.

Her father had left her at the front door of the manor to freshen up for supper as he went to unhitch the horses from their breeching. She sneaked quietly to her room, eyeing the hallway. The last thing she wanted was to run into her stepmother after such a nice time. Nothing like a slap in the face to ruin a joyful afternoon!

She lifted her small hand mirror and looked at her reflection. Her father had commented earlier how she looked more and more like her mother every day. Even she could see her face changing, no longer a little girl's. Her cheeks had lengthened over summer; her legs often ached from growing pains. She no longer had to scoot a stool over to reach the top of her dresser. Some of her dresses stretched tightly across her chest, and the hems hovered over her knees instead of below. She looked more intently, trying to see the resemblance to her mother, and feeling despair that Mama's beautiful face faded from her memory a little more each day.

And then a hand yanked hard on her hair and knocked her off her chair.

Jadiel cried out as Huldah nearly dragged her halfway across the bedroom floor. Her stepmother abruptly dumped her in a heap on the wood floor and straddled over her, glaring.

Jadiel curled up in a ball as Huldah gave her a swift kick in her side with a heavy, iron-toed boot.

"I've grown tired of your arrogant disrespect," Huldah growled. Jadiel cringed, awaiting another kick. Tears streamed down her cheeks and a sob stuck in her throat. She dared turn her head and look up at Huldah, whose scowl turned into a sinister grin. "But I won't have to put up with it any longer. Get up, you stupid brat!"

Jadiel scurried to her feet before Huldah could assist her with another yank of her hair. She backed into a corner as Huldah picked up a strange-looking book she had dropped onto Jadiel's bed.

She shoved the open book into the girl's face and screeched, "You see this tree?"

All Jadiel could manage was a terrified nod. It looked like a drawing of any one of the expansive oaks on the estate.

"Well, my child," she crooned in a falsely sweet voice, "study it well, for you have until the next full moon to find this tree and bring me back a satchel full of leaves."

Jadiel frowned. What in the world did she want with oak leaves?

"I see you're not getting it through your thick head!" Huldah swiped at Jadiel, smacking her hard on the side of her head with the back of her hand. Jadiel yelped in pain and bit her lip.

"This," Huldah hissed, "is a very unique tree—the Tree of Eternal Youth and Beauty. And, no doubt, it will require you to muster all your clever talents to find it. But I suggest you hurry and pack and be quickly on your way if you are to return in time."

Jadiel's heart sank like a boulder falling off a cliff. "Wh-what do you mean?"

"Why, my dear Jadiel, if you do not show up in this house by the next full moon with those leaves, your dear, sweet Papa will die the following morning. And that would be *such* a shame, wouldn't it?"

Jadiel gasped in horror. Huldah couldn't mean to kill her Papa, could she? Would she? Fear and panic struck her so hard she reeled. "But—however am I to accomplish such a task? I'm only twelve years old. I know nothing about the wide world beyond the manor . . ."

Huldah pushed her face up close to Jadiel's and hissed. "Well, you better learn fast. Why, you were clever enough to worm your way out of my other traps. Surely someone so smart and beauti—" Her stepmother gagged on the last word. "—*determined* will manage. Unless you don't mind living out the rest of your days as an orphan . . ."

The thought of losing Papa after having lost her mother was unbearable. One look told her Huldah was serious. There would be no clever way to sidestep this threat.

"Where will I go? How will I eat?" Jadiel asked these questions more of herself than of Huldah.

Huldah shrugged and snickered. She snapped the book shut and turned to walk out of the room. She spun around to face Jadiel, who still cowered in the corner. "And if you breathe a word about our little 'agreement,' or try to outsmart me, I won't wait for the full moon to kill Ka'rel. No running teary-eyed to Papa—or anyone else for that matter. Just keep your end of the bargain and I'll keep mine. You *do* understand?"

Jadiel nodded and watched Huldah stomp from the room, slamming the door behind her.

A deep shaky breath escaped her chest. Her whole world crumbled around her, leaving her shocked and in disbelief. How in heaven would she find some magical tree? And in thirty days' time? Huldah had given her a hopeless task—and a death sentence for her father. And what would her father think of her sudden disappearance? Surely he would become frantic and come searching for her. Jadiel knew deep in her heart that Huldah would carry out her threats. She could not risk her father's life, but what hope could she harbor for success?

Jadiel stood on trembling legs and managed to stumble over to the window. Her head ached from Huldah's slap.

"Grork," she whispered as tears kept flowing. "Are you there?"

Jadiel heard nothing for a moment, then the bushes rustled and the little hoptoad came bouncing over. He positioned himself under her sill and looked up.

"I heard everything, miss. Oh, the evil woman certainly means your death—and your father's." Jadiel cried harder, gulping air.

"But, miss," the hoptoad said, trying to encourage her. "Take heart. Heaven favors the honest and valiant. Go, look for the tree, and I will get word to your father of your quest. Perhaps once he knows the truth about your stepmother and what she has done to you, he will find a way to thwart her—and bring you back. Look, I have hidden a pouch of coins under the yellow rosebush by the kitchen window. Take those for your journey, and don't forget the gifts from your mother—and your flute! You may find they will come in handy."

Jadiel nodded and wiped her eyes. "Thank you, Grork. Please tell my father I love him. I will try somehow to get word to him of where I am, but—" Tears pooled once more in her eyes. "I don't have any idea where to go. I've never been outside the vale."

Grork nodded in sympathy. "Neither have I. But perhaps if you inquire of trustworthy people, they may be able to assist you. But beware, not everyone would be your friend."

Jadiel shuddered thinking of all the possible dangers that could meet her out in the wide world.

Grork croaked softly. "I hear someone coming. Go, hurry and pack, and don't forget about the coins!"

Jadiel watched the hoptoad scurry under a bush and then she shut tight her window. The sun was an hour from setting; already the afternoon sky grew dark, and gloomy clouds gathered overhead, matching her distraught mood. As if in a daze, she packed her satchel with warm clothes, an extra pair of sturdy shoes, and the things Grork had told her to take. She tied a rolled-up blanket to the top of her satchel. With her heavy cloak draped across her arm, she quietly snuck out the back door and hurried to the side of the manor where, under the yellow rose bush, she found a small velvet pouch filled to the brim with gold coins. Jadiel guessed Grork had stolen them from Huldah's room somehow. She wished she'd thought to thank him, or even given him a kiss on his bumpy cheek. But she had no time to look for him.

One peek in the window showed the cook preparing supper. The thought of food set her mouth watering, but she dared not attract anyone's attention. She knew she would burst out crying and the cook would pry her story out of her. No, supper would have to wait. But there were ripe apples still hanging from trees in the orchard. And with the coins she could find lodging and food along the way.

Jadiel hurried to the orchard and picked apples, stuffing a dozen into her satchel, weighing it down. She hefted the load onto her back and walked down the dirt road to the south entrance of the estate. Behind her, her papa was upstairs, getting ready for dinner. What would Huldah say to keep him from worrying? Jadiel fumed. Surely the witch would just put Papa under one of her spells. He would probably never even notice her absence.

With that thought, Jadiel stomped the ground, steeling her resolve to hurry and find the leaves and return. And maybe, in the meantime, Grork would get through to Papa and they'd come find her. More tears fell. Oh, it all seemed so hopeless!

In the evening dusk, the little hoptoad stuck his head out from under the camellia bush. Sensing the way was clear, he hopped gingerly to the dining room window to listen. There he pressed his sleek head against the wall, trying to hear to the voices of those at the table, but the words were garbled. He would wait until the meal ended and then find a way to sneak inside and speak to Ka'rel. The girl's father often retired to his study after dinner, a room three doors from the dining room, but he rarely opened his window. Perhaps he could kick some pebbles and attract his attention, the way he had done with Jadiel. Somehow he had to warn Ka'rel, as he'd promised Jadiel, for hoptoads are always true and trustworthy.

Suddenly, Grork felt the ground shake. He turned his head and, looming over him, stared the evil stepmother, her hands on her hips.

"Well, what have we here?" Her voice made Grork shiver. He quickly dug into the soft dirt, burrowing until only his eyes peered out.

"Don't think you can hide so easily." She scooped him out and grasped him in a stranglehold. "I suspected some conspiracy. That brat couldn't have escaped my traps without help."

Grork croaked as Huldah squeezed tighter around his throat.

"Please," he whimpered.

"Oh, it speaks! How endearing." Huldah spat in the toad's face.

"Aren't you afraid of getting warts?" he asked in a broken, frightened voice.

Huldah yelped and threw the toad to the ground as if he carried the Plague. Grork kept a straight face, containing his laughter. Why did they always fall for that?

Huldah leaned down and sneered at the toad. "Well, you can wipe that smug expression off your face. You'll not be the girl's fairy god-frog any longer—"

"Madame." He interrupted her in an offended voice. "Excuse me, I am *not* a frog. I am a hop—"

Huldah didn't let Grork finish. She lifted a heavy-booted foot and smashed it down hard on top of the toad. He squished under her sole, flat as a pancake.

Huldah lifted her shoe and saw bits of hoptoad sticking to her boot. As she wiped her boot in the dirt to clean it off, she said to herself, "Such a waste. Frog legs are quite a delicacy."

ELEVEN

CALLEN SHOOK out the cramp in his wrist. He had been drawing so intently for the last few hours without a break that the muscles in his hand ached. He set down his sketch pad and took out his knife. With short strokes, he whittled away the wood and sharpened the lead in his pencil.

As he sat on a hard bench alongside the river Heresh, people walked past him, looking over his shoulder at his drawings. Occasionally one would mumble a compliment or engage him in conversation. He answered in short, polite words, but they quickly understood they were disturbing his concentration and moved on. From this vantage point he could make out the bridge's scrollwork in perfect detail. Most of the stanchions that rose from the bridge displayed intricate carvings, as did some of the smaller balusters. Presently, he focused his attention on the corbelled arch closest to him, one bearing flowing designs that resembled clouds or swirls in water.

Nearby, a steeple rang out a rhythm of six bells, prompting some of those walking across the bridge to liven their steps. He watched tired workers heading home, where, possibly, a hot meal and bath awaited them. Callen knew he should start thinking about quitting for the day, but he just had to finish the one topmost pattern while the light lingered. Beren had been right; this bridge displayed parallel themes and designs to his mysterious bridge, but the intricacy and sophistication paled in comparison. There was something—well, perfect—about the strange drawings he carried in his pack, that now, after seeing the Heresh bridge up close, made him hunger even more to find trace of the ancient, puzzling suspension bridge.

As Callen picked up his sketch pad to continue, a shadow fell across the page. He turned his head and found himself staring into the ugliest face he had ever seen.

A strange man bent over him, looking curiously at his drawing. Rags hung off his lean frame. Scars ran across his cheeks and forehead where a tangle of dirty brown hair fell into his eyes, and his trim beard had been cut in choppy fashion. He seemed Callen's age, but his eyes carried pain that made him appear much older. A heavy dark cloak draped across his shoulders and appeared to weigh the man down. Callen recoiled in surprise and jumped to his feet. For some reason the closeness of this unpleasant person set him on edge. Was he a thief, a beggar? Would he try to steal Callen's pack?

And then the man tipped back his head and chortled, giving Callen pause.

As a precaution, Callen pushed his pack with his foot so it was no longer between him and the stranger.

"What do you want?" Callen snapped.

The man fastened his dark-brown eyes on Callen's. He spoke softly. "What do *you* want?"

"What?"

The stranger pointed a gnarled finger at the sketchbook. "I see you are seeking something. Your drawings make that evident."

The man's accent was thick and odd. Callen stepped back and studied him, his baggy tunic and pants, his worn sandals. Clearly, he wasn't from Sherbourne. Callen tried not to stare at the man's repulsive face.

"What do you mean?"

The stranger sat on the bench. He carried nothing with him—no pouch or pack or water skin. He seemed both feeble and agile at the same time, moving with deliberation and thoughtfulness.

"There was a man," he said, looking out across the river, "who found a tiny seed. The tiniest seed in existence. Yet when he sowed it in his field, it grew to become the greatest tree in the world, so that birds of every kind came and found lodging in its branches."

Callen shuddered at the man's words. *The terebinth tree!* The stranger looked back into Callen's face. "The Ke'sher."

"Are you referring to this river, the Heresh?"

The man patted the bench for Callen to sit. "Come, let me tell you a story. Do you like stories?"

Callen reluctantly sat beside the stranger, though he would have preferred to shoo him away and finish his sketches. Yet he spoke of a great tree—perhaps alluding to the terebinth legends. Why would this stranger mention something that consumed his own thoughts? Was this odd, repulsive man some kind of prophet or holy man? Callen had heard stories of such men wandering the deserts ages ago, but surely those were children's tales.

Callen noticed the man sat still, waiting. Once he saw Callen poised to listen, the stranger stared back over the water and spoke.

"Long ago, there was a wealthy landowner, who had need to travel to a faraway country. So he hired caretakers to tend his vineyard and orchards, men he thought were trustworthy. At harvesttime, he sent a servant to them, asking for the profits from his estate, but the caretakers beat him badly and sent him away. The landowner heard of this grave news and sent another servant on the same mission, along with a stern warning, but the caretakers laughed and beat this man also."

Callen turned and stared at the stranger as he told this story, wondering what on earth he was rambling on about. Perhaps the man was addled in the head!

If the stranger was aware of Callen's scrutiny, he didn't show it, gazing at the water as he finished his tale. "Now, word came to the landowner that the ruthless caretakers had beaten his other servant. Well then, he thought, I will send my son; surely they will respect and listen to him. But when the men saw the young man, they conspired together, saying, 'This is the heir. Let us kill him; then we can have this place to ourselves and keep all the profits.'"

At this, the stranger turned and caught Callen's gaze with such a severe look that Callen's breath caught. He felt the man peered into his very soul, and it made him squirm. "What do you think the wealthy landowner did to those men who killed his son?" the stranger asked.

Callen shrugged uncomfortably. The man's eyes bored into him. What did he care about some dumb story about a landowner?

"Come now," the stranger said. "What would you do if you were that wealthy man?"

Callen couldn't take it anymore. He stood back up and started gathering his things. "I just want to sketch this bridge. Why are you annoying me with your silly stories?"

The man gave Callen a sad, lopsided smile. Something in that smile made Callen feel instantly remorseful for being so curt. Perhaps he was just a lonely eccentric looking for company. With that repulsive appearance, Callen was sure most people kept their distance.

The stranger set his hands in his lap as his eyes wandered to the bridge. "That landowner is the one who also built the Ke'sher." He turned to Callen once more. "Ke'sher, in the ancient language, means bridge."

Callen's jaw slacked. Just what was this man inferring?

"And the same evil men who murdered the heir to his estate destroyed his bridge." His eyes smiled but his twisted mouth remained in a frown. "That is what you seek, is it not?"

So this man must truly be a prophet or seer! How could he know about Callen's quest? Questions tumbled from Callen's mouth, demanding the stranger tell him about this bridge, where it could be found, why it was built. But the man only sat quietly and slowly shook his head.

"You are not ready to hear answers to those questions."

"What!" Callen had had enough of this man talking in such riddles. Clearly, the fool was only teasing and goading him. Well, he would just keep searching his own way—without this ugly man's help.

He hurriedly put away his pencil and sketch pad, then hoisted the pack onto his back. As he turned to walk away, he heard the stranger call out sharply.

"Callen!"

A stab of fear pierced Callen's heart. "How—how do you know my name?"

He answered Callen as he struggled to his feet, balancing against the back of the bench. "There sits a circle upon a circle within a circle. There lies a promise of a crown on the backs of kings . . ."

Callen shook his head as the words tumbled into his brain. In his mind's eye, a vision intruded, of a desolate plain, windswept and hungry. A hill rising up in the middle. And under the ground, the bones of ancient kings, waiting.

"The King's Plain . . ." Slowly the vision was whisked away, as if blown off by the plain's howling wind. His body slumped in weakness. Callen's words were a vapor of breath. "Who are you?"

The stranger bowed his head. "I am Ebed, a lowly servant. I was once a prophet in a land far from here, and for a time respected among my people."

Callen sensed the man would say no more. He fought the urge to shake him and make him spill all his secrets.

"Go there, then." He met Callen's frustrated eyes. "To the Valley Perilous. Seek the circle upon a circle within a circle. But know that you are taking a great risk, one that may cost you your life."

"Why?" Callen felt fear crawl up his neck. "Why is it such a risk? Is the plain that dangerous?"

The ugly man shook his head. "It is not the land that is dangerous, Callen. The danger lies in your heart. Others have lost their lives searching for the bridge. Are you certain you are prepared to pay that price?"

Callen snorted. What was all this mysterious talk about his heart harboring danger? And that searching for a bridge could cost him his life? Perhaps this prophet—or whoever he was—had spent too many years in the hot sun, or perhaps whatever injuries had been inflicted upon him had damaged his thinking faculties.

"Will you not heed my warning? Are you not afraid?"

Callen shook his head and started walking upriver, toward the inn where his supper awaited him. "Of course not." He waved Ebed away.

After a moment, Callen glanced back to make sure Ebed was not following him. He'd had enough of the man's taunts and riddles and warnings. But when he looked over at the bench, the repulsive man was gone. Callen stopped in his tracks and swung his head around, but only a few people strolled the water's edge. Ebed was nowhere to be found.

"Humph," Callen muttered. He quickened his pace, feeling the evening air settle around his neck, giving him a chill. He shook off his thoughts of Ebed and let his mind drift toward the image of warm fare and a pint of ale. Yet the vision of the King's Plain seeped into his awareness, pushing out those tempting comforts, and stirring in him a hunger he knew a hot meal and drink would fail to sate.

TWELVE

WHEN KA'REL stepped through the front door to the manor he stopped abruptly. There, standing huddled together in the entryway, were Huldah and her daughters, their faces distraught and tear-streaked. Fear clutched his heart, sending his thoughts reeling to the day he learned of M'lynn's death. *Please, not another tragedy!*

When Huldah cast her eyes to the ground, Ka'rel looked frantically around.

"Jadiel. Where is Jadiel?"

Huldah nodded solemnly to Kinna, who trudged down the hall and came back carrying a bundle in her arms.

Ka'rel's heart threatened to burst at the sight of Jadiel's coat, ripped to shreds and streaked with blood. He questioned Huldah's eyes, and what he saw there summoned a scream to his throat.

"No!" His anguished cry reverberated off the walls. He lunged at Kinna, frightening her as he grabbed the garment from her hands.

He spun around and grasped Huldah's shoulders. "Where? Where is she?"

Huldah spoke in a consoling tone. "Gone." The words seemed to lodge in her throat. "The girls were out playing and found this."

Ka'rel ached to scream, to fill the manor with the pain bursting from his heart. "Please, show me . . ."

Kinna questioned her mother with her eyes. Huldah threw open the front door and ran down the steps, with Ka'rel and her daughters close behind her. She led them down the lane, past the stables, to a field adjacent to the horse pasture. There, by an oak tree, in the evening twilight, Ka'rel knelt and searched the ground. Blood covered the gnarled roots protruding from the ground, but search as he might, Ka'rel could find nothing more. No other traces of clothing or flesh.

Huldah and her daughters stood silently as Ka'rel dropped his head to his knees and wept. After a long while of grieving, he raised his stricken face.

"Did any of you see her—see what happened?"

The women shook their heads.

"Did you make a search?"

Again they shook her heads. Ka'rel leapt to his feet. "But she may only be injured, lying somewhere around!"

Ka'rel turned in frantic circles. "Huldah! Go and find Azar. Tell him to gather all the workers before they leave, and to search the grounds."

Huldah hesitated. "But, Ka'rel, my love . . ." She gently touched his shoulder. "Surely, with this much blood . . ."

"Do as I say. Hurry!"

Huldah stiffened at his recrimination. "Yes, Ka'rel." She turned and headed toward the carriage house.

Ka'rel looked intently at Kinna and Ramah. "How long ago did you find this?"

Kinna shrugged and looked at Ramah. "An hour ago?"

Ka'rel grabbed onto any scrap of hope he could gather. "Then she may still be alive!"

Ka'rel ran back to the manor as fast as he could. Inside, he lit a lantern and found the cook, telling her what had happened. She nearly swooned at the news.

"Oh Jaddie! I saw her not two hours ago!"

"Go and find anyone you can. We must search for her!"

Ka'rel rushed out of the kitchen, buttoning up his coat. As he ran back outside, he heard voices shouting and men running. He spotted Azar down by the carriage house with a lamp in his hand, hurrying toward him. *Jadiel, please be alive!*

The next morning, Huldah listened patiently as Ka'rel raged and grieved about his missing daughter. But by the end of the week, her patience grew brittle and threatened to break as Ka'rel refused to stop searching for Jadiel. Every morning, before dawn, he rode out on his horse, scouring the countryside, questioning neighbors. And every night, well after dark, he would straggle in, discouraged and heartsick, but unwilling to quit his search. Huldah had had enough of his whining and his foolish hope. Why couldn't he see Jadiel was lost and just forget about her?

She tried to give him draughts, claiming they would calm him, but he refused. Yet these were more than sleeping potions; they would make the last few days fade away, like the remnants of a dream upon awakening. Hard as she tried, she couldn't find a way to get him to drink, or even eat the soup she laced with her elixirs. Ka'rel swore not to touch food or drink except water until he found either Jadiel or her remains.

Huldah fumed, sitting in front of her mirror brushing out her hair. She had slit the throat of that calf, spilling more blood than an injured girl could lose and still live! How foolish men were; in a crisis they lost all sense of reason. She had to do something to end Ka'rel's stubbornness. In a matter of days, Ka'rel would have the whole countryside aroused and, with everyone out searching, someone would stumble upon Jadiel on the road. And that would ruin her plans! No one, she swore, would stand in the way of her getting those leaves. Especially not a weak, sentimental fool like Ka'rel.

She looked out the window as night cast a pall over the estate. In the distance, she saw a tiny light wiggling. Ka'rel returning on his horse. Huldah seethed and knit her brows together. She considered one way to get Ka'rel to stop—a spell she had used nearly a hundred years ago on one of her wayward husbands. It might arouse suspicion, but time was running out, and this untenable situation called for desperate measures.

Huldah opened the door to her armoire and searched in the back for a small pouch. She reached her hand in and withdrew a tiny wide-banded leather collar, cracked and aged. Attached to the collar was a thin chain made of iron links. Huldah fingered the collar thoughtfully and stood just as she heard Ka'rel's horse clomping across the driveway.

Later that night, when the rest of the household had gone to bed and the searchers had abandoned their efforts, Ka'rel came dragging into the bedroom. Huldah sat on the edge of the bed, in her robe, watching Ka'rel strip off his tunic and unlace his boots. She waited for him to splash water on his face and wipe the grime from his forehead and neck before she came up behind him.

With a wave of her arm, she shut her eyes and muttered words that made the candle on the nightstand flicker. Ka'rel turned around, and with a weary, defeated grimace looked in bewilderment as his wife filled the air with strange mutterings.

Huldah smiled at Ka'rel as his form wavered and changed and a look of horror rose in his eyes. He fell back onto the bed, clutching his throat and thrashing his arms wildly—arms that turned into flecked wings. Huldah held her breath as man changed into bird. Before the frightened hawk could fly away, she clasped the collar tightly around its feathered throat and gripped the iron leash in her hand.

On the bed stood a shaking bird, small and trim, with a sharp beak and two yellow beads for eyes. The hawk pulled frantically against the collar, flapping its wings and snapping at the air.

Huldah laughed and grabbed the bird around its waist, pinning its flailing wings as she carried it to her dresser, where she tied the chain to the furniture leg. The bird opened its beak and tried to cry out but no sound issued from its throat.

"Your voice has been erased. Do you think I want to hear your pathetic screeching day and night?" She grunted, looking the hawk over. "You make a handsome raptor, Ka'rel."

The bird's eyes went wild with fear. Once more it fought against the tether, without success.

"Save your strength. You'll not get free." She came closer, but kept a safe distance from the sharp beak. "I thought you'd give up on searching for that brat, but you wouldn't quit. I couldn't very well let you find her."

The bird's eyes widened.

"Oh yes, your dear precious daughter is alive. She's off to fetch something I need." Huldah tipped her head. "But now that you know, what am I to do with you? The last thing I want to witness is a teary-eyed, mushy reunion between father and daughter when she returns before the next full moon." Huldah frowned. "That would cause a problem for me and my daughters, wouldn't it?"

The bird shook its head emphatically, pleading with its little yellow eyes.

"Well, I can't take the chance that you might whisk me out of the manor, after I've grown so accustomed to this comfortable lifestyle. So . . ."

Huldah narrowed her own eyes to match the bird's beady ones. "You may not want your lovely daughter to come home. For the moment Jadiel steps across the threshold of the manor, your life will drain from you—and you will die."

As the bird shook from crown to talon, Huldah shrugged in amusement. "Sorry." She then blew out the candle on the nightstand and climbed into bed.

THIRTEEN

LAERA PICKED up a melon and tapped it, listening to the hollow sound with her ear against the lime-green rind. On such a warm breezy day, the marketplace bustled with shoppers. She didn't even realize someone was tugging her sleeve until she heard Azar's voice behind her.

"Laera. Beren told me where to find you."

One look told Laera he bore terrible news. The wizened caretaker's haggard face showed exhaustion and despair. She let Azar lead her away from the fruit stand to a shady, uncrowded spot under an oak and faced him.

"It's Jadiel," he said, the words catching in his throat. His rheumy eyes filled with tears, and Laera clung to his arm, dizziness engulfing her.

"Tell me," she managed to whisper.

Azar told her of Jadiel's disappearance, of the bloody coat, and how he and Ka'rel and all the workers had searched for her all week.

"There's no trace of the girl." A great sadness laced his voice.

Laera stood and cried, filling her mind with self-recriminating accusations. "I should have come and taken her away. I *knew* she was in danger."

Azar raised his gray eyebrows. "Laera, she was killed by some wild beast—"

"—She was killed by Huldah!"

Azar trembled, crumbling into himself. "Could the woman truly do such a deed?"

"Believe it." She let herself drop to the soft, leaf-strewn dirt. All her strength ebbed from her body, leaving a giant pain in her heart. *Oh Jadiel! First M'lynn, now you!*

Azar stood politely and looked away while Laera wept. After a few moments he spoke, even more agitated.

"There's more."

Laera stiffened. What could possibly make this news worse?

"Ka'rel's gone."

"Gone? Gone where?"

Azar shrugged. "I asked the wife and she said he took off on a long trip, to buy seed."

"What! That's preposterous! He loses his daughter and he goes shopping?"

"That's what she said," Azar answered. "But I think he's out looking for Jadiel. He left without a word."

Laera shook her head. "What if Huldah has done something to him as well?"

Azar calmed her with his hand on her shoulder. "Now why would she do that? It's obvious she loves him, and frets night and day over his absence." He added with a scowl. "Never a lament over Jadiel, though."

"Of course not! She hates Jadiel, jealous of the love Ka'rel gives her." Laera looked sternly at Azar. "Tell me—did Ka'rel truly think Jadiel was still alive? That perhaps she'd run off?"

Azar shrugged. "He wanted to believe it. But the blood . . ."

"Who knows where that blood came from? And if Huldah had threatened the poor girl's life, then she just may have run away." Laera stood, lost in thought. "We must remain hopeful. But Azar, this news of Ka'rel's leaving distresses me. Without Ka'rel to manage the estate, what will happen?"

"I'll do my best to watch over Ka'rel's affairs. But Huldah has already taken charge and yells at the workers. Some are grumbling and planning to quit."

Laera imagined the sorry state of affairs Ka'rel would return to. Oh where had he gone? Would there be a way to find him?

She turned to Azar and spoke in a quiet, firm voice. "Azar, you must be very careful. But when you have a chance, go through Huldah's things."

Azar's eyes filled with fear. Laera laid a hand on his wrist.

"You must. I am certain Huldah has done something to Jadiel, whether or not she has killed her. But Ka'rel's leaving makes no sense. She is up to more trouble, and I fear if she is allowed to go on unhindered, she will bring ruin to Ka'rel and the manor."

He nodded in agreement. "I'll do what I can. See if I can find some clue as to Ka'rel's whereabouts."

Laera wrapped her arms around the bony old man. "Bless you, dear friend. Please send word if you learn of anything."

Laera watched Azar wend his way through the hordes of people. Then, lowering herself back to the ground, she let her tears stream down her face, thinking of Jadiel and praying heaven would watch over her—whether she be in this world or the next.

Huldah breezed into her dressing room, her face flushed. Of all the stupid people! She had spent the last hour ordering the servants around, demanding they stop sulking and obey her. They acted as if she had no authority. Well, she would show them who was in charge. Ka'rel was gone, she told them. They would now take instructions from her, whether they wanted to or not. And the first order of business was to examine the ledgers and cash in every needless thing in the manor.

She grew tired of drumming up suitors for her daughters. Few would even come to the estate to meet them. No doubt, word had spread of their ugliness. Well, there was little she could do until Jadiel returned. Soon her daughters would turn into beauties—and then they could pick and choose their husbands. In the meantime, though, she would gather as many coins as possible to have gowns made for them—and new shoes. She would hire the most costly seamstresses and shoemakers in the land to outfit her daughters for their weddings.

She pulled out her bottom dresser drawer and felt around. She stopped and pursed her lips. Where was her pouch filled with gold coins? She yanked out the drawer and dumped the contents on the floor, rummaging through the dainty handkerchiefs and linens. The pouch was gone!

Huldah clenched her teeth and fists. Who had been in her room?

She stood and pulled the drapes apart, revealing her mirror. "Show me!"

She watched the mirror grow cloudy in response to her command. Soon it cleared, and Huldah observed a hunched man slowly open the door to her room and tiptoe in. Her mouth twisted into a cruel smile as she watched Azar look gingerly under her bed and in the closet. She didn't need to wait for the mirror to show the rest. Clearly, her husband's caretaker was a thief and a sneak! Well, he would pay. Huldah fretted for a moment, knowing that Azar alone kept the estate running. But how hard could that be? Nothing would be planted until spring. Only the house and the animals needed care. Surely any simpleton could tend to those duties.

With her mind made up, Huldah broke her hold over the mirror and snapped shut the drapes.

Late into the night, as Azar retired to his small room off the carriage house, he poured himself his usual glass of brandy. He had done what Laera asked—searched Huldah's room for anything that would tell him where Ka'rel could have gone—but he'd found nothing. Azar sighed, feeling his age press upon him. Twelve years he had managed this estate, and they had been some of the more joyous years of his life. Ka'rel was a kind and considerate employer and now—would he ever see Ka'rel again?

As he sipped his drink, a burning sensation gripped his throat. Azar clawed at his neck with his hands, trying to suck in a breath that wouldn't come. He felt heat rush to his face as he gasped for air. Wide-eyed, he fell off his chair to the floor and tried to crawl toward the door. As he lay dying, his eyes lighted on the bottle of brandy, and he noticed the strange hue of the liquid. Before all went dark, understanding settled over him, and he realized, too late, that Laera had been right.

FOURTEEN

JADIEL JERKED awake and found herself jostling around under something itchy. She clawed at the fabric above her and popped her head out from under a canvas tarp littered with straw. It took her a moment to remember how she had climbed into the back of the grocery wagon, so exhausted and depressed, with just enough strength left to burrow under some crates of bogberries and drop off to sleep. Every muscle ached from the miles she had walked yesterday. And now, an early morning sun baked on her head, making her sweat. From where she sat, she could see through the wood slats to the driver, who jiggled the reins and clucked at two small mules.

After leaving her home, she had hurried south, toward Kettle-bro and the marketplace, thinking she could inquire about the tree. Then, when she straggled into the main thoroughfare, she pondered what would happen if she ran into someone she knew—and they tried to take her home. Huldah's warnings rang in her head. Staying in the vale meant someone, at some point, would recognize her as Ka'rel's daughter. And word would get back to Huldah and her father's life would be forfeit. So she hid under the hood of her cloak and strayed off the main road, keeping to herself. By nightfall she had neared the center of town, knowing she could not take the chance of rooming at an inn.

She had hid behind a tree, looking down the road where, only a few hundred yards away, stood the two-story wood shop owned by her uncle Beren. Oh, how she longed to throw her arms around Aunt Laera and pour out her heart! But instead of running down the road, she turned away, then noticed the cart parked in front of a lone cottage down a dead-end lane. She must have slept soundly, for she never heard the driver hitch up the mules and leave Kettlebro. Who knew how many miles they had traveled—and where they were headed?

As the driver urged the mules down the road, Jadiel took a drink from her water jug and ate some nuts. The strong aroma of bogberries baking in the hot sun tempted her, but she knew it would be wrong to eat what she hadn't bought. She tried to formulate a plan, now that she couldn't stay in the vale. She had no idea where to go to learn of this strange tree. Her father had read to her of many lands; she knew Sherbourne was the regional center where the king ruled, but the idea of wandering around a big, crowded city frightened her. There were smaller kingdoms south and east— should she try to go to one of them?

Huldah had given her thirty days to accomplish her task. Jadiel's eyes filled with tears. Despair overwhelmed her, and she missed Papa. She would never find this tree; she may as well give up and go home. Huldah could kill her and Papa for all she cared. At least they would be rejoined with her mother in the next world. How bad would that be?

Jadiel took out her comb and mirror and tried to untangle her hair strewn with straw. *Mama,* she pleaded with the mirror, *tell me what to do.*

A hazy shape took form behind her reflection in the glass. Her mother, once more, reached out and stroked Jadiel's head. Jadiel felt the warming touch and her heart leapt. Her mother's fragrance drifted into her nose, calming her distress.

"Be brave, Jadiel. And do not fear. Trust your heart and you will succeed."

Her mother's image faded. *But, Mama! Wait!*

Jadiel stared at the mirror, but all she saw were her own sad blue eyes. She put her things away and looked out on the countryside, keeping low to avoid being seen.

Hours drifted by and the sun rose high in the sky. The few hovering clouds had moved north. Jadiel could tell by the sun's path that they were traveling south. They passed many carriages and riders on horseback heading the other direction. Finally, the cart slowed and Jadiel hid, listening as the driver got down from his bench and walked to the door of a cottage. Hearing the exchange of coins, Jadiel realized he would soon be coming to unload his carts of berries, so while the two men talked and made their exchange, Jadiel slipped out. She hunched low as she ran down the road to hide behind a tree. After a while, she heard the driver cluck at the mules and continue on. When the sound of the turning wheels grew faint, she came out and looked across the land.

Fields stretched out around her, overgrown with brown grasses. In contrast to her estate's pastures and fields, this land seemed untamed and unplowed. A handful of cottages dotted the landscape, set back off the dirt road, but there were none of the huge oaks of Logan Valley, just small bare-limbed trees that clumped together in patches throughout the fields.

Jadiel laid her cloak over her arm in the warm sun and marched along the road, continuing south. She doubted anyone in this region would know her or Papa. She let her feet fall into a rhythm and tried not to think about her father. She would end up somewhere, a place where, hopefully, someone would have heard of this Tree of Eternal Youth and Beauty. She now understood Huldah's desperation—an old, ugly woman who valued beauty over everything else. Jadiel couldn't help but think what an empty, joyless pursuit that would be. Everyone grew old and aged. Everyone died. To try to outwit and beat mortality went against nature. And to try to make the outer appearance beautiful while the inside remained ugly and hateful was sure to fail. It reminded Jadiel of a white-washed grave—beautifully ornate on the outside, but inside full of rotting bones. No wonder Huldah was such a miserable person!

Throughout the day, many on horseback and in carriages passed her, giving her a nod or a friendly wave. Jadiel wondered where they were all going. If only she had a map; perhaps that would give her some idea of the nearest town. As she came upon a crossroads, she stopped. Now she had the choice of turning three directions. Should she continue south? She sighed in frustration, hoping the men who slowed their carriage behind her could help her somehow.

A tall man holding the reins called down to her. "You look lost."

Jadiel studied the two men on the buckboard of a wagon pulled by one huge draft horse. A covered shell enclosed the back, like a delivery wagon. The other man, short and squat, jumped down and came to her. He cocked his head, and Jadiel studied his grizzly unshaven face and stringy dark hair that looked unwashed.

"Yes, what's pretty little thing like you doing standing in the middle of the road?" He smiled, and Jadiel cringed at the few blackened teeth remaining in his mouth.

She backed away a few feet, deciding these weren't the right people to ask for help. The man on the bench called down to her.

"Perhaps we can give you a ride." The smile he cast in her direction did not look friendly.

Suddenly, Jadiel had an urge to run, but before she could act upon it, the short man grabbed her arm tightly. Jadiel looked frantically around, hoping someone would notice her predicament, but the roads were empty in all directions.

Jadiel realized the two men were also scanning their surroundings. Her heart sank in terror. She struggled to get loose. "Let me go!" With her free arm she managed to swing at her captor's face and scratch his cheek with her nails.

"Ooh, this is a live one, Merl." He laughed as he wiped blood from his face.

Merl threw something down to the man still pinching her arm. A rope landed at her feet. Jadiel's eyes widened and she struggled harder, but it only made the men laugh. "Hurry, Gerb, tie her up. With a face like that, she'll fetch at least fifty silvers."

Gerb pulled a strip of cloth from a back pocket of his trousers and shoved it into Jadiel's mouth. She screamed as loudly as she could, but the filthy rag he tied in a knot at the back of her neck muffled her cries. He pulled her hands behind her and bound them tightly together with a scratchy rope, making her yelp. As he dragged her, kicking and wiggling, to the back of the wagon, he pulled her satchel off her shoulders.

"Just throw that in the back for now. We'll go through her things later," Merl said. "Look, someone's coming."

Jadiel could see dust kicking up a ways up the road but knew that it would be minutes before those travelers arrived at the crossroads. Gerb picked Jadiel up with a grunt and heaved her into the back of the wagon, flopping her onto a hard floor between a couple of large wooden trunks. As she struggled to sit up, Gerb grabbed her hair and pulled her close. She smelled his rotted teeth and unbathed skin and cringed.

"Now, you behave, if you don't want me to knock you out with a slug to the head." He took another line of rope and tied it around her waist. The free end he looped through one of the wooden wagon slats, then tied a big knot. "You'll not be going anywhere for a while, so just enjoy the ride."

Jadiel shook with terror as Gerb let go of her hair and touched her cheek. "Yep, you sure are one pretty little thing. And you'll fetch us a pretty coin, there's no doubt of that."

He pulled the two pieces of draping canvas together, enclosing her in the stuffy, hot space. She heard Merl yell at the horse and the wagon lurched forward, racing down the road with Jadiel knocking about like a sack of turnips. Tears poured down her face as she tried to brace herself with her legs against the floorboards. Her head reeled with the understanding that these men planned to sell her! Where on earth did people sell children—and for what purpose?

Jadiel's imagination filled her with terrifying images of what lay ahead for her. She would have fared better taking her chances with Huldah than in the arms of these evil men! With that thought, Jadiel's head spun and she fainted, hitting her forehead hard against one of the wooden trunks.

The merchant handed over the quiver full of beautifully fletched arrows as Callen laid the silvers on the counter. Moments earlier Callen had deliberated in front of the window displaying bows made from yew wood. It had been many years since he'd practiced with bow and arrow, but the elegant lines and the richly oiled red-tinged wood had called to him. He was not one for spontaneous purchases, but when would he find another bow as well-crafted as this? Besides, he told himself as he slung the bow and quiver over his shoulder, he was heading out into desolate land. Whether for defense or food, he would be foolish to venture forth without a weapon of some kind. He could just imagine trying to fend off a wolf with a carving gouge!

He had only indulged in one other purchase, and as Callen walked out of the store, it pawed the ground restlessly and nickered at him.

The mare was a five-year-old buckskin with a sleek conformation. One look had told him she was spirited, but eager to please. The owner had brought her to market with three other horses to sell at a fair price. In addition, the seller offered a pack saddle and headstall as part of the deal. How could he resist? It had never occurred to him before to buy a horse, but now it seemed a practical decision. He could travel far and wide much faster, and if he needed to, he could sell her later.

Callen rearranged the bag of feed to accommodate the bow and quiver across the back of the saddle. His pack and food fit in the ample side pouches. Down the cobbled lane, the south gate tower loomed over the tops of the thatched-roof shops. He mounted the mare and then rode around the corner, where the huge stone wall rose thirty feet before him. He felt a little sad to leave Sherbourne behind, but now that he had been here, he planned to return. Beren had been right, also, about the abundance of inspiring architectural styles of the buildings and along the footpaths. Next trip he would fill his sketchbook before heading home.

As he walked his horse through the southern gate and onto the dirt road, he thought about his destination. The King's Plain—The Valley Perilous. Za'ker had told him to look for a village called Rumble on the southern road to Ethryn. A cool wind whipped at his tunic. Callen untied his cloak from the saddlebag and draped it around his shoulders. A few clouds gathered, casting shadows on the ground. The farther from the city he rode, the fewer people he passed. After an hour, he stopped and let his mare drink from a creek. He realized that the seller had failed to tell him the mare's name. Well, he would think of something, once he got to know her better. For now, he was pleased with his purchase. She had kept up a strong pace and responded with a sensitive mouth to his leadings. Apart from straining to eat a tuft of grass now and then, she seemed content to be on a journey. Perhaps she'd spent much of her life in a boring stall. Maybe, Callen thought, she'd enjoy a good run.

Callen gave her a nudge with his boots on her flanks. "Come on, girl, let's see what you can do." He whooped at her and leaned forward, and she took his hint. Soon they were galloping down the empty road, with the wind blowing through Callen's long wavy hair and cooling his face. He gave the mare her head and let her run until she tired. Finally, she slowed to a trot and huffed, tossing her ebony mane. Callen patted her neck and smoothed back his hair.

A wagon travelled the road not far ahead. Callen kept enough distance to let the stirred-up dust settle as he walked his mare, letting her cool down. He reached into his pack and brought out one of the pasties he had bought from a woman with a stall set up along the river. She and her daughter had rambled on excitedly about the coronation ceremony, surprised Callen hadn't attended. The whole city seemed abuzz over the crowning of Prince Adin. Well, he thought wryly, he had other kings to visit—those sleeping and waiting under the ground.

A pounding headache woke Jadiel. She tried to touch her head and found her hands bound behind her. The events of her capture rushed into her mind, and she jerked alert, looking around the inside of the covered space in which she found herself. The wagon rocked and jiggled, making her wonder how long she'd been holed up inside this stuffy compartment. Sweat had soaked her blouse, and her hair stuck to her cheeks. Her throat cried for water.

She studied the rope around her waist and followed it with her eyes. She felt around with her hands, squirming on the hard wooden floor until she found the bulky knot tied at her back. She could barely reach it with her fingers. As she worked at the knot, tugging at it, she bit down on her lip, forcing back tears. The faces of those men invaded her thoughts—their mean sneers and rough hands. Jadiel shivered with fear, knowing she *had* to get away. Why oh why was she so beset with misfortune?

She attacked the knot with furious determination and finally loosened it enough to free her waist from its tether. With her leg, she pushed aside the canvas flap and looked out. She would have to jump and run off the road before those men realized she had escaped.

Her satchel lay a few feet away. With one foot, she dragged it close, then hooked her shoe around the strap. If only she could free her hands! Balancing herself against the wagon's rattling, she lifted her foot and swung the satchel toward the opening in the canvas. The pack flew out of the wagon and landed with a thud in a poof of dust, quickly retreating behind her as the wagon continued down the road at a fast clip. Jadiel crawled to the far end of the compartment and squatted to look out. There was no way she could jump and land on her feet as she cleared the low wooden slats that separated her from the road.

She would just have to tumble out and hope for the best.

Callen bit into his pasty, enjoying the explosion of meat juices. As he walked the mare behind the wagon, the face of the ugly man came to his mind—the man with the repulsive scars running over his nose and cheeks and forehead almost like stripes from a whip. But what a strange fellow! Speaking in stories and riddles. Taking about circles in circles. And just who was that landowner he'd mentioned, the one who had built the bridge? Callen gritted his teeth. Why wouldn't that pest tell him how to find the bridge and who the builder was? *"You're not ready to hear those answers."* What nonsense! The deranged man was probably pulling his foot with all that gibberish, just enjoying rattling him. Callen tried to push away the man's words, but as he walked his mare down the road, they lingered. Those warnings tickled his thoughts. Ebed had warned him of danger. That he should be afraid. Well, why would searching for a bridge prove dangerous? It made no sense.

Callen's thoughts were interrupted by something that caught his eye. Down the road, he spied movement in the back of that wagon. One of the flaps blew open and he thought he saw a leg, a human leg, sticking out. *Probably just a passenger fooling around.* He closed the distance a bit between him and the wagon, curious at the sight of the leg kicking at something—a package or a box? Then, to his surprise, whatever that parcel was, out it tumbled from the back of the wagon and plopped down onto the middle of the road.

Fifteen

JADIEL STEELED her nerve and took a deep breath. Then she leapt out through the canvas flaps, curling into a ball as she met the hard ground with a thud. A sharp pain shot through her shoulder as she tumbled side over side, then rolled to a stop.

Dust filled her nose and gummed her eyes. She wiped her face on her shoulder as she shakily got to her feet. Her hands were still bound behind her, but the gag had slipped from her mouth as she tumbled. The pounding on the side of her head made her squint in the bright sunlight. And then, the jangling of the wagon ahead ceased.

Jadiel realized in horror that the driver had stopped. No doubt he had heard or felt her escape. In the settling dust, Jadiel looked around her, trying to make out her surroundings. She had to run, but where? The land around her was flat and empty. She froze in fear, staring at the wagon as it materialized out of the dust and stopped on the road not a hundred feet ahead.

Just as she spun around to run the other way, she found herself facing a galloping horse—coming toward her! But as she cringed and started to flee off the road, the horse skidded to a stop before her and a tall man with dark hair waving in the wind slipped quickly off his mount and picked her satchel up off the ground. He looked her over and offered his hand.

"Here, let me help you up on my horse. I'll take you someplace safe."

Jadiel shook her head in terror. Strange men were everywhere, trying to steal her! What horrible land was this that men searched the roads for children to snatch?

The man's face showed surprise when Jadiel began running across a field.

"Hey," he called after her, getting on his horse with her satchel slung over his shoulder. He kicked at the mare's sides and took off after the girl. "I just want to help."

Jadiel looked back as she ran. The two other men had clambered off the wagon and were hurrying toward her, closing the distance and paying no heed to the rider on the horse. Now she had three men after her!

With nowhere to hide and no one else on the lonely road, she spun futilely in place. She could either let those men recapture her or take her chances with the pursuing rider. Either way, in her heart, she knew she was doomed. Her knees buckled and gave way, and she fell to the ground in a heap.

Two strong arms lifted her and swung her onto the horse in front of the saddle. Her legs straddled over the mare's neck, and she gripped its withers with her knees. As the man jumped into the saddle behind her, he kicked the horse hard and yelled at it to run. Jadiel pressed her cheek against the mare's neck and watched as the two evil men stopped their pursuit and threw their hands up in apparent anger. Her new captor swung the horse in a wide circle, overtaking the wagon and picking up speed as the horse reentered the road. He pressed his forearms against her, holding her firmly as he gripped the reins and urged the horse on. Jadiel struggled against him, but for naught. She was pinned in place, at the mercy of this new abductor.

After a long while, the man drew in on the reins and brought the panting and lathered horse to a walk, mumbling praises and patting its head.

"Now," he said to the back of Jadiel's head. "Where can I take you? Are you lost?"

Jadiel lifted her chin and turned enough to see the man who spoke. His eyes smiled at her, but his face was etched in concern. He slid the satchel off his shoulder and offered it to her after loosening her bindings. She took it from his hands and sighed a deep breath of relief. Maybe he really did want to help.

Jadiel coughed. Her voice came out in a raspy wheeze. "Do you have any water?"

The rider brought the horse to a halt and slipped off the saddle to the ground. He scanned the barren countryside filled with scrub brush and tumbleweeds. Off in the distance, a rutted narrow road led to a half-collapsed barn. The man pointed.

"Let's go over there and get you untied and washed up. I can keep an eye on the road from there. Don't worry about those men coming after you. I can take care of them." He patted a large wooden bow tied to the back of his saddle. He pulled the reins over the horse's head and reached into a side pouch. As he held the horse still, he uncorked the jug and brought it to Jadiel's mouth.

She drank gratefully, reveling in the cool water slipping down her parched throat. "Thank you."

He clucked at the horse and walked her quickly toward the barn. In moments they were inside the dilapidated building, in a shady spot where sunlight streaked through the broken slats in the roof. Before the man could assist, Jadiel swung off the horse and landed on the ground, tripping and falling at his feet.

He helped her up and turned her so he finish untying the rope still wrapped around her wrists.. "My name's Callen. What's yours?"

"Jadiel."

Callen stopped and dropped his hands. The rope at last fell free, and Jadiel rubbed her chaffed fingers together, bringing blood to her numb extremities. She looked up and saw surprise in Callen's face.

"What?" She looked into his dark eyes and studied him. He wore nice clothes, not fancy ones, but he was neat and trim. Dust coated his bronze skin and his hands looked soft, so he was not a laborer like her father's workers. She wasn't good at guessing ages, but he was surely younger than Papa.

Callen shook his head, puzzled. "Is that a very common name?"

"I don't think so. I've never met anyone else by that name. It means 'may God cause to rejoice.'"

"Jadiel." His voice sounded soft and worried. "You aren't perhaps Beren's niece, are you?"

Now it was Jadiel's turn to be puzzled. "Beren! Yes, he is my uncle. But how do you know him? How do you know my name?" How odd that here, so far from the Logan Valley, she had chanced upon someone who knew her family.

Callen loosened the horse's girth, then poured water into his hand for the mare to drink. He cocked his head and stared out at the road through a cracked window. Jadiel noted the keen attention in Callen's stance. She came to his side and peeked through a broken board in the wall.

"There's the wagon," he whispered, as if the men could hear him.

They watched in silence as the wagon tore off down the distant road until it disappeared from sight. Callen and Jadiel both sighed in relief.

He turned and gave Jadiel a stern look. "What happened to you? How did you come to be captured by those men?"

Jadiel clammed up. What could she tell him without revealing her whole story? Even this far from home, she feared trusting this man. What if he took her back to the manor by force?

"Does your father know you have gone? I overheard Laera worrying over your safety."

Jadiel's stomach lurched at the mention of her sweet aunt. "When? Do you know my father?"

Callen huffed and pulled a sack from the horse's saddlebag. "Here, let's sit and eat something. Are you hungry?"

Jadiel nodded and sat on the ground, leaning her back up against the barn siding. Callen lowered down beside her and handed her a cold meat pie and an apple. She bit into the pie and sighed. She *was* starving! Callen ripped a piece of bread from a dark loaf.

"I am one of Beren's apprentices. I've been working at the shop for four years." He added, "I've heard a little about you and your father. That your mother died . . ." His voice filled with tenderness. "I was sorry to hear about the accident. Your aunt grieved for many months. Well, she still grieves—and she worries so over you." Now he furrowed his brows at her. "So, what are you doing here? You're a bit young to be off on your own, aren't you? And shouldn't you be home with Ka'rel? He must be frantic over your absence."

Jadiel ached to pour out her heart. It pained her to hear how sorrowful her aunt was. Heaven must have sent Callen to her rescue, for if he worked for Uncle Beren, then he was surely a friend. But could she trust him?

"I—I can't return until I find something. My father knows I am gone." Or so she hoped. *If* Grork had told her Papa the things he promised to disclose.

Callen let the matter rest. Jadiel could see his mind churning with questions, but she ate in silence and drank more water. When she finished, she turned and looked at him.

"Thank you for rescuing me. If you hadn't come to my aid, those men were going to sell me."

"Sell you? To whom?" She could tell by Callen's expression that he was just as surprised that such things occurred.

"I don't know. They didn't say."

Callen's voice was stern. "I should take you home. Now."

Hearing the word *home* stabbed her gut. Tears filled her eyes and flowed out onto her cheeks.

"Here." He handed her a cloth from his shirt pocket and studied her. "For your face. We should find some water and get you cleaned up."

She wiped the tears from her cheeks. "But I can't go home . . ."

Callen stood and walked to the open barn door. "Then where are you going? I'll take you *there*. And *then* I'll take you home. Laera would never forgive me if I didn't bring you home safely." He shook his head. "And how could your father send you—a small girl—off to find something for him? What kind of parent would whisk his child off into strange, dangerous lands—"

Jadiel jumped to her feet. "It wasn't my father!" She clamped her mouth shut.

Callen looked into her face and frowned in understanding. "Huldah. You father's new wife. She's the one, isn't she?"

Jadiel could tell by Callen's tone that he'd heard about Huldah and didn't like what he'd heard. She had sworn not to say anything, but her eyes clearly told all. Callen whistled.

"Well," was all he said. He spotted something and waved her over. "Look, there's an old pump handle. Maybe we'll find a spring."

Jadiel followed, bringing along her comb and mirror, and mulling over the last two days' events in her mind. She thought of her father back at the estate and hoped he was waiting to hear from her. Somehow she would get word to Papa that she was safe and not to worry. But how would she do that? And what could she tell this apprentice of Beren's who intended to watch over her? Would he be willing to wander the world searching for some tree that probably didn't exist? And why was he riding a horse on some desolate road and not working in the shop in Kettlebro?

Callen grabbed the iron handle and pushed on it. After a few hard tries he managed to get the handle to lower, then worked it up and down until a spray of brown water gushed from the spout. After a few minutes of pumping, the water streamed out clear.

"I'll go get a bowl and a towel and let you wash up," he said.

Jadiel pumped with one hand and stuck her head under the flow of warm water. She let it stream down her neck until it ran cool, washing the grime away and refreshing her. She nearly gasped when she looked into her little mirror and saw a lump swelling on the side of her face. Her head still throbbed and her legs and shoulder were bruised, but she was alive. And—she fretted, while combing out the tangled mess of hair—she had about twenty-eight more days to find the leaves and return home to save her father.

She lifted her head and looked across the barren fields, trying to ignore the boulder-sized lump in her stomach. Where, oh where, would she find that tree?

SIXTEEN

THE HAWK hopped from his perch and jumped onto the windowsill. He sidestepped along the edge until his tether pulled tightly around his neck. From this vantage point he stared out over his fields, but saw no one.

For the last few days he had listened with his keen ears to the voices around him. The thick stone walls of his estate muffled out words, but he could sense heated emotions reverberating through the manor. Most often he heard Huldah's shrill yells, and boot steps pounding the tiled floor. What disturbed him most was the absence of his workers. Shouldn't they be out in the fields? Azar would have them weeding and turning over the furrows by now. From this window he had seen neither Azar nor anyone else going about their daily chores.

He strained at the linked chain, trying to peer over to the carriage house, but all he could glimpse was the corner of the building and none of the driveway. Lately, he had heard no horses or carriages rattle on the cobbles. Surely Azar was doing his best to keep the estate in order. But now—with Huldah in control . . .

Ka'rel squeezed his eyes together, wishing hawks could cry. Instead, the anguish and guilt lodged in his throat, constricting his breath. How blind he had been—letting himself fall under the wiles of such an evil temptress! Surely losing M'lynn had torn him to pieces, had made him weak and vulnerable. Oh, if only he had listened to Laera's warnings. At the time he thought Laera jealous, wanting to protect her sister's memory. And poor Jadiel—

Thinking of his daughter's sweet, trusting face sent a stab of guilt through his heart. Huldah had stripped away more than his human form; a veil fell from his eyes the moment she transformed him. Now, with a hawk's astute perception, he saw through deceptive appearances to the glaring truth. The last nine months came at him in a rush of revelation—months spent under Huldah's consuming enchantment, a bewitching that had lured him away from the one person he loved more than any in the world. Now he saw Jadiel's misery and pain; he had failed to pay attention to her suffering all this time. She depended upon the comfort and protection of her father, and he had failed her.

The small hawk pressed its feathered cheek against the cool glass in defeat. Even if Jadiel found a way to return home safely, he would never hold her in his arms again. Instead, what awaited his daughter was more grief and horror. She would have to watch him die, and then her fate would rest in Huldah's hands. Ka'rel shuddered to imagine what Huldah would do to his daughter once he was dead.

Frustration roiled up, followed by rage. He would not—could not—let this happen to Jadiel! There had to be some way of getting word to Azar—or to Laera. But how? He was chained to a table, and his voice was gone. Even if he could manage to find pen and parchment, how could he write with a talon? And who would deliver his messages? Moreover, who would believe him?

He heard the door to the dressing room swing open and turned. Huldah walked to the window and cocked her head, a smirk on her face.

"Well, enjoying the view? I brought you lunch." She reached into the folds of her gown and brought out a mouse, dangling it by its tail. Ka'rel took one look at the terrified creature and turned away.

"You mustn't starve yourself, my love."

Ka'rel cringed at the sarcasm in her voice. Not a week before, that alluring tone had sent his heart racing. Now, it made him want to disgorge the contents of his craw—which consisted only of some seeds he had eaten yesterday.

Huldah grunted and dropped the mouse into the empty water jar on the dressing table. "For later, then, if the mood strikes you." She came alongside him and looked out the window. "However did you manage to keep this estate running with all those disagreeable workers? A shame I had to let most of them go. A bunch of lazy, disrespectful peasants."

Ka'rel glared at Huldah. No wonder no one was out in the fields! Huldah had either fired them or yelled at them until they couldn't bear staying. But where was Azar?

Huldah must have read his thoughts. She narrowed her eyes and drew closer. "Oh, and that most despicable old man. Doddering around the place as if he owned it. Why, the gumption of that fellow."

She smiled at Ka'rel. "He's dead."

Her words hit like a blow to his gut. Dead?

"I found him snooping in my room. Imagine the nerve!"

Ka'rel gasped for air and tugged frantically at the tether. Huldah laughed at Ka'rel's feeble attempts to peck at her with his beak.

"Good riddance, I say." She left, with her skirts swishing the floor.

Ka'rel grew lightheaded, wondering how she had managed to kill Azar, his kind and faithful caretaker. *Oh Azar! What evil have I unleashed in this accursed house?*

Anger seethed deep in his little hawk's heart. He hopped back to the dressing table and knocked over the jar with his wing. The mouse scurried away, leaping to the floor and running out the room. *Escape while you can, little one. If only I could be so fortunate.*

He searched the tabletop, but Huldah had been careful not to leave any sharp objects within his reach. She had attached the end of his chain to the piece of wood he used as a perch. For days now he tried to pull the chain out, but an iron hasp kept it secure.

He caught his reflection in the glass jar that lay upon the table. The leather collar wasn't loose enough to worm out from under, but maybe . . .

Ka'rel rolled onto his side and kicked his leg at his throat, catching a talon between the collar and his neck. He pushed with all his might against the leather, hoping to stretch it, but it wouldn't give.

Jadiel's face came to his mind—her sad, woeful eyes, crying over her mother's death. If he died, it would surely break her heart beyond repair. He would *not* give Huldah the satisfaction of ruining their lives further—he would not!

With a grunt propelled by fury, the hawk whacked at the collar with his talon—again and again. Ka'rel panted hard, feeling blood rush to his head. The stiff, cracked leather resisted, until one swift kick caught a nick along the edge and ripped it. Ka'rel felt the leather give under his claws, loosening the collar a tiny bit. Encouraged, he lashed away with renewed fervor until the tear lengthened halfway down the collar.

He freed his tangled talon and collapsed, catching his breath. He could feel his tiny heart thumping against his chest. If he had hands he could remove the collar with ease by sliding it over his head. Instead, he had to hang his head over the side of the dressing table and wiggle, but ultimately, he achieved the same result—freedom!

Ka'rel watched the collar fall to the floor, still attached to the sturdy iron chain. Huldah had made sure his lead would not wrench free from the perch, but had failed to take into consideration the aged leather. No doubt she had too little experience with animal hide to know it needed oiling to keep it pliable, something Ka'rel did regularly with his harnesses, saddles, and breeching used on his horses.

The hawk jumped down from the table to the floor and hesitated. When he determined the house was quiet, he did what came naturally to creatures with feathers—he stretched out his strong, sturdy wings and flew out the door, down the hall, and soared effortlessly through the nearest open window, leaving Huldah and his home behind.

As Za'ker balanced on the ladder, shelving the last two books, he paused. He finally realized what niggled at his mind. He pulled the large tome back out and stared at the raised geometric pattern on the cover, an interlocking design that formed a border around the edges. Images flitted through his mind of similar patterns, and as Za'ker sifted through them, he chewed his lip in frustration. Just what significance did those patterns have, and why did he find himself growing anxious?

He climbed down the rungs, aware of the silence permeating the library. He thought that strange, as the library was nearly always quiet. Yet this silence emanated from a growing unease within him and a looming presentiment of dread gathering around him, as if the long-dead spirits contained within the volumes around him had awakened.

That's it! The disparate images in his mind suddenly pieced together like the interlocking patterns on the book's cover. Za'ker's hand shook as he ran a finger along the spines of one column of books after another. He tried to picture the odd assortment of parchments, scrolls, and references spread out around the table where he and that young man, Callen, had sat the other day. Callen had asked him about those buried in the King's Plain. He read they were not dead but were waiting—for something.

Then he remembered. He hurried to a cabinet and found the slim volume he sought tucked back in the recess of the shelf. The materials within this cabinet were ancient and fragile. Anyone wishing to study them required Za'ker's supervision—and special gloves. But some books on these shelves were hidden away for another reason. They contained strange elements that had aroused the suspicion of the former librarian when he had discovered them in a broken crate abandoned by the library doors decades ago. The librarian instructed Za'ker not to show them to anyone but refused to explain why. True, his mentor had been an odd sort of fellow, with his quirks about cataloging and tedious methods of preserving old scrolls. But Za'ker always wondered about the fearful tremble in the old man's voice when he told Za'ker to be careful, mumbling something about dark magic and trapped powers within the pages of the books. At the time, Za'ker dismissed it as superstitious hogwash. He never gave the books more than a cursory glance.

But in that momentary glance, Za'ker had seen an illustration that now forced its way to the forefront of his memory. He hid the book under his arm as he walked quickly to his small office and shut the door. There, in those private confines, he laid the book on his desk. An inexplicable fear washed over him as he stared at the worn linen cover.

Set against a blood-red background stood a dark terebinth tree, its branches full and outspread, with nestling birds of many kinds. Za'ker ran his finger over the chipped painting and jerked his hand back, stunned by the iciness of its surface. Encircling the tree— which grew upon a barrow of land—rose a ring of what looked like tall slabs of stone, somewhat smooth but of varying heights. Za'ker stared at the strange array of stones, some of which were capped with horizontal blocks in no apparent pattern. From the scale, the stone circle would be of formidable size; if a man were to walk its circumference, it would take him perhaps fifteen or twenty minutes to arrive back where he started.

Za'ker puzzled at the strange construct, wondering if it had ever truly existed and what meaning it held. Then he chuckled, for no human or even an army of men could raise such weighty rocks into that formation. Or could they?

As he pondered this, he noticed his hands shaking. The same icy sensation that met his fingertips now returned, but this time the cold traveled up his arms and spread across his chest. Soon, his whole body shook, as if a sudden blast of frosty wind assailed him. He jumped from his chair and distanced himself from the desk, eyeing the book warily. Surely his imagination was running wild, what with the enigmatic warnings of his predecessor rattling around in his head!

Za'ker lifted his cloak from the wall hook and draped it around his shoulders, dispelling the lingering chill. He poured himself a cup of lukewarm tea from the kettle sitting near the oil lamp and sipped thoughtfully. Then, steeling his nerve with humorous self-chastisements, he sat back down and, without hesitation, flipped open the book.

Za'ker's breath caught in his throat as the pages fluttered to a stop and the book rested open, revealing a finely detailed ink drawing of what appeared to be a tomb or vault. The structure looked to be made of marble or some similar hewn stone and was accessed by six steps retreating into the earth. He picked up the magnifying lens from his desktop and leaned closer to peruse the illustration, and there, in the center of the half-buried structure, was the geometric pattern he had seen in the corners of Callen's parchments.

Was it a design etched into the stone? Za'ker looked closer and determined that the pattern stood out in relief from what looked like a door, perhaps one or two feet in diameter. And judging by the texture implied in the drawing, this puzzle pattern was made of dark stone, perhaps stained in different shades to distinguish the interweaving lines. The design itself was a random assortment of rectangles, some long and thin, others short and wide. Most ran horizontal, but a few interlocked vertically. Za'ker had no idea of its portent. An insignia? A family crest? That seemed likely if it were a tomb.

Surrounding the drawing were lines of flowing handwriting. It took Za'ker a minute to identify its regional dialect and origin, placing it far back to the earliest written languages. Some of the words confounded him, but as he read, he got the gist of the emphatic message ascribed to one Me'lek Ko'hane, a virulent warning surrounding this tomb and its occupant.

The blood drained from Za'ker's face. The teacup fell from his hand and clattered to the floor, spilling minty liquid around his feet. But Za'ker hardly noticed his soft boots become sodden.

"Oh, that poor man," he muttered, narrowing his eyes as a vision of evil swirled out from the drawing in the book, putrid black vapor that made Za'ker gag. He pictured Callen wandering the King's Plain and now understood, in horror, why some called it The Valley Perilous. He had to warn Callen before he met with such unthinkable peril! But how?

Za'ker snapped the book shut with shaky hands and sank deep into his chair. As he stared at the cover with its dark terebinth tree, he tried to think of someone to send to warn Callen. He felt compelled to go, but he had no one to manage the library in his absence. Who in their right mind would undertake a journey to that forbidden region, for any amount of silver?

No one, that's who.

Za'ker dropped his head into his hands and shuddered. His heart pained him, for he liked the young inquisitive man, Callen. A man soon to meet his demise.

• PART TWO •

"A Promise of a Crown

on the Backs of Kings . . ."

SEVENTEEN

UPON CALLEN'S urging, Jadiel and her erstwhile captor-turned-champion spent the night in the dilapidated barn. Callen wanted to ensure the kidnappers were long gone and not hunting for their lost prisoner, and Jadiel was too exhausted to travel. She had slept so soundly she hadn't heard Callen saddle up the mare. Not even the aroma of fried sausage woke her, although the moment Callen tapped her shoulder to hand her the bowl, her mouth watered. How many days had passed since she had eaten more than a few bites of fruit or bread? She wolfed down her breakfast, aware of Callen's amused expression. And as she ate, Callen told her about his brothers back in Tebron, and the work he did for her uncle Beren.

Jadiel could tell Callen had more questions, but he busied himself cleaning up and packing the dishes and food. Once they mounted the mare, they spoke little. Jadiel asked where they were headed, and he told her. They were traveling south to a village called Rumble, to inquire for directions to a place called The King's Plain.

They journeyed at a slow pace in consideration for the mare. Even though Jadiel was light and trim, with the added weight of the saddlebags Callen worried they were taxing the horse's feet. By late morning, the road meandered through a low pass between two hills, then straightened out. For the bulk of the afternoon they traveled south along flat, uninteresting terrain, enduring a day of hot sun void of wind or shade for relief.

Upon arriving at Rumble, just before dusk, Callen rode to a woman shaking out a rug on the front porch of her rundown cottage. He inquired of the villager where he could purchase another mount. She pointed him to the tavern, a thatched, weathered building that looked similar to the homes that dotted the dusty roadside. The small mud house had a stable alongside it, and as they rode up, Jadiel glimpsed patrons through the windows, sitting at tables in a brightly lit room.

Callen brought the horse to a halt and dismounted. "Wait here. I'll be back in a moment."

Jadiel looked nervously around. "Is it safe? I mean, what if those men are inside?"

Callen's mouth drew tight. "You're right. Stay with me." He stepped back while Jadiel swung off the horse. Her legs ached and wobbled as she straightened. She hadn't ridden horseback for that many hours in a long while, and never straddling the bony ridge of a mare's neck. If they couldn't buy another horse, then maybe she would walk instead.

She waited while Callen secured the saddlebags and tied the mare to the tavern's signpost. They hadn't seen anyone riding on the road, but they did pass a few horse-drawn carts. How likely were they to find a horse for sale in a tiny village as this? From what Jadiel could tell, the tavern was the only commercial business around. Where did people shop at market, or did they grow all their own food? Considering the dust and barrenness of the land, Jadiel doubted much would grow here. She glanced up at the high, crumbling cliffs backing the village covered with scrub brush and other scraggly plants. Such a depressing place in contrast to her lush, green land.

Thinking of home released a rush of emotion. During the day she'd let her mind empty and avoided thinking of Papa, and of

Huldah's horrible threats. But now, tired, sunburned, and hungry, she couldn't hold back the tears from splashing her cheeks. She was farther from home than she'd ever been and harbored little hope her quest would succeed. Even if she told Callen what she sought, would he be much help?

Callen gestured toward the door. "Come, let's go inside and see if we can find lodging."

Jadiel cringed as wary eyes scrutinized her in the smoky room. She slipped behind Callen and dared look at the assortment of grizzled, tough-looking men drinking at the tables. Callen turned and questioned her with his eyes, and Jadiel shook her head.

She let out a sigh. "I don't see them here." Even though her kidnappers were absent, Jadiel tensed. Any one of these men might wish her harm. A strong urge to flee overtook her, but at that moment Callen took her arm and led her past the men to the counter.

"Jadiel, relax. I'll keep you safe," he said. "Just sit here and I'll buy you some supper. How does that sound?"

As she sat on the stool, she caught a whiff of something delicious cooking in the kitchen mingled with the sweet scent of pipe tobacco. Her stomach grumbled loudly. A few men in a corner laughed amid the noisy banter floating around her. Callen leaned over the counter and spoke to the man filling glasses from a keg perched against the wall. Ale frothed and spilled over the edges of the glasses as Callen asked about rooms and horses. The man called to the back room, and a boy a few years younger than Jadiel came out, wiping wet hands on his long apron.

"Skif, go with this fella here and bed down his horse."

Jadiel stood to go with Callen, but he motioned her to stay. She sat back down, aware of the irritation on Callen's face. It made her heart sink. No doubt he had important things to do, places to go. She was an unexpected burden he'd taken on and he probably resented her. Well, she mused, no one made him save her from those men, but he did. She appreciated his kindnesses, but she had something important to do as well—and little time in which to do it. Traipsing along with Callen to some plain would not bring her closer to finding the Eternal Tree or whatever it was called.

Jadiel's attention snapped back as a short stocky woman brushed against her. She set a plate of steaming stew and a mug of cider on the counter. "Here, luv, dig in." The woman pulled utensils from her apron pouch and set them beside the plate. She lowered her voice and leaned closer. Jadiel smelled charred wood smoke and grease.

"He's a bit young for your pa, no? Your brother, is he?" Jadiel felt the woman's eyes bore into hers.

"A friend of my family." From the corner of her eye she caught some of the patrons' glances. Maybe they didn't get many strangers passing through their village. Jadiel shrank lower on her stool.

"Not safe to be traveling the land at night. Not 'round here." The woman's eyes twinkled with warning. "Where you be headed?"

Jadiel picked up her fork and took a bite of the stew, which tasted more like a bland soup with overcooked vegetables simmering in meat stock. A far cry from her cook's savory cuisine.

"Um, the King's Plain, I think."

As the woman gasped, Jadiel noticed a telltale hush envelop the room. How she longed to slip off her stool and hide beneath the counter!

"Ah, you'll not be wanting to go there. Not on your life." The woman backed away from Jadiel, as if afraid to touch her, and bumped into Callen as she turned to hasten off.

"Go where?" he asked, setting his pack down on the floor.

The barkeep stopped pouring ale and glared at Callen. "Surely you're not taking a child into the Valley Perilous? Man, have you lost your beans?"

Jadiel turned her head and caught the wide-eyed expressions on the faces around her—disapproving, incredulous glares that made her shiver.

"Callen, what is that place—"

He stopped her with a squeeze of her arm. "What business is it of yours where I go?" he asked the barkeep in a tone that made Jadiel stiffen. She hoped Callen wasn't prodding this man into an argument. She'd endured more than enough yelling and screaming these past months.

"Here in Rumble, anyone venturing onto the plain is our business. Why do you think this place is called Rumble, as such?"

Callen sat down on the stool next to Jadiel and scrunched his face. "I don't know. Why, then?"

The man set down a tall glass of ale before Callen. His voice softened, but his eyes remained full of judgment. "Because the foolish likes of you go stirring up the dead, making the ground shake and the animals spook." He snorted and pointed a finger in Callen's face. "All you adventure seekers, looking for the thrill of danger. Just go home and stand in front of a runaway carriage. That's danger enough." He grunted and wiped the counter with a towel.

Jadiel spooned more stew into her mouth as those in the room resumed their conversations. Was that what Callen was doing—seeking danger and adventure? Was this his idea of a holiday from work? And what did the man mean by stirring up the dead? What a superstitious lot these villagers were! Everyone knew the dead were unable to think or feel or speak. They probably experienced earth shakes, like the ones back home, shakes caused by the land settling, as Papa had taught her.

The woman who served Jadiel returned once more with a plate of stew for Callen, and a wooden board holding a small crusty loaf of bread. Callen mumbled his thanks and the woman huffed, shaking her head as she retreated into the kitchen.

Callen tore off a piece of bread and dipped it in his stew. As he chewed, he whispered to Jadiel. "Friendly bunch, aren't they?"

Jadiel ate the rest of her meal in silence, wanting to tell Callen the things pressing on her heart, but she would wait for a more private place. She sensed Callen's ire and wondered what had compelled him to this forsaken land.

"I've arranged for a cottage with two bedrooms. There's one behind the stable. We can sleep in beds tonight—and even boil up some hot water for bathing." He kept his voice low and his eyes on his food.

"And then what? Are we really going to that place?"

He met her worried eyes with a warning look. "We'll talk later." His face brightened. "Oh, and I found a mule. So you can have your own mount now."

Gratitude welled in Jadiel's heart. "Thank you. I can't remember when a stranger has treated me so kindly."

"I'm not a stranger. I'm practically family." He tousled her hair affectionately and scowled sternly. "Now, eat your supper like a good lass, and then it's off to bed with you!"

Jadiel couldn't help but smile at his imitation of Uncle Beren. Maybe Callen was right—he was almost family. And maybe she would risk trusting him with her secret. Maybe.

"You said you would tell me once we got far enough away," Jadiel complained, shifting on the scratchy blanket covering the mule's back. "Isn't this far enough?"

Callen turned in his saddle and scanned the landscape. Rumble receded to the east, the cottages barely visible in the swelling ground fog that nearly engulfed their mounts' legs. Across the bleak terrain, a tight ring of ragged cliffs rose before them. Callen could just make out the narrow pass the boy Skif had told them to watch for. The villagers only huffed in anger at Callen's request for directions to the Plain. One man even spat upon him and muttered what sounded like a curse. Fortunately, in the early morning's dusky light, as they transferred one of the saddlebags onto the mule, Skif snuck over to the stable, eager to share his tales of woe and mystery surrounding the Valley Perilous. Callen listened politely but inwardly scoffed at the exaggerated stories of men swallowed up in pools of blood and hands emerging from the ground eager to grab unwary trespassers' ankles. Jadiel, though, had turned ashen at Skif's telling.

"There're some flat rocks we can sit on. I want to show you something," Callen said. He dismounted and led the horse through a thicket of pricklybush; Jadiel followed.

"How can anyone stand to live out here?" she asked. "And why don't those villagers leave, if they so fear this place?"

"Good question."

Jadiel sat on a rock and fastened her cloak, throwing the hood over her head. "This place is creepy—and cold." She hugged her knees to her chest as Callen pulled out his pack and the rolled-up parchments from his saddlebag. The horse and mule snuffled the ground, tugging at bits of scraggly vegetation. The scarcity of grasses made him glad he bought that bag of feed.

Callen set the parchments next to Jadiel and rummaged through the pack. He pulled out two apples and then handed Jadiel a small wooden box.

Jadiel turned the box in her hand, studying the design made by the pieces of inlaid wood. "What is it?"

Callen put an apple on the rock beside her and bit into his. They had skipped breakfast, not wanting to face another round of scowls and harsh glares. In between bites he said, "A puzzle box. Have you ever seen one?"

Jadiel shook her head. "I don't understand. Does it open?" She poked at one side and a piece of wood moved.

"See if you can figure it out." He smiled, knowing she'd have little luck. Both Eliab and Dariel had tried for weeks and failed, and once Callen showed them the sequence they had dropped their jaws in awe. He had worked these last few years at mastering his design after seeing one Beren had in the shop. Beren told him that, in ancient times, kings often kept valuable signet rings and seals in these boxes, hidden away from prying fingers. Only the kings were shown by the craftsman how to unlock it.

Callen watched Jadiel work at the puzzle while he finished his apple and drank water from his jug. She managed to find two of the trigger releases, but couldn't locate the third.

"Here." She handed the box back to him. "I can't do it. Did you make this?"

Callen nodded and took it from her. She watched him flip it from side to side, pushing on various sections of wood and unlatching hidden locks. Her eyes widened as the top popped open on gold hinges to reveal an empty chamber of oiled ebony wood.

"That's amazing. But there's nothing in it."

"You can put whatever you want in there and no one will find it." Callen added, "I'm considering making these to sell; what do you think?"

Jadiel took a bite of her apple and nodded. "I'd buy one. It's beautiful as well."

Callen put the box back in his pack and untied his cloak from the saddle. A chill breeze drifted down from the cliffs and Callen's fingers numbed. He wondered at the sudden change in weather and eyed the pass. Somehow he sensed the fog and cold emanated from the plain, just beyond those crags, like a cauldron spilling over its contents. A shiver ran up his spine and he looked at Jadiel. Her eyes rested on the cliffs, too, and her face relayed concern.

"So, tell me why we are here," she said.

Callen came over and unrolled the drawings. "I'm searching for a bridge."

"A bridge? Out here—in the middle of a flat, empty land. Are you mad?"

"Hold on; there's more." Callen pointed at one of the parchments and Jadiel leaned over. As she looked at the sketches, Callen explained what he had learned about the bridge, showing her the designs and odd letters in the scrollwork, the mysterious notation of the king-priest of Antolae, and telling how he found references in the library leading him to The King's Plain, where this king, among others, had supposedly been buried.

"But I don't understand. If you seek the bridge, then what do you care about finding this king's grave? What's to be learned from venturing into some dangerous place?"

Callen wasn't sure how to answer Jadiel. For some reason he resisted telling her about Ebed, the ugly stranger who spoke riddles and challenged him to seek the circle upon a circle within a circle. A man who knew his name and warned him of danger in his own heart. The vision of the hill rising up from the plain came unbidden to his mind. Callen shuddered and wrapped his cloak tighter. A noise off in the distance startled him, a low moan that swelled along the ground. Callen jumped up from where he sat on the rock and looked down at his feet, which seemed to be shifting.

Jadiel's eyes filled with fear. "What was that? Look!" She pointed to where the horse and mule stood, their heads raised, faces tense and alert. Callen paled as a small ripple in the earth traveled beneath the animals' feet, almost like a creature burrowing beneath the surface. The horse shied and whinnied, sidestepping with the mule as the surge passed and petered out.

"I'm sure that was just the wind caught in the crevices of the cliffs."

Jadiel's voice trembled. "And that—thing in the ground?"

Callen shrugged as he tried to quell his nerves. It wouldn't help for Jadiel to see him rattled.

Jadiel grunted. "Well, I'm not going over there. And I don't think your horse will want to go either. This is stupid."

Callen saw her eyes glistening with tears. He sighed and sat beside her, speaking tenderly. "Jadiel, please tell me. What are you looking for? You said you have to find something."

He watched Jadiel struggle with her thoughts. She swallowed hard and found her voice. "Huldah sent me to fetch leaves from a tree." She grunted in frustration and rolled her eyes. "Leaves that are supposed to give eternal beauty and endless life."

"Is she serious?"

"She showed me a picture in a book. If I don't return with those leaves by the next full moon she . . . will kill Papa." Jadiel's voice cracked and sobs followed. Callen pursed his lips together in anger. Huldah! He'd never met her, but his low estimation of her now fell even lower. He sat quietly, wanting to put his arm around Jadiel, but wondered if she would want his comfort. What she really needed was her father.

"Jadiel, surely there must be some way to stop Huldah. If we go back, we can get Beren and others—"

"No, Callen!" She wiped her face with her sleeve and scowled. "You don't understand. She has powers. She swore if I told anyone or tried to stop her she would kill my father—and I believe she would, with all my heart. Please, don't tempt me with your words. I want to go home more than anything. I—I just can't."

Callen took her small hands in his and squeezed them. "All right. Then I'll help you find this tree. Tell me what it looks like." Clammy fog swirled around them, dampening Callen's hair and eyelashes. Beads of moisture laced Jadiel's black tresses in a net of pearls. A faint odor carried on the air, of something rotting.

Jadiel sniffled, and Callen handed her his handkerchief. "Here, for your nose."

Obediently, she blew into the cloth. "I don't know how I'm supposed to find some magical tree. The drawing she showed me looked like a big oak tree. But the leaves were a little bigger, not jagged, but glossy like oak leaves, and the branches weren't gnarly but smooth and straight."

Callen's breath caught.

"What?" Jadiel asked.

"Do these look like the same leaves?" Callen lifted one sheet of parchment from under another and held it in front of Jadiel. He pointed to one of the tree motifs, with leaves splaying out of branches that twisted up a column.

"Yes!" Her eyes flitted as she looked over the scrollwork. Her voice filled with excitement. "And these branches—they're the same too."

Callen exhaled, suddenly aware of the muted silence around him, as if time stood still, holding its own breath. What a strange coincidence! How had he chanced upon this young girl searching for the same tree he hoped to find? Surely heaven had arranged their meeting; there could be no other explanation.

One look in Jadiel's eyes told Callen she had come to the same conclusion.

"Jadiel, the bridge I seek was fashioned from a terebinth tree. I saw pictures of them in the library—giant trees with huge boughs." He heard Ebed's words in his head, describing the tiny seed that grew into a mighty tree that housed the birds of heaven. "In ancient times they were considered sacred, and a valuable oil was obtained from them—from their leaves, I suppose. And kings were often buried under them. They were sometimes called 'the king's tree' for that reason."

Jadiel frowned. "Then, I still don't understand. Are you look-ing for the bridge, or for the tree it was made from? And you still haven't told me why you want to venture into that valley."

Callen hesitated. "I met a man in Sherbourne. He told me to come here."

Jadiel huffed. "So you're risking your life—our lives—just because some stranger sent you here?"

"You wouldn't understand." Irritated, Callen gathered up his parchments and returned them to their sheath. He stuffed his pack into the saddlebag and tightened the horse's girth. Jadiel called out to him.

"What—because I'm a child? I'm not stupid."

"I never said you were." He wondered at the edginess in his voice. Was Jadiel right? Was he heading recklessly into danger? He felt his conscience prick for taking a young girl, now under his protection, into a land wiser people feared to tread. Well, if Jadiel wanted to wait for him out here, she could. But he had to go. Something deep within him pressed him toward that Plain, as if it called to him.

He looked over at Jadiel, who stood holding the mule's reins, and saw a small girl trying to be brave.

"Look," he said gently. "I just have to go. You can stay here, or I can take you back to Rumble to wait for me there."

Jadiel led the mule to the nearest rock and used it as a mount-ing block. She swung onto the beast's back and glared at Callen. "What if those kidnappers return? No thanks. I'd rather take my chances with you—and the dead kings. If that's okay."

Callen nodded and set his face west. As he clucked at the mare, an icy wind rubbed against his neck. He shuddered.

The wind felt like a hook, pulling him toward the cliffs that enclosed the King's Plain.

EIGHTEEN

"DOES THIS come in a larger bottle?" Huldah held up the delicate blown-glass jar for the shopkeeper to see. The woman tipped her coiffed head and peered across the counter to where Huldah stood fingering the assorted perfumes and colognes.

"No, I'm sorry. Those fragrances come all the way from Ethryn, so are quite costly and hard to acquire, as you can imagine."

"All the way from Ethryn," Huldah mimicked in a sassy tone under her breath. *Probably mixed in the back room of the shop for a pence.* Still, Huldah had to admit, "Evening Lotus" gave off a wickedly sinful scent. Ramah needed something overpowering to cloud the minds of her suitors—with a little help from her mother's stash of potions. A drop of this, mixed in with that, and—voila! Men would be putty in her daughter's hands.

Shopping—the best way to take her mind off things, she mused. Especially things that upset her. And right now, thinking about Ka'rel's sneaky escape made her want to smash every fragile bottle in this pretentious, overpriced shop, but she forced herself to remain calm and poised as she doled out three silvers into the shopkeeper's waiting palm.

"I'll take these—and one of those powder puffs there."

The woman handed her a round box from the shelf. Huldah flashed her cloying smile and stuffed the purchases into her carry bag. She gave a friendly little wave as she stepped out of the stuffy shop and into the breezy street running through the Kettlebro marketplace. *Must keep up appearances.*

The bells in the nearby chapel rang, announcing noon. Huldah quickly trotted over the cobbles, careful not to trip in her high-heeled boots. She picked up her skirts, avoiding puddles from the street washers' unsuccessful attempts at cleaning away the dirt and animal wastes that muddied the wide lane. Her corset pinched too tightly, forcing her to take quick shallow breaths. And her whole body shook from the exertion of running; her physical beauty was only an illusion that did not extend to her aged muscles and bones beneath. With each aching step she longed for the leaves that would truly restore her youth and grant her natural loveliness. No more of this painful charade. So what if Ka'rel had flown the coop? What trouble could he cause? Peck out a few eyes? Huldah laughed at her unnecessary agitation. Even if Ka'rel could find someone to warn, or miraculously locate that brat, how would he speak to them?

Still—it was a matter of pride. She wanted her husband back, even if just to watch him die the moment Jadiel returned to the manor. How dare he break free and mock her? She would show him!

Huldah arrived at the chapel as the last bell sounded. There, standing in front of the statue of some revered saint, was the man she had arranged to meet. Her eyes quickly took in his muscular physique, the proud chin and high cheekbones, the shock of golden hair swept back from his broad forehead. Here was Gilad, son of a wealthy merchant, suitor for Ramah's hand in marriage, and—best of all—an expert sharpshooter with a bow. Slung over his shoulder were an impressive well-worn crossbow and a quiver of arrows.

Huldah sidled up to the young man, batting her eyelashes and brushing a hand along his cheek. She heard the telltale catch in his breath and watched his eyes glaze over.

"You must be . . . Huldah." His breath wavered as his hungry eyes drifted from Huldah's face down to her feet.

"Yes." She tried to mask her impatience. *Who else did you think I would be, idiot?* "So, have we come to an understanding?"

"Your daughter in marriage for one hawk."

She waggled a finger at him and his eyes followed her movement like a cat stalking a moth. "One *live* hawk. You may shoot it, but must not kill it."

"Well, now that I've met you, I can only imagine your daughter must be as lovely—as you declared." He drew a deep whiff of Huldah's perfume and rolled his eyes.

Huldah clenched her teeth and forced a smile. Any moment now, the man would become a drooling, blathering fool. "Here." She took his hand and opened it flat, placing a round object in his palm.

The man tore his gaze from Huldah's face and stared at the glass casing he held. A small black twig, thin as a pine needle, floated inside it.

She leaned closer and ran a hand through his sun-bleached hair. "This will show you the way to the hawk. Point it toward this mark here and off you go . . ."

Gilad looked up and once more met Huldah's eyes. She brushed a swath of long red hair from her cheek and brought her lips against his ear. Huldah felt his body shake like a leaf. "Don't forget, I must have him back within a fortnight." She pulled back and raised her voice. "Or the deal's off!"

The sharp tone shook Gilad's attention, snapping him awake.

"Now go," she said, waving him off like a pesky fly.

Gilad bowed graciously and scampered away. Huldah watched him, nodding in approval. The man was stupid, like most men, but plenty handsome. Once they married, he'd take Ramah to his home in Wolcreek to immerse her in wealth and luxury. Ah, what more could a doting mother wish for?

Jadiel heard Callen curse the fog under his breath. She didn't mind the haze as much as the stench. What was that horrible smell? She kept her cloak over her mouth and took shallow breaths. Even her eyes watered at the pungency of the air.

They wended their way through the steep, narrow pass, only to find the valley below engulfed in a blanket of white. The scramble of boulders made riding impossible, so they dismounted and led the horse and mule slowly, listening to echoes of their faltering footsteps. More than once, Callen's horse tripped and nearly fell head over heels. Callen slowed to a worm's pace. Without a visible sun westering overhead, Jadiel couldn't tell how long they trudged down the rocky path, but at least the terrain had flattened out some.

"I can't see my nose on my face with all this fog," Callen complained.

"It was your idea to come here."

She kept her eye on the little bit of horse tail swishing in front of her, which was all she could see. Callen's voice sounded muffled.

"You could have stayed behind."

"Too late now." Jadiel almost bumped into the horse's rump as Callen stopped abruptly. She stepped backward. "At least you could warn me when you plan to stop."

"I think the fog is lifting." Callen sounded much closer, but all Jadiel could see was more horse tail.

However, she could soon make out Callen's hooded head as he strained to see through the murkiness. The mist at her feet thinned, revealing a flat expanse littered with rocks. A few boulders lay strewn among the lumpy barren ground. Jadiel stood on tiptoe to try to see around the horse. "Can you see anything at all?"

Callen walked forward a few paces and his horse resisted, pulling against the lead. "Come on, girl," he said to the mare. He tugged harder, but she yanked back and rose up on hind legs in protest. "Whoa, calm down."

Jadiel's mule flattened his ears against his head, and his eyes darted nervously.

"Maybe we should tie them up here, while we explore," Callen said.

Jadiel handed her mule's lead rope to Callen and waited while he tied them to a rotted branch of a fallen tree. He took a bowl from the saddlebag and poured water into it from his jug. The horse and mule drank warily, lifting their heads nervously as they slurped.

"Here, you should drink, too." He handed Jadiel the water jug and she took a long draw. Her throat stung from the acrid air.

"Why do you think this place smells so bad?"

"Look." He pointed to a wet puddle on the ground. "See those bubbles? Something is festering from under the dirt, some mineral deposits maybe."

"More like moldering dead things." She wrinkled her nose. "Now what?"

Callen retrieved his pack, bow, and quiver from the horse's bags. "Well, the way I figure it, these mountains form a ring, a circle. I was told to look for a circle within a circle. So, whatever it is, we should find it out there. This way." He walked ahead into the gloom.

Jadiel watched him vanish after just a few footsteps. "Hey, wait up."

Jadiel drew close to Callen, listening to the strange sounds rising from the ground around her feet. She shot Callen a questioning glance, but his eyes were focused ahead. Shivers raced down her back as she recognized voices—murmurs and moans rising in pitch the more they walked onto the plain and away from the cliffs. How could those sounds be coming out of the earth?

"Callen, the voices—"

"Shh, I hear them. Just ignore them."

"Ignore them!"

Callen grabbed her arm and squeezed. He opened his mouth to say something, but just then the ground lifted Jadiel and rocked her to one side.

"Help!" Jadiel tried to balance as the rocks below her feet rose and rumbled. Callen held on to her arm as they floundered together, slipping and tripping until, finally, a quiet settled upon the plain. Behind them, the horse neighed and the mule strained on his tether, clearly frightened.

Jadiel was too afraid to move, or run back. Callen tried to pull her along unsuccessfully.

"Jadiel, it's just an earth shake, you know that." He looked into her tear-streaked face. "Just a little farther, okay?"

"What do you expect to see, anyway? Some dead king who will tell you where to find your dumb bridge?" Jadiel knew she was whining but couldn't help it.

Callen dropped his hand from her arm, and she fell to the cold ground in a huff. "Go. I'll wait here," she said.

"Don't be difficult, Jadiel." He slid the bow from his shoulder and pulled an arrow from the quiver. He held them in one hand while offering Jadiel the other. "Please, stay close to me."

Jadiel pressed her hand against the ground to lift herself up to standing, then froze.

Her voice rattled. "I feel something."

Callen dropped to his knees. "What?"

Jadiel felt the blood drain from her face. A rhythmic pulse pounded against her wrist; the ground was unusually warm. A heartbeat.

Jadiel quailed and jumped to her feet. "There's something alive!"

Callen narrowed his eyes in disbelief and gingerly placed his hand on the ground. She could tell he felt it too.

"The kings are not dead; they are waiting . . ."

Jadiel grew hysterical. "Waiting? For what? To eat us?"

Callen tried to laugh, but stopped when earth raised his foot in the air. Jadiel watched him step back abruptly, gasping in fear.

She followed his gaze to the ground, where a dark liquid pooled around his feet. The thick fluid oozed from the earth and soon encompassed them both, edging toward their boots. In the distance, she heard what sounded like swords clanging and hooves pounding the plain. Jadiel clung to Callen's cloak, shaking uncontrollably. Her eyes went wild when Callen dared touch the liquid with a tentative finger and brought it close to his face—the color of blood.

"That's it!" She pulled away from Callen and jumped over the growing puddle. "I'm leaving this place." She started back to where the animals were tethered, but couldn't see more than a few feet in front of her. More "blood" seeped from the ground, creating puddles on all sides. She turned and spun around, but there were no landmarks to indicate the way. Which direction to go? She clucked and nickered, hoping the horse would respond, but all she heard on the putrid air was more moaning, followed by shrieks and yells that sounded barely human.

Callen ran to her and shook her gently.

"Jadiel, stop screaming."

Jadiel closed her mouth and located Callen's worried eyes. He said with a touch of cynicism in his voice, "You're making enough noise to rouse the dead. Bad idea."

She nodded, unable to speak. Her body stiffened, and she found herself incapable of moving her limbs. Terror raced over every inch of her body like an army of ants.

Callen again took her arm, and she let herself be led. For a long time they walked, silently stepping with care as the ground moaned and rumbled around them. The clang of swords carried on the muffled air, coming from one direction, then another. Jadiel heard a loud thud close by and felt the ground respond in a shudder, as if something—or someone—heavy fell. The mist wrapped them, closing behind and opening paths in front. Callen kept his bow at the ready, darting his head from side to side. Jadiel stared at the ground, expecting any moment to feel a hand grabbing her ankle. Maybe that boy, Skif, had spoken the truth. Now she understood why those villagers were terrified of the plain.

Callen paused and Jadiel looked up. Appearing out of the fog directly ahead stood a huge flat stone, so tall Jadiel could not see its top. Callen ran his hand across the practically smooth surface of the gray rock, then circled it. The stone was at least ten feet wide, and as more mist thinned, she saw another to the right, a few feet away. The stones rested on a raised berm of ground, at least two feet higher than the land around them.

"This is odd," Callen said, returning to her side. "There are many of these stones. Look." He pointed to the left and Jadiel now saw three more, sentinels in a curved line. Callen took her hand and led her along the outside of what appeared to be a ring of rock. Two lay on their sides, fallen over, perhaps five feet thick and a dozen feet long.

"These have been carved or chipped away to form slabs," he said. "But why? What purpose do they serve?"

After walking for a few minutes, Callen ducked between two stones, pulling Jadiel along with him. Inside the ring, a short stubby grass grew, carpeting a hill that rose toward the center. As they walked up the hill, Jadiel noticed the sponginess of the grass under her boots, so different from the jagged and sharp terrain outside the ring. She could now make out more of the towering pillars of rock, clearly encircling the mound upon which they traversed. The awful smell subsided, leaving a tingling fresh scent on the air. Jadiel almost felt they had entered a different world.

A snuffling sound burst out behind her. Callen jerked to a stop and, in one quick motion, raised his bow and nocked an arrow. Jadiel fell behind him as the snorting and huffing grew louder and came toward them. Soupy fog engulfed them. Jadiel stared into the gray, trying to see what approached, feeling Callen tense beside her, his bowstring taut and vibrating near his cheek.

A dark, low shape ran at them. Jadiel strained to make out its form, then called out. "Wait, Callen."

She could see legs trotting, and a long snout belonging to an odd-looking creature. Two white pieces of what looked like bone curved along the sides of its mouth. Beady dark eyes bore down on her, surrounded by tufts of coarse brown fur.

Jadiel turned to Callen and gasped. "What are you doing?" She threw her weight against his shoulder the second the arrow released from the bow, sending it flying askew. "Are you crazy, shooting blindly at some helpless animal?"

Callen shoved her back. "Helpless?" He quickly pulled out another arrow from his quiver. "It's charging at us!"

Jadiel looked back at the beast, which seemed to be slowing down, huffing as it approached. "Callen, you can't just shoot and apologize afterward."

Callen snorted in disgust. "You're kidding, right?" He nocked the next arrow. "Look at the beast's eyes—and those tusks! Boars can spear you through in an instant, without blinking."

Jadiel had never heard of a boar or what it could do—and she didn't care. She stepped in front of Callen and forced him to lower the bow. "Just wait for one moment; will you do that for me, please?" The anger in her voice made him halt, but he kept his gaze on the creature with his bow at the ready.

Jadiel crouched level with the boar's eyes. The beast wheezed and panted a few feet away, waiting. She thought of how she had used her mirror to calm the bear, then realized her satchel was buried in one of the saddlebags. But she had her flute in the hidden pocket of her cloak. Maybe music would pacify the boar. Maybe it was just frightened, having strangers disturb its home. Why didn't Callen know that animals usually meant no harm? Humans were more often the ones to invoke fear.

Jadiel sat on the grass and took out her flute. From the corner of her vision, she saw Callen reposition himself, arrow still pointing at the boar. *He must think I'm mad, trying to pacify such a creature.* Well, maybe her playing would calm Callen as well—and whatever stirred under the ground. Just imagining bodies lying in wait underneath her, their hearts beating and their blood flowing, made her hands tremble. But she placed the flute under her lip and soft clear notes sang out, filling the air with a melancholy tune that thickened around her.

The boar cocked its head and trotted a few small steps closer to Jadiel. Jadiel eyed the huge beast as she played, surprised at its size. Why, its haunches probably came up to her chest, and it was nearly as long as a horse. The face was so ugly it was almost funny, with its long hairy snout and patch of wiry fur that flared out on top of its head. Jadiel smiled, reminded of Papa's hair after he removed his hat at the end of the day.

As she played, her fears melted away, drifting into the air with the sweet clear notes. She closed her eyes and imagined herself back in the manor, sitting on the rug beside her mother, who had always listened in rapture to Jadiel's playing. Her heart wrenched in sorrow, and she let this sorrow feed and fuel her music.

Jadiel finished her melody, letting the last note fade out. When she opened her eyes, the boar walked toward her. Jadiel cast a stern look at Callen, who kept his arrow fixed on the creature. She turned back to the boar and said kindly, "I hope you liked that song. My mother taught it to me."

Jadiel's jaw dropped when the boar opened its mouth and in a gravelly voice said, "Then your mother taught you well."

The hawk soared over the Logan Valley, sensing the lift under its wings. At first, the confusion of temperatures and crisscrossing currents made him falter and drop, but after many hours he had learned to adjust quickly to the wind's subtle nuances and to exert less energy by riding the updrafts that lifted him over the rolling hills and cascading rivers.

With his sharp eyesight he made out small mice scurrying across the fields far below him. He circled the tiny villages and studied the manner in which the villagers walked, looking for a familiar human. From the heights of the clouds he studied all their faces, aching to find one special face among them, but so far, he had not located Jadiel.

Now that he knew she lived, he grew more anxious each minute, worrying for her safety. How would Jadiel make her way in the wide and unfamiliar world—a girl of twelve all alone? How far could she travel in a week? Already, Ka'rel had flown low over all the roads leading north and west of Northvale. After dark he surreptitiously listened at the lighted windows of inns and taverns, hoping to hear her voice, or hear some word of her, but his efforts yielded nothing so far. He knew even his keen eyes would be unable to find her if she happened to be indoors, or under the boughs of a large tree. As he dipped into a downdraft, he wondered if he'd already passed her by. Now, nearing the sprawling city of Sherbourne, he gave a heavy sigh, wishing he could screech, imagining how hard it might be to spot his daughter among the crowds and shops and other obstructions that would block his view. If she was even there.

The brown ribbon of road stretched out below him. Noises from the city reached his ears—voices calling out or singing; cart wheels turning; pots clanging; men pounding on stone, repairing the city walls and streets. The sounds swirled on the breeze around him, mingled with smells of cookstoves and vegetation and the Heresh River in the distance. Ka'rel marveled at his heightened senses, although sometimes the sounds and smells assaulted him all at once in a dizzying wave. He still had trouble sifting through them and identifying their sources. A sense of hopelessness filled his little hawk's heart, but he pressed on. He would find Jadiel and somehow save her. He made a little frustrated noise in his throat. *And just how would he manage that?*

Suddenly, one sound grabbed his attention. He circled lower and listened intently, picking up the current that carried the sound, a hint of music different than the lute strumming and bawdy singing drifting toward him from the east. He singled out the breathy melody, a thin strain wafting his way—from the south. His heart pounded faster as he stilled his wings, floating in rapt silence with every nerve alert, daring to hope.

The farther south he glided, the more sonorous the music. Now he was certain he heard a flute, its crystal-clear notes stringing into a tune that resounded deep within his soul. A tune his wife, M'lynn, had sung many nights in the drawing room, beside the fireplace. Ka'rel squeezed his beady eyes shut at the heartbreaking memory, letting the grief spur him onward, praying he would find Jadiel before the last few notes diminished into thin air.

NINETEEN

CALLEN LOWERED the bow, letting the arrow drop from the bowstring to the ground. The fog dispersed and a streak of sunlight peeked through, turning the grass a shimmering green all around them. Awed, Callen traced the ring of massive stones with his eyes, the towering slabs brilliantly lit as the lichen and mosses coating their surfaces caught the sun's rays. Now he could make out the swelling hill upon which he stood, a sight that matched the vision seen in his mind's eye back in Sherbourne. Through the spaces between the gray stones, the King's Plain stretched out in all directions, abutting the ragged cliffs a league away.

Callen looked back at Jadiel, who sat on the grass, flute in hand. Then he studied the boar that rested back on its haunches, its snout raised in the air. He feared to move, for the speech and intelligence of this beast unnerved him more than its grunting and charging. And now, the creature set its gaze upon Callen, and that piercing look fluttered his stomach.

"Who has trampled the kings?" Rumbly words—almost a growl came from the creature. "Seekers, do you not know?"

Callen observed Jadiel bow her head to the boar.

The beast tilted its wiry head and scrutinized Callen. "You have disturbed them in your passing, mere ones."

Mere ones? Callen ventured a hesitant step closer. The boar tipped its head back and cleared its throat. "How long has it been since we've spoken? More years than we can remember."

"Please." Jadiel held out her open palm towards the boar. "My name is Jadiel, and this is Callen. What may we call you?"

The sides of the boar's mouth lifted into what Callen guessed was a smile. He breathed out in relief. Maybe no one would be gored today. The hairy beast ambled to Jadiel and stopped inches from her face, its head level with hers.

"What name are we called? So long since asked; we don't remember." It scrutinized Jadiel, straining its eyes to look her over. "You are a human child. Come to find the tree? Shame, it was cut down ages ago, don't you know?"

Jadiel jerked her head to face Callen. He met her look of sad shock.

"How do you know what we seek?" Callen came alongside Jadiel and helped her stand.

The boar got to its feet and shook its coat. Bits of dust and debris scattered from its fur, making a small dust cloud that lingered in the still air. Narrowing its eyes and snorting, the boar turned its snout up to Callen. "You seek the old vision, that one. But how can a flimsy reed stand firm in the rising floodwaters? It cannot, don't you know?"

"Know what? What floodwaters are you talking about?"

The boar pushed past them and headed up the hill. Jadiel tugged Callen's sleeve and they followed. The land around them lay in uneasy stillness; Callen sensed alert attention, as if a hundred pairs of eyes watched his every move.

"Yes," the boar bellowed, not looking back, "the kings are waiting. Waiting for what?" The boar stopped and turned, lifting its head in recitation.

"'The kings await a prince. Fathers await an heir. Captives await a deliverer.' Yes, that is also disclosed in the old vision." The boar continued up the hill, its stubby legs squishing the damp grass. "Once, there was a foolish man who chose to build a house on the far side of a small creek. Why was he foolish? Because he did not expect the flood, and built his bridge from small sticks and twigs and thin pieces of twine. What happened when the floodwaters rose? That bridge splintered, shattered, and collapsed, don't you know?"

Callen's gut twisted at the mention of a bridge. He quickened his pace to walk alongside the boar, which seemed intent on cresting the hill. "Tell me . . . please," he added, not wanting to offend the creature, "what do you know of a circle upon a circle within a circle?"

The boar stopped and sat, wheezing with each shallow breath. "Where sits the circle upon a circle within a circle? Why, just look." It motioned with its snout.

Jadiel left Callen's side and walked a few steps to where the hill leveled out. There, in the middle of the summit, sat a huge stump, very old and poorly cut, as if a dozens axes had been used to hack through the tree's girth. It spanned perhaps eight feet across. Jadiel touched the stump, and then sat upon it. Tears poured down her face.

"Mere one, why is your face wet? Because you mourn the tree. But have you not heard? The old vision discloses 'For there is a hope for a tree, if it is cut down, that it will sprout again and that its shoots will not cease though its root grows old in the earth and its stump dies in the ground.'"

The boar sidled up to Jadiel, standing nearly aligned with her shoulders as she sat on the stump. "'Yet,' the vision discloses, 'at the scent of water it will bud and put forth branches like a young plant.'"

Jadiel blurted out, "But what hope is that? Even if such a stump as this could grow and sprout, how many years would it take to bear leaves? Too long, I fear."

Callen caught up to them and confronted the boar. "Wait, I asked you about the circle. I'm looking but I don't see it. Do you mean the ring of stones?" Perhaps they comprised one circle, but what did it signify? Callen pinched his lips together. The boar spoke in confusing riddles, like Ebed had. "Why all the riddles? Why not speak plainly!"

"How does the riddle go?" The boar shook his head as if to help him remember. "'There sits a circle upon a circle within a circle. There lies the promise of a crown on the backs of kings. There awaits a stone, a pillar, a star, a name, for those who cross the bridge.'"

"Yes, the bridge!" Callen squatted down and looked the boar in the eyes. "What is the promise of a crown on the backs of kings?"

The boar chuckled. "Mere one, the girl sits upon it. What is the promise? The holy seed is its stump."

"What holy seed are you talking about? A seed from that tree?"

The boar lifted its short legs and pounded the ground with its hooves. "Why is that one so blind? Because it is a flimsy reed. Look, mere one!"

Callen turned to watch the place where the boar gazed, down the hill. A swirl of fog erased three of the mighty stones, revealing the plain in amber twilight. A snarling wind ripped down from the cliffs and tormented the Valley Perilous, the place where countless battles had been fought and precious lifeblood spilled upon thirsty ground. Callen watched as hordes of men on steeds charged across the plain, clashing swords with their opponents. Screams carried on the air, cries of the wounded and fallen.

Callen's eyes riveted on the march of history unfolding before him. Then, one lone man, afoot, in rich crimson robes, walked between the warriors, heading toward the stone circle, bearing a crown on his head and something small dangling from a chain in his hand, an incense censer, perhaps. Callen somehow knew without question that this was the king-priest of Antolae. As the king trudged up the mountain, Callen turned and watched him walk toward them. The king reached the stump, then vanished, the vision shredded by the assailing wind. Twilight shifted to sunlight, and the hill was once more bathed in brilliance.

"Who is the king-priest of Antolae?" the boar asked quietly. It turned and looked at Callen, who glanced over at Jadiel, sitting unusually silent upon the stump. "The holy seed is its stump, don't you know?"

Callen huffed and slumped next to Jadiel. Ebed had spoken of a tiny seed that grew into the largest of trees. His head pounded as he sifted through the tangle of words.

"Mere one, that is the *old* vision. What does the new vision disclose? This . . ."

Callen's head swooned, and suddenly he found himself alone on the King's Plain, far from the circle and the boar and Jadiel. He spun around on the rocky ground, trying to find his bearings, but he was utterly lost. The hazy twilight returned and Callen squinted. Before him, draped in obscurity, stood the appearance of a man. But Callen knew he could not be real—or human. His raiment shone radiantly and his face was obscured, masked by illumination. But the man spoke to him in a voice that seemed to come from inside Callen's mind, a strong, instructive voice that mollified Callen's fear. A hand touched his shoulder, but it felt as if it touched a place much deeper inside him, in his very soul.

"Look around you, mortal."

Callen startled at piles of bones materializing at his feet. Littering the ground as far as he could see were the bleached ivory bones and skulls of humans.

"Mortal, can these bones live?"

"Only you know this," Callen answered as if by rote, hearing his voice far away, as in a cave.

"Prophesy to these bones and say, 'O dry bones, hear the word of heaven: I will cause breath to enter you, and you shall live. I will lay sinews upon you and will cause flesh to come upon you, and cover you with skin, and put breath in you and you shall live.'"

Callen spoke the words to the bones and watched in wonderment as a rattling arose and the bones came together, bone to its bone. Sinews wrapped the bones, then skin enveloped sinews.

"Call the four winds, mortal, to breathe upon these slain that they may live."

Callen obediently called the winds. From on high, the winds gathered and coalesced, then raced down to the plain. Breath came into the multitude of bodies and they stood on their feet, a vast array of men and women in regal clothing.

In unison, the living slain ones spoke: "Our bones were dried up and our hope was lost, but now our spirits are returned."

Callen felt a nudge against his leg. He looked down and found himself on the sunlit hill, with the boar's snout rubbing against him.

"What hope was lost, and how was it restored?" the boar asked. "The promise of the crown on the backs of kings, don't you know?"

Suddenly Callen understood. The king-priest buried under the terebinth tree—the king's tree. *He* was the promise of a crown, buried in this plain, literally on the backs of fallen kings. And the circle?

Callen's eyes rested on Jadiel who sat on the stump—a circle of wood. He looked at the hill, then down to the ring of rock. His jaw dropped. The tree stump was the circle upon a circle of hill, within a circle of stone.

"Then, does this king return somehow?" Callen asked the boar.

"What king?" Jadiel said, speaking for the first time in many minutes.

"The King of Antolae." He turned to the boar, excitement in his voice. "Did he build the bridge? Was it made from this tree?"

"Mere one, what odd questions you ask. How could the bridge be made from this tree?" The boar cackled in delight.

"What?" Callen asked. "What's so funny?"

The boar snorted and plopped down next to Jadiel. It pushed its head up to meet her hand, and she dug her fingers into its thick fur. The boar groaned in delight.

"How long has it been since we've been scratched? More years than we can count." Its voice deepened and grew stern. "And do we await the king-priest of Antolae? No, he but stands as a shadow of the One to come."

What one to come? Callen wondered. And what was the meaning of these visions, old and new? He questioned the beast with his face and it answered.

"Take heed, for there is still a vision for the appointed time. It speaks of the end and does not lie. If it seems to tarry, wait for it. Why? Because it will surely come. Mere one, what does the new vision disclose? 'Thus says the Most High: I myself will take a sprig from the lofty top of the tree and I myself will plant it on a lofty hill in order that it may produce boughs and become a noble tree. Under it, every kind of bird will live; in the shade of its branches will nest winged creatures of every kind. All the trees of the field shall know me, for I bring low the high tree, I make high the low tree; I have spoken it and I will accomplish it.'"

Callen's head swam with images: the king-priest buried under the terebinth, with its boughs in the heavens. The tree cut down, but sprouting again. A king returning, blowing breath into dry bones. But not the king-priest of Antolae—a different king. The boar's words swam dizzily in his head: *The kings await a prince . . . Fathers await an heir.* Instantly Callen was reminded of Ebed's parable of the wealthy landowner who sent his heir to deal with the evil tenants—and was killed. How were all these stories tied together?

And the one image that wouldn't come was the one he yearned for most—the bridge. He was no closer to finding the bridge than the day he left Loganvale. What was it the boar said? Something about a stone, a pillar, a star, and a name. For the one who crosses the bridge. Did that mean the bridge *did* exist? And why did that creature laugh with such amusement when he asked if the bridge was built from this tree?

The boar came and nudged Callen again, this time with a sad, tired expression on its face. "Why is the man swept away in the flood? Because he built his bridge with flimsy materials, perishable things. The bridge you seek is made from unblemished, imperishable materials, at the cost of much blood, don't you know?"

"No, I *don't* know," Callen answered in frustration.

It took a long look at Callen. "How can a mere one, a flimsy reed, stand fast in the flood of waters? By becoming a solid tree, unwavering and firm." It added, with warning in its dark eyes, "If you do not stand firm in the faith, you shall not stand at all."

Faith in what? Callen turned and looked into Jadiel's confused eyes. Clearly she made no sense of the boar's confounding patter, either.

"You must leave this place, now. The kings are waiting—but not for you," it said pointedly.

"But where do we go?" Jadiel asked, her voice filled with hopelessness.

"Mere one," the boar crooned sweetly to Jadiel "Where do they go to find answers? In the hidden city of Ethryn, inked upon a lost scroll, don't you know? Ten branches, ten words."

Callen ached to ask more, but the boar abruptly stood and trotted quickly down the hill. Just before it slipped between stones out of the circle, Callen caught a flash of silver, of something encircling the boar's neck.

He stood, hands on hips, sensing the restlessness of the plain under his feet.

He recalled the warning tone in the boar's words. "We should go." When Jadiel didn't answer him, he turned and saw she had her head buried in her hands. He went to her and touched her shoulder.

"Don't cry, Jadiel."

She didn't look up. "Why not? You heard what the boar said—that this was the tree I seek. Now it's just a stump."

"Surely there must be more of these trees. We'll keep looking until we find another."

Jadiel looked at Callen. He saw little trace of hope in her face. "We won't give up, Jadiel. I promise."

Callen walked a few feet away, torn between the urgency to leave and wanting to allow Jadiel a few moments to herself.

"Callen!"

Jadiel leaped up and wiped her face. "The stump is moving!" She pointed at the wet spot on the wood where her tears had fallen. A small crack opened between the rings of wood, and something wiggled out.

Jadiel hung onto Callen's cloak and together they watched as a slender, dusty green sprout inched its way out of the crevice, twisting upward as it sought the light. Within a minute, the branch stopped moving, hovering a foot above the stump. And then, a solitary leaf unfurled from the tip of the sprout, a shiny leaf that matched the ones on Callen's parchments.

The boar's words came to him. "*Yet at the scent of water it will bud and put forth branches like a young plant . . .*"

They waited in silence to see what would follow, but nothing else occurred. Jadiel took a deep breath and straightened.

Callen fidgeted as a disturbing sensation clawed at his neck. A dark cloud drifted in front of the sun and the wind kicked up, bringing with it the foul smell from the plain. "We really need to leave—now."

"But, Callen, I can't just take one leaf back home! Surely more will sprout—if we wait . . ."

As if in response, the hill groaned and creaked, and a chasm opened up in front of Callen as he sought purchase with his feet. A rift traveled outward from the dark rent in the ground, pulling the hill apart around them.

"You're right," Jadiel said, dodging the fissure, "we should leave. Now!"

Jadiel plucked the lone leaf and stuffed it in her smock pocket. They ran down the hill and out of the ring of stones, catching their breath at the bottom. As Jadiel readjusted her cloak and set her eyes on the ring of stones, Callen admired the determination in his companion's young face, imagining how her heart pained. Well, he would do all in his power to help her find another terebinth tree and return her safely home.

The boar told them to go to Ethryn, to find a scroll. *Ten branches, ten words.* Callen snorted and waded into the mass of fog. More riddles! Somehow he doubted terebinth trees grew in the desert city, but where else would they go? Perhaps this lost scroll would tell them more.

For Jadiel's sake, he truly hoped so.

Jadiel watched her footing as they trudged, slow as snails, back over the rocky terrain. As soon as they had left the grassy mound and the circle of towering stones, the fog once more swallowed them up, making her worry they would never find their way back to the pass—and their frightened mounts. The fetid air once more assaulted her nose. She was grateful, though, that the rumbling had ceased, and so far she had not felt any movement under her boots or seen more pools of blood. Maybe the boar had quieted the restless kings under the earth—but for how long? Already she and Callen had been slogging through this swampy ground for over an hour. Her boots were soaked, her stomach grumbled, and they had finished off the water in Callen's jug. There was plenty to eat and drink in one of the saddlebags—*if* they could find the animals. Jadiel feared the poor creatures had bolted, frightened at all the disturbing goings-on in this bewitched valley.

"I can see the cliffs; they're close," Callen said.

Jadiel looked up from her feet and saw the crumbling sandstone through a clearing in the fog. She whistled and called to the horse and mule, listening for a response.

Callen shrugged. "I'm sure they're here somewhere. Let's hug the base of the cliff. We're bound to run into them, even if we have to circle the entire valley."

Jadiel groaned. Surely it would not come to that!

"Wait." Callen held up his hand. "What's that?" Up ahead, a dark shadow recessed into the rock rose up from the ground, arching at the top. Jadiel followed Callen, but as she drew closer to the hillside, her gut lurched with trepidation. A tingling spread over her skin and she shivered.

He stopped suddenly. "This is interesting."

"Something's not right," Jadiel whispered. "We should go . . ."

Callen ignored her as he peered into the dark depression in the rock. "Look, there are steps leading down."

The instant Callen placed his foot on the first step, Jadiel's heart raced in panic. She suddenly felt claustrophobic, as if something hemmed her in.

"Callen, don't go down there!"

"Why not?" He skipped down the steps and stopped at the bottom.

Jadiel looked down to the small excavated landing where Callen stood. Before him, set back into hewn sandstone, rose a smooth face of marbled gray rock, reminding Jadiel of a door, although wider than most.

"Maybe this is an entrance into the cliff—a way through it." He called up to Jadiel. "If it's tall enough, we can lead the animals through and not have to tackle that difficult pass."

Jadiel watched Callen study the "door." There was something odd in the center of it, but from where she stood, she couldn't tell what it was.

"Jadiel! You won't believe what I found."

"What?" She noticed her anxiety growing greater with each second they tarried. "Callen, let's go find our mounts, please. I'm worried about them."

"Wait a moment." Callen ran his hand over the protruding part of the door. "It's like a puzzle box! See—there are blocks of mitered stone pieced together, but they move! Maybe it's some kind of lock, a way to open the door."

Jadiel's shivering heightened, making her teeth chatter even though the day grew warm. She tried to call out to Callen, but the words stuck in her throat. Something was very wrong; her feet were poised to run. But she stayed there at the top of the steps, and watched Callen slide the pieces from side to side, top to bottom, shifting their positions into different geometric patterns. "I don't think you should try to open it," she managed to mutter.

"Whoever made this was quite clever." His face knotted in concentration. "But not clever enough . . ." At those last words Jadiel heard a loud click, like a latch releasing. She watched Callen step back from the door as it swung open into the black void behind it.

Instantly, an icy knife struck Jadiel's gut, making her fall to the ground in agony. But when she felt around for a wound she found nothing untoward. What was that? She struggled to her feet and looked down at the open door—and Callen was gone!

Blood rushed to her head and she nearly swooned. Then Callen emerged from the darkness.

Disappointment laced his voice. "It's only an empty chamber. There's nothing in it." He closed the door behind him and Jadiel heard the lock catch. She saw him turn and look back at the pattern he had assembled with the puzzle pieces, a three-pronged shape set against horizontal stripes. "Odd, there's something familiar about this design. I can't put a finger on it . . ."

Jadiel found her voice, but her words shook as violently as her limbs. "Callen, you . . . you shouldn't . . . have gone in there." She looked at her boots. A film of ice grew beneath them, spreading like spilled ink.

Callen rushed to her side. "Jadiel, what's wrong? You look ill."

"Please, let's go."

He helped her stand and walked her away from the steps, following the base of the rocky wall. "Maybe you've just had too much excitement for one day."

All she could do was nod. She trudged in silence alongside Callen and then heard a welcome sound.

"There's the horse." Callen pointed at the nickering mare. "And your mule."

Jadiel noticed the animals had broken free from the branch and stood huddled together against the cliff with their leads dangling. They looked distraught but relived to see their caretakers.

Jadiel went over and stroked the mule's forehead, watching the fear leave his face. Callen slid the bow off his shoulder and reached into the saddlebag. He handed Jadiel a large slice of rye bread and a chunk of hard cheese. She ate in silence as Callen gave the horses feed and water, then sat on the ground and ate with her. But whatever relief she felt at finding her mule was tainted by the certain sensation that something lingered near them. Something evil.

The one in the dark chamber stirred. Centuries had passed in silence, in blackness. Outside, while he waited, kingdoms rose and fell; seasons turned in rhythm as the earth wheeled around the sun through the vast void of space; humans married, raised families, buried their loved ones, flitted away like chaff in the wind. But the one imprisoned in the dank rock chamber did not notice. Nor did he care. For time meant little to him; his imprisonment passed as a watch in the night; all the while he awaited the dreaded moment of his release.

Like some dormant beast long trapped in sleep, he barely noticed the snap of the door echoing deep in his mind, a tiny ripple on the surface of water. Slowly, that ripple reached the shore of his dreaming, lapping against his consciousness, coalescing his thoughts. Although he had no human eyes with which to see, he sensed light spilling onto the dirt floor, a quality of excited particles in the air.

A being entered his cell, rousing surprise, then curiosity, then—dare he think it? Hope. For the one entering was not the one appointed to remand him to his accuser, the promised one who would annihilate him. Instead, the composition of this being was human. Puzzling. Unexpected.

Somehow, a mere human had unlocked the forbidden door. With this stunning realization, the prisoner gathered himself together, pulling himself into present time and space, becoming gradually aware of walls and floor, of substance and weight—and fleeting opportunity.

As the human opened the door, a shadow, black as the chamber, slithered along the floor, edging up the wall, gliding ever so quietly beside the human shape standing in the threshold of the cell. The sudden exertion of intent caused him to stop at the base of the steps, searching for strength that would move matter in this earthly realm. In his mind's eye, he struggled to differentiate between light and dark, but could only sense movement and shadow upon shadow. He felt the vibration of the door shutting behind him and of human footsteps leading upward and away.

Above him, at the top of the steps, a form gelled against a lighter background. Thoughts of freedom energized him, stirring his imagination with the havoc he would foment, as he had centuries ago, knowing his disguises would once more conceal him. Then a troubling thought nudged him. What if this human spoke to others of how he opened this door? Word would spread to high places, to those with eyes fixed on other lands. To those with the authority to capture him.

This was something he must not allow! He studied the figure on the ledge above him, too weary to move. But he could make out the size and shape of the human, and something he carried, something long and curved. Before his mind drifted out of time and space, he imprinted the shape on his memory.

The shape of a man in a cloak, carrying a bow.

• PART THREE •

"Ten Branches, Ten Words . . ."

TWENTY

A HOT SUN baked Callen's shoulders. For four days now, they had trudged along a dusty road invaded by sand drifts, leaving behind the barren plains. The small mountains they first spotted now loomed before them—sharp pinnacles of beige and ochre rock, whipped about with swirling winds that pelted them with stinging sand. He and Jadiel covered their faces with cloth, copying the other travelers they passed coming down from the mountains. Callen's clothing itched; he had brought only heavy woolen shirts and trousers that made him sweat profusely, clothes for the Loganvale fall. Jadiel looked equally miserable, with a shirt draped over her head to keep the sun off her face. At least she had a thin smock to wear. Fortunately, there were cisterns along the road at intervals, for they only carried the one water jug. Only the horse and mule seemed unbothered by the heat, comfortable with their thin coats and tough hooves. What irritated Callen the most were his chafed lips, already so cracked that they bled.

The people they encountered spoke little but nodded politely as they passed. They had olive skin and thick black hair, similar to his own. Despite his weariness, he found himself growing excited as they neared the entrance to Ethryn. His ancestors were from this city; perhaps he had family here. Callen sighed. If only they had more time to spend in this fabled land. As with Sherbourne, he would have to look to a future trip for his exploring.

"Callen, I think my eyes are playing tricks on me." Jadiel pushed the piece of shirt from her face. "Look ahead."

Callen stopped his horse and watched the sandy face of the mountain shift in shadow and light. A crevice closed up and another opened, and, to his surprise, what appeared a solid wall melted away, revealing a man with a herd of small goats emerging out of the rock. Callen stared in confusion as the man entered the road, prodding his noisy herd with a stick. On the opposite side, a woman with a huge basket on her head merged into the mountain. Only then did Callen realize the road upon which they traveled ended abruptly a half-league ahead. No gate, no opening—just solid pinnacles of sandstone rising up in spires to the heavens.

Jadiel sucked in her breath. "Did you see that?"

Callen nodded. "How did they do that? Is that how you get in—walk through solid rock?"

Jadiel pulled the shirt off her head. Callen noticed her puffy eyes, and the exhaustion written across her face. He knew she slept little at night, often tossing from side to side in her bedroll on the hard ground. And last night she'd had a terrible nightmare, crying out for her father in her sleep. His heart wrenched for her, but he felt helpless to comfort her. Maybe, he prayed, someone in this kingdom would have knowledge of terebinth trees and where in the world they grew. Maybe this "lost scroll" of which the boar spoke would tell them more. He wanted to believe it. As much as he doubted the success of their quest, he made a point to show Jadiel a hopeful and confident demeanor.

An old man riding a strange animal came alongside him. He wore a turban on his head, and a robe striped in brilliant colors, the threads interwoven with gold. His beast was unlike any Callen had ever seen—taller than a horse, with a long neck and broad lips—and a huge hump protruding from its back. The man's face, dark as ebony, shone with kindness as he spoke in an accent that crisply enunciated each syllable. "Peace be with you, my friends. You must be strangers to Ethryn."

"We are," Callen answered, catching Jadiel's wide-eyed stare at the beast. His horse shuffled nervously at the strange smell of the man's mount.

"What is that animal you ride?" Jadiel said. "And why does it have a bump on its back?"

The man chuckled in delight, showing large shiny teeth. "This is my camel, Melora. Say hello, girl," he told the beast.

The camel opened its mouth and stuck out a fat purple tongue and bellowed. Callen put his hands over his ears at the grating sound.

Jadiel laughed. "She's funny."

"This," the man said, patting the hump, "is where she stores her water. She can travel through the desert for weeks without a drink. Of course, by then, her hump has deflated and sags to one side. Like a water skin, no?"

"Yes, it is. But when she does get a drink, I imagine it takes a very long time for her to fill up."

The man laughed again. "Nearly all day. But come, don't let these shadows deter you. Ethryn is a hidden city of shifting sand. Centuries ago, while it was under siege, the powerful ones shrouded the city in trickery, to befuddle their enemies. Most of the enchantment wore off, but a little remains to this day. We are used to its idiosyncrasies—ah, its fickle temperament, one could say. You wake one morning and find your house has moved, or the door is on the other wall." He shrugged. "Makes life interesting, wouldn't you agree?"

He smiled and kicked hard at the camel's flanks. "Follow me."

Callen looked at Jadiel and for the first time in days saw a smile on her face. She clucked at the mule and joined Callen behind the man and his camel.

"What a strange land," she said. "I wonder what it is like on the other side."

"I suppose we'll soon find out."

The wind abated as they left the road and waded through sand. Hot shimmers of heat rose and flushed Callen's face. The air thrummed with insects as they neared the rock face striated with colors of burnt orange and red clay. Ripples in the rock reminded Callen of carved gouges dug into the hillside.

The man bobbed up and down on the camel as it walked. He twisted back to look at Callen. "There's no trick to it, really. You picture the other side and walk toward it. Simple."

Simple? Callen took a deep breath and clutched his reins tighter as he continued forward, watching his guide neatly disappear before him. Jadiel squeezed her eyes shut, but their mounts showed no concern. They walked a steady pace—right through the rock.

For a moment, Callen was immersed in blackness. The air turned instantly cool and clammy. He heard muffled sounds—of sand shifting and slipping, of water dripping, of other travelers, perhaps passing nearby. He saw nothing—not the man in front nor Jadiel beside him, but he heard her words.

"Callen, are you here?" Her voice sounded as if she were at the bottom of a well, but he sensed her near.

"I'm right beside you."

She chuckled uneasily. "This is very unnerving . . ."

A minute passed, and another. Then Callen pushed through something thick and yielding as he emerged from the darkness into the bright glaring sunshine that gleamed upon a vast city stretched out before him. A tall palace painted in gold and indigo stood in the center of a valley, surrounded by hundreds of round clay buildings. Beside the palace, with its pointed spires and tall windows, spread a huge lake bordered by giant frond trees.

Jadiel gasped beside him as they stood on a ledge overlooking the hidden city. "Oh, Callen, have you ever seen anything so beautiful?"

The old man drew alongside them. "That wasn't so hard, no? Tell me, what brings you to Ethryn? May I help you find someone?"

"Thank you for your offer," Callen said. "Well . . . we are looking for a scroll." As obtuse as the words sounded, Callen could not think of anything better to say. But his guide seemed unperturbed.

"Ah, friend, you seek the Great Hall. Scholars from the world over come to visit the famed Scroll Room. You'll find it in the annex behind the palace gardens." He pointed to a small patch of green in the center of the sand-laden city. "Peace be with you." With a nod, he kicked hard at his camel and headed down the hill.

Callen meant to thank him, but the man hurried off too quickly.

Whether due to the mirage of sweltering heat waves or the residual magic, the city wavered before his eyes like an apparition. Surely a city this large would have lodging and fare for weary travelers. And, he hoped, enough water for a bath. A thin film of grit covered every inch of his exposed skin and made him itchy. Apart from the large oasis, Callen guessed water would be drawn from wells and stored in deep cisterns. Off in the distance Callen made out rectangular patches of greenery, most likely where food was grown. But, no doubt, with such a desert environment, most staples had to be imported and traded. How odd this place seemed compared with Tebron, where dense forests of trees stretched into the heavens and vegetation grew lush and abundantly.

Jadiel fell quiet as they descended toward the city. The heat made Callen sleepy as he rocked along with the rhythm of his horse's footfalls. They followed a narrow trail that switched back on itself again and again until they reached the bottom, a flat basin of small dunes and stubby flowering groundcover. Callen noticed no official entrance, only small lanes that dissected the rows of round clay houses, many that were adorned with glossy ceramic tiles framing their doors and windows. Sand invaded everywhere, piled in doorways and on windowsills, capping the tops of the homes like cake icing. The first people he saw were men with great brooms, sweeping sand off the huge flat bricks that composed the street upon which they trod. They were dressed in the same white gauze clothing, with their heads wrapped in cloth.

As they headed toward the palace, the lane widened. They passed women in long dresses of the same fabric in pale shades of wheat straw and eggshell; many covered their faces with veils attached to their headdresses. They were tall and elegant, with penetrating dark eyes. Clearly, strangers were common, for few gave them more than a cursory glance. Just when Callen's thoughts turned to a tall glass of ale, he saw a sign ahead, with strange symbols on it. One symbol, though, was a cup and another a bed. Now, instead of homes on either side, shops that displayed exotic clothing and furnishings lined the widening lane. All had signs and notices in their windows in those odd symbols.

"Oh Callen," Jadiel said. "I know we need to find that scroll, but can we take some time to rest? I am so tired of riding."

Callen stopped and dismounted, then helped Jadiel dismount. She groaned as her feet touched the sandy ground. "I'd like to find us a hearty meal, and a place to stable the animals," he said. "I wonder how costly things are here." He didn't want to tell Jadiel he hadn't brought enough coin for such a long journey; his funds were getting low.

Jadiel pinched her lips together. "I completely forgot, with all the recent events. Here." She reached into her mule's saddle bag and found her satchel. After fishing around, she pulled out the small velvet pouch and handed it to Callen. "I don't have any idea how much these coins are worth, but I can't have you pay for everything."

Callen's eyes widened as he looked inside and found, not silvers, but gold coins. He had seen few of those in his life, and never expecting to hold so many in his hands. One coin alone was more valuable than a bucket of silvers.

"Jadiel," he whispered, eying the people in the street, "you carry a fortune—and one we shouldn't speak about." He took her hands in his. "I will safe-keep these for you, if you wish, but they are yours to spend as you like. Perhaps you might consider buying a gift for your father, for when we return home."

Callen saw a flash of hope in Jadiel's eyes. "I suppose we could take a few minutes and look in the shops—after we eat. Callen, I'm starving."

"Then let's first find a stable, then some food. And what do you think about a proper bath?"

Jadiel sighed. "I don't even think I will be able to find my skin under this crust of sand. And my hair is so tangled I will probably want to cut if off. I can see why the people here shave their heads."

"Well, I think one day of indulgence is called for. The afternoon is already waning, so perhaps after a good nights' sleep we can go to the Great Hall and see if we can find that scroll the boar told us about."

Callen and Jadiel walked along the lane until they found a large clay building with wide doors. Callen's horse whinnied and two other horses responded from within the stable. The mule quickened his pace at the exchange; Callen correctly guessed the animal smelled hay. In little time, they had their mounts comfortably cool within a paddock, stripped of their headstalls, saddles, and bags. Jadiel chuckled as the horse and mule rolled in the fresh straw, wiggling in delight.

Their animals now boarded, Callen led Jadiel along the brick-lined street back to what looked like a tavern. He yearned for cool ale to slake his thirst, but at this moment, anything wet would suffice. Tomorrow they would look for a lost scroll with ten words and ten branches. But for now, the most ambition Callen could muster involved ordering a huge plate of food and collapsing upon a very soft bed.

The hawk made lazy wide circles over the road snaking far below him. To the west lay a ring of cliff, buried in a blanket of cloud. A narrow path twisted up and over the mountain, but he doubted Jadiel would wander there, far off the road and into some remote, desolate wilderness. A small village appeared on his left, tucked into the hills, but few people walked the lanes between the thatched houses. Frustration welled up inside him, but he refused to be discouraged. He had heard Jadiel's flute—of that he was certain. And only hours ago. It was only a matter of time before she would show up on a road somewhere near. He would just have to be thorough and diligent, not allow even one person to pass by without scrutiny.

He slept little, and only at night, trusting Jadiel slept the same hours. He dove after small rodents and ate them quickly, knowing he needed to keep up his strength, yet not wanting to risk missing sight of his daughter. Far off in the south, the road climbed to a dizzying height, ending in a wall of crinkled rock. A steady stream of travelers journeyed in both directions. Unless Jadiel had turned north, back toward Sherbourne, she was here, so close. But where?

Gilad yanked on the reins and skidded his steed to a halt near a grouping of small thatched cottages. He hoped this small village had fare and ale, for his throat was parched and the last meal he'd eaten in Sherbourne roiled in his stomach, a poorly cooked roast not fit for a peasant. Evening approached, and he needed supper and lodging. He was not one to tolerate sleeping in poor accommodations, and certainly not on the cold, hard ground. He had plenty of coin and always insisted on the best room.

He took out the small round glass and watched as the tiny stick swiveled to a rest, pointing southwest. With a swipe of his hand, he pushed his golden bangs from his face and pouted. The stick shivered, then swung due east, then north. What was this useless thing Huldah had given him? Gilad doubted it worked, for it moved erratically, never settling on one direction for long. If it did follow the hawk's movements, then this bird was flying in circles, back and forth, retracing its paths. He had yet to see sign of it.

Gilad huffed in frustration. Why did that woman need him to retrieve this silly bird anyway? He was accustomed to kings and noblemen commissioning him to slay huge beasts that threatened their lands. Or to rescue princesses abducted by ogres and the like. But to ride off in search of a meager raptor—really, what was the point?

Gilad dismounted and walked his destrier through the village until he spotted what looked like the only tavern around. Well, no matter, it was time he married, and if all he had to do to win the hand of the beautiful Ramah was bring back a dumb bird, then so be it. There would be other, more challenging, adventures once he married.

He pocketed the glass vial and pushed open the door to the tavern, relishing the cool temperature of the room. Sweat beaded on his forehead and dripped into his eyes. He pulled out a neatly starched white handkerchief and dabbed his forehead. As he approached the counter, a barkeep looked up and wiped his wet hands on a towel. Gilad exhaled and sat on a stool, forgetting the hawk, forgetting Huldah's warm breath tickling his ear. He would think of them later—after a meal, an ale, and a good night's sleep.

The one long-confined inched along the ground, sensing heat and dust. He easily wearied, lethargic after years of imprisonment in a cool chamber. Perhaps he had acclimated to the temperature in that rock enclosure, for this heat sapped his ability to hold shape and move quickly. He still only detected shadow and light, but found he moved with greater ease in shadow, more akin to his nature.

So upon leaving the ring of mountain, he slipped from shadow to shadow—of rock, of shrub, slithering in the late mornings or afternoons when the shadows grew long and accessible. At high noon and at night he rested, rallying strength, slowly thawing out of his ethereal slumber.

He came upon a road, recognizing the feel of packed dirt and the vibration of human and animal footfalls. He latched onto the shadow of a man walking, catching a ride, merging his own essence with the darkness cast upon the ground. Here he rested and sighed, conforming his shape to the other, blending in unseen as they traveled, yoked together. As it suited him, he left one shadow and became another, all the while watching for the shape he sought—of the human carrying a curved object on his back. Although a tinge of urgency pressed him on, he knew he could remain undetected in this manner and so took careful thought with each action. Only when he grew too weak, unable to bear the strain of clinging to shadow, did he strike.

Late in the afternoon, he inched his way along the shaded ground until he reached the place where the man's boots touched dirt. In his weakened state, he could not sense if others were close by, but he cared not. What would an observer notice? As he slid his way up the man's legs and reached through the chest cavity to grasp the pumping heart, a bystander would only see a man choking and clutching his chest, then falling dead to the ground. Heart failure? Perhaps.

Now energized from the human's life force, the evil one would wait patiently for his next victim to come by, ready to merge shadow to shadow, his unseeing eyes ever searching for his unsuspecting liberator.

TWENTY-ONE

AS THEY entered the spacious inner courtyard, Jadiel tried to shake off the residual fear that trailed her. What was that strange thing she saw in the mirror last night as she untangled her hair? She had called out to Mama, but instead of a lovely, reassuring face, the mirror had grown cloudy, then turned black, nearly smothering her own reflection. A foul smell had saturated the air and the surface of the glass iced over, burning Jadiel's fingers, causing her to drop the mirror onto the tiled bathing room floor. What disturbed her most was the horrid sensation that this shadow was somehow alive. She almost sensed malevolence, and some inhuman hunger driving it. Her sleep that night had been more troubled than ever, invaded by images of great slaughter and screaming victims. Surely, these imaginings must have been triggered by their visit to the King's Plain. Hopefully—she reassured herself—they would fade in time.

Jadiel pushed those thoughts away and let her eyes linger on the airy, sun-filled courtyard. A three-tiered rock fountain spewed water in the center of the lushly landscaped square, emitting a soothing bubbly sound. Smooth, glossy mosaic tiles depicting frond trees and ferns comprised the floor. Music drifted on the air, a stringed instrument strumming somewhere outside the courtyard. The moist warm air carried the fragrance of sweet blossoms, an intoxicating perfume. Callen wandered the room, studying walls covered with paintings of the desert in tones of orange and purple, the dunes casting soft shadows under a fiery sinking sun.

Through a large archway in the adjacent stone wall, Jadiel made out rows upon rows of rolled scrolls, stacked neatly from floor to lofty ceiling. As she walked to the entrance of the Scroll Room her eyes widened in awe, for the room went on for such a long distance that the end was nowhere in sight. She had never in her life seen a room so large. There must be thousands of scrolls within this room.

Callen came alongside her and whistled. "Well, I can see how our 'lost' scroll could get lost in such a place."

Jadiel wandered ahead and noticed, to her right, another large room with round, puffy couches and low tables. Dozens of people reclined, perusing unrolled scrolls and talking quietly. Some looked like scholars, hunched over parchments and writing in ink. Their garb varied as much as their features and hairstyles. Most were dark-skinned and wearing the clothing prominent in Ethryn, but others were clearly from faraway lands, with light skin and strange outfits. None dressed like the farmers of Logan Valley, though.

"What do we do now?" Jadiel asked.

Callen lowered his pack to the ground, the rolled-up bridge parchments protruding from the top. "Wait here. I'll see if someone can assist us."

Jadiel turned and noticed another beautiful mural on the wall over the archway. This one was even more panoramic than the one in the courtyard, stretching across the entire span of wall and spilling onto the other walls. Rather than a desert, this scene depicted meadows with tumbling creeks, splashes of wildflowers, and distant snow-capped mountains. The wall to her left caught her eye, for the mountain range, with its jagged peaks, looked exactly like the view from the road leading to the abbey west of Logan Valley, facing the Sawtooths.

Jadiel turned at the sound of footsteps. A tall man with a shiny bald head and long striped robe walked beside Callen, nodding as he listened.

"—And so, we hope to find someone who can help us locate this scroll."

The man tipped his head politely at Jadiel and spoke. "I'm afraid that without more information you will find the task impossible. Our archivists are attending to other visitors, ones who made their appointments many months ago." He smiled with a proud air and clasped his hands together. "The renowned Scroll Room of Ethryn receives hundreds of visitors a day. You can only imagine the demands placed upon the archivists."

"We can wait until someone can help us," Callen said.

The man smiled again, this time with an air of disdain. "Then, perhaps, you would give me your name and your place of lodging. When an opening presents itself, we will notify you."

"Can't we wait here?"

"Sir, I am afraid it will be many days before we can help you."

"Days?" Jadiel bristled. "We don't have days, Callen."

He touched her arm. "I know." He whispered in her ear. "Leave it to me; I'll find a way."

Callen reached into his pack and withdrew the pouch of gold coins. He took out three and offered them to the man, saying, "Please, this is urgent. Her father's life is at stake."

Jadiel watched the man's eyes burn with anger as he slapped at Callen's hand, knocking the gold coins to the ground. Heads turned and people stared. Jadiel cringed. "How dare you insult the servants of Ethryn with your attempt at bribery? Leave this place, at once!"

The man turned in a huff and marched away, his head held high. Jadiel glanced around and saw many of the visitors glaring, their eyes narrowed in irritation.

Callen's face looked stricken with embarrassment as he gathered up the coins. "I had no idea . . ."

Jadiel took his arm and tugged him. "That's all right, Callen. We'll figure something out."

Callen picked up the pack and put it on his shoulders. Jadiel walked back into the courtyard and sat down on the fountain ledge, letting the mist of the water cool her face. Morning sun streaking through the towering glass windows radiated heat that Jadiel felt rise off the tiled floor. How many days had it been since Huldah sent her on this impossible quest—a week, two weeks? Jadiel had lost count of the days. But the waning moon shining through her window last night was less than a crescent. And here she was, in a treeless land, far from home.

She put her head in her hands and let the tears flow, not caring if anyone watched. After a few minutes, she felt a hand rest on her shoulder.

Callen spoke gently. "Maybe we can speak to someone else and ask about the terebinth tree. Who cares about that scroll?"

Jadiel raised her head and gave Callen a weak smile. She knew he was trying hard to keep her hopeful. Just this morning he had gone shopping with her, helping her think of something to buy for Papa, all the while asking what she planned to do for the holidays. Deep in her heart she wanted to believe she would be reunited with Papa and all would end well, but her mind insisted she was fooling herself. Huldah's vicious sneer loomed over her, shriveling her resolve. What was to stop her stepmother from murdering them both, even after receiving her bag of precious leaves?

Jadiel's attention turned at the sharp retort of a boy's voice. She scooted over on the fountain's ledge and saw an elegantly attired child being attended by a robed servant. His head was shaved and it shone with oil, and he wore sandals on his feet with straps that wrapped his calves to the knees. He wore a finely stitched tunic made of gold and silver threads.

"Leave me. I grow weary of your lessons. I've had enough for one day!"

Jadiel couldn't hear the man's reply. Apparently he was the boy's teacher and was trying hard to persuade the child to cooperate. Jadiel almost giggled when the boy, a little younger than she, stuck out his tongue in the universal gesture of dismissal, then, with a sweep of his braceleted arm, knocked a scroll to the floor.

As the teacher bowed and backed away, Callen tapped Jadiel's shoulder.

"Here." He handed her the small puzzle box. "Why don't you try this awhile? You did well the first time. Could you hear the latches open?"

Jadiel took the box from his hands. "Well, this will surely help us find another terebinth tree."

Callen frowned. "It's just something to take your mind off things for a bit. I'm going to inquire of that teacher, see if he can help us."

Callen hurried after the boy's instructor, who had left the courtyard in a huff. Jadiel looked at the box, trying to remember how Callen had opened it the first time. The peaceful quiet of the courtyard calmed her as she pushed and pulled the slats of wood. So deep was her concentration that she didn't notice the boy watching her hands, standing only a few feet away.

When he cleared his throat, Jadiel looked up into big, curious eyes.

"Would you like to try it?" she asked.

The boy lifted his chin and cocked his head. "It's just a silly toy. For children."

Jadiel smirked at the boy's haughty demeanor. Clearly he was the child of some important person—and well he knew it.

"All right," she said, "if it's a silly toy, perhaps you can show me the solution. It sure has me stumped."

She held out her hand and dropped her eyes as the boy turned the box over in his hands. She didn't think it polite to stare and worried she would receive recriminations as Callen had earlier. It wouldn't do to have this boy snap at her as he had at his teacher.

Jadiel let her gaze wander the room, studying the murals as the boy fretted in frustration. "This is—unacceptable!" he said, preparing to throw the box to the ground.

"Wait!" Callen ran toward them. He held out his hands in front of him and the boy halted. "Let me show you."

The boy gave Callen the box and pursed his lips together. He stood with feet apart and hands on hips as he watched Callen work the puzzle. When the lid popped open, the boy demanded, "Show me!"

Callen raised his eyebrows at the boy's show of impatience. Jadiel scooted over to let them sit beside her.

"Here." Callen put the box in the boy's hand. "Start here. Always face the box this way. The pieces revolve around each center slat, here, here, and here. Each time you move an outer piece that shifts the center, be sure to move it back to where it was. The center pieces are these shapes, so the first task is to get them in their proper position—like so."

The boy's eyes fastened on Callen's hands as he scrambled the slats. "Now you try it."

In no time, the boy had all the center pieces aligned. "Perfect," Callen said. "Now watch what I do." He turned the box on its side and moved three pieces. "Hear that click?" The boy nodded, clearly enraptured with the box. "You do this with all four sides, remembering to reposition the center piece, like this, got it?"

The boy nodded again and grabbed the box from Callen. He followed Callen's directions precisely and within a minute, the top latch opened, bringing a flush of joy and pride to his face.

"Where did you buy this?"

"I made it."

The boy's eyes brightened. "However did you create such a wonder? Would you make one for me?"

Jadiel smiled at the change in the boy's attitude. Gone was the haughty, impatient boy. Instead, his face held all the wonder of a young child discovering a treasure.

"Take it. A gift," Callen said, then added with a bow of his head, "Your Majesty."

Jadiel's mouth dropped open. *Your Majesty?*

The boy bowed back with a regal air, then giggled. "Let me try it again—so I don't forget how to open it."

As the two leaned over the box, with Callen politely reminding the boy of the sequence of moves, Jadiel watched two men approach, guards with large silver shields, each carrying a long pointed spear.

Jadiel nudged Callen. "Uh-oh." She pointed at the scowling, burly men hurrying in their direction.

Callen abruptly stood and backed away from the boy. Just as the men reached out to grab Callen, the child cried out.

"Halt! These are my friends."

The men stopped, tapped the ends of their spears on the floor, and straightened to attention. One man spoke. "Pardon me, Your Majesty. These two are strangers, and we could not tell if they intended you harm." He turned to Callen. "Our apologies."

Callen shook his head. "You are doing your job. No offense taken."

"Look, Fahad." The boy showed the box to the guards, his face glowing with excitement. "Watch me solve this puzzle."

As the boy demonstrated his newly acquired skill, Jadiel whispered to Callen. "Who is this boy?"

"He's the crown prince of Ethryn, first heir to their throne."

"Oh! Well, that was a nice gesture, giving him your box."

Callen lowered his voice even more. "I was afraid he would have his guards spear me if I *didn't* give it to him." Jadiel could see by Callen's expression that he was joking. "It must be tedious, being groomed for the monarchy. Probably never gets to play and joke around like ordinary kids."

Jadiel nodded. Perhaps his was a lonely life with heavy burdens laid on his shoulders. Still, what a gorgeous palace to live in!

Finished with his demonstration, the prince turned back to Callen and Jadiel. "Tell me, strangers to Ethryn, why are you here?"

Callen watched the guards back away and take their stance at a more generous distance as he explained to the crown prince their quest. The boy drank in every word. Clearly, the hint of adventure set him to wild imaginings.

When the prince heard how they had been turned away from the Scroll Room, he leapt to his feet. "*That* is unacceptable!" He shouted to his guards. "Fahad, bring me the Chief Archivist immediately." Fahad nodded and scurried off, leaving the prince with a smug smile on his face. He tipped his head to Callen. "We'll find your lost scroll. I must admit, I do love puzzles, and this bridge you seek intrigues me. I wish . . . I could go with you to find your bridge." He straightened in a perfect, well-trained posture. "My name is Kael-al-Falad, and I thank you for your gift. By what names are you called?"

"This is Jadiel, and I'm Callen."

The prince smiled at Jadiel. "I don't see many girls. My sisters live in the east wing of the palace and I am not allowed to play with them. We dine together for important functions and holy days, but they have their own tutors and attendants." Kael sighed. "You have such light skin. Are you not allowed to play outdoors under the hot sun?"

Jadiel laughed. "That's just my color."

Kael glanced over Jadiel's head and clapped his hands. "Ah, the Chief Archivist, Fasial." Another tall bald man approached, his face lined with broad wrinkles.

"Your Majesty." He bowed deeply to the prince.

Kael put on a sour face. "Fasial, attend to these visitors at once. They are on a vital mission and must find a particular scroll."

Fasial bowed low, his nose nearly touching his knee. "As you command, Your Majesty."

Jadiel followed the archivist into the Scroll Room alongside Callen. The prince sidled up to her and whispered in her ear.

"This will be like a treasure hunt." He turned to Callen. "What did that boar mean by 'ten words, ten branches'? Where did you learn of this scroll?"

Callen met Jadiel's worried eyes, but he apparently saw no reason to withhold the truth. "We went to the King's Plain, and found the grave of the king-priest of Antolae."

Kael's face brightened with excitement. "Did the king speak to you? I heard he is not dead, only sleeping. Is it true?"

Callen chuckled. "No, he's quite dead and buried under the stump of the type of tree we seek."

The archivist stopped halfway down the first columned chamber at a small table. He asked Callen questions, then requested a look at the parchments. After Callen unrolled them and explained their search for the terebinth tree and the mysterious bridge, Fasial left to find scrolls for them.

Jadiel turned to Kael. "Thank you, Your Majesty, for helping us. My father is in grave danger, and only the leaves from this tree will save him."

Kael fidgeted and turned the box around in his hands. "It may be a while before Fasial returns. I will summon lunch and we will dine together."

Jadiel shrugged at Callen, who nodded in agreement. "How gracious of you. Many thanks."

The boy marched off, head high and proud. People he passed bowed and lowered their eyes respectfully. Jadiel reached into her smock pocket and pulled out the leaf. She laid it on the table and sat, studying its veins and running a finger along the shiny surface. Such a simple leaf, but her every hope depended upon it. She lifted it to her nose and smelled an aroma of lemon and fennel. Callen paced nearby, his arms folded across his chest.

Nearly half an hour passed before Fasial returned. He carried three long, yellowed scrolls in his arms and set those on the low table. "We have nothing that fits your description of the bridge." He made a little clearing sound in his throat. "We have no use for bridges, you see, and grow few trees. However, these scrolls do make reference to the terebinth. And I found a particularly interesting one regarding the king of Antolae."

Callen brightened. "May I see that one?"

Fasial unrolled the largest scroll and Callen held the corner for him. Callen's face showed dismay, as the scroll was covered in odd symbols. "I cannot read this."

"I will summarize it for you," Fasial said. He let his eyes trace over the lines of faded inked symbols. "It speaks of two warring kingdoms in endless struggle. The king-priest of Antolae served as mediator, negotiating peace. However, when he left to return home, an unknown army descended upon the two kings as they met to seal their treaty and annihilated thousands of their subjects, then decapitated the two kings. Evidently, the hard-won treaty was for naught, for both rulers and their subjects were destroyed." His eyes traveled down to the bottom of the scroll and then darkened in concern.

He exhaled and rolled the scroll back up, as if something upset him.

"What else did it say?" Jadiel dreaded hearing the answer.

"The king of Antolae returned to the place we call 'The King's Plain' upon learning the grim news. He discovered something terrible and troubling, for the attacking army hailed from a dark realm, not of this world, not human, but immaterial and powerful. No human weapon could harm the destroyers, and their motive was unclear. Somehow the king found a way to capture them, but it is not said how. He trapped the dark leader and imprisoned him, to be held until the appointed time of his execution."

Jadiel's skin crawled. She looked at Callen and saw his face stricken and perspiring.

Callen asked quietly, as if worried about listeners, "Does it mention where this dark one was imprisoned?"

"In a vault in the mountain, locked and secure."

Callen stammered. "Bu-but that was centuries ago. Surely this prisoner could not still be alive? Perhaps he was removed and executed."

Fasial shook his head. "It is written: only when the true king returns to take his throne will the prisoner receive his punishment. No king has since sat on the throne at Antolae—or in the King's Plain. It speaks of a future time."

Fasial shook off his somber mood. "Well, it is said no man can open the vault. And that is a good thing, for if this evil were unleashed upon the world, we would all be in grave danger." His reassuring smile hung heavy on the air, and Jadiel felt it as the weight of a boulder.

Instantly, a cold knife jabbed her gut, the same sensation she had felt while standing at the top of the steps facing the stone door. She struggled to calm her breathing, but panic raced through her veins. Had Callen loosed someone from that chamber?

"And then again," Fasial added, "that is one scribe's account. He may have been embellishing a tale he had heard, recording a fable, yes?"

Callen nodded, saying nothing. Jadiel saw him tremble.

"Ah, here is something curious." He picked up the leaf Jadiel had placed on the table and studied it. "This is from your terebinth tree, is it not?"

Jadiel nodded.

"The other two scrolls confirm your legend of the tree and its leaves, but they contain nothing alluding to ten words or ten branches. However . . ." He rubbed his bald head and thought for a moment. "Come with me."

Jadiel and Callen followed Fasial down the hall, passing one massive marble column after another. The archivist turned and went down a long aisle, then turned again. Jadiel trotted, trying to keep up. Eventually he slowed and, holding up the leaf, compared it to the glyphs painted on the beams running across the top of each large shelf. Jadiel saw how the sections of scrolls were catalogued by different symbols. Some depicted animals and birds, some looked like tools and pottery, others had lengthy combinations of glyphs. But the shelves directly before them each displayed a different shaped leaf.

Fasial kept walking, his gaze roaming up and down. Finally he stopped and a smile formed on his face. He knelt at one of the smaller compartments, a short shelf with only one scroll resting inside the cubicle. "Look, your leaf matches."

Fasial held the leaf up next to the painted glyph, and it matched the symbol perfectly in size, shape, and color. He handed the leaf back to Jadiel and pulled out the scroll. It was small and ancient, more yellowed than most of the scrolls on the shelves. Callen stood quietly at Jadiel's side while the archivist unrolled and perused the parchment.

After a long moment, he turned and showed the scroll to Callen. "Well, here are your ten words and ten branches."

Gilad stood by his horse, cracking his neck and stretching out the kinks in his back. Well, this was one village he couldn't wait to leave. They call that a bed? The mattress he slept on last night was little more than a sack stuffed with itchy straw. And they dared charge five silvers! His meager breakfast sat in a greasy lump in his stomach: cold toast with congealed butter, rubbery goose eggs, sour juice made from rotten fruit.

Gilad shook his head in disgust, but it did little to erase the vile aftertaste in his mouth. Good riddance to this place. He pulled the glass vial from his pocket and laid it flat on his palm. The small twig swung south, quivering but holding steadfast. Well, south it would be. Ethryn.

He had visited the hidden city years ago and remembered well their fine cuisine and comfortable goose-down beds. With a huff of anticipated pleasure, he swung the bow over his shoulder and mounted his horse. He swatted his golden locks away from his eyes and looked east. The sun inched over the peaks, splintering light that illuminated the ground, promising a warm, clear day.

As he whistled a little tune and urged his horse down the lane, he did not notice the odd shadow drifting along the dirt toward him, edging ever so slowly up his horse's flank. A shiver ran up his spine, but he attributed it to the putrid breeze coming from the western ridge far off in the distance. He tightened his cloak at the neck and, upon entering the wide road that led to Ethryn, spurred his horse into a gallop, eager to cross the mountain before the heat of midday bore down upon him.

However, as fast as he rode, kicking up dust on the nearly deserted thoroughfare, he couldn't shake the chill that settled on his neck or the sensation that someone hovered close by. With a nervous laugh, he shrugged off his fear, chastising himself for imagining danger where there clearly was none. He was Gilad, son of Ren, the bravest man in Wolcreek.

Nothing frightened him.

TWENTY-TWO

CALLEN HELD his breath as he studied the scroll, with Fasial leaning over his shoulder in curiosity. The ancient parchment crackled and resisted his handling, but Callen carefully laid it out on the table. The archivist reached for several of the pyramid-shaped glass weights lying about the table and used these to pin down the corners of the parchment.

As the men opened the scroll, Jadiel pointed to the drawing it revealed. "Another picture of the terebinth, and those symbols look like the ones on your bridge parchments."

"They are!" Callen pulled out the sheaf from his pack and unrolled the three larger parchments, laying them alongside the small, simple outline sketch of the tree with ten evenly spaced branches, each branch with the unusual block lettering above it.

Callen looked up at Fasial. "Sir, do you know how to read this language? Is it related to your own?"

The archivist shook his head. "I have seen samples of this written tongue, but it is a very old, dead language. I'm afraid none here would know how to decipher it."

Callen sighed and took out his sketchpad and pen set. He dipped the pen in ink and copied the strange letters into a list. Jadiel watched him as he concentrated on capturing the flair of each letter just so.

Finally he completed his list:

בוה

צגע

צכה

ענה

דכא

יבל

חלכ

לקח

ערה

חיה

"See if you can find these on the bridge, Jadiel."

Callen double-checked his strokes as Jadiel searched the drawings.

"I found the first one in two places, there—and there." She pointed at the arch on the first sheet, and a different arch on the second. "I wonder if they have to be in a certain order—if they form a sentence."

Callen joined Jadiel in searching for matches. "If we can't drum up anyone to decipher this, then what's the point of finding this scroll? What if it tells us where the bridge was built but no one can read it?"

Fasial cleared his throat. "Do you see these murals? A visitor from the north appeared in Ethryn one day and lived here for a number of years. He was from Sherbourne, a great painter. Ta'man was his name. He left quite recently to return home. A shame you missed him, for he seemed to know something about this language that he called *law'az*. Maybe there are some in Sherbourne who have studied this tongue and know how to read it."

Sherbourne? Callen grunted in frustration. He was just there a week ago, and now it looked as though they would need to return—unless they could uncover any other clues that would point them to another tree. He recalled that Za'ker, the librarian, had no acquaintance with the symbols on the parchments. If someone as knowledgeable as Za'ker didn't know, then who would?

"Well, I found eight matches. I think you are missing some of the bridge drawings," Jadiel pointed a few inches off the page. "See, the other two words would have been over here. On the next section of bridge."

Callen nodded. "Yes, I think you're right. Well, whatever the words mean, they are linked to the bridge—and from this scroll, they clearly link to your tree. They are invariably bound together, tree and bridge."

Callen watched Jadiel's face cloud over in despair. Now what? All these clues and parchments and drawings. Nothing that told them where to go.

Another bald-headed servant approached. He bowed to Callen and Jadiel. "The prince summons you for lunch. Please accompany me."

Callen rolled up his drawings and placed them back in his pack. "Fasial, do you have any idea where we might find this tree? Any suggestions at all?"

The archivist thought deeply for a moment, then looked at Callen with a kind and sorrowful expression. "I believe your only hope will be to find Ta'man, or another scholar who may have learned the *law'az*." He lowered his head in dismissal. "Heaven bless your journey."

Callen swung the pack onto his back and motioned Jadiel with his head. "Then our business is done here. After we dine with the prince, we should depart. Thank you for your assistance, Fasial. We would not have found that scroll without it."

Jadiel nodded and followed Callen down the long hallway, escorted by the servant. As they passed under the archway, he looked up at the expansive mural overhead, wondering who Ta'man was and how, in such a large city as Sherbourne, he could be found. *If* he could be found.

Gilad pulled his horse to a stop under the partial shade of a withered tree. High above, with wings backlit by the afternoon sun, a hawk circled. Gilad took out the glass vial and the twig spun wildly, unable to lock onto any direction. Surely that was the hawk Huldah wanted, and now was the perfect opportunity to shoot it down.

He untied his bow and quiver from the back of his saddle, then nocked an arrow on the block. He held the bow with a steady hand and narrowed his eyes, fixing on his target, waiting for the bird to circle back around toward the tree.

Suddenly, an icy pain pierced his chest. He gasped for air and loosened his grip on the bow. With a cry of anguish, he dropped the weapon to the ground and sent the arrow lobbing a few feet into a scrub brush. An excruciating throbbing fomented under his ribs, almost as if a hand had torn through his flesh and taken hold of his heart.

Gilad clutched his chest and expelled an agonized scream, then slid to the dirt with a thud. But he did not feel the jolt of his back hitting the hard ground, for by the time his shoulder touched earth, he was already dead.

The fire crackled and sparked as Callen fed it bits of wood. Jadiel shifted on the hard log, every muscle sore. The residue of the day's travels weighed her down—the hours of riding in the glaring sun, annoying flies that had buzzed mercilessly around her ears, feelings of hopelessness tugging at her heart. Why had no one in Ethryn heard of the Eternal Tree? The young prince had even called in his wisest tutors during their extravagant lunch, but their suggestions were couched in apologies. The only advice they concurred on was to journey to Sherbourne to search out the meaning of the strange words inked on the scroll. And yet, Callen had told her about the librarian who knew nothing of the ancient tongue. If this ancient language could not even be found in the great library, then the task seemed insurmountable.

She lifted her eyes to the sky, where stars splattered the dome of night. The half-moon lay hidden under the horizon and in two weeks would wax full. Two weeks left! Never had Jadiel dreaded the moon's radiance as she did now. Her father's death drew closer every day.

Callen stood and picked up the pot resting on hot coals. "Jadiel, won't you eat more? You barely touched your food." His eyes pleaded with hers.

She nodded reluctantly. Callen poured the thick green liquid into her bowl. Worry had diminished her appetite, but she forced herself to swallow the bland pea soup. She needed her strength to keep going. Her father's life depended upon her. Huldah had to be stopped. She drilled this litany of reminders into her head day and night. Now, looking at the dry, desolate surroundings in the faint starlight, leagues from home, she doubted she would ever see the manor—or her father—again. She was so tired of clinging to hope. How much easier it would be to quit and take her chances with Huldah's wrath.

As Callen walked off to wash dishes, Jadiel reached into her satchel and pulled out her flute. The silver gleamed in the firelight, warming in her hand. She put the instrument to her lips and played, letting her anguish and despair fill the night air. The notes drifted, sweet and sorrowful, giving Jadiel little comfort. Her thoughts drifted as well: memories of her mother laughing, holding her hand as they walked through the woods; her father galloping his horse across the fields, his hat flopping in the wind. Rather than comfort her, the melody brought an upwelling of fresh grief to her heart.

Jadiel put the flute down and cried. She was never going to find this tree. She would return empty-handed to Northvale and watch her father die before her eyes. Why even return, if that fate awaited her? Maybe Callen's first idea was not so preposterous. They could rally a band of neighbors and storm the manor. Maybe their efforts would fail to save Papa, but if they could seize Huldah and constrain her, she might release him—to save her own life. Wasn't that worth a try?

Jadiel looked up as Callen approached the fire pit.

"I checked on the animals and gave them some feed. Not much for them to graze on here." He sat on the log beside her. "You play that flute well. Adds a bit of cheer in this gloomy place."

"Callen, I've been thinking—"

A whoosh of air blew her hair about her face. Soaring out of the dark, over the fire, a bird swooped, just missing her head. She shrieked and jumped to her feet.

Jadiel swung her arms in the air as the bird returned and made a pass near her shoulder. "Callen! What is that?"

Callen jumped up and grabbed his bow. "It looks like a hawk, but it's behaving oddly." He pulled an arrow from the quiver propped up against the log. The night grew still. They peered into the darkness, listening as silence spread like a blanket over the barren landscape.

"It's coming back!" The whoosh of wings beat in fast strokes on the night air. Jadiel ducked as an outstretched wing nicked her cheek. "Since when do hawks attack people?" Callen stood in front of Jadiel, who cowered behind him. "Why does it keep diving at me?" she asked. "It doesn't seem to notice you."

When Callen raised his bow and positioned the arrow, Jadiel put a hand on his arm. "Callen, don't hurt it. It's small. Maybe it's hungry."

Callen grunted. "Hawks have sharp talons. It could gash your face." Jadiel saw him tense as the sound of pumping wings drew close once more. "Maybe it's diseased or starving."

"Well, still. How much harm could—"

The hawk suddenly appeared before her, flapping hard as it dove directly at her head. Callen bumped her aside, knocking her to the ground. Jadiel screamed as Callen, poised and keen-eyed, loosed an arrow at the hawk in flight. The bird screeched and veered sharply, falling to the ground somewhere past the fire pit in the dark terrain.

Jadiel scrambled to her feet and brushed dirt from her leggings. "Why did you do that? Why are you always shooting at helpless creatures?"

"Oh, for goodness' sake, Jadiel. That bird was barreling at you. What did you expect me to do—wave it away with a dishcloth?"

Jadiel reached into the pit and pulled out a fiery branch. "I sure hope you didn't kill the poor thing." She snorted in a huff and tromped off, using the light of the flame to search the ground. She heard Callen following behind, grumbling.

"It's just a bird, Jadiel."

The small flame died out on the branch, leaving a glowing tip. By that dim light she searched the ground, bent over, listening for sounds of an injured creature. Then she saw it—panting on the dirt, belly up, with the arrow sticking out of one wing.

Jadiel rushed over and, dropping the branch, scooped up the bird and cradled it in her arms. Pain laced its eyes—eyes that peered into Jadiel's with such intensity that she shuddered. The hawk's beak opened but no sound came out. Not even a tiny squeak. As Callen came alongside her, she stroked the slick feathers on its head. The hawk squeezed its eyes shut and nuzzled into Jadiel.

"See—it's so sweet—and you shot it!"

Callen threw up his arms and huffed. "Bring it over to the firelight. I'll take out the arrow, but I don't know if it will be able to fly."

Jadiel followed Callen with her lips pinched tightly, and then calmed the bird as Callen studied the wound.

"Try to hold it still." He repositioned the bird on Jadiel's lap, wings outspread. The hawk lay quiet and unresisting.

Jadiel kept her gaze on the hawk's face as Callen wiggled the arrow, loosening it. She feared the bird would peck her and try to squirm out of her grasp, but it only met her eyes with a strange concentration. Jadiel had an uncanny sense the bird was trying to tell her something, but how could that be? As Callen worked at the arrow, she crooned softly to the hawk. Before long, Callen extricated the arrow from the feathers and wiped off a drop of blood from the tip.

"I did the best I could, but that wing is pretty mangled."

Jadiel lifted the bird and hugged it to her chest. "Well, we'll just have to care for it until it can fly again."

Callen sighed again. "Great."

Jadiel shot him a stern look that caused any further words to fade before they reached his lips. Not a chance that she would leave this helpless creature to waste away and die. She walked to the fire pit and picked up the water jug, then poured a trickle of water over the wound and dabbed it dry with her blouse. Why in the world had that hawk swooped at her? And why did Callen have to shoot it? She looked at Callen, who was gathering the washed dishes and pans and stacking them by the fire while he grumbled to himself. As much as she cared for him and appreciated his efforts to help her, he sure acted impetuously at times. Her father was so different: careful, thoughtful, never acting on anything until he examined every angle. Callen's hasty manner took getting used to.

Instantly, her earlier fatigue rushed back and washed over her. After placing the bird carefully on the ground, she crawled into her bedroll and readjusted her coat into a pillow. To her surprise, as she slipped under the wool blanket, the hawk hopped over and sidled up to her shoulder. Jadiel pulled the blanket up and over the hawk as it settled in beside her, pressing its slick cheek against her neck. With gentle fingers, she tucked in its errant, injured wing and closed her eyes, feeling the hawk's tiny rapid heart beating against her skin.

TWENTY-THREE

CALLEN'S EYES snapped open as a noise shook him out of a drowsy stupor. He had dozed off; rocking in his saddle in the warmth of the afternoon made his eyes droop. Up ahead, a handful of people huddled in the middle of the road, speaking in loud voices.

Jadiel trotted on her mule and came alongside him. "What's happening?"

Callen reined in, stopping his mare. A handsome white stallion picked at tufts of grass a few yards off the road, its reins still draped over its neck. By the look of the saddle—its fine quality and leather-punched detailing—this horse belonged to a wealthy man. No one paid the horse any mind, which made Callen curious. In the space between the milling onlookers, a shape lay on the ground. A body.

Callen clucked at his mare and approached. He dismounted and craned to see. On the dirt lay a finely dressed man, well-coifed and quite dead. His ashen face was drained of blood, but Callen could not make out any telltale wounds from his vantage point.

Two men worked to drag the fallen rider to a cart. When Callen asked what had happened, no one could say. Perhaps he suffered sunstroke, or fell from his horse and broke his neck. One old woman shook a finger at the men as they hoisted the body onto the cart.

"Mind you, this is not the first." She raised her voice to address the crowd. "Over in Rumble, it's said another young man was found—just like this poor sod—right smack in the middle of the road. Dead as dust, no cuts or bruises." She spat on the dirt. "I tell you, some evil's at work."

"Oh, hush, Nettie," One of her companions, a young man in farming clothes, tried to quell the hysteria. "You and your superstitions. You'll have us hiding behind doors for the rest of our lives."

The woman humphed. "Mark my words, Geral, or you'll be next." With a fling of her long silver hair, she spun on her heels and strode toward a cluster of cottages set back off the road. People shifted uncomfortably, worry in their faces.

A young woman raised her hand. "What if Nettie's right? Don't you recall the old tales—of the Golgoth? The one that slips unnoticed along the ground and rips your heart out, leaving no mark?"

Callen shivered as a nervous chuckle broke out in the crowd. He thought about the scroll in Ethryn that spoke of evil beings who annihilated thousands—and of the vault in the cliff. His heart pounded hard in his chest. One of the men who loaded the body latched the small gate on the cart and climbed up onto the buckboard. He raised his voice over the din of his neighbors' arguing. "Just children's stories, is all. Stories out of Rumble, I'll gather." He pointed. "Someone best be getting the man's horse yonder. Geral, why don't you keep it in your stable until we can suss out who this fella was and where the horse belongs?"

Geral nodded and fetched the horse. Callen walked back to Jadiel and mounted his mare. Jadiel questioned him with her eyes. He was reluctant to tell her what he'd heard.

"A man's dead. They're seeing to him."

Jadiel stroked the hawk that sat on the saddle pommel. She looked around, scanning the distance. "Something feels wrong."

"What do you mean?"

She shook her head as if a chill had just raced up her neck. "I don't know. Let's just leave this place, okay?"

Now that Jadiel mentioned it, a creepy feeling grew in Callen's gut. He urged his mare forward, veering off the road to bypass the dispersing crowd. But he couldn't wrench his gaze from the shadows cast across the plain. The dark blotches seemed to waver and lengthen in odd fashion. Surely his eyes were playing tricks.

They rode north, leaving Ethryn and Rumble behind—along with all the superstitious talk and wild stories about evil beings from dark realms. Callen's hands cramped from clenching his reins in tight fists. He relaxed his grip and turned his thoughts to Sherbourne, wondering where to start looking for a painter named Ta'man.

"Look, Callen. There's a man needing help."

Callen glanced up the road where a man in a long gray robe hunched over a pile of belongings strewn on the ground. "He's probably just reorganizing his bundle."

"No, he's having trouble, can't you tell?"

Jadiel kicked her boots into the mule's flanks and trotted to the man. He lifted his head and his stringy brown hair fell to the side, revealing his scarred, repulsive face.

Callen snorted. Ebed. The annoying man he'd met at the Heresh Bridge. What was he doing wandering the southern road?

Callen called to Jadiel. "Come on, Jadiel, leave him be."

As Callen approached, the man looked up at him and smiled, recognition in his face. Callen turned away, intending to pass by. A shiver traveled up Callen's spine. The man gave him the creeps, with his gaze that pierced deeper than eyes should. Callen felt naked and exposed by Ebed's unwavering stare.

Ebed stood next to Jadiel, who had slid off the mule. He spoke in a raspy voice. "Callen, did you find the circle in the King's Plain? What did the Keeper say?"

Callen froze.

"You know his name," Jadiel said to the man, her eyes wide. She called to Callen, her voice a chastisement. "Come back; where are you going?"

Callen swung his horse around and returned to Jadiel. He raised his eyebrows at her and gestured to Ebed with his head. "We've met before."

With a sigh, he dismounted. The last thing he wanted was a lecture and a bunch of meaningless riddles from some lunatic prophet wandering the world. And what on earth was a Keeper?

Callen watched Jadiel reach over her saddle and take down the water jug. "Here," she said, handing the container to the weary stranger. "You look flushed. Are you unwell?"

Ebed took the jug from Jadiel's hand and patted her arm. "Bless you, dear girl. What a kind heart you have." He looked deeply into her eyes. "Are you not repulsed by my face?"

Callen fought an urge to whisk Jadiel away from the ugly man's proximity. Ebed was leaning close to her, but she didn't seem to mind. How could she tolerate him?

Jadiel chuckled. "Of course not. You can't judge a person by their appearances, can you? Better to be ugly on the outside and beautiful on the inside than the other way around, my mother always said."

Ebed clapped his hands in delight. "What a wise girl you are." He tipped the jug and took a long drink. "Ah, that refreshes. Tell me, Jadiel—that is the name Callen called you?" Jadiel nodded. "Do you know the story of the great king who built a bridge spanning eternity?" Jadiel shook her head in eager anticipation of a forthcoming tale. Callen snorted. If only she knew what silliness his stories bespoke.

Ebed sat down in the midst of his pile of clothing. Callen watched as other travelers passed by, eying them curiously, some with expressions of disgust. He led his mare off the road and took the mule's reins from Jadiel, then tied the two mounts to a bush. He sighed deeply. Something told him they were going to be there awhile.

Jadiel sat on the dirt close to Ebed, her eyes wide with interest. Callen stood by the animals and listened. *Oh, great.* Now they would hear another confusing tale. And followed, no doubt, by some masked warning. Some danger about to consume them. Why was Jadiel so keen on paying mind to this wanderer? She looked like a child eager for her bedtime story.

Ebed lifted his chin and spoke into the air. "There was once a great king who built a beautiful bridge over a raging river chasm. But this bridge did more than link land to land; it spanned eternity. It was the king's great love for his people that moved him to fashion such a bridge as his gift for them. The king promised that the bridge would connect to the eternal world—a place where death held no power and peace ran like a river through a golden city." Ebed gestured widely with his arms, then narrowed his eyes and riveted his gaze on Callen. Callen squirmed and stared at the dirt. He felt like a mouse cornered by a hungry cat. Ebed's crisp voice sang in his ears, and Callen felt the words seep deeply into his mind.

"But the people scoffed, accusing the king of treachery. They claimed he spoke lies to get them to do his bidding, making empty promises so they would be loyal and pay him tribute. Soon the grumblings grew into riotous rebellion, and they amassed and took counsel against the king and his son, saying the bridge came at too great a cost. That a person would have to sell his soul for such a gift." Ebed paused, catching Callen's attention. He watched the ugly man turn to Jadiel and smile in a lopsided manner.

"So the people destroyed the bridge, hoping to remove all trace of its existence. Imagine that."

Callen grunted. "Why would anyone destroy such a thing? It makes no sense."

Ebed smiled at Callen, and this smile was full of sorrow. "No, it doesn't. But, then, the bridge was built to be destroyed."

"What?" Callen shook his head. "Come, Jadiel. Let's leave this babbling fool. He'll only confuse you with his stories." As much as he wanted to ask Ebed if this tale had to do with the bridge he was seeking, he knew he would only get hazy answers at best. No doubt the man was making these stories up, just to confuse and tease him. And really! How foolish to believe anyone would build a bridge for the purpose of destroying it.

Jadiel jumped to her feet. "Callen, you are rude and insulting! Perhaps I'll stay here with Ebed and let you go on to Sherbourne alone."

The stranger fumbled to his feet and laid a hand on her shoulder. "Fearful people often strike out at others. He doesn't mean harm."

"Fearful?" Callen said. "What on earth am I fearful of? I certainly am not afraid of *you*."

Ebed chuckled. "No, that's quite apparent." He stooped and gathered his things, pulling up the edges of the cloth and tying them off with a knot. "I'll be on my way, then. Good day."

Ebed hoisted the bulky load over his shoulder and bent over from the weight pressing against his shoulders. He took slow, faltering steps. Callen untied the mounts and swung up into his saddle. His face flushed hot and he pursed his lips.

"Are you coming, Jadiel?"

Jadiel ignored him and hurried after Ebed. "Please, Ebed. Let me put your load on my mule and you can ride."

Ebed stopped, wonder in his eyes. "But then you would have to walk."

"Oh, I am quite tired of jostling around on the back of this beast. Where are you headed? Surely you can accompany us." She helped Ebed lower his bundle to the ground.

Callen rolled his eyes at the thought of hours in this wanderer's company.

Jadiel picked up Ebed's things and carried them over to the mule. "I insist." With a grunt, she hoisted his bundle behind the saddle and patted the seat. "Here, I'll help you up."

Ebed hobbled to Jadiel and, with her help, got into the saddle. "What a kind heart you have, Jadiel." He looked at Callen with a gleam in his eye. "To where are you heading?"

Jadiel took the reins and led the mule, with Ebed riding contentedly in his seat.

Callen shook his head. *As if you don't already know, you with your secret knowledge.* He answered, "To Sherbourne. To find a painter named Ta'man."

Ebed shook his head in dismissal. "You won't find that elusive hermit; he has left the kingdom, never to return. But since you seek understanding of the *law'az*, there is only one place to go."

Callen narrowed his eyes and gritted his teeth. He was no longer surprised at Ebed's uncanny knowledge of their plans. "And what place is that?" He didn't bother to mask his irritation, but Ebed only chuckled.

As Jadiel led the mule along the road, passing Callen, Ebed pointed north. "To see the king. King Adin. He alone knows the ancient language."

Callen blurted out a laugh. "Right. As if the king would grant us audience."

Ebed only smiled in response. That smile was beginning to grate on Callen's nerves. Callen continued, "I heard the king abandoned his sister in a faraway land, and for that heaven cursed him with infirmities."

Jadiel yanked her reins and stopped to glare at him. "Callen, heaven doesn't punish people in that manner. Misfortune befalls all, and many who should be punished live long lives fomenting trouble. Was my mother so evil that heaven sent a horse to trample her? My mother was the kindest woman in the world, yet she died a cruel death."

Callen watched big tear stream down Jadiel's face. "I didn't—I'm sorry, Jadiel." How did this conversation end up here? "Sorry."

Jadiel dropped her head and hurried past him.

Ebed turned back and looked at Callen. "King Adin will see you. He's a kind and gracious man."

Even though Ebed's voice was gentle and uncritical, Callen couldn't help feeling reproached. A stab of remorse poked him, remorse over the hasty words he had spoken. He looked into Ebed's scarred, misshapen face and felt strangely that he, Callen, was the ugly, repulsive one among them.

TWENTY-FOUR

"CALLEN, IF Ebed says King Adin will see us, then you should believe him." Jadiel glanced at Ebed, who stood quietly by the gate with the reins of both their mounts in his hands. The robed prophet smiled at Jadiel, encouraging her with his eyes. Something about those eyes filled her with comfort and hope, beyond understanding. Ebed had said little on their journey to Sherbourne, but just his presence had eased her fears and anxiety. The earlier creepy sensation of evil had vanished, making her think her imagination was overwrought. Or that this odd man had some special gift to dispel fear, apart from his ability to know hidden things.

Callen adjusted the pack on his back, securing the parchments in their pouch. "We'll see when we get there."

As they stood on the road near the south tower, Jadiel looked up the hill to the palace, where the stone fortress gleamed in the sunlight. The little hawk on her shoulder shifted its weight and settled against her throat. Jadiel didn't want to admit her hesitancy to enter such a magnificent edifice, but they had just come from Ethryn, where they had dined with the crown prince. Maybe King Adin would be just as welcoming as Prince Kael. But even if he wasn't willing to see them, they had to try to gain an audience. What else could they do? Callen had no other ideas, and time was fast slipping away.

Callen motioned her to follow him up the wide cobbled road leading to the palace. She turned her head and spotted Ebed still standing next to the tall stone wall encircling the city. If her heart wasn't so weighed down in worry over her father and her quest for the leaves, she would run with excitement through this city she had only seen once as a very small child. But now, nothing held her interest. She focused on her footsteps and marched straight to the palace courtyard, keeping up with Callen's long stride.

As they crested the hill, they passed many well-dressed visitors on horseback and in carriages. Jadiel shriveled under their gazes, keenly aware of her dirty boots and simple garb. Perhaps they should have shopped in town for more presentable clothing. Jadiel's heart sank even lower. One look at their appearance and surely the guards—or whoever screened the king's visitors—would shuffle them off without delay. But Ebed said King Adin would see them, and he didn't tell them they needed any special clothing. She would trust him.

Callen stopped at the massive oak doors and turned to Jadiel. He smoothed his tunic and hair and looked Jadiel over. "Are you ready?"

Jadiel nodded. Callen exhaled and opened one of the doors. A cool breeze greeted them as they stepped onto the smooth stone floor of a large entryway. A few people milled about, studying the gilt-framed portraits on the towering walls. Jadiel took in the enormous room that stretched past the entryway, with its long staircase off to one side. Heavy velvet drapes flanked the beveled windows that ran the length of the room, letting sunlight spill onto the gray stone floor. The sight took her breath away.

From around a corner came a short, pudgy man close to Callen's age. Jadiel noted his green and brown attire and a firebird stitched on his tunic. His expression was friendly and meek—not what Jadiel would expect from someone guarding the palace. In fact, she was surprised to find, as she looked around, that there weren't any dour guards on the alert. The palace seemed to radiate a friendly, relaxed atmosphere. Hopefully, King Adin would be just as accommodating.

The uniformed man extended his hand and Callen shook it. "Welcome, friends," the man said. "My name is Merin, and I am the Palace Greeter."

"I'm Callen, from Tebron. And this is Jadiel."

Merin's eyebrows raised slightly. "Tebron? That's a ways from here. The king knows your village, he does." He smiled at Jadiel. "And where do you come from? Also Tebron?"

"I live in Northvale, in Logan Valley."

"Ah, where the best beer hops are grown." His eyes twinkled. "But, I gather you are here on important business. You don't look like tourists."

Callen cleared his throat and Jadiel sensed his nervousness. "We do have an urgent matter and would like to see the king."

Merin's eyes filled with sympathy. "Ah, I see. You and so many others. Always some matter that must be settled, that requires only the king's attention. He is a very busy man."

Jadiel's countenance dropped and she fought back tears. "Please," she begged, "my father's life is in danger, and we need the king to tell us what a scroll says." She struggled to speak through the lump growing in her throat. "Just ten words. In the ancient *law'az.*"

Callen added, "We heard the king was somewhat of an expert in that language."

Merin clasped his hands together and smiled. His eyes filled with wonder. "You have found something written in the ancient language? I am certain the king would be interested. The *law'az* is one of his most consuming hobbies." He studied the faces of the other visitors; Jadiel noticed that none seemed to be waiting for an audience with the king. "The king is presently in council with his advisors. But wait here. I'll return shortly."

Jadiel watched Merin straighten his tunic over his bulging waist and spin on his heels. As he marched off down the hallway into the large chamber beyond, Jadiel turned to Callen and shrugged.

"Now we wait," he said, letting his eyes roam around the room. "There's a bench there, if you'd care to sit."

Jadiel shook her head and moved aside to let three uniformed men hurry past her. A group of elegantly dressed and coiffed ladies strolled toward them, coming from one of the adjacent chambers near the front doors, chatting gaily among themselves. Jadiel heard hushed whispering behind her and the mention of the Queen. One quick glance told her the older woman with the long auburn hair was the Queen, King Adin's mother. And she was coming this way!

Jadiel pressed herself against the wall and tore her eyes from the beautiful serene face that caught her glance. She lowered her head and stared at the floor as the Queen and her entourage passed by, watching the crystal glass slippers tap on stone across the threshold and out the doors. After a moment she raised her eyes and caught Callen's surprised expression. How out of place she felt.

Her attention was caught by the figure hurrying toward her from the end of the hall. Merin, out of breath, wiped a hand across his perspiring forehead. He tugged at the collar that seemed to press tightly against his flushed neck. "The king asks to see you. If you'd follow me, please."

Jadiel smiled at Callen, and they trailed after the greeter. She surveryed the massive room that looked like a banquet hall. Huge bouquets of flowers overflowed from urns all along the walls and from vases on the large hewn-wood tables. Jadiel recognized that much of the furniture was crafted from the oaks that grew in her valley. A giant crystal chandelier hung overhead with dozens of lit tapers. She could just imagine the number of servants needed to keep the palace so clean and beautiful.

They followed Merin down another high-ceilinged hallway and stopped at an open door. Through the doorway, Jadiel caught a glimpse of King Adin, standing behind a massive desk in a breath-taking round chamber lined with stained-glass windows perched high near the domed ceiling. Each window depicted a figure in artistic detail, and the sun streaming through the glass spilled col-ors over the chamber floor. Jadiel risked a long look at the king, worried he would notice her stare. But his attire intrigued her, for he did not wear kingly garb; instead, his simple cotton pants and light-gray woven tunic resembled commoner's clothing. Jadiel expected him to be lavished with rich velvet robes and a shining golden crown atop his head. True to the rumors, his back seemed hunched, forcing him to strain forward, and one side of his face appeared to pull up along his cheek. However, the king was a strik-ingly handsome man, despite his deformities.

Callen leaned over to whisper to Jadiel. "This must be the Council Chambers I've heard about. A circular room. Isn't is amazing?"

Jadiel nodded, speechless. Was she really standing inside Sher-bourne's palace, about to speak to the king of all the land? How would she ever find her voice?

They waited at the doorway with Merin until the last of the dark-robed councilors had exited the room, leaving the king alone at his desk. Then Merin ushered them in and presented them to King Adin. Jadiel bowed her head as Merin introduced them.

"Please, friends, sit." Jadiel raised her eyes and looked at this bright-eyed man. His dark red hair was pulled back in a clasp behind his neck and trailed down the collar of his shirt. She tried not to stare. As the king circled to stand in front of the desk, she noticed he limped slightly, as if one leg were longer than the other. She recalled the callous remark Callen had made about the king's deformities.

She stole a quick glance at Callen and saw his face was flushed, as if embarrassed. King Adin gestured with his hand to invite them to take the large velvet upholstered chairs positioned near the desk. The king walked slowly around the table toward them and said, "I hear you have something written in the *law'az*. May I see it?"

Callen set down his pack and extracted a small sheet of parchment. "Your Highness, thank you for taking time to see us. We have just returned from Ethryn, where we were shown a scroll with ten words upon it. We were not allowed to keep the scroll, but I did write down the words on this page." Callen handed the parchment to the king, who stopped walking and studied the writing.

Jadiel sat quietly, waiting as the king read with narrowed eyes. When finished, he looked up at them both. "I am not that learned in reading the actual letters; I'm more familiar with the spoken language. But I do have a primer." He walked behind his desk and took out an old bound book from a drawer. Jadiel's nerves were a jumble, being this close to the king. But he smiled kindly at her and opened the book, displaying pages of the same writing, with notations scribbled alongside in the common tongue.

"Will that primer contain these words? " Jadiel asked, her voice trembling.

"Ah, no," The king said, "but that's the fun part. I can look up these letters and sound them out. Once I hear the word, I may be able to tell you what it means. But it may take some time. Let's take a look at your first word."

He set the parchment down on the desk and motioned for Callen and Jadiel to come closer. He thumbed slowly through the pages of the primer and stopped at one section. "See—all the words on this page begin with the same letter here. This is pronounced 'bah.' Like the sound a sheep makes." He gave Jadiel another lop-sided smile, then pursed his lips together. "Tell me, Jadiel. Why are these ten words so important?"

Jadiel exhaled and looked to Callen for help. She knew if she opened her mouth she would begin to cry. Callen spoke up. "It's a long story, and we wouldn't want to take up your precious time, Your Highness. We have to find leaves from a terebinth tree—a tree that may not exist anywhere in this land. And we met something called a Keeper who sent us to Ethryn to find this scroll, which displays branches from that very tree."

King Adin's eyes widened in surprise and he grabbed the edges of the desk. After a moment, the color returned to his face and he composed himself. "I see. I can tell you must have a very interesting story, one I would be quite intrigued to hear. But it will have to wait for another time, as you said. Perhaps you can come back on another occasion and I can listen to your entire tale."

Callen lowered his head. "Thank you, Highness. I hope we will be able to return and enjoy your presence another time with more leisure. You are too kind."

King Adin let out a breath and Jadiel wondered about his reaction. He certainly seemed to know what a Keeper was. Had he been to The King's Plain and met that boar? She longed to ask him questions but held her tongue.

"Now," the king said, studying the parchment and looking back at the primer. "This first word is *ba'zah*." He paused and furrowed his brows. "I think that is correct. He looked again. "Strange, but yes, that's the word. *Ba'zah* means 'despised.'"

Callen shook his head. "Despised? That's an odd word to be etched into a bridge."

"A bridge?" the king asked.

Callen shrugged. "The ten words found on that scroll match ten words illustrated on some drawings I have of a bridge. I know this sounds confusing, but it's important we learn what these words mean. Hopefully by translating them we will be able to locate this bridge and its maker."

The king shook his head slowly. "I've never heard anything about a bridge of importance. Or of any structure with the *law'az* written upon it. What a strange thing to discover, one that piques my curiosity." He turned to Jadiel. "My greeter said your father's life is in danger. How can finding this bridge help save him?"

Jadiel's mouth dropped open. How could she even begin to explain? But when her eyes met the king's, he waved his hand in dismissal.

"I can only imagine the intriguing tale you two have to share. But tell me, Callen, did this Keeper say anything more about the ten words?"

Callen shook his head.

Jadiel found her voice again. "We met it on the King's Plain, down near Rumble. I think that's who the Keeper was . . ." She looked at Callen and he shrugged. "The boar. That's the one who spoke to us while we stood in the circle of stones."

King Adin leaned closer to Jadiel and his face radiated such interest that she instinctively backed away. He seemed nearly speechless. "A boar? A talking boar? And in a circle of stones?"

"Have you met it too?" Jadiel asked, feeling her nerves tangle in a knot.

"No, but I am acquainted with a talking pig. Always spoke in riddles and drove me mad."

"Sounds a lot like the boar we met," Callen said.

The king shook his head as if clearing his thoughts. "Callen, do you have those drawings of the bridge? Would you kindly leave them with me for the day and return tomorrow?"

Callen removed the sheaf of parchments from his pack and handed them to the king. King Adin gently laid them on the desk.

"I'll look over your list this evening. Return in the morning and, hopefully, by then I'll have figured out your words."

Jadiel cleared her dry throat. "May I ask one more question, Your Highness?" When Adin nodded to her with warmth in his face, Jadiel continued. "Have you ever on your journeys encountered a terebinth tree? A large oak-like tree?"

King Adin shook his head in puzzlement. "No, only the oaks that grow in your district." When Jadiel dropped her head, she heard him add, "I'm sorry."

He clapped his hands twice and a guard entered from outside the room. "Please escort these visitors back to the entry." He turned to Callen. "I'm sorry I have to cut our visit short. The delegation from Wentwater will be here soon, and there are many preparations to be made." He took Jadiel's hands and compassion filled his eyes. "I am sorry about your father. I hope I can help in some small way. Be brave and trust heaven. Heaven always finds a way for the true of heart."

The king's words fell like soft petals on Jadiel's ears. Tears filled her eyes, and she mumbled a thank you. She startled at the touch of his hand upon her shoulder. "I will see you tomorrow, then," he said in conclusion.

She nodded and let the guard escort her out alongside Callen. As the tall chamber door shut behind her, she let out a trembling breath. Images of her papa filled her mind, his warm touch and comforting embrace. She clamped down on her feelings and bit her lip as the guard led them through the hall to the entrance. The doors opened to a warm fall afternoon, and a burst of fragrance enveloped her as she marveled at the lavish landscaping and sweeping view of the city below. She turned and looked at Callen, who seemed overwhelmed by his encounter with the king.

"I don't see Ebed anywhere." His voice sounded irritated. "I'll bet he took off with our animals."

Jadiel glared at him and was about to say something mean, but shut her mouth. She was too tired to argue about Ebed again. "Let's just find a tavern and get some food, Callen. I'm starving. I'm sure we'll find Ebed before we leave. I have little doubt he'll know where to find us when he's ready."

Callen huffed and stopped searching the road. "Fine, but all our things are on those mounts."

Jadiel shook her head in frustration. "Look, there's a tavern right there." She pointed at a sign that read "The Golden Boar" near the end of the long block below. On the sign was a wood carving of a boar that looked much like the animal they met in the King's Plain. "I'd never seen a boar before, and now they're every-where. Come on, Callen." She tugged at his shirtsleeve.

"I'm coming," he said. "At least I still have your pouch of coins."

Jadiel ignored the scowl on Callen's face and strode toward the tavern. She was too tired to think about boars and ancient writ-ing and terebinth trees. Her stomach grumbled, turning all her thoughts to just one thing—food.

TWENTY-FIVE

IN THE dim tavern's light, Callen cradled his frosty mug of ale.
"More roast, luv?"

He looked up through his hazy stupor at the smiling face
of the young maid who served him earlier. What was she so happy
about? He shook his head as she cleared the empty plate and utensils from his table, then watched her wend through the crowd in
the smoky room.

A blazing fire crackled in the huge stone hearth across from
him. The flames mesmerized Callen's eyes. Thoughts flitted
through his head—disturbing thoughts he had been trying to
drown out these last few hours by plowing through three pitchers
of Loganvale dark ale.

Jadiel had retired in exhaustion to her private room upstairs,
and after Callen had made sure she was safe and had all she needed,
he went back downstairs to mull over recent events. Images of the
finely dressed man lying dead in the road burned in his mind, as
did the words of the archivist in Ethryn telling him of the evil one
confined in his prison. The villagers that huddled around the body
had spoken of a legend concerning a creature called the Golgoth.
Even the word gave Callen the creeps. Yet, of all the images, the
one that most unsettled him was the look on Ebed's face and the
way the old prophet's eyes had bored into him, making him feel
like a bug speared and wriggling on the tip of a knife. Ebed's words

replayed over and over, but they made no sense. "*The danger lies in your heart . . . You are not ready to hear answers to those questions . . . Are you prepared to risk your life for the bridge?*"

Callen grasped his mug and downed the rest of his ale. His head spun in a heavy cloud, and the incoherent voices of the other patrons swarmed around him in the stuffy room. What was the matter with him? Here he was, on a journey to seek knowledge. He should be enthralled with the sights and sounds of new lands. Instead, anger and frustration hemmed him in. Surely, he was worried for Jadiel and knew aiding her was much more important than seeking his own pleasure. But it wasn't concern over Jadiel's plight that dampened his spirits. It was this obsession with finding that blasted bridge—

Callen's ears pricked. He spun his head around and saw three bearded old men laughing boisterously at a booth a few feet away. They wore dark robes with hoods that gathered around their shoulders, and a strange insignia marked the cords hanging from their necks. A pot of tea and a plate of shortbread crumbs sat in the middle of their table.

One of the wizened men—a tall, lanky fellow—caught Callen's gaze with his watery gray eyes. "Ah, young lad, come join us." The other two nodded and waved him over. A stouter man patted an empty chair beside him.

"Yes, lad, you're too young to be wallowing alone over a pitcher of ale. We'll cheer you up." His fellows grunted in agreement.

Callen snorted and straightened in his chair. "And what makes you think I need cheering?" He gestured with his arm and knocked over his empty mug. Callen quickly righted it, feeling his face flush hot. His action inspired another round of cackling from the old men. Why did he have the irritating feeling that everyone was laughing at him?

"What's so funny?" he demanded.

The tall man smiled a challenge. "Come, join us. Pose us a question and see if we can answer it."

Callen narrowed his eyes at the men, then stood and found his balance. Somehow he staggered across to the other table and plopped down in the chair. "What do you mean—pose a question?"

The tall man tipped his head by way of introduction. "I am Antius and these are my associates, Arbulus and Anthanus. We are regents of the Antiquities Board. Historians visiting Sherbourne from the Heights above Wentwater. What may we call you, lad?"

"Callen."

Antius continued, his smile stretching across his face and revealing a mouth missing a few teeth. "Well, Callen. Quiz us on any topic. Test our knowledge!" Antius's companions hooted and slapped the table. Callen puzzled at these strange men who couldn't seem to stop chortling. He had never met anyone from Wentwater and, for that matter, had no idea where Wentwater was. Were all the people of that land so . . . jovial?

He looked into their faces and saw eager eyes. No doubt, they hoped to stump him in some test of knowledge and show off their great education. Well, he had just the topic for them.

What was that name Ebed used for the bridge? He cleared his throat. "Tell me about the Ke'sher."

A moment of silence ensued. Then, as if unable to contain their hilarity a moment longer, the three men guffawed so boisterously that the table rattled under Callen's hands, making the cups and teapot nearly topple over.

The one called Arbulus caught his breath as tears streamed down his cheeks and soaked into his white beard. "Ah, the Ke'sher. We haven't had anyone quiz us on that in ages, isn't that right?" His companions gasped for air and nodded with fervor.

Antius finally found his voice and calmed down enough to speak. He dabbed at his moist eyes with his napkin. "Let's see.

The Ke'sher. The bridge. An ancient tale out of Antolae. Spans across a deadly chasm and connects to Paradise. Leads the mortal to immortality and all that nonsense." He furrowed his brows as if straining memories from his mind. "Built somewhere between the first and second Age of Kings—"

Arbulus interrupted. "Before the *first* Age—"

Anthanus, who had yet to speak, piped up in a squeaky voice. "Fools, that bridge was never built. Just a tale recorded in the Alexander Romances, fourth century. You recall Alexander sought to find the water of life, and discovered it in the Land of Darkness . . ."

Antius bellowed with laughter again. "The Land of Darkness! Yes, that's where the bridge was said to be built. Point and score, old boy!" Antius slapped Anthanus's hand in congratulation. "Let's see what I remember about that tale." He stared up at the ceiling and recited. "The Ke'sher, built from the mighty terebinth tree, was said to be invisible."

With that remark, Antius's companions huffed and nodded. Callen's jaw dropped as he listened in amazement. *Invisible?* Antius continued. "Legend states the bridge is under a spell, buried in myth and folklore. The bridge builder was a mighty king, and the bridge was his life's work—"

"No," Arbulus said, halting his friend with his hand. "The bridge was built by a poor, destitute man of low station. It was left uncompleted due to lack of funds, and so eventually was torn down. Platoch's *Annals of the Age* states that the man building the bridge fell from a high cornice to his death—or was pushed, as some suspect—landing into the chasm the bridge spanned."

Anthanus pounded his fist on the table, making the dishes jump once more. "No, I beg to differ! You have it all wrong. The *Collected Songs of Ancient Realms* tells how those in the Land of Darkness hated the bridge builder and destroyed the bridge to spite him. The builder then disguised himself and went into hiding, and he's still there—trapped in the Land of Darkness."

"—And the second volume of *Northern Myths and Legends* describes the fellow as a liar, a lunatic, and a phony. Made outrageous claims of immortality, and for that the villagers attacked and killed him," Arbulus added.

Words tumbled through Callen's head. "Wait, I did hear something like that. But, I'm confused. What is 'the Land of Darkness'? Is this a real place?"

Through another bout of laughter, Antius spilled out his words. "Of course not, lad! How could such a place truly exist? People stumbling around in perpetual shadow, never aging, never able to leave! Let me recite from the oldest recorded prophet about the place called *Shamma* or *Araf'el*: 'Their memory perishes from the earth and they have no name in the street. They are thrust from light into darkness and driven out of the world. They have no offspring or descendent among their people. And no survivor where they used to live. They of the West are appalled at their fate, and horror seizes those of the East.'"

Anthanus clapped his hands in delight. "And don't forget the words of Ishi'el: 'They will see only distress and darkness, the gloom of anguish. And they will be thrust into thick darkness.' Lad, there are myriad tales of the accursed land. In books and song, inscribed on ancient tombs."

"Then surely, there must be some truth to all these legends?"

"Pahh!" Antius said. "Legends like these start with superstition, and soon grow in a measure proportionate to the fear and ignorance of those telling them. No doubt someone, somewhere, disappeared on a foggy night, and another's overactive imagination concocted such a tale as a caliginous land that swallows the unsuspecting, causing them to forever wander in darkness—"

Arbulus chortled. "Reminds me of the fool tale of that snake creature up in the northern Wastes—what was it called?" He turned to Anthanus, who threw up his hands and guffawed.

"Vitra! Ah, yes. Whose chopped-off head turned any to stone who dared look upon her."

Arbulus added: "Recorded over three hundred years ago in the tomes found in the ruins of Paladya. Wasn't there a bit in those tales about a sea wyrm?"

Antius slapped the table. "What a precise memory you have, old friend!" He chuckled until tears dribbled down his cheeks. "A sea wyrm . . . of all things . . ."

Arbulus shook his head. "More superstitious rot." He turned suddenly to Callen and said, "So it is with the Land of Darkness. Tell me, Callen, how could such a place exist?"

Callen shrugged. He thought back to his discussion with the librarian. Za'ker had said something about a curse near the land of Antolae. Could this curse have something to do with this strange land?

"Can you tell me how to get to this place—this Land of Darkness?"

Antius nearly dropped the teacup he was lifting to his lips. Now the smiles fell from all three of the old men's faces. "You're not serious, lad? The place is a myth. From time to time stories surface of those who wander near Antolae and vanish. But they are just bal'derdash—stories meant to frighten small children into behaving."

Yes," Anthanus added, pouring himself a cup of tea. "You'd best be forgetting that place. A waste of time, indeed. This is the Age of Science, lad! It's one thing to learn and acquire the knowledge of the ages—no task is more noble and worthy. But truly another thing to go chasing phantasms."

Antius stood and brushed a lapful of crumbs to the tavern floor. His companions followed suit. Antius smoothed out his beard and threw his hood over his head. "Well, Callen, my boy, my old bones are finally feeling the brunt of the day's travels." The other two men nodded and Anthanus yawned.

"Take a word of advice—and caution." Arbulus took Callen's hands in his own weathered ones and gripped them tightly. He lowered his voice. "Forget the bridge. A fool's errand, that. Devote your time and youth to pursuing more noble pursuits. Ishi'el, one of the greatest of all wise men also said, 'But those who are noble plan noble things, and by noble things they stand.' Your task, lad, is to find that noble pursuit and stand by it."

Antius patted Callen's shoulder. "Chasing off to some silly imaginary land would only bring you trouble."

Callen looked at Antius as the old man pushed in his chair. A strange look of warning seemed to emanate from the man's face. Their eyes remained locked for a moment, then, with anther burst of laughter, Antius turned to his companions. "Shall we?"

He gestured to the door and the three men wobbled toward it, chuckles of mirth following in their wake.

"Jadiel, are you finished?"

The knock at her door came as Jadiel chewed her last bit of cheese. In between bites, she called to Callen, "Come in. I'll be ready in just a few minutes.

The door swung open and Callen entered, wearing his cloak with his pack slung over his shoulder. He reached for Jadiel's satchel. "I'll be downstairs. I'd like to get started. Who knows how long it will take to find that Ebed—if we can find him at all in this tiresome place."

Jadiel wondered at Callen's tone. He had been kind enough to awaken her with a breakfast tray, but had left in a huff when she asked him about his evening in the tavern.

"Callen, I'm sure he'll be waiting for us at the gate as he promised. But first we're visiting with King Adin, remember?"

"Of course I remember." He shut the door behind him and Jadiel let out a sigh. The hawk hopped off her shoulder onto the small side table, where it pecked at the crumbs on Jadiel's plate.

"Oh, sweet thing, I'm so sorry. You've been stuck here in this room while I was visiting with the king. I haven't even thought of your hunger. You haven't had much chance to hunt within these city walls, if you can even hunt at all. I wish I had more to give you."

The hawk stopped pecking and tilted its head at Jadiel. It acted as if it understood her words, showing eyes filled with sadness. Jadiel's heart went out to the poor creature. If only Callen hadn't shot it down with his arrow!

Jadiel took one last look around the room and remembered her mirror and comb on the dresser. She picked up the mirror and stared at her reflection. Her hair was a tangled mess. Callen may be in a hurry, but she was meeting with the king. Surely he could wait a few minutes more for her to neaten up.

As she held the mirror and combed her tresses, a shape wavered behind her reflection. At first she thought her mother was appearing again, but this time, the shape formed a different face—and her breath caught. A head of straw-colored hair framed her papa's face, and his deep green eyes overflowed with pain.

"Papa!" Jadiel spun around, half-expecting to see her father standing in the doorway. But only the hawk stood on the edge of the table, its eyes widened in surprise. The little bird began to hop up and down in excitement, thrashing its wings in the air and jerking its head up and down.

"Oh, little bird," she said, rushing over to scoop up the hawk in her hands. "How frustrated you must be, not able to fly. I promise we'll get you healed—and then off you will go, back to soaring the heights."

Jadiel stuffed her comb and mirror into her smock pocket and set the hawk on her shoulder. "It's time to see King Adin. And let's hope he has made some sense of those ten words."

As she skipped down the stairs and out the front door of the inn, she felt the little hawk's talons grip her shoulder tightly, as if hanging on for dear life.

TWENTY-SIX

"I'M AFRAID I can't make much sense of your words, but perhaps they will hold some meaning for you."

The king handed the rolled-up parchments to Callen, who placed them back into his pack. "Come, sit." He motioned Callen and Jadiel to the two chairs in front of the massive red wood desk in the Council Chambers across from his finely carved wooden chair. Jadiel sat, aware of the welling despair rising in her throat. If King Adin could not make sense of the words, how could she and Callen? The whole walk to the palace, Jadiel had been unable to wrench this feeling of hopelessness from her heart. And now—noting the king's apologetic expression—all she wanted was to flee home as fast as she could and face whatever consequences would greet her. In less than two weeks her papa would be dead. Two weeks, two days—what did that matter? Huldah had sent her on a fool's errand. She determined that once they finished visiting with the king, she would persuade Callen to take her home.

The king laid Callen's list of words on the desk beside another sheet of writing. Callen leaned across the desk as King Adin pointed at the scribblings.

"They seem to be a rhyme of sorts, at least in the *law'az*. First, let me read them to you." He picked up the sheet of parchment and recited:

"*Ba'zah, na'gah, na'kah, a'nah, da'kah.*" He paused and looked at Jadiel. "Those are the five words found on the right side of the page, the ones that would have been positioned over the branches as you described. The other five, on the left, are *ya'bal, cha'lal, la'kah, a'rah,* and *ka'yah.* The words of the *law'az* read from right to left, so I am guessing these would be read in the same order. But I could be wrong. I can't see how it would matter in what order these words should be read."

"So, Your Highness, how are they translated?" Callen's tone sounded much softer this morning to Jadiel. She looked up in his face and detected an odd expression—almost of shame or embarrassment. What was Callen thinking?

"Here is my list, although I could not decipher the last word. I wonder if that word holds the key, somehow, to this puzzle." He handed the sheet to Callen, who read the words aloud.

"Despised. Stricken. Smitten . . . "

The king interrupted. "I wasn't sure how to translate that word. It means to strike sharply with a hand—like a slap across the face—or with a sharp instrument, as with a knife or sword." He waved at Callen. "Continue, please."

"Afflicted. Bruised. That's the first five words." He frowned. "Carried away. Wounded—"

"Actually, that word means pierced, I think. But perhaps it has a more general meaning of injury."

Jadiel spoke. "How is it, Your Highness, that you have learned these words? We were told the ancient language has all but disappeared, and that no one—except maybe a Sherbourne man named Ta'man—can speak it."

The king's face grew ashen. "Ta'man! How in the world did you hear of that fellow?" One look told Jadiel the king knew of this man.

"In Ethryn," Callen said. "He spent many years there, painting beautiful murals on the Great Scroll Room walls. We were told about him before we came here, to Sherbourne. Told that he knew the *law'az*."

Jadiel waited as the king wandered in his thoughts, his face troubled. She exchanged glances with Callen and waited politely.

"Well." The king let out a long sigh and shook thoughts from his head. "You didn't perchance find this man and speak to him, did you?"

"We didn't try. A . . . man we met told us Ta'man had left the kingdom. For good."

Jadiel noted a look of disappointment drop like a shroud over the king's countenance. "That's what I gathered, when I had gone to call on him, and his cottage lay empty and abandoned." He cleared his throat. "But, to answer your question as to how I learned the *law'az*. That is a long and fantastic story for another time. Callen, continue," he said, gesturing at the parchment.

"Let's see: the next word means 'taken.'"

"More like 'snatched,' I would say." The king nodded for Callen to go on.

"And the last one is 'emptied.'"

"Or 'poured out,' or 'laid bare.' I cannot quite make that one out. And as you can see, I did not write anything for that last word: *ka'yah*. I'm afraid that one will have to remain a mystery for now."

Callen sighed. "Not that it will matter. I haven't the faintest idea what all those words mean. Why carve such strange words onto a bridge? And why did the boar imply these ten words would answer our questions and lead us to the terebinth tree?"

The king stood. "I wish I could tell you. But if you truly did encounter a Keeper, then I believe its words have great import— at least to you and your quest. I would mull over them and pay attention to what you hear on your journey. The Keepers know much more than they let on."

"Please, Your Highness, just what is a Keeper?" Jadiel asked.

Just as the king opened his mouth to answer, Merin, the greeter who had once more shown them into the Chambers, poked his head in through the doorway.

"The regents from Wentwater are here to see you."

King Adin looked toward the open door and listened to the sound of raucous laughter filtering into the room from down the hallway. Jadiel looked over at Callen, who only rolled his eyes.

"Well," the king said. "I suppose that answer will also have to wait until another occasion. I'm afraid, my friends, this is all the time I can give you. I don't know if I've been any help, but I pray your journey will lead you to your tree, Jadiel. And that your father will be returned to you, safe and sound."

Callen gathered the parchments and put them in his pack. He and Jadiel stood and shook the king's hand. "You've been gracious and kind to see us, Your Highness. Thank you."

Jadiel nodded and felt tears squeezing out the corners of her eyes. She tried to speak, but the words jammed thick in her throat. The king gave Jadiel a lopsided smile as he signaled Merin to escort them out.

As they followed the perky young greeter, they passed three tall old men with long beards and wearing dark robes. Their laughter trailed in the hall behind them as she and Callen approached the front door. How wonderful to have such a light heart and no worries, to be able to laugh so freely. Jadiel sighed, wondering if she would ever laugh like that again.

"I told you he'd be waiting for us."

Callen noticed Jadiel did not bother to hide her ire. One look at her face told all. Why did she feel such affection for this repulsive, arrogant fellow? Without a word or nod of his head, Callen took the reins from Ebed's hands and busied himself reattaching their small packs.

"Ebed, we met King Adin!" Jadiel threw her arms around the old prophet and hugged him. "And he told us the words of the scroll, but they didn't make any sense." Callen cringed. How could she even touch him? From the corner of his eye, he watched Ebed return her embrace and pat her head with his scarred hand. Just what was that irritating man up to, and why did he ingratiate himself with Jadiel? Surely he had some ulterior motive in pestering them. Free food, use of their mounts? Well, enough was enough.

"Come on, Jadiel. Let's get going."

Jadiel turned and watched Callen swing up into his saddle. "Where?"

He shot Ebed a look. Hopefully the old man would get the hint. "I'll tell you once we leave these city walls. But I think I now know where to find the bridge."

Ebed lifted a half-amused smile, but Callen read it more as a challenge. "Oh, pray tell, Callen. Do you hope to locate Araf'el—and dare to take this young, innocent child into such a land?"

Jadiel's eyes narrowed at Callen. "What land? Is it dangerous?" She stood resolute next to her mule, gripping the reins. The air fell still and a few flies buzzed near her head. The weak autumn sun baked his shoulders. Callen waggled his finger at her. "Jadiel, I'll tell you *after* we leave Sherbourne. Not here."

Jadiel turned and looked at Ebed. He stood without speaking, his face masked of emotion. The little hawk sidestepped along his shoulder, then flew to gently land on one of Jadiel's.

"Ebed, tell me. Will we find the bridge there? And the terebinth tree?" she asked.

The prophet picked up his bundle from the cobbled street and smiled at Jadiel. "Would you still go—even if a great danger awaited you?"

Jadiel didn't hesitate with her answer. "Yes. If I can save Papa, I'll do anything."

Ebed rested his eyes on Jadiel, lost in thought.

Callen waited. He knew how stubborn Jadiel could be.

"Then I shall show you both the way to the Land of Darkness," Ebed said, tying his bundle to his back with a rope and setting off toward the north gate of Sherbourne, bent under the weight of his load.

In a heartbeat, Jadiel swung the reins over the mule's neck and mounted into her saddle. She kicked the mule's flanks and headed after Ebed, leaving Callen in a cloud of dust. Callen mumbled under his breath and followed. *Great, just great.*

• PART FOUR •

"You Must Stand Firm in the Faith, or

You Will Not Stand at All . . ."

TWENTY-SEVEN

SINCE EBED refused to ride, they made slow progress. By late afternoon of the third day since leaving the city, after a long journey battling a headwind, they had reached the junction branching north into Loganvale—and home. Jadiel resisted the strong urge to turn aside and gallop north, back to the manor and to her papa. How easy it would be—to forget this insane quest and take her chances with Huldah. But Ebed had said something earlier to her, and his words soothed her mind with power and comfort. *"Will you trust me, Jadiel?"* He told her nothing more, just looked at her with eyes filled with knowledge and reassurance. Callen kept asking why she listened to him, but how could she explain it? Ebed somehow made her feel safe. Being by his side was like having her arms around Papa as she rode behind him on his horse. No matter how fast they would race across the fields, her hair blowing wildly and her body jouncing, she knew Papa wouldn't let her fall. She didn't have to know where they were headed or when they would get there. Her papa knew, and that was enough. That's what being near Ebed was like. Callen would never understand.

Callen reined in his mare a few feet off the road. He turned back to look at Jadiel, who struggled to gather all her hair into a clip. Wind whipped Callen's clothes like sheets on a clothesline. Ebed walked his steady pace, catching up to Jadiel and turning his gaze north.

Callen yelled over the wind. "Now's your chance, Jadiel. What do you want to do?"

A tear ran down her cheek. "What about you, Callen? Do you want to go back? I can't ask you to risk your life just to help save my papa."

"Jadiel, I made you a promise. If you want to trust . . . Ebed to show us the way to the bridge, well, I'll stick with you until the task is done." He slid off his horse and stretched in the evening twilight, his shirt billowing in the wind. "Take your time. We can make camp close by. The nearest inn, however, is in Wheatsheaf, and that's at least an hour north, out of our way, if we're not planning to go home."

Just hearing the word *home* punctured Jadiel's tenuous resolve. She buried her head in her hands and sobbed. Ebed reached up and lifted her from her saddle, then led her over to a fallen log half-buried in a field of brown-eared grass where she sat and wiped her eyes. Wind howled mournfully across the fields, and Jadiel lifted her face and smelled winter on the air. She pulled her coat tightly around her neck, wishing for the sweltering heat of Ethryn. Ebed sat quietly beside her and took her hand in his. Her stomach rumbled noisily, and she felt her face flush in embarrassment.

Ebed walked over to a small, gnarled old apple tree. A few pieces of withered fruit hung by thin stems, wavering in the breeze. A pile of rotted apples lay around the trunk.

Jadiel called to Callen, who had his back turned, looking off at the horizon where the sun was setting, a burnt orange globe against a cerulean sky. "Let's make camp here, Callen. Then we can wait until morning to decide which way to go."

Callen turned to Jadiel. "Fine. I'll start dinner."

Jadiel watched him collect the animals and set up a high line a hundred yards off across the field where a small copse of trees stood. The little hawk that had been sitting quietly on the pommel of her saddle suddenly took off in the air, spreading its wings and catching an updraft. "Look!" she called out to Ebed, "its wing has healed." She sighed and a strange feeling of loss filled her. "I will miss that little bird. But I suppose I should be happy for it. It can go back to its family now."

Ebed watched the hawk fly in circles above them. "Jadiel, you are the only family he has. He will be back."

Jadiel shrugged. From where she sat, with the light fading, she could just make out Callen stooped over, preparing a campfire.

"Here," Ebed said, his hand outstretched. In his palm lay a bright red apple, plump and shiny. Jadiel pursed her lips in confusion, then looked over at the tree where Ebed had been standing. She shook her head. Surely that tree had been withered and the apples wrinkled and dry. Yet now the small tree bore dozens of ripe apples, and its branches were smooth and sturdy, full of pliant green leaves shimmering in the breeze.

"How—"

Jadiel searched his face, noting his eyes shone with a light that defied the night gathering around them. "A secret," he said. "Is it good?"

She took a big bite and delicious flavors exploded in her mouth. Juice dribbled down her chin, and her heart instantly lightened. "It is! Try it." She handed the apple to Ebed and he took a bite and laughed. She leaped up off the log and ran to the tree, picking apples and spreading her shirt to hold them. "Let's take some back to Callen."

Ebed helped her. "Perhaps we should leave a few—for other hungry travelers."

Jadiel stopped picking the fruit. "Good idea." A dozen remained on the tree. "Come, Ebed, let's go eat."

Jadiel dumped the pile of apples next to the pit where Callen had a roaring fire going. After she fed the horse and mule each an apple, she returned and reached for the sack of potatoes.

"I've already washed those, Jadiel. Just cut them in small pieces and throw them in the pot."

Jadiel sat on a log Callen had positioned beside the fire and began chopping the potatoes.

Ebed walked across the field. Jadiel watched the way his soft robes flapped in the wind. Callen balanced the pot of water on two rocks, and the hungry flames flared underneath it. He straightened and stared after Ebed, whose shape was now a dark shadow against the landscape.

"Jadiel, why do you want him along? He slows us down. Why can't we just go to this place by ourselves?"

Jadiel huffed and picked up a large spoon to stir the potatoes she had dumped into the water. "Well, for one thing, you don't know the way—and Ebed does. And, for another, he makes me feel safe."

Callen snorted. "Like he could really protect you? He's weak and . . . feeble. Well, maybe one look at his face and any wild beast would high-tail it and run away."

"Callen, that's just plain mean! I don't understand you. Your answer to every threat is to shoot arrows. All you've done is hurt a poor little hawk. And what about that door you opened in the mountains! For all we know, you could have let some evil thing get out—"

"That's just an old tale and you know it!"

"And what if it's not? That's not the point. What matters is that you act without thinking first. You're impulsive."

"And you're twelve years old! If I hadn't saved you from those bad men in that wagon, where would you be now!" Callen stomped off toward the road, kicking dirt into the fire as he left.

"Callen, wait. I'm sorry . . ."

Jadiel let out a rush of breath and looked at her clenched hands. Above her, stars dotted the sky. In the flickering firelight, she caught sight of the hawk high above, winging toward her. With a soft whoosh, it back-flapped its wings and landed on the ground at her feet, a juicy little mouse pinned in its beak.

"Well, you did come back. But I hope that's not a present for me." She stroked the hawk's head and it hopped up onto her knee. She pointed past the fire. "Why don't you eat that over there?"

As if it could understand her words, the hawk promptly flew to the other side of the fire, and in a moment, the mouse had disappeared down the bird's throat.

After a few moments of listening to the snap and crack of the fire, Jadiel saw Callen emerge from the inky shadows of night to check the boiling pot. He rearranged some of the burning sticks and coals to lessen the heat. The roiling in the pot reduced to a simmer. Callen reached into his pack and pulled out a package of sausage they had picked up from a butcher's shop in Sherbourne earlier that day. As he sliced the meat and dropped the pieces into the pot, he spoke quietly to Jadiel, not looking at her.

"Jadiel, I'm sorry I got angry. I guess I felt slighted. Here I've been trying to look after you and help you find those leaves and we're running out of time—"

Jadiel laid her hand on his arm. "Callen, you don't have to explain. I understand. I'm sorry too. I just—I just want to go home." Her throat swelled with the words and she gasped for air. She heard soft footsteps behind her and saw Callen look up.

Callen gestured Ebed to sit, and Jadiel noted his eyes soften. Maybe, in time, he'd get used to their guest's strange ways.

Ebed cleared his throat. His words came out raspy and tender. "The darkness is not real, you see. It originates in their hearts."

Callen stopped what he was doing and stared at Ebed. "What darkness? You mean in the Land of Darkness?"

"If the light in you is darkness, how great that darkness will be."

Callen shook his head and stared at the fire. "Riddles. Why do you always speak that way?"

"I will open my mouth in a parable; I will utter dark sayings of old. Things we have heard and known, that to us our ancestors told."

Jadiel perked up. "That sounds like a rhyme from a song."

Ebed turned and smiled at her. "Why, it is, Jadiel. From the seventy-eighth Song of the King."

"What are the dark sayings, then?" she asked.

"Things held in mystery, waiting to be revealed. If your eye is dark, your whole body will be dark. As long as it is dark inside, it will be dark outside."

Callen grunted and stirred the pot. Jadiel frowned. "I don't understand, Ebed. Are my eyes dark?"

He gently moved a lock of hair off her forehead and studied her. "Not at all. You have two of the brightest eyes I've seen in a long while."

Callen picked up a towel and removed the pot from the fire. "Food's ready. Ebed, you are just like your parables—an enigma, making no sense."

"Tell me, Callen. How do you manage to get through life using only your eyes to see?"

"Huh?" Callen spooned stew into bowls, and Jadiel's mouth watered at the aroma. "That's what eyes are for—seeing. What else can you see with?"

Ebed smiled and accepted the bowl from Callen's hands. He bowed his head and closed his eyes. Jadiel watched him, worried. When Ebed lifted his chin, Jadiel said, "Are you all right?"

"Yes, I was just thanking heaven for providing this meal."

Callen muttered under his breath, but Jadiel heard him. "*I'm* the one providing the meal."

Ebed chuckled. "Thank you, Callen, for feeding me."

"Yes, but I'd like to see you make a potato!" Jadiel laughed and dug into her bowl. "Where do you think all the good things in life come from?"

"From the world around us. Food certainly doesn't drop out of heaven and onto our plates."

Jadiel chewed the food appreciatively and swallowed before answering. "Well, in a sense, it does. Rain falls from above and waters the plants. The sun in the heavens gives heat. The grass grows, which the cows eat. You could say that heaven makes all the food grow."

"Whatever." Callen stuffed stew into his mouth and chewed quietly.

Ebed set down his half-eaten bowl of stew and looked at Callen. "The last word—*ka'yah*—means 'restored to life.'"

Callen nearly spit out his mouthful of stew. "What! Are you telling me you know the ancient language—that you can read the words on that scroll?"

When Ebed nodded calmly, Callen slammed down his bowl. "Then why didn't you tell us? Why send us off to the king and make us waste all that time?"

"You needed to see King Adin, Callen."

"Why? And since you're so smart, maybe you can tell us just what those stupid words mean. And why they're etched into a bridge—a bridge built to be destroyed, or invisible, or buried in myth." Callen paced by the fire, challenging Ebed with a glare that matched the fire's glow on his cheeks. "Tell me—how can you build an invisible bridge?"

"I'll ask again," Ebed said kindly. "How do you manage to get through life using only your eyes to see?"

Callen fumed and said nothing. Ebed continued. "The things seen are temporary. The things unseen are eternal."

"That makes no sense! How could you know something is eternal if you can't see the confounded thing?"

Jadiel finished her stew, but her stomach turned in circles. Why did Callen have to be so troublesome? "Callen, there are lots of things that are invisible. The wind, for one. And the most important things in life, like love, loyalty, trust. And hope." She sighed. "Don't you think those things are eternal? Maybe some day this entire world will vanish or crumble away, but maybe long after all this is gone, there will still be those other things."

"Not if there's no one around to feel them," Callen retorted.

"Eternal things require faith, Callen," Ebed added. "Your eyes can deceive you and your heart may lie. But you must trust most in the things you cannot see, if you are to stand firm in the floodwaters of this life."

Callen's eyes widened at Ebed's words. "The floodwaters . . ."

Jadiel jumped to her feet as she remembered. "The boar said something like that, 'How can a flimsy reed stand firm in the floodwaters? It cannot.' That's what it said to us on the King's Plain."

"And she was right," Ebed said.

Jadiel's eyebrows rose. *She?* Come to think of it, that wiry old boar did seem like a female, the way it crooned and behaved. Jadiel wouldn't be surprised if Ebed knew that boar well.

Ebed added, "You must stand firm in the faith, or you will not stand at all."

"Yes," Jadiel added, feeling a prick of excitement in her heart. "She said 'You must become like a solid tree.' Was that what the boar meant about standing firm in the faith—having faith in the things unseen? Believing more in the power of love—and holding on to hope, even when hope seemed utterly futile?"

Callen grunted, and Jadiel could tell he had enough of this talk. She gathered up dishes and forks and reached for the pot. "I'll clean up, Callen. Do you want to check on our animals?"

"Gladly." Callen wiped his hands on the towel and stomped off in the dark. Jadiel heard the horse nicker in the distance. She turned to Ebed, who stared in silence at the last few flickers of flame in the fire pit. His scarred face was filled with lines of shadow, yet she couldn't help but notice a radiance of beauty peering through.

"Ebed, if I go with you to the Land of Darkness, will you keep me safe and help me find that tree?"

His face lit up from the ember glow. "All you have to do is ask, Jadiel. Ask, and you will receive."

"Then I will go with you and trust you."

Ebed's eyes seemed filled with great joy. Jadiel threw her arms around this odd man and hugged him tightly. Somehow, she knew everything would turn out all right. She didn't know where they were headed or when they would get there. Ebed knew, and that was enough.

TWENTY-EIGHT

B Y NOON the next day, they approached a lone wooden shack positioned at a crossroads in a barren land. Callen wiped a mat of sticky hair out of his eyes. Sweat trickled down his neck and his shirt stuck to his back. A hazy sun streaked down from a cloudy sky, but the air was as still as death. Tall, jagged mountains formed a partial ring around this valley of scrub brush and tumbleweed. The road south and west he knew led to Tebron—and home. This outpost was one of the delivery station stops en route between his forest village and the Logan Valley. But another less-used road turned northwest, leading toward a pass off in the distance and to lands he had no knowledge of.

He turned in his saddle and watched Jadiel catch up on the mule, with the hunched-over prophet walking steadily by her side. He had to hand it to that stubborn man—he walked endless miles without complaint. Jadiel had been able to convince him to let the mule carry his load, but he refused to ride. Judging from the wear of the man's sandals, he wouldn't be surprised if Ebed had walked the length and breadth of the entire kingdom many times over.

Jadiel reined alongside him and heaved a great sigh. "I'm so sick of plodding along and getting nowhere." She swiveled her head around to take in the sweep of scenery. "This place is so empty. Ebed, which way now?"

The prophet pointed north. "Into those mountains, there."

"Are there any more villages along the way?" she asked.

Ebed shook his head. "We should arrive in Antolae in two days."

Callen took a quick mental count of their stores. "Then I better hunt up some food," His mare stretched her neck and chomped at a clump of scraggly grass. "At least there's a bit of grassland here for the animals. Maybe we should let them graze a bit while we rest. This overhang on the building may be the only shade we get for a while." Callen dismounted and unstrapped his bow and quiver. He checked the tautness of the string, then swung the bow over his shoulder.

Jadiel nodded and slid off the mule. "I'll hobble them." She untied her water jug from the saddle. "Here, Ebed. Drink." She handed him the jug, and he tipped his head in gratitude. When he was sated, he handed the jug back to her.

"I would suggest leading your mounts over there." He pointed to a tumble of large boulders surrounded by thick brush. "You'll find a creek there."

"Water! That's good news," Jadiel said, gathering up reins. "Do you want to come, Ebed, and wash up?"

Ebed took hold of Jadiel's outstretched hand and Callen watched them lead the animals off the road and into the brush. *Humph! He must have been here before, to know about that creek.*

Motion to the north caught Callen's attention. He glimpsed two huge jackrabbits with meaty flanks leap over a dry creek bed a hundred yards from him. Ever since they left the rolling hills and meandered through this plain, he had lost count of the rabbits he'd seen hopping in all directions. He smirked and hunched down, then set off in the direction of the hares. Now, at least, he could hunt something that would meet with Jadiel's approval.

Ebed handed the towel back to Jadiel after wiping his face. He sat on a patch of grass at the water's edge and gazed afar in silence. Jadiel studied him. Where was Ebed from, and was he was all alone, without family? He didn't seem especially sad. But she did find it curious that he willingly chose to accompany them—into a land said to be dangerous.

Araf'el, Ebed had called it. Earlier that day, she had asked him questions about their destination. The name meant "thick darkness," but that region had once been a part of Antolae, a thriving city now in ruins at the foothills of a towering mountain range. He said those dwelling in the north called the ruins *Shamma*—desolation. Few lived nearby, and fewer ventured within a league of Antolae. They feared the curse.

"Ebed, is there really a curse on the land?" She leaned over a rock and splashed cool water on her face. She couldn't see the horse and mule but could hear their hooves kicking rocks nearby, and by their snuffling and snorting knew they were grazing contentedly.

Ebed spoke, yet his eyes rested on the water as it trickled over stones in the creek. "An ancient prophet told of the curse: 'We look for light, but there is darkness! For brightness, but we walk in blackness. We grope for the wall like the blind, and we grope as if we had no eyes. We stumble at noonday as at twilight. We are as dead men in a desolate place.'"

Jadiel wiped her face and pulled out her mirror and comb. She tugged gently at the tangled mess of hair. "But you said the darkness is inside, not outside. I don't understand."

"There is an old proverb: 'The way of the wicked is like deep darkness. They do not know what they stumble over.' Jadiel, many live in darkness and don't even know it. They choose darkness over light. Those in Araf'el could leave at any time. Nothing but their own blindness holds them back. But it is a choice. It is a true saying that some men love the darkness more than the light."

"But that makes no sense to me. Why would anyone choose darkness over light? Don't those people want to go home? You told me earlier they are trapped there, wandering aimlessly. That those in the land had been punished by heaven. Punished, why?"

Ebed turned and looked deeply into Jadiel's eyes. For a moment he said nothing. Then he spoke. "The great king of that land, at great cost, built that bridge Callen seeks. A bridge unlike any other—it spanned the deep chasm to the land beyond, a land formerly out of reach. A land of such beauty, the sight of it would take your breath away. There, on a hill, stands a palace of gold, surrounded by orchards and vineyards as far as the eye can see. A golden light bathes this kingdom day and night. A fountain of water bubbles up in the courtyard in front of the palace— the waters of life. And a wide lane, paved with gold and precious stones, leads up the hill to the palace."

Ebed searched Jadiel's face. "And lining the lane, on both sides, are mighty trees, whose leaves are 'for the healing of the nations.'"

Jadiel gasped. "Terebinth trees! Ebed, tell me—are they really there? Is this a real place, or another one of your parables?" She felt her heart thump wildly but dared not hope. How could such a place be real?

"Jadiel," Ebed said gently, "this kingdom of which I speak has been prepared for you from the founding of the world."

"For me?"

"And for any who would desire to live there. One day you will rejoice to see your mother again, for she will join you there, in good time."

"My mother . . ." Jadiel's throat closed like a vise. A flood of tears streamed down her face. "Ebed, I miss her so much . . ."

The prophet approached Jadiel. He knelt and gathered her into his arms and she cried, a great flood of grief pouring from her heart. As she heaved and sobbed, Ebed stroked her hair.

When she had run out of tears, she lifted her head. "I don't understand. You told us the bridge was destroyed. That it was meant to be destroyed. If that is so, how can we cross it to get to that land? I can't wait until some day in the future, when I will see my mother again. I only have a few days left to get those leaves before my papa will die!"

Ebed released Jadiel and walked back over to the creek. "You will just have to wait until we get there, Jadiel. You will have to trust me."

Jadiel picked up her mirror and looked at her red puffy eyes and tear-streaked face. "I will, Ebed. I'm sorry I ask so many questions."

In the mirror, behind her reflection, she saw Ebed smile. "The asking of questions is the beginning of wisdom."

Jadiel sighed and resumed untangling her hair. Surely Ebed would not lead them into a dangerous land without being certain of a way out—and a way to the terebinth trees. Oh, if only she could believe with all her heart that everything would turn out all right—that she would get the leaves and save her papa in time. What if Callen was right, that Ebed was spinning stories? Maybe he was good-hearted with kind intentions, but could it be that nothing he said held truth?

She tilted the mirror and watched in the glass as Ebed sat on a rock. Her doubts rested heavy on her, a weight she wished she could fling away. How she wanted to believe in him, to believe she would see her mother again, to trust she could save her papa.

Suddenly, the mirror brightened, filled with light as if the sun shone upon it. Jadiel shielded her eyes with her hand but could not look away. A man's shape appeared, in white glowing garments, and a rich gold crown rested on his head of dark hair. Behind him, she saw a brilliant green hill of grass, not unlike the hill she and Callen had walked upon inside the circle on the King's Plain. Off in the distance, she saw a golden tower, rising into the clouds and shimmering like sunlight upon water.

Jadiel's breath caught as she stared at the image in the glass. She thought of the king the boar had spoken of—the one who is to come. *The kings await a prince, captives await a deliverer . . .* She pictured the sleeping kings waking and bowing to this one. She stared harder and saw that the man held something in the palm of his hand. A small stone, round and white, with a word written on it. Jadiel could not make out the writing, but somehow she knew the man was offering it to her. Then she looked up from the stone and into his face and startled. He looked so familiar! But the most odd thing was, she felt she had known this face her entire life, better than her own, better than her papa's. An ache—one she did not even know she had—stopped hurting.

Then, just as quickly as the light appeared, it vanished with an eerie sucking sound. Jadiel watched the glass cloud over, then darken, and that terrible sensation of evil returned. An icy chill raced up her fingers and into her chest. A putrid smell seeped from the mirror, and before Jadiel could throw it down, the glass cracked with a loud noise and shattered in her hand.

Ebed leaped to his feet. Jadiel screamed and threw down the broken mirror. The horse neighed in fear and thrashed in the underbrush.

With startling speed, Ebed raced back through the boulders, and Jadiel rushed after him, bolting through the brush and out onto the prairie. By the time she emerged from the rocks, she saw Ebed running past the small building, where he then dropped in a heap beside a shape lying prostrate on the dirt.

Callen!

TWENTY-NINE

JADIEL NEARLY collided with Ebed, her eyes transfixed in horror upon Callen's pale face. Now she understood the expression "white as a specter." She never knew skin could turn so wan and nearly translucent. An expression of terror lay across Callen's features, frozen on his unmoving face.

"Ebed, do something!"

The prophet, on his knees, studied Callen from head to toe. Jadiel held her breath, wanting to scream out. Was Callen dead? How could this have happened—with nothing around, no one, no animals, no sign of a struggle or injury? Callen's bow lay on the ground next to a speared hare a few feet away. Her eyes roamed the prairie, seeking out answers but finding nothing. A hush had fallen over the land; not a bird called or stirred in the brush.

Ebed turned his head and looked at Jadiel, who hovered over him. "Don't let your heart be troubled, Jadiel. For he is only sleeping."

"Sleeping! No one looks like *that* when they sleep!"

The prophet laid a tender hand on Jadiel's wrist. "Jadiel, fetch me the water jug." He pointed to their packs piled on top of the bench. She ran, her heart thumping furiously in her chest. Her legs felt like jelly as she stumbled over rocks and sagebrush.

She pushed the packs and her satchel aside and found one of the water jugs. She turned to run back, then halted at the curious sight that met her eyes.

Ebed had one hand on Callen's chest. His head stretched to the heavens, as if in supplication, with his stringy hair tumbling around his shoulders. Streaks of sunlight filtering down to the ground lit up the dusty terrain in patches around him. A breeze kicked up and a mass of clouds parted overhead, allowing the sun to shine unhindered. The sight was surreal, illuminating the two figures and bathing them in radiance. Jadiel approached cautiously. The air grew oddly calm, but she detected a buzzing, or a hum. The air around her vibrated with energy, the way it felt in a lightning storm. Even the hairs on her arms stood on end, electrified.

Jadiel dropped by Ebed's side and looked into Callen's face. A bit of color had returned, but she couldn't see him breathe or his chest rise. Time grew thick and muddled and Jadiel waited, holding her breath.

"Callen, arise," Ebed said, with a commanding tone Jadiel had not heard in his voice before. Instantly, Callen opened his eyes and sat up. Jadiel clamped her hand over her mouth to stifle a scream.

Ebed tipped his head and gave a smile that radiated a calm joy. "As I said, he was merely sleeping."

Callen clutched his chest. "W-what happened . . .?" He blinked a few times and squinted in the glaring afternoon light. "Oh! I remember—" A gasp caught in his throat and he searched the ground around his feet. He locked his eyes on Ebed's.

"What *was* that? That . . . shadow . . ."

Ebed helped Callen stand and nodded at the jug. Jadiel handed it over, and Ebed carefully brought the jug to Callen's lips.

Jadiel watched Callen guzzle the entire contents. With a trembling hand, he set the jug on the ground and let Ebed help him to the bench, where he lowered onto the hard seat with great care.

Ebed stood before Callen and said nothing.

"What shadow? What did you see?" Jadiel asked, sitting down beside him.

Callen squinted his eyes in memory. "I had just released the arrow—and killed the hare. I had been kneeling along the side of the building, in the shadows. Just as I stood to retrieve the hare, something caught my eye. I thought my mind was playing tricks, for the shadow of the roofline shifted—and changed shape! How can that be? It was not as when a cloud moves and shadows follow. This one, this shadow, *followed me.* I backed away from the building, but it spread across the ground like an inky dye, pursuing me. I-I tripped and fell on my back. The last thing I remember . . . so cold and the pain!" Callen clutched at his chest and looked into Jadiel's eyes, but he also looked past her, to something beyond, something frightening. "I swear it felt like a hand had grabbed my heart and squeezed the life out of me—"

Jadiel's voice came out a whisper. "The man we saw, dead in the road . . ."

Callen rubbed his forehead. "I'm so dizzy—and weak."

Jadiel rummaged through her satchel and found one of the last remaining apples. "Here." She handed the fruit to him and turned to see Ebed walking back to where Callen had lain. He seemed to be studying the ground, then raised his eyes and looked into the distance.

Callen's voice came out a whisper. "They called it the 'Golgoth,' those villagers near Rumble. They said it slips along the ground unnoticed, then rips your heart out." A moan grew in Callen's throat and Jadiel saw tears form in his eyes. "Jadiel, it has to be my fault. You were right and I didn't want to admit it. But something escaped from that vault in the mountains, and I fear those legends must have some truth in them. What if I accidently let this evil creature out of its prison—a monster that killed all those people long ago and was then captured by the king-priest of Antolae? What if those tales aren't mere legends or myths, but are true?"

Callen buried his head in his hands and sobbed. Jadiel put an arm around his back, feeling uneasy and fearful. She had tried these many days to shake off the memory of that icy chill she had felt while standing above the steps of the rock vault, and the eerie sensation that someone or something was following them. She didn't dare hold Callen's words true—for they portended unimaginable horror.

Huldah glared at the mirror, willing it to reveal Ka'rel's location. The crumpled missive lay at her feet on the bedchamber floor, but, for good measure, she trampled on it again. How could this have happened? How! Gilad of Wolcreek—dead! An unforeseen accident, they called it. What would she tell Ramah? Not that her daughter had any feelings for this suitor she had never met, but what were her chances of snaring another one? Especially if that brat Jadiel failed to return with the leaves . . .

Huldah ground her teeth so hard she felt bits of tooth grit slide over her tongue. *Jadiel!* That snot-faced kid had something to do with this. And so did her despicable father. Somehow they had killed Gilad, for how else could so accomplished a hunter succumb on a lonely road, with no witnesses or evidence of foul play?

She watched intently as the mirror shimmered with a dull green sheen, but no images rose to its surface. "Pig's breath! I should have paid the extra fifty silvers for the long-range model. This mirror is useless. Pah!"

She spat at the glass and watched as her own image reappeared, one that revealed more of her true ugliness than the last time she checked—only two hours ago. Time was running out. Even her strongest potions failed to mask most of her flaws now. Every muscle in her flaccid body jiggled with anger. She didn't dare let herself be seen by anyone—not even her daughters. Not after she caught the look on the cook's face yesterday morning at breakfast. The foolish woman's jaw hung open like a codfish, and then she dropped a pot of oats on the floor, mumbling apologies in an agitated flurry. Huldah surveyed the mess in her chamber— dirty dishes piled by the door, heaps of smelly, unwashed clothing draped over the furniture. Every so often, her daughters pounded the door, but she ignored their pitiful pleas for her to come out.

One peek through the closed curtains told her most of the field workers had fled the estate days ago. The neatly turned furrows were already beset with jumbles of weeds, plows lay abandoned between rows, and the trees in the orchard swelled with heavy boughs of ripe, unpicked fruit.

She could kill that brat for taking so long. A twisted smile lifted her sagging cheeks. Yes, she could—and she would—the moment those precious leaves were in her clutches. Jadiel's innocent face appeared in the mirror, conjured by Huldah's will. Those ruby lips, her unblemished skin, her long black hair that fell around her delicate shoulders. Huldah felt a scream gather in her throat like erupting lava. *It's not fair! Not fair!* All that beauty wasted on that dolt of a child. On one who neither deserved nor appreciated it.

Ka'rel was history, and good riddance. Let him live out his raptorial days eating smelly rodents. Once she killed Jadiel, the estate would be hers. Five more days until the full moon. Surely that brat was on her way back with the leaves, anxious to save her dear daddy's life. Huldah could wait five more days. And if the girl didn't show, she'd call all her powers to bear upon finding her.

She slumped in her overstuffed chair and smoothed out her wiry, lifeless hair. Yes, she would wait five days. But no longer.

Callen heard water before he saw it. The sound thrummed the ground under his boots as he clambered up another slick rock. Up ahead in the cloying, sticky mist, he watched Jadiel struggle with handholds, finally pulling herself onto a ledge on the mountain's flank with Ebed's assistance.

For two days they climbed higher and higher. The forests of alder and birch thinned as the temperature plummeted; the ground was blanketed with brittle, discarded leaves. Callen was glad for the wool cloaks they bought in Sherbourne, for they certainly needed them now. Yesterday afternoon, they took the packs off their mounts and let the animals go, watching until the beasts were out of sight. Ebed had assured them the beasts would find their way back to Sherbourne, where someone would care for them. Callen had been upset at the time, complaining they'd have to carry all their supplies on their backs. But he had to concede to the logic of Ebed's decision; the horse and mule would never have made it up these gargantuan crags.

The words of the scroll flitted in and out of his thoughts these past two days. *Despised, stricken, smitten, afflicted, bruised, carried away, wounded, snatched, emptied, restored to life.* Clearly, these depicted the mistreatment of some poor fellow, but why carve them into the bridge like a worthy design? It irked him that Ebed knew these words, and no doubt understood their implication. Why wouldn't he tell them their significance? Or maybe it didn't matter now. Ebed said he would lead them to the bridge—and supposedly to the trees Jadiel sought. Wasn't that what mattered?

Jadiel called down to Callen, patting the sloping ledge. "Come here. I'm taking a rest." He scrambled up a sharp crevasse, straddling the fissure with shaky legs and leaning hard into his walking stick. He looked up and saw Ebed vanish into gray just beyond Jadiel. The small hawk, which had been circling them the whole journey, flapped its wings as it alighted beside her. Callen frowned. Why wouldn't that bird fly away home?

Callen muttered, "I'm sure we're lost. He's leading us deep into trouble."

Jadiel dropped her head and sighed. "I wish you'd stop saying that."

"We're running out of food. It's freezing up here and we don't have warm enough bedding. If you haven't noticed, there's no real shelter anywhere around. At least a cave would provide some protection from the elements."

"Ebed says he knows the way. We're getting close."

Callen grunted. "Look, we're almost to the snow line. We'll be frozen icicles by the time we reach the land. Then what?"

Jadiel tightened her cloak around her neck as a bitter wind blew up from the reaches below. Callen strained to see down the canyon, to determine how far they had come this morning. He couldn't even tell the time of day, or how many hours had passed since they'd eaten their cold, meager breakfast of nuts and cheese. Since they left the crossroads and ventured northwest, they'd seen no one and no sign of wildlife—no tracks, no deer trails—nothing. Callen had never seen a land so inhospitable.

As he sat beside Jadiel, he listened to the moaning wind and what sounded like the rush of a waterfall. For hours, he had mulled over whether to tell Jadiel about the letter he posted in Sherbourne before they left that city. Would she be angry with him for writing her aunt Laera? Or would she be relieved that those she loved learned she was alive and well? He still didn't know if he should speak of it. Maybe his had been a hasty act, but once he'd heard those old men warn about the Land of Darkness, he thought someone should know where they were headed. Perhaps if they didn't return by the full moon as planned, Beren would send a search party out after them. Hopefully, his employer wouldn't find three frozen bodies lying among a pile of boulders.

Ebed emerged from the mist. "This way; the ruins of Antolae are close."

Callen stood and brushed off his cloak. He readjusted the pack and bow on his back. As he helped Jadiel to her feet, he wondered how Ebed could bear the cold with just that thin linen wrap. But the prophet seemed unbothered by the elements and had kept up a steady, unfaltering pace for two days now. Callen knew he should feel some gratitude for what Ebed had done. Jadiel said Ebed saved his life, that she saw the prophet lean over and revive him. But was that true? Callen remembered nothing but the cold, clammy sense of doom and that creeping shadow . . .

He shuddered and squeezed his eyes shut, forcing the images away and fighting the fear yearning to overtake his heart. He didn't want to worry Jadiel, but he knew someone was following them, stalking them. Perhaps it was only his railing guilt over opening that vault, but the sensation unnerved him, making him startle at every little sound. He kept spinning around, expecting to be attacked.

Callen followed Ebed and Jadiel around a corner of towering rock where the noise of water clamored in his ears. High on a ridge, a waterfall tumbled hundreds of feet in cascades, like a messy braid down the mountain's spine, emptying into a roaring river. He stepped carefully along the slippery plateau of wet, pitted rock until he met up with Ebed and Jadiel at the edge of the rapids. A fine web of mist settled on Jadiel's hair. The hawk swooped low to perch on her shoulder, pearls of water dripping from its beak. It nuzzled and edged its way under her cloak.

"You're not thinking of crossing this?" Callen asked. Water churned and spilled over boulders, moving at a fast and frantic clip. Twigs and debris tumbled in the current. If there was any safe place to ford, he couldn't spot one. The river wasn't all that wide but was certainly uncrossable.

"What now?" Jadiel asked Ebed.

Ebed looked at Callen and smiled. He pointed across the river to what looked like an old cart road leading up a hill from the south. The mist lifted enough for Callen to make out the shapes of structures, perhaps buildings long abandoned. The stonework looked like broken, jagged teeth against the dark background of sky.

"The ruins of Antolae," Ebed said. "And the way in to Araf'el."

As Ebed took a step toward the raging river, Callen raised his hand in protest. "Now I know you're crazy. What do you plan to do—swim to the other side? You'll be swept away before you get halfway across!"

But Ebed only chuckled as he turned to Callen and took the walking stick from his hand. Callen's face loosened in wonder as Ebed touched the water with the stick and instantly the mighty flow abated, exposing the tops of previously submerged boulders. Now a jagged pathway of stepping-stones lay before them, spanning from one side of the river to the other. The waterfall still roared in the distance, and cold spray rained as Callen followed his companions, stepping from rock to rock, securing each footstep with care. One look at the icy water set his head reeling.

As Callen's boot touched dirt on the other side, Ebed handed the stick back to him and wiped damp matted hair from his eyes.

"How—how did you do that?" Called asked, watching the surge of water resume and the stepping-stones vanish under a powerful current.

"Faith," he said simply.

"Faith? What has faith got to do with it?" he grumbled, mesmerized by the sight of the last boulder swallowed up by the rising waters.

Jadiel tugged on Callen. "Look! I see the city."

Ebed was already cresting the top of the hill when Callen wrenched his eyes from the river and turned. The fog thinned and the air smelled drier as he trudged up the dusty road. Suddenly, he stopped and dropped down to examine the ground.

At his feet lay the edging of a cobbled road made of ochre stone. He brushed dirt in a semicircle before him and exposed a beautiful pattern of brick. As he stood back up, a heavy sense of foreboding came over him, making him want to run away.

He inspected the crumbling buildings of a once-great city. He could tell from the detailed scrollwork of the remnants of inlaid wood that the city must have boasted great craftsmen. The architecture of the crumbling edifices spoke of elegant design and sophistication.

"Antolae," Ebed said, walking down the middle of the wide lane toward a broken, chipped fountain. "The city of the great king-priest."

Jadiel went up to Ebed, who had stopped at the obsidian fountain. Etched into the glasslike rock were intricate whorls of wind and wave and clouds.

"A wondrous city it was, in its time. A land of prosperity and peace in olden days."

Callen couldn't shake the chill that danced down his back. He looked into the eyes of his companions and wondered how they could be so relaxed. Jadiel seemed almost excited to be here. Callen had told her what the old men of Wentwater had said, that the land was dangerous. And hadn't Ebed also warned him that day in Sherbourne, saying he risked his life by seeking the bridge? Yet here was this lunatic prophet—about to stroll nonchalantly into such a fearsome place.

Jadiel sat on the sculpted rock ledge of the fountain. "What happened to this city? Is it also under a curse?"

"No," Ebed answered. "But after its king died and lay buried in the King's Plain, neighboring bands began raiding Antolae, with one skirmish after another. Families left and the population dwindled over time. Without a king to lead them, the people grew fearful and eventually abandoned the city. This was centuries before the cursing of Araf'el."

Ebed continued walking along the lane. In the distance, Callen saw what appeared to be an iron gate, swinging loosely on a wooden post. The cobbles underfoot ended just as he heard a soft, high-pitched voice float on a sudden lift of wind. He jerked around, searching for the owner of the voice, but the sound merely tickled his ears and fled away.

Ebed stopped at the gate. Callen narrowed his eyes at the sight before him and another shiver raced across his neck.

Just beyond the gate, a blackness pooled in the air, strangely swirling and viscous, and too opaque to peer through. Jadiel stopped beside him and grabbed his sleeve.

"I don't want to go in there. It's creepy." She craned her head toward the gate. "Do you hear that?"

"What?" Callen asked, straining to listen.

"I hear bells. And a chicken—I think. Don't you hear that?"

A menagerie of sounds floated out from the soupy darkness, soft voices talking and laughing, boots clicking on stone, sheep baaing, horses neighing.

Jadiel gasped. "There are people in there—and animals!"

Ebed blocked the gate as Jadiel looked about to run through it and into the gloom on the other side.

"Jadiel, listen to me. Do you remember what I said—that the darkness is not outside but inside?"

Jadiel nodded. Callen's eyes caught on an arm appearing out of the darkness.

"Callen!" Ebed's voice was sharp. "Pay attention to how you listen."

With difficulty, Callen pulled his gaze from the gloom and focused on Ebed's stern face. A stupor settled over him, distracting his mind and making it hard to concentrate. He shook his head, trying to clear the wooziness.

"You may see what seems to be an ordinary village, its residents living ordinary lives, going about their daily affairs. But, know this: Araf'el is under a curse of darkness. Those living here do not know they are cursed. Only those outside this land know that people in the Land of Darkness are forever trapped and cannot get out. These cursed ones do not even know they live in darkness, that they should have died long ago."

"Are they bad people?" Jadiel asked.

"If you asked them, they'd tell you otherwise. They believe they are good, decent folk. But they are walking dead." He added, "They are dead in their sins."

"You say this with warning in your voice," Callen took a step backward, wondering what Ebed meant by that last remark. "And if they are trapped, won't we suffer the same fate?"

"An ancient prophet said, 'The people that have walked in darkness have seen a great light. They that dwell in the land of the shadow of death, upon them hath the light shined.'" Ebed sighed and swung open the gate. "They had their chance, but rejected the light. For 'a child has been born to us, a son is given to us; authority rests upon his shoulders.'"

The boar's words resounded in Callen's mind: *The kings await a prince. Fathers await an heir. Captives await a deliverer.* His heart skipped a beat. *The One to come.*

Ebed pushed open the rusty gate and Jadiel walked through and stopped on the other side. Callen watched in fascination as wisps of darkness danced in the air around her, never touching her skin. "You mean when the subjects of that king attacked the bridge builder—and destroyed the bridge?" she asked.

Callen frowned. Somehow the people of Araf'el had seen the promised heir, the bridge builder's son. And if that parable Ebed told was true, then they massed together and killed him. But why did the boar give him the vision of the dry bones and tell him the kings are still waiting to be revived? Surely that event was yet future. And if the heir was dead, then what? What did the Keeper mean by *the holy seed is its stump*? How can a seed *be* a stump? Callen's head swam in confusion.

"Yes, now your eyes are starting to see," Ebed said. "But come, we must not tarry here. Stay close to me and do not allow anything to distract you from your purpose."

"What purpose?" Jadiel asked, waving a hand through the air as the shadows encircled her. She took a few hesitant steps into the murkiness and nearly vanished from sight. "This is strange, Ebed; I can see the people and the town, but they don't seem to see me. They walk past me as if I'm invisible."

Ebed ushered Callen in through the gate. "Our purpose is to get to the chasm on the other side of the town as quickly as possible. We will not be welcome here. Hurry."

Callen took a deep breath and shut out the sounds of the village as he entered through the gate. His boots touched a dirt path once more and the air grew as still as death. He steeled his nerves and plunged ahead into shadow, trailed by a presentiment of evil. As he came alongside Jadiel, his jaw dropped. Ebed's words fell on the hushed air like a pebble dropped down a deep well. The blackness sucked up the sound so quickly, Callen was unsure they had been uttered aloud.

"Woe to those who trade darkness for light!"

THIRTY

"SHE'S ALIVE, thank the heavens!"

Laera rushed down the stairs of the root cellar, where Beren was hefting a musty bag of potatoes onto his shoulder. He stopped and let out a low breath.

"Who? Who's alive?"

Laera waved a sheet of parchment in the air and nearly jumped into his arms. "Jadiel! Oh, I could kiss the ground."

Laera could barely make out Beren's perturbed face in the cellar's dim light. He set the potatoes down on the coal bin and took the letter from her hand.

Laera paced as he read. Jadiel alive! For weeks her heart would not be consoled. Nor could she constrain her anger. She had mustered every bit of resolve to hold back from driving to Northvale to do something hurtful to that witch. But each time the thought tempted her, she'd recall Huldah's threat. She never told Beren of her encounter and feared if she took matters into her own hands she'd end up dead like M'lynn. But now! Hope coursed through her veins.

"Callen, is it? How odd for him to have found the lass."

"Odd, no, my love. It's heaven's doing, can't you see?"

"Appears to be, that. But what is this nonsense about a tree with magic leaves? And a place called the Land of Darkness. Where in creation would that be? In all my years . . ."

Laera tugged on Beren's shirt. "Callen expects to be at the manor in four days. We must go, and take as many brave friends as we can gather. You read for yourself—he says Huldah plans to kill Ka'rel . . ."

"But, Laera, no one's seen hide nor hair of him in weeks. He's run off, no doubt, in search of the girl. Surely, he won't return empty-handed."

Laera sighed deeply. "If only he had told us where he went, then we could get word to him. Do you know anything of his family, where he may have gone?"

Beren shook his head and ran a hand through Laera's hair in a sympathetic gesture. "He could be at the ends of the world by now, love. But, I agree—we mustn't let Jadiel return to face Huldah alone—even if she is with Callen. The lad's no match for such a creature." Beren tugged on his beard. "Ah, it's heaven's kind mercy that she's in Callen's care. He won't let the lass come to harm. Don't you fret now."

A rush of relief caused Laera's knees to buckle, and she fell into Beren's hefty arms, unable to stop the flood of tears from gushing out.

"There, there," Beren said in a soothing tone. "Our niece is safe. And I'll wager Ka'rel will learn the news somehow and return to her. She means the world to him."

Laera dried her face on Beren's shirt as he patted her head. He stepped back and lifted the sack of potatoes with a grunt. "Well, I wondered why the lad had been gone so long. He set off to find a bridge and now he's looking for a tree."

A small chuckle escaped Laera's mouth as she followed Beren up the cellar steps and into the cool afternoon sunlight. "And acquired a tag-along girl in the bargain."

She stood and watched Beren walk through the herb garden and in through the kitchen door. *The Land of Darkness.* Just the name sent a shudder of fear through her weary bones. *"Heaven, help Jadiel,"* she prayed. *"And please find Ka'rel!"*

The one who for so long was mere shadow and motion now grew substantial and took heft and shape. He had found the one with the bow, but his victory had been short-lived. Another had intruded and yanked him from his quarry. Oh, he well knew *that* one, disguised or not. He'd know that one anywhere. But what was he doing, traveling with a pair of humans? And, more puzzling, why had that one let him go? He had felt not just power but recognition in the touch.

The evil one nursed his wounds deep in the shadows of rock, for he had been fully joined with the human when that powerful hand ripped him away. In a turmoil of heat and pain, he slunk across bunchgrass and gravelly ground to rest in a thicket of brambles. There he tended his wounds, gathering the essence of life from what little he could scrounge—from shrubs and beetles and worms in the packed dirt beneath his form. Small bits of life that took effort to absorb but finally nourished him enough to allow him to coalesce and stand upright.

Their trail was easy to follow. Up, up, and up the mighty mountain, hunched over and sniffing, he latched onto the stench of human sweat lingering in the air, a strand of scent that seeped through the cracks in boulders. All the way, the evil one pondered and plotted. Entering Araf'el would be to his advantage. A place of traps and treachery, of easy minds to lead in conspiracy. He'd done it once before; he would do it again.

Something like a laugh rumbled from his chest. The irony of it. Just as centuries ago, the scene would replay again, but this time his nemesis would lose. Every smoldering wick would be stamped out, every crushed reed broken. The sleeping kings would die in their sleep, their rotted bones left to bleach white and grow brittle, disintegrating to dust. Their promise would die with them, forever moldering under a blood-stained ground.

He reached a plateau, then turned a corner and faced a swath of roaring water. He waded through, feeling the current tug at his legs but catching on nothing. He pondered the odd sensation of water: its cold bite, its strange consistency, the way its transparency distorted what lay beneath.

He had never been to Antolae—only read of it in the mind of the king that day on the plain. Even in the midst of bloody battle, the king's thoughts had dwelt ever homeward, pulling him in distraction before heaven narrowed his concentration and granted him unwarranted victory. As the evil one trekked up the wide dusty road, it took little imagination to rebuild the abandoned city, erect in his mind the towers and gates and courtyard as he passed them, barely noting the appearance of cobbles underfoot. He hesitated at the wrought-iron gate, letting his fingers run along the cool metal and already noticing the change. He tapped finger to metal, felt resistance, hardness, temperature. Then, he pushed open the gate and entered.

He watched as a village materialized before him like an apparition. Haze dissolved into clarity, with a bright sun glimmering off puddles in the street, off the shiny nails of cartwheels as wagons rolled down the lane, off the metal trappings of the horses ridden by peasants and farmers. The gate swung closed noiselessly behind him as he entered the town in the glare of a hot summer day. Heat beat on his shoulders, and he smiled at the way the warmth penetrated his shirt and touched his now-human skin. A sensation gripped his stomach. Hunger. He laughed again. He had forgotten food and ale and sensual pleasures.

With a deep breath came aromas too many to count, and his mind swooned in memory. The Unnamable One had erred. He had foolishly thought humans would feel gratitude for the generous abundance of delectable gifts he provided without reservation. He had thought by giving them free will they would turn their hearts to him. How ludicrous an idea! No wonder so many of the evil one's own kind had forsaken their proper place and latched onto human existence, with its wondrous sensations and yearnings.

But his yearning for revenge surpassed those worldly temptations, giving him perspective and sobriety. He knew he had little time. He could not allow anything to distract him. Why *that* one had returned to Araf'el was a mystery. But whatever compelled him to return held little import. The evil one knew he had to act quickly. No matter. These lost souls were putty in his hands. They would do his bidding.

And so he began. In only moments, faces turned and gazed at him, spotting him suddenly in the middle of the lane. Riders reined in their horses and shopkeepers spilled out their doors into the street, summoned, curious, and expectant. Young and old gathered to listen, aware of a growing unrest in their hearts and unable to identify its source. A seed of panic, of fear, of threat, disrupting their complacent lives and ripping their veil of ignorance.

Oh, how easy to mold their minds.

Jadiel grabbed the sleeve of Ebed's tunic and clung tightly. The air had the quality of a dream, thick, like moving through water. The village blurred in the strange half-light, neither night nor day, but not dark. As she stepped into the muddied street, the darkness had thinned, leaving an odd haze. Like looking up from the bottom of her pond to the wavering sky above. Callen stood beside her, his mouth gaping. The village looked like Kettlebro, but of an earlier time, perhaps. People walked by them, everyday sort of folk, dressed in simple garb and going about their business. Some nodded perfunctorily, but most ignored their arrival. Many wore peculiar clothing, robes and long tunics, with strange hairstylings and jewelry adorning their necks and wrists. And others appeared to be wanderers or farmers or soldiers. As if this town held captive people from every land and time in history.

Ebed started down an uneven narrow lane, toward what looked like the center of town. Shops lined the lane, made of dull clay, and looked more functional than ornamental. A wooden boardwalk ran along each side. And the people moved about in a slow, perfunctory manner, almost as if they were sleepwalking. Jadiel tried to form a picture of their inner darkness. How could you be blind and still see your world? Or did Ebed mean that their dark minds and hearts prevented them from seeing the truth of their captivity?

"Keep up," Ebed said, eyes focused ahead. Jadiel let loose his sleeve and turned to Callen.

Callen leaned into her and whispered. "Those old men I spoke with in Sherbourne said they never age or die. They just wander about in gloom, never knowing they are trapped."

Jadiel looked around furtively, but no one seemed to hear Callen speak. He recited in a whisper, "'Their memory perishes from the earth and they have no name in the street. They are thrust from light into darkness and driven out of the world. They have no offspring or descendent among their people.' That's what they said. Can it be true?"

"I don't know, but this place spooks me. The sooner we leave, the happier I'll be."

Callen nodded in agreement. They hurried after Ebed, who kept up a quick pace, making turns as if he had been here before. Jadiel breathed hard; the thick air caught in her chest and gave her the sensation of suffocating.

"Look. Those people." Jadiel pointed as the villagers stopped abruptly and raised their heads as if hearing something.

"What is it? What are they doing?" she asked.

Callen shrugged. They slowed as those around them abandoned their brooms and carts and even left their sheep and goats to stray while they heeded some unvoiced call. A crowd formed in the lane, unspeaking, eyes glazed, all turning in one direction, back toward the entrance to the town.

"Come, Jadiel. Ebed is way ahead. Don't mind them." Callen put a hand to his head and faltered.

"What is it? Are you ill?" As she spoke these words, her head spun and her eyelids grew heavy. When she forced her eyes open, Ebed was standing beside her. How had he come to her so quickly? She had seen him turn a corner just seconds ago. The sky grew dark and clouds melted into a pool of silver. A foul-smelling wind kicked up, reminding her of the putrid odors of the King's Plain. She strained to see as a throb assaulted the backs of her eyes.

Ebed's voice sounded distant. "Callen, Jadiel. The darkness is an illusion. These people have chosen darkness, yet they could leave at any time. Don't be fooled."

Jadiel looked in Ebed's eyes and her head stopped spinning. He added, "When a person wanders into Araf'el, he grows deluded. The darkness he first sees eventually dissipates, for those around him ignore their peril and convince him of light. Surely, he thinks, these people can't *all* be wrong. Surely *I* must be the one who is mistaken. Such is the power of the masses." He took Jadiel's wrist, and his touch was warm and comforting. Jadiel grasped his hand tightly.

Callen huddled closer. "I think I am sick . . ."

Ebed pressed his palm to Callen's forehead and Callen let out a deep breath. "There is much evil at work here, and not just from the villagers. You sense him following you."

Callen's eyes widened. Jadiel's stomach clenched in fear. What did Ebed mean?

The color drained from Callen's face. "We'll never escape!"

Ebed's expression showed no sign of concern. He looked in Callen's eyes and spoke sternly. "The danger lies in your heart."

Callen's eyes sparked. "You said that to me, back in Sherbourne."

Ebed nodded. "The heart is treacherous, and men love the darkness rather than light because their deeds are evil. All who do evil hate the light and avoid it, so that their deeds may not be exposed. But those who do what is true come to the light so that their good works may be seen."

Jadiel spoke and her words were swallowed up as they left her mouth. "I don't get it. How do you fight the darkness?" Her heart sank in hopelessness. Now the sky had turned black and a thick mist gathered around her, occluding her vision. A sense of melancholy engulfed her as she squeezed Ebed's hand fiercely.

Callen muttered, defeat in his voice. "Then we're doomed. There's no way out."

"That is what the evil one wants you to think. His lies fill the land like a choking vapor, blanketing their minds, stopping up their ears so they cannot hear, blinding their eyes so they cannot see, hardening their hearts so they cannot feel, making it impossible for them to be healed. You must resist."

Ebed gestured for them to follow, but Callen stood steadfast in place. "I can't . . ."

Jadiel tried to lift her leg. "Ebed, my feet won't move." A noise behind her drew her attention. She turned her head and saw a mob of people, countless numbers filling the lane, running toward them.

To her horror, Callen turned and began walking toward those approaching. Jadiel sucked in her breath as fear made her heart race. The faces of those coming at them reflected anger and hate and fury.

Jadiel grabbed Callen's arm with all her might and pulled hard. "Callen! Run!"

Darkness engulfed Jadiel as she spun around with Callen in tow. He shook his head, breaking the spell, and met her eyes and nodded. They sprinted after Ebed down the lane and around the corner, hearing jeers and shouts close behind them. Ebed stopped in a shadowed doorway and held up his hand.

Jadiel listened as the mob noise escalated, but from the pitch of the voices, their pursuers appeared to have stopped at the corner. She couldn't make out their words, but their hysteria flooded the lane. She looked at Ebed. He seemed calm and unruffled.

"This will detain them awhile. Callen," Ebed said, putting his hands on Callen's shoulders. "Will you trust me?"

To Jadiel's shock, Callen pushed Ebed away. "Trust you? You brought us here, to this insane place. A land of darkness with no way out. Now I know you are mad! We should have never listened to you. Jadiel will never return home in time to save her father, and it's all your fault! All your empty promises and confident talk and stupid parables. I'm sick of it! I'm sick of you! Just leave us alone and go away!"

Callen slumped to the ground and banged his head against the stucco wall of the building. A lump formed in Jadiel's throat. How could Callen say such things? Was he right? What if they were trapped here forever, just like all the others?

A groan escaped her mouth and despair swallowed up her last vestige of hope. She would never again see her father, her home. Never. Doomed to wander these streets. And just like all the others, she would probably forget she was trapped, forget about the darkness, and live out her days in denial and delusion. Oh, why had they come here?

Callen was right. There was no bridge, no terebinth trees, and no beautiful kingdom waiting for her on some sun-drenched hill.

Ebed had led them to their doom. She should never have trusted him!

The pain settled heavily on Jadiel's heart and she wept in misery.

Callen raised his head. He realized he had nodded off and had no idea how long he had sat huddled there, his head buried between his knees. Beside him, Jadiel knelt in silence, wretchedness written across her face as she stared into the soupy haze. Maybe it was the middle of the night—who could tell? A quick glance told him Ebed was gone. He grunted. Some surprise. The ugly, repulsive prophet had abandoned them to their fate. Ebed had known what danger awaited them and he didn't care. Perhaps they weren't the first ones he had lured to this place and forsaken. What perverse pleasure did Ebed get from that? Maybe he was in league with that evil being that hunted them.

Callen chuckled and realized he didn't even care. So what? Maybe he should welcome death at the hand of that creature. Better than wandering in darkness for eternity. One thing was certain—he would never get out. There was no way in the world anyone could escape the Land of Darkness, despite what Ebed said. *"They could leave anytime they wanted."* Sure. Just walk right out.

Callen stiffened, then jumped to his feet. Well, why not?

Jadiel turned and looked up. "Hey, where are you going? Don't leave me!"

Callen pulled Jadiel to standing. "Then come. Ebed said anyone can leave whenever they want. So, I'm leaving!"

Jadiel hesitated, then nodded. "I guess I'm coming. You were right. There is no bridge. And I'm not going to find those leaves here. I may as well just go home—if we really can get out of here."

"And, then again, Ebed may have been lying about that as well."

Misery seeped out of Jadiel's voice. "Where is Ebed? Don't you think we should wait until he returns? What if those people spot us and chase after us again?" She took a few steps out into the gloomy street. An eerie quiet draped the village, like a thick fog.

Callen ventured out and joined her. "Where is everyone? Something's wrong. And I'm sure that prophet has something to do with this."

"Maybe we should wait," Jadiel said, stepping back toward the shadowed doorway.

"Fine. You wait. I'm leaving. Let Ebed save you."

Callen strode back the way they'd come, watching for any signs of movement in the murk around him. He heard footsteps and looked behind him. Jadiel ran up to him, breathless.

"Wait, I'm coming."

He took her hand and together they wended through the now-deserted streets back to the place they had entered. The silence hung ominously around him; he sensed someone watching, and it sent a shiver across the back of his neck. Callen stopped where he guessed the gate would be. "Well, seems simple enough. Let's just go through."

Callen took a few steps and felt around with his hands. The edge of the town was drenched in such dark pitch that Callen could not even see his fingers in front of his face. He stumbled over a rock and caught his balance, but his groping hands found nothing upon which to light. He fought a nameless, irrational fear that made his legs quake.

Jadiel's voice sounded muted, as if coming from a deep cave. "Did you find the gate yet? Do we even have to go out that way?"

Callen snapped back. "How should I know? I thought all we had to do was walk out."

"Well, then let's just walk out—"

"I'm trying to!"

He felt Jadiel's hands touching his shirt. She stopped and drew close. "Ebed said something at the crossroads when you were off hunting. How the people look for light, but find only darkness. That they grope for the wall like the blind and grope as if they had no eyes. As dead men in a desolate place." He felt her shudder. She hung on to him as he fumbled around, feeling his way and finding nothing.

After a few minutes Jadiel spoke. "There's got to be a trick to it."

"Trick, nothing. It's just a lie." Callen moaned in exasperation. "This is hopeless. We may as well go back where we can at least see."

"Remember what Ebed said about unseen things? That we have to have faith in what we can't see—that our eyes and hearts may deceive us, but the unseen things are eternal."

Callen pulled Jadiel back into the lane and found her face in the dim light. A tremor of relief brought calm back to his heart as he distanced himself from the boundary of the town. "And how is that supposed to help us?"

Jadiel shrugged. "I'm not sure. Maybe we don't have enough faith that we can leave. We don't believe it."

"Well, you can't *make* yourself have faith. You can't make yourself believe something you just don't believe. That's stupid."

Callen let his eyes light on Jadiel's and he felt instant remorse. "I'm sorry, Jadiel. I've failed you. I wanted to get you home to your father and now . . ." Tears forced their way out of the corners of his eyes. "I'm sorry for being so rude and angry. I'm just so frustrated and I'm scared . . . after what happened on the prairie . . ."

Jadiel put her arm around Callen's waist and leaned into him. "I understand. It's okay. Let's just stick together and try to figure something else out. I think we should go back to that doorway and see if Ebed shows up."

He felt the last thread of frustration snap. He had tried so hard to control his choices, his emotions. Failure sat heavy on him as he realized he was completely at a loss. He had nowhere to turn; he'd run out of ideas. If he could just surrender somehow, that's what he'd do. He mouthed the words to no one. *I give up.* He felt his heart drain of all determination. "If that's what you want, then let's go."

Callen walked in silence with Jadiel, glad to be out of that suffocating blackness. He didn't want to admit how terrified he had been in that eerie absence of light. It was as if the world had vanished altogether, leaving nothing but a vast, hungry emptiness that hollowed out his gut. That sense of emptiness had frightened him more than anything, even more than his recent brush with death.

As they arrived at the building where they had last spoken to Ebed, Callen strained to see into the shadows. There Ebed stood, calm and composed, in the doorway. Ebed seemed neither surprised nor relieved to see them. As if he knew they'd be back. Callen let out a big sigh.

Maybe Ebed was right. Maybe there was great darkness in his own heart, some nebulous danger inside him that he needed to face. But how would he know? He was a good person, not evil. Surely, many of those wandering Araf'el were good people too. Why should they be cursed? Was it their fault? It seemed all those people were being punished for things that they had no control over. They were under a curse they didn't deserve. Wasn't there any way to be free of it?

This time Jadiel didn't run to Ebed and throw her arms around him. She stood quietly at Callen's side, looking defeated and heartsick.

Ebed caught her eye and smiled. Callen grunted. "*What is he smiling about? Happy we're so miserable?*"

"Well, my friends. You are now ready." Ebed's expression puzzled Callen. Rather than exuding victory and arrogance—as Callen expected—the prophet's gaze held only warmth and compassion as he turned and reached out an inviting hand.

"Ready for what?" Jadiel asked in a weak and sorrowful voice.

Ebed grasped their hands in his.

"Why, to cross the bridge."

• PART FIVE •

"Long Ago, a Wealthy Landowner Had Need to Travel to a Faraway Country . . ."

THIRTY-ONE

JADIEL RAN as hard as she could, but with each turn she fell farther behind. Her boots were soggy from thrashing across the puddles that marred the lanes. Mud splattered her leggings, and the satchel on her back weighed her down as if filled with rocks. Ebed had told them to hurry, but she couldn't keep up. She stopped at the last row of small cottages and doubled over, catching her breath. Something moved in the sky, shadowed by cloud. Jadiel peered through the mist as the little hawk floated on a draft and landed with a thud on her shoulder.

"It's you! I thought I'd never see you again. Why did you come here?" She stroked the hawk's head as it nuzzled against her neck. "You should have stayed down on the prairie." The hawk gripped her shoulder with its tiny claws, and Jadiel stifled a giggle. "You're tickling me."

She heard Callen call her from down the road. The little sod cottages sat in a neat row, with flowers in bloom and fronted by manicured lawns. The air was still and ominously silent; not even a bird chattered from the trees lining the lane. Back home, she would have considered this a beautiful scene. But here—an under-tone of illusion tainted all she saw. And where were the people?

When she caught up to Callen and Ebed, she got her answer.

At the far side of the road, beyond the last home, lay a field of overgrown weeds. Beyond that, barely visible through the haze, a mountainous ridge of jagged peaks formed a semicircle far in the distance. But between the field and the mountains a chasm stretched, wide and menacing. Even from where Jadiel stood, she could tell that treacherous depths awaited any who fell into that giant maw of doom. The huge rent in the earth ran as far as the eye could see, and Jadiel could hear and smell moving water leagues below in the canyon made by the great fissure. It was as if a giant had split the land asunder with a mighty axe.

And blocking the gaping chasm stood all the inhabitants of the Land of Darkness.

Jadiel quailed and clung to Ebed as he faced the mob. Their faces churned with malice, and they waved pitchforks and shovels in the air.

Jadiel whispered, "Why are they so hateful? We haven't done anything to offend them."

Callen laid a hand on her shoulder, and she felt him shudder.

Ebed's voice reflected calm as he gazed out at the crush of people. "Because they know there is a way out, and they don't want you to find it."

"But why?" Jadiel asked.

"Because they refuse to take the steps to freedom themselves, they block the way to any who would dare to do so. They hate the truth, even though the truth would set them free."

"What truth?" Callen asked.

Ebed's face radiated a fierce intensity that startled Jadiel. "That there is a bridge spanning eternity. That they murdered the heir of the great king and feel no remorse. That all they have to do is open their eyes and they will see."

Ebed stepped forward, and Jadiel gave Callen a grim look. "They'll kill him!"

The mob moved toward Ebed as one. Someone picked up a rock and hurled it, just missing Ebed's shoulder.

"Do you come at me with shovels and picks? When I have walked among you and done nothing to merit your hate?"

An outbreak of yelling rolled like a renegade wave over the mob. "You think that disguise fools us? We know who you are!"

Another called out, "Why did you return? We thought we were rid of you—"

"Did you come to taunt us again?" An old woman waved a horse-whip in his direction. "To denounce us with more of your curses?"

Jadiel could barely hear Ebed over the roar of the crowd. Many hurled shouts of accusation at him, and a frustrating feeling of powerlessness held Jadiel in its grip. "Callen, we have to do something."

Ebed took three more steps toward the surging crowd. "Where is your leader? Too afraid to come out of hiding?"

The sea of bodies swarmed and parted, and a man of indeterminable age stepped out and faced Ebed. Jadiel gasped. His features were dark and blurry, nearly formless, and his black hair fell about his shoulders in a shimmer. Jadiel couldn't make out his face but sensed something thoroughly evil about him. An icy pang wrenched her stomach and she wrapped her arms around her waist in pain. Then she sucked air in recognition.

This was the exact sensation she had felt when Callen opened the vault in the mountain. And the same blast of evil she had encountered when she had looked in the mirror in Ethryn, and when her mirror cracked by the creek. All those warnings and fears and ancient legends crashed upon her and she fell to the ground, every muscle in her body shaking with terror. Callen dropped down beside her and wrapped shaky arms around her shoulders. She felt his pounding heart against her back.

All the blood left Jadiel's face in a rush. The archivist in Ethryn had said these beings were from another realm, and they had wiped out armies and nations using supernatural power. What in the world was Ebed thinking to challenge this one?

The dark man took a stand before Ebed and lifted his head proudly. He opened his mouth to speak and his words bellowed across the field and echoed through the canyon behind him.

"You were foolish to bring those humans here. Now you are all trapped and will serve me forever."

The whip of power and authority behind Ebed's words surprised Jadiel. "No, it is you who are the fool. As you slept away the ages of time in your prison, you underestimated the power of the High One. You failed to grasp his mercy and love for his people."

Ebed nodded for Jadiel and Callen to follow. Jadiel cringed as she walked through the parting mob, expecting hands to grab her or a shovel to land on her head. But the villagers only cursed and grumbled as the three passed through the angry throng and stopped at the edge of the chasm.

Jadiel dared to look into the bottomless depths. Fear clenched her throat in a viselike grip. A few loose rocks tumbled down, bouncing off the cliff walls until their ricocheting grew faint and then silent. The hawk craned its neck to see, and then buried itself under Jadiel's hair. The sky lightened enough for Jadiel to view the other side of the rift, causing her to gasp in wonder. Apparently, the mob of people saw it too, for, behind her, she heard sounds of awe and surprise.

Callen put a protective arm around her as the dark man drew near to Ebed. Jadiel whispered. "Do you see it, Callen? The great city shining on that hill?"

Callen nodded and stared at the crevasse. The span of the chasm stretched over a league. Jadiel fought the fear rising in her heart. She glanced at Callen and they shared an unspoken thought. Ebed had said he was taking them to the bridge. So, where was it?

Ebed pointed a finger at the dark leader. "I have the authority to bind you and return you to your cell. But I choose instead to leave you here, to wander the darkness until the end of time. This will be your imprisonment and your chains of judgment."

The dark leader laughed and then stopped when Ebed took a step toward the edge. "Hah!" he said. "And what do you plan to do? Throw yourself into the canyon below? Or sprout wings and fly? Perhaps you could manage that stunt, but what of your charges? Will you leave them behind?"

"They will accompany me," Ebed said evenly.

His words evoked raucous laughter from the crowd.

The dark leader pointed a finger at the prophet. "You are trapped here—along with all the others. But first, I will make you pay for the years of imprisonment . . ."

A crack of lightning rent the sky in two. A whorl of agitated cloud spit fire and flaming, oozing rock down upon Ebed. Jadiel screamed and covered her head. The grass erupted in flames, sparking and sputtering around her feet. Callen threw his cloak over their heads as they huddled; pellets of hard rock rained down on their backs, and the heat of the fires ignited the hem of Jadiel's shirt. Jadiel slapped at the flame.

"We'll be burned up! Ebed, help!"

From under the burning cloak, surrounded by choking smoke and ash, Jadiel heard Ebed yell. She could not make out his strange words and dared not peek out from under their makeshift tent. But his words reverberated in power, void of fear, and as those words filled the air, they loosened the very sky, and the ground rumbled and quaked.

When the battering of rocks ceased, Jadiel heard screams and cries of anguish around her. Callen tugged at the scorched cloak, and they ventured a look.

"What happened?" she whispered, staring at the hordes of people, their arms outstretched before them, running in mayhem.

Jadiel saw dozens of villagers run headlong into the chasm and fall, screaming as they plunged down to the ravine. Others clawed and scratched at one another, yelling in panic and fear.

"That evil man made the sky rain fire and rocks. But we're safe, Jadiel." Even though the onslaught of elements had stopped, the residents of the land seemed not to notice. They kept rushing about in panic, directionless and confused.

Ebed stood in his same place and faced the dark leader. "Now, return to your darkness. May it prove as dark as the pit of your heart."

The smirk of vengeance left the evil one's face. He grabbed at his cheeks, trying to hold the skin together with frantic fingers. "NO! What have you done to me?" He hurled a scream into the air and the sound stabbed Jadiel's gut. She clung hard to Callen as the dark man faded and merged into shadow, losing shape and substance as a swirl of emptiness sucked him out of sight.

Ebed came over and Jadiel asked, "Where did he go? Did you destroy him?"

The prophet shook his head. "Here he will remain. Among others cursed by darkness." Jadiel watched the crowd. The villagers whimpered and moaned; many fell to the ground and begged for help. Ebed waved an arm in their direction; the crying lessened and then stopped. A hush fell over all. They turned their gazes toward the prophet as he stood at the edge of the precipice.

Ebed turned to Jadiel. "It's time. We must go."

Callen gripped Jadiel's arm. "Go? Where?" he said.

Ebed pointed to the mountains across the ravine. Then, without a moment's hesitation, he took a step out into midair.

Jadiel gasped. Ebed stood suspended in the air, two feet out from the edge of the cliff, his sandals resting on nothing.

Suddenly, the crowd murmured, and once more Jadiel felt angry gazes upon her.

"Come, Callen, we better hurry." She tugged on his sleeve and approached the edge of the cliff, stepping carefully through the scorched grass.

"No way!" he said.

"Callen," Ebed called over. "You must stand firm in the faith, or you will not stand at all. Step out onto the bridge."

"I can't see anything. Are you crazy?"

"Stop looking with your eyes and see with eyes of faith. The things unseen are eternal."

Ebed looked at Callen with warmth radiating from his scarred face.

"Will you not trust me, Callen? Just this once?"

Something amazing happened within Jadiel's heart and mind. She stared at Ebed, struck with realization. The man she had seen in the mirror, radiant and beautiful, stood before her with his hand outstretched. She looked beyond the scars and deformities and saw, beneath, the beauty of his spirit. His was the face she knew so well. Knew to be a face full of honor and love and truth.

Every last vestige of doubt vanished, and her heart flooded with assurance and peace.

Without a moment's hesitation, Jadiel stepped out into the air next to Ebed. The little hawk edged over to her shoulder, then soared up and circled her. A great screech escaped from its throat, and Jadiel could almost feel the bird's weightless joy. The prophet smiled at Jadiel, then turned his back to Callen and began walking across the chasm.

Jadiel yelled to Callen, her face tingling with excitement and relief. "What are you waiting for?"

"I don't believe it!"

"You'd better believe it," she answered. "Or you will fall to your death."

"Trust me."

Callen fought Ebed's words with every ounce of logic. There *is* no bridge. You can't walk across a gaping chasm in thin air. It has to be a deception. Yet, there was Jadiel, walking on nothing.

Callen grew aware of the crowd closing in. Fear and shock held them back, but Callen knew if he waited any longer, they would grab him and his chance for freedom would be lost. The boar's words haunted him. *How can a flimsy reed stand firm in the rising floodwaters? By becoming a solid tree, unwavering and firm.* She then had added, with warning in her dark eyes, *If you do not stand firm in the faith, you shall not stand at all.* The very words Ebed had just spoken. She had laughed when he asked if the bridge had been built from the terebinth tree. Why? She said the bridge was built from imperishable materials, at the cost of much blood.

Now he understood why the bridge was invisible. It could only be seen with eyes of faith, for it was not made of wood after all.

A hint of peace and calm settled on his heart, and the fear that had gripped him melted away. Before hands could grab him and pull him from the edge, he took a huge breath and walked out, feeling substance under his boots. As he strode toward Jadiel, who waited for him yards away, the thick mat of clouds parted and a bright warm sun lit up the bridge under his feet. Callen's mouth dropped open in utter awe and his words fled. "Whaa . . ."

Appearing in all its intricate detail and magnificence, the bridge unfolded before and below him. He turned and looked back and saw its spandrels and columns and balustrades and parapets form- ing. Towers stretching to the heavens holding two silver cables spanned from land to land. Callen had never imagined a bridge so huge and spectacular. As he walked the narrow parapet wall, he reveled in the elegant scrolling of the terebinth tree and its boughs of leaves, materializing in the structures around him as if a hidden hand carved out the lines as he stared. Curiously missing, though, were the block letters, the words in the ancient writing. He reached down and touched the wood, smooth and silky to his fingers, and yet warm and pliable. The rich red-brown tones of the wood shone as if oiled and rubbed.

He hurried to Ebed and shook his head. "This is amazing." He looked back at the mob still crowded at the cliff's edge. "Why aren't they following?"

Jadiel answered. "Because they can't see it. And they can't believe their eyes."

Callen ventured a look over the bridge railing. Far below, a ribbon of river snaked through the canyon. His feet froze. He was on an invisible bridge, not made of wood. Made of what? He was standing in the air thousands of feet above that river. One false step and he'd tumble to his death. How can this be happening? This wasn't possible . . .

Suddenly, the bridge began to dissolve beneath his feet. He stared down at his boots in horror as the wood melted away, erasing the parapet on which he stood. Wind whipped at his back and made him wobble.

"Help! Save me!" He started to fall through the spaces opening between his feet, his arms flailing above him.

A hand clasped his. He jerked his head and looked up into Ebed's calm eyes. With little effort, the prophet pulled him up to stand once more on the wooden surface. "Why did you doubt?" Ebed asked. The prophet gently released Callen's hand.

Callen looked down and the bridge reformed into solid wood beneath his feet. His heart pounded in his throat. He didn't know what to say. Suddenly, he felt weak and fearful, doubting himself and all his abilities. Doubting all he ever believed, wondering if the world around him was real or just a fabrication of his mind. Was he losing his mind? His understanding of the world lay shattered before him—tiny broken pieces that could never be reconstructed into anything recognizable. How in the world could he go on?

As he followed his companions in silence, a deep sadness overcame him and he wept, wiping tears as he walked. He was nothing, nothing. All that pride over his meager accomplishments, his boasting over his skills at woodworking, his puny knowledge of such unimportant things. These all glared at him in the harsh light of truth.

He took one more step and touched upon spongy grass. He spun around and looked back to where the frustrated crowd on the other side of the chasm back in Araf'el, the Land of Darkness, dispersed and headed back to their daily routines, steeped in ignorance and denial. The bridge faded, then vanished from sight, leaving only wisps of fog floating over the river on a mild breeze.

Callen's pride lay dashed and broken. For what did all his knowledge and accomplishments—and even his life—amount to? Nothing worth bragging about. He felt so very empty as he let go of everything he had ever held on to. Let each and every worrisome thought and care drift slowly down into the unreachable chasm.

Then he smiled.

Now there was room for something else to fill him, and he felt it rush into his soul like a gushing flow of water filling an empty well.

A flood of peace.

THIRTY-TWO

CALLEN LOOKED up the sparkling lane to the magnificent castle stationed high on the hill. Never in his dreams had he envisioned such splendor. A street made of gold and silver and gems. A palace of gold so expansive it encompassed an entire mountain. A river as bright as crystal running through the center of the lane, and on either side, huge terebinth trees with massive boughs bursting with leaves, leaves that shimmered in the sunlight like diamonds. A surreal light, intense and radiant, lent a glow to everything around him, as if the sun itself poured down liquid gold from the heavens.

He watched as Jadiel plucked leaves from the trees and stuffed them in her satchel. A deep joy filled his heart to overflowing, just seeing Jadiel run about in delight, gathering leaves and chattering with Ebed.

"Jadiel," Ebed said, nodding at the trees. "You understand that only those who cross the bridge can partake of the leaves' healing properties."

Jadiel stopped picking and nodded to Ebed. "I remember. But Huldah sent me on this task, and if I return home empty-handed, she'll kill Papa."

Callen frowned. *And when those leaves don't work? Then what? She'll accuse Jadiel, and take out her anger on the poor girl.*

"Ebed," Callen said, coming up beside the prophet, "is there anything else Jadiel might do, or that I might do, to protect her from her stepmother?"

Jadiel searched Ebed's face, which was longing for a word of hope. After a moment's thought, Ebed said to Jadiel, "Be faithful in your task, and trust that heaven will reward you."

Any other day Callen would have scoffed at the ugly man's words. But now—after crossing that bridge and seeing this unbelievable land, Callen felt his wall of resistance crumble just a little. He had to hand it to this strange prophet—everything he said had come to pass. Was there any reason to doubt him now?

Callen studied Ebed as he stood under one of the towering terebinth trees—the King's Tree, according to Za'ker's ancient books. Callen let his gaze wander over his threadbare tunic, his worn sandals, his bruised and scarred body . . .

In that moment, Ebed turned and caught his look, and a vision came upon Callen as suddenly as a sweeping wind. Glaring sunlight blocked out the surrounding countryside and Callen squinted. He heard Ebed's voice in his head as a scene unraveled that gripped his attention.

"Long ago, there was a wealthy landowner, who had need to travel to a faraway country. So he hired caretakers to tend his vineyard and orchards, men he thought were trustworthy."

Callen watched from a distance as a young man in a long, simple tunic stood on a dais in front of an ornate temple. A pressing throng of angry people yelled and jeered, but Callen couldn't make out their words. Yet, their anger burned. Had the man done something wrong to merit their hate? He watched as two soldiers in shining mail grabbed the man's hands and tied them behind his back with a thick rope.

"At harvesttime, he sent a servant to them, asking for the profits from his estate, but the caretakers beat him badly and sent him away."

The soldiers dragged the unresisting man behind the temple and whipped him with vicious fury, ripping the skin off his back and ignoring the man's cries of pain.

"The landowner heard of this grave news and sent another servant on the same mission, along with a stern warning, but the caretakers laughed and beat this man also."

After they had thoroughly beaten him nearly lifeless, they placed a purple robe across his bloodied shoulders and pressed a crown of thorns on his head. They laughed and mocked him and called him "King" and "Your Highness." The man dropped his head and said nothing.

"Now, word came to the landowner that the ruthless caretakers had beaten his other servant. Well then, he thought, I will send my son; surely they will respect and listen to him."

The soldiers threw the battered man to the hysterical, angry mob that surrounded the temple. In silence, the beaten man allowed the crowd to force him to walk up a hill outside the city, a place where criminals and those dishonored were punished. A place for the disgraced, unworthy, and detested.

"But when the men saw the young man—the landowner's heir—they conspired together, saying, 'This is the heir. Let us kill him; then we can have this place to ourselves and keep all the profits.'"

Callen watched in horror as they took this man and nailed his hands and feet to a stake, then left him in his agony to die a criminal's death. Yet, somehow, Callen knew this man was innocent of all the crimes they had charged him with. A stab of pain and anger ripped through Callen's heart as he glared at the hateful faces of those watching. Why wouldn't anyone save him? How could they do this terrible thing? And why did this man not resist? It didn't make any sense!

Ebed's voice grew quiet in his head. The words of the scroll fell into place, like a key fitting a lock. Ten words, ten branches. Ten words that fell so short of describing what this man had to endure. Callen waited, the minutes moving in agonizing slowness, as the condemned man finally drew his last breath and died. Callen felt his own heart break at the sight. He glanced up at a crude carving someone had gouged into the stake above the man's head. Callen's eyes narrowed, then widened when he recognized the simple geometric pattern he had seen on the vault door when he fit the pieces of that lock in place. A three-pointed star—which was also the symbol stamped on the corner of the bridge parchments.

A crown. *The promise of a crown on the backs of kings.*

Callen recalled the question Ebed posed that day by the bank of the Heresh River. "*What do you think the wealthy landowner did to those men who killed his son?*" He glanced back across the chasm to Araf'el. Now Callen knew.

"There's more to the story. But you weren't ready to hear it then," Ebed said, walking toward him.

"I suppose you're going to tell me—in another one of your puzzling riddles." This time Callen's words were lighthearted and free of accusation.

"No. No more riddles for you, Callen. For you, I now speak plainly."

Jadiel came running down the hill, breathless and radiant. "I have the leaves. We can go home now!"

Ebed rested a hand on Jadiel's head as she held out her satchel stuffed with leaves. "Do you see now how the bridge was built to be destroyed, but since it was made of imperishable material, it could never truly be destroyed?"

Callen nodded. He thought he understood. But the bridge was still a puzzle. Just like his wooden box—there had to be a way to arrange all the pieces into their proper places to open the lock.

Jadiel chuckled and took Ebed's hand in her own small one. "Don't you understand, Callen? The key is in the last word of the scroll—*restored*. The great king restored his heir to life—and set him on that throne, up there." Jadiel pointed to the palace on the hill. The sunlight reflected off the golden walls so brightly he had to shield his eyes.

Any other day, Callen would have said such a feat was impossible. But after crossing that chasm over the invisible bridge, he knew better. There *were* unseen, eternal things in this world, and they certainly appeared to be more substantial than the visible structures around him. Maybe Jadiel was right when she said those invisible things like love and faith and hope endured forever, while the material world around them could crumble away.

Callen's mind swam with so many new ideas and concepts. He needed time to sort through them, but that would have to wait, for he saw Ebed walking down the hill, along the river's edge, leaving the palace and trees behind and holding Jadiel's hand. He hurried after them.

"Ebed, when will the promised one take the throne and wake the sleeping kings?" Jadiel asked.

"The vision is yet for the appointed time. But, if it seems to tarry, wait for it, for it will surely come."

Callen followed them down the grassy slope to a narrow pass squeezed between two huge crags.

Ebed stopped and turned. "Follow this trail and it will lead you to the north edge of the prairie. From there you will find your way home."

Jadiel surprised Callen by throwing her arms around Ebed and crying. "I wish you were coming with us. I'm scared."

"Do not fear, Jadiel. Be brave and go save your father." Ebed pulled back and looked in her eyes. "And, one day, I will see you again. Here, in this kingdom."

Ebed turned to Callen. "A wise prophet once said, 'A shoot shall come out from the stump, and a branch shall grow out of his roots. The spirit of the High One shall rest on him, the spirit of wisdom and understanding, the spirit of counsel and might, and with righteousness he will judge the poor and with equity the meek of the earth, and his dwelling shall be glorious.'"

In his mind's eye, Callen saw the stump, sitting atop the hill in the King's Plain. He took one last look up the hill, now behind him. The palace shimmered like an apparition in the brilliant mid-day sun. Yes, it was truly glorious. A longing grew wildly in him, like the sprout that had emerged from the stump that day, twisting in desperation toward the light. He wished to stay, for this place called to his heart, but he knew he must help Jadiel and return to his life back in Kettlebro.

With a sigh, he wrenched his gaze away and took Jadiel's hand. Ebed kissed Jadiel on the cheek as the little hawk dipped its head toward him. The prophet stroked the bird and turned to Callen.

The words of the boar came to Callen's mind. *The holy seed is its stump.* Callen chuckled. The meaning was now so obvious. He grinned and shook his head, humbled and awed.

Ebed took Callen's hands in his own scarred ones. "Well, you found your bridge. Now that you see, do you believe? Happy are those who do not see, yet believe."

With those words, Ebed turned and walked up the hill toward the palace. Callen and Jadiel watched until the hobbling prophet reached the massive marble steps. Then Callen adjusted his pack on his back and walked through the crags, with Jadiel following close behind.

THIRTY-THREE

DAWN CAST a pink streak on the horizon as Jadiel forced open her eyes and looked out from under her cloak. The carriage's jostling startled her awake, and she threw the cloak off her head, smelling snow.

"Well, looks like the lass is up. Almost at Northvale now." The grizzled driver pointed at the hills above the Logan Valley. "Snow. A bit early this year, wouldn't you say?"

Jadiel caught a whiff of something delicious. She looked behind her and Callen was sitting up, munching on a chunk of steaming bread.

"Nice to get a lift from a baker, isn't it? Here." He ripped off a piece of the moist dark bread and handed it to Jadiel. She gobbled it down and realized she was starving. During the last two days of trekking, they had finished off all that remained in their packs. Jadiel was tired of nuts and moldy cheese. She had walked with great anticipation last night as they neared Wheatsheaf, thinking of hot stew and chocolate pastries. But just before the village came into sight, this baker had stopped and offered them a ride to Northvale. Her stomach would just have to wait for that big hearty meal.

"Well, my last delivery's not more than a tick from your manor. I'll drop you both there, if you don't have a care."

"That's perfect," Callen said. "We're grateful."

Cold air bit Jadiel's cheeks as they climbed down from the carriage and walked the road north. Fat flakes of snow drifted onto her eyelashes and cheeks. The little hawk buried itself under her hair. A wave of homesickness welled in her heart, seeing her neighboring farms and knowing her own home was just around the next corner. She felt she had been away years, not weeks. But fear rushed in on top of that longing for home. For who knew what awaited her there? Was her father safe? Had Huldah already killed him? She dreaded finding the answers.

Jadiel steeled her nerve. She would just have to walk in and find out.

When they arrived at the wide wooden gate to her drive, Callen stopped her with his hand. "Jadiel, it may not be safe to march in. Maybe we should sneak over someplace safe and take a look."

She nodded. "Let's go around the orchard to the carriage house. We'll be able to see the manor from there."

Callen opened the gate and Jadiel led the way. She pulled her cloak tighter around her chilled neck. When they got to the far side of the carriage house, they dropped down and looked out over the fields.

Jadiel's countenance fell in shock. "Oh, Callen. Something's very wrong. Look at the furrows! They're overgrown, and no one is here. What if Huldah's killed all the workers?"

Callen laid his hand on Jadiel's wrist. "Stay calm, Jadiel. We'll suss this out."

"Where's Azar? He should be in the carriage house." Jadiel jumped up and ran inside. Her papa's carriage sat gathering dust. The sight twisted her stomach in a knot. The hawk lifted off her shoulder and flew to the small door in the back of the building. Jadiel ran off and knocked, then tried the latch. The door swung open to an empty, disheveled room.

"That's not like Azar to leave such a mess." Clearly, someone had been through his things, which meant he was no longer around.

The hawk now squawked at Jadiel as if trying to tell her something. Somehow, it had regained its voice, and seemed to have something urgent to say.

Jadiel returned to Callen.

"There's trouble here," Callen said. "Perhaps your father's inside. Maybe we should leave and head for Kettlebro—and get Beren."

"No, Callen. Last night was the full moon, and it's setting now. We have no more time. I have to give Huldah the leaves before it's too late."

Callen sighed and nodded. "As you wish. But I'll be right by your side."

Jadiel let the satchel drop from her back. The strong smell of fennel seeped out from the pile of leaves. She carried the bundle in her hands as she approached the front door. As she made to press the latch, the hawk flew into her face and batted her with its wings.

Jadiel shrieked and waved her arms. "What are you doing?" she cried. "Stop it!"

Callen waved his arms too, but the bird kept at her, flying back and forth between Jadiel and the door, screeching and nipping at her and creating a commotion.

The front door flew open.

The sight struck her like a blow to the face. There stood Huldah, ugly and fat, her gray hair wild and flapping against her hideous wrinkled face. Jadiel almost didn't recognize her.

"So the brat has returned!" Huldah put her hands on her hips and eyed the hawk. A sickening smile pushed up her saggy cheeks. "And you've brought a little companion. How nice."

Callen swatted at the hawk, which still flapped and screeched and dove at Jadiel. "She brought you the leaves," he said. "Now, where's Ka'rel?"

"And who might this young fellow be? Your champion and rescuer?" Huldah's voice grated on Jadiel's ears. Gone was her stepmother's soothing, lilting tone. "Leave!" she ordered, pointing a gnarled finger in Callen's face.

"Not until you show us Ka'rel."

"Fine," she said, gesturing them into the hallway. "Just step inside and I'll go get him."

The hawk again flapped wings in Jadiel's face and pecked at her head. "Callen! Get this thing off me!"

Huldah laughed, and her chortling shook the walls. Then her eyes narrowed in impatience. "Give me those leaves—now!"

Jadiel struck the hawk with her arm, and she gasped as it crashed into the threshold of the door. She took a step inside and heard a pitiful screech behind her. The hawk fell in a thud on the top step and died.

Huldah laughed even louder. She grabbed the satchel out of Jadiel's hands and opened the flap. "The leaves! You found them!"

Jadiel knew she should warn her stepmother that the leaves wouldn't make her young and beautiful, but she knew Huldah would never listen. She would just have to chew them and find out—and then Jadiel would be in bigger trouble. Oh, where was Papa?

She glanced over at the little hawk lying still on the stone. It must have hit its head hard on the wall when she pushed it away. A pang of guilt and sorrow ate at her gut. But why had it railed at her so? Its behavior made no sense.

Callen pulled Jadiel into his arms as Huldah stuffed leaves into her mouth. Jadiel yelled at her. "Where's Papa? You promised to get him."

Huldah stopped chewing and spoke with a stuffed mouth. "Why, little brat, he's over *there*." She pointed at the hawk, and Jadiel frowned.

"I don't under . . ."

In an instant, the body of the hawk shook and rattled, then transformed before her eyes into the shape of a man. Jadiel nearly swooned.

She struggled out of Callen's arms and fell to her papa's side. "Oh no! Papa! Callen, he's dead!" She spun around and lunged at Huldah, but Huldah knocked her to the ground. She scrambled to her knees. "What did you do? You killed him!"

Huldah laughed so hard that tears squeezed out her eyes. She chewed and gagged on the leaves, trying to clear her throat. The words puffed out between gasps. "He . . . He made a nice hawk, didn't he . . . couldn't have him run after you now, could I?"

Jadiel made to lunge again but stopped suddenly and stared at Huldah's face as it turned a shade of blue. Huldah reached for her throat and scratched at it, gasping for air. "He was destined to die . . . when you walked . . . through door . . ."

Tears poured down Jadiel's face as she looked back at her father. *Oh, Papa, I never could have saved you after all.* She turned to Huldah, wanting to wring the old witch's neck. But when she caught the frozen expression of terror in her stepmother's face, she knew she needn't bother. Huldah stiffened and fell backward as her eyes rolled into her head. Her bulging and wrinkled body lay lifeless on the ground.

Callen whistled and put his hand on Jadiel's shoulder. "I'm so sorry about your father. That hawk—he was your father. That means the whole time we traveled . . ."

Jadiel turned away from the disgusting sight of Huldah's sprawled body. She knelt beside her papa and stroked his soft hair. "You were trying to keep me from stepping inside," she whispered, her words lodged in her throat. "I wish I had understood you. I'm so sorry. Oh, Papa . . ."

Callen startled and grabbed Jadiel's shoulder. "Jadiel, the hawk—it crossed the bridge, didn't it?"

Jadiel looked up at him. What was he trying to say?

"I remember. He perched on your shoulder, then flew around a bit. But he did cross over, right?"

Suddenly, understanding came over her. "Ebed said the leaves would heal—but only those who crossed the bridge!"

Callen reached into the satchel that lay on the stone floor at Huldah's feet. He handed some of the terebinth tree leaves to Jadiel.

"But Callen, he's dead. He can't chew these."

"You can," he said, nodding at her hand.

Jadiel stuffed the leaves in her mouth and chewed hard. After a minute they wadded into a paste tasting of licorice and lemon. Her heart pounded so hard she thought it would break in her chest.

She took the pasty lump out and opened her papa's mouth. Carefully, she placed the wad of leaves on his tongue and waited. *Oh, Ebed, help me!*

The entry hall grew silent as a tomb, but Jadiel heard sounds down the road, the jingling of breeching and wheels turning. Someone was coming.

Callen knelt beside Jadiel and took her hand. Together they waited and watched and hoped.

Jadiel startled as Ka'rel's eyelids fluttered. "Callen, look!" She put her hands on her papa's cool cheeks and watched color come back into the flesh. "Oh, Papa, please live!"

Callen gripped Jadiel's shoulder. "He's alive. He is!"

Just then, footsteps bounded up the stone stairs of the manor. "Jadiel! Are you here?"

Jadiel turned to see Aunt Laera and Uncle Beren rush into the hall. They halted abruptly at the sight of Ka'rel on the ground, then looked across the threshold. Other people Jadiel didn't recognize came up behind them, mumbling at the sight of Ka'rel lying sprawled.

"Heavens!" Laera cried. "Is that Huldah?"

Beren rushed to Jadiel's side as Ka'rel fluttered and opened his eyes.

"Now here's a sight," Beren said in his gruff voice. "The witch is dead, is she?" He narrowed his eyes at the lifeless body.

Ka'rel struggled to sit upright, with Jadiel supporting his back. She wrapped her arms around him and felt warmth and life emanate from him. "Oh, Papa, you're safe."

Ka'rel pulled back and searched his daughter's eyes. "Jadiel, you saved me. Will you ever forgive me? I was so wrong . . ."

"Hush, Papa, everything's okay now. We're home."

Laera rushed over and gave Jadiel a crushing hug. Beren patted Callen on the back. "We got your letter, lad. Sorry we arrived a bit late, by the looks of things. I imagine you have quite the tale to tell, venturing into the Land of Darkness, and all." Beren's eyebrows raised in wonder. "Is there truly such a land?"

Callen nodded. "There is. But the telling will be a long one."

Laera pulled Jadiel back into her arms and rocked her, her face beaming with happiness. "Well, we have all day. And I'm not budging until I hear the whole tale."

Ka'rel stood on shaky legs and stretched out his arms. "Oh, that feels so good, but I'm a bit wobbly on my feet."

Jadiel laughed. "But, Papa, how fun it must have been to fly!"

"Fly?" Beren said. "Now I know there's a long tale to be told." He gave Laera a nod toward the kitchen. "Maybe we should make some breakfast for this bunch."

Ka'rel walked over to Huldah's body. The room grew still as they all stared at the creature who had once been Ka'rel's beautiful wife.

Jadiel pointed. "Papa, look at her feet."

All eyes peered at what was left of Huldah's toes. They lay crumbled to dust on the smooth tile floor. As Jadiel stared longer, the rest of Huldah's legs turned to powder, followed by her hips and torso, and finally her head. Even her hair disintegrated into silver dust.

"Who knows how old that witch really was? Now she's caught up with her age," Laera said, shaking her head.

More footsteps came running up the steps. Heads swung around as Kinnah and Ramah, dressed in outrageous gowns and sporting jeweled shoes on their feet, nearly crashed into each other in the doorway. The two girls gasped at the sight of their mother turned to a mound of powder, and screamed. Without a word, they fled down the steps and out the drive.

"I think we've seen the last of those two, lass," Beren said, ruffling Jadiel's hair.

"Come," Laera said to Beren, "Let's make breakfast for these hungry travelers. And then they can tell their tale with full stomachs!"

Laera pulled on Beren's shirt and dragged him into the kitchen. "Woman, stop yanking on my shirt. You'll rip it, you will!"

Jadiel laughed and hugged her father. Now that she had him in her arms, she wanted never to let him go.

Ka'rel pulled back and rubbed his right arm. He caught Callen's concerned glance.

"It's still sore, where the arrow went in. But it will heal properly in time."

Jadiel wagged a finger at Callen. "I'm glad you're a poor shot. A little to the right and that arrow would have pierced his heart."

Callen smiled and shrugged. "Maybe I'll sell that bow and stick to wood carving."

"Good idea," Jadiel said—and meant it. She took Callen's hand along with her father's and led them both into the dining room. "Now—let's eat!"

Ka'rel stopped at the dining room entry and looked up and down the hall in confusion.

He turned to Jadiel. "Where did all the furniture go?"

THIRTY-FOUR

"JADIEL, look who's come!"

Jadiel peeked up from her pile of weeds and saw Callen's curly head bobbing her way. Behind him, her aunt and uncle waved, walking carefully over the muddy furrows. Yesterday's rain had left the fields soggy, but Jadiel had on her muck boots and didn't care if mud covered her from head to toe. She was with Papa, and nothing would dampen her spirits.

Already, in just the one week, they had cleared out the two lower fields and even found time to ride to the spring. Snarl, her mare, took her saddle without complaint, and Jadiel was thrilled when her papa told her the horse was hers to keep. Now they could ride together, side by side, over the fields and around the villages. Word spread as fast as wildfire, and by midweek, many of her father's workers had returned, happy to help bring the estate to order under Ka'rel's management. Even her beloved cook rushed back into the kitchen, eager to stuff Jadiel and her papa full of food. Oh, the horror stories they told about Huldah. And her papa still reeled over Azar's death. They held little doubt of Huldah's culpability in the poor caretaker's sudden demise.

Her wicked stepmother had sold all that was valuable in the manor, but Jadiel produced the pouch of gold coins, which was more than enough to replace the losses and buy seed for the winter and spring crops.

Callen came to Jadiel and hugged her.

"I'm surprised to see you so soon," she said. "Aren't you back at work in the shop?"

Callen nodded. "I missed you. When Laera told me they were paying a visit, I had to come. You look well—and happy."

She laughed heartily. "I am."

Ka'rel lifted his pitchfork laden with sodden weeds and dumped the mess into the cart parked next to his daughter. He took off his muddy gloves and offered his hand to Callen.

"I didn't thank you enough for what you did. Saving Jadiel from those men, and watching after her, helping her find her way." Jadiel noticed her papa's eyes glistened with tears.

Callen smirked. "She wasn't the easiest of charges. Took a lot of looking after." He punched her arm playfully.

Jadiel punched back, but harder. "Ow!" he said.

"And *you* took even more looking after—shooting everything in sight and dragging me into dangerous places."

"And, Laera," Ka'rel said, giving her a hug, "I should have listened to you and not sent you away. If only I had—"

Beren raised a hand in the air. "Hindsight's always better than foresight. Besides, the witch had you flummoxed. Who could resist those spells of hers?"

Laera chuckled and pinched Beren's ear. "Well, you certainly didn't. In under five minutes, she had you wrapped around her little finger . . ."

"Did not!"

Laera rolled her eyes and Jadiel laughed. "I brought you something, sweetheart." She held out her hand and led Jadiel over to the cart. Jadiel jumped on the flatbed as Laera handed her a wrapped package. Jadiel wiped her grimy hands on her work trousers and opened the pink wrapping.

"Oh, Aunt Laera, it's beautiful!" She turned the silver hand mirror over and looked at the tiny painted flowers trailing the mirror's rim. Her aunt had heard the tale of her mirror shattering.

Laera reached into a pocket of her sweater and pulled out a matching comb. "Now, let's neaten you up," she said, laying a hand on Jadiel's head and running the comb through the thick black hair. Jadiel held the mirror and watched her aunt work out the tangles. Tears came to her eyes as she recalled the last time her mama had done this.

No images formed in this glass—no shimmers, no fancies, no evil smells. All Jadiel saw was the reflection of a twelve-year-old girl who looked a whole lot older and wiser than the last time she peered in a mirror.

Laera crooned, "Mirror, mirror in my hand, who's the fairest in the land?"

Jadiel turned and questioned her aunt with her eyes. Laera shrugged. "Just a little rhyme your mother and I would recite when we were girls. We always fought over who was prettiest." Laera handed Jadiel the comb. "Silly, now that I think of it."

Jadiel was reminded of Huldah and her big mirror. Papa didn't want to sell it at market, saying it was cursed. And when they tried to break it to pieces, nothing would shatter it. They ended up burying it in a sewage sump at the far end of the estate where it would trouble them no more.

Beren wrapped his arms around Laera. "You'll always be the most beautiful lass in the land, in my estimation."

Laera kissed him on the cheek. "Even when I'm old and wrinkled and ugly—like Huldah?"

Beren laughed. "You'll never look that way to me. Beauty's in the eye of the beholder, folks say."

Jadiel thought of Ebed and how Callen had been so repulsed by his appearance. *Beauty's only skin deep.* Her heart warmed thinking of Ebed. She knew what lay under his disguise. And why he carried that disguise. You had to take the time to look past those outer layers, to get to the true person underneath. You had to care enough to look. And use the eyes of your heart, to see the things unseen.

Jadiel smiled. Far away, where the mountaintops scraped the heavens, a bridge spanned a wide, gaping chasm, linking a dark, hopeless world with an eternal one full of hope and joy. A king would one day rule, and those asleep in the ground would arise. Jadiel would rejoice to see her mama again and live in that kingdom. She longed for it with every bit of her heart. But, for now, she was more than content to stay here, on this little patch of earth, with her papa, her aunt and uncle, Callen, and so many she loved, knowing the bridge awaited them. Awaited all with the eyes of faith to see it.

Callen felt a tap on his shoulder and lifted his pencil from the block of cherrywood clamped to his table.

"Beren told us tales at lunch yesterday. Did you really find the bridge?" Eliab leaned over the worktable to examine Callen's sketch. His curls bobbed in Callen's face.

Callen scooted his stool back and studied the youth's face. "I did."

Eliab exhaled and his eyes widened. Dariel, the redheaded boy, came over from his bench. A sudden hush fell over the shop as heads turned to listen. Callen waved a hand in the air.

"I'm sure Beren gave a good tale. You know how he likes to, uh, embellish."

Eliab and Dariel huddled closer, hemming Callen in. "Oh, come on, tell us," Dariel begged. "Was the bridge really invisible?

And is there really a land of darkness, where people wander forever and never get out?"

Callen looked into the boys' excited eyes. They were always eager for a wild story.

"Please, Callen, tell us!" another boy shouted from across the room.

Callen looked at the young faces, so eager and open. Only weeks ago he thought of these apprentices as naïve and full of silly dreams. He thought he was so much older and wiser than they. What did he know? Now a fondness and warmth welled in his heart for them. They were naïve and trusting—true. But they also yearned to learn and were easy to teach. Not stubborn and head-strong as he often was.

He recalled Ebed's patience with a stab of guilt. All those many times Callen had chided and criticized the prophet. Yet, Ebed had responded to his taunts and jeers with kindness and forgiveness. Ebed had taught him humility and compassion by example. Callen only hoped someday to be more like him. It would take some effort; that was for certain.

Callen looked back into a room of eager, waiting faces. He smiled, cleared his throat, and in a soft voice, began.

"Long ago, there was a wealthy landowner, who had need to travel to a faraway country . . ."

THE END

Acknowledgments

A writer's journey is often beset with trials and disappointment. Often we writers must traverse our own "land of darkness" to arrive in the place where we can bask in the warmth of God's light. We sometimes lose our way, and lose heart when gloom descends and hope is nowhere to be found. I certainly am no exception. Yet, wonderful people are put on our path to help guide the way, sometimes carrying a small lamp to shine on the narrow road a few steps ahead. Other times these friends just hold our hand, let us cry on a shoulder, and strengthen us with a few kind words of encouragement. I could fill pages with the names of friends who have walked alongside me in this manner, and although I can't list them all, I am truly grateful to each and every one.

My deepest gratitude to AMG publishers—Rick, John, Dale, and Trevor—for such wonderful support, prayers, kindness, and letting me express myself through my writing and set my creativity loose without hindrance. Every writer should be so blessed to have such a supportive team. And I am truly appreciative of my agent, Susan Schulman, for working tirelessly on my behalf and expecting nothing short of excellence in all I write.

A special thanks to my friends who read, critique, counsel, advise, pray, laugh, and cry with me: Ann Miller, Renae Brumbaugh, Kathy Ide, Cathy Leggitt, Sandi Greene, Jeanette Morris, Pam Walls, MaryLu Tyndall, Helen Bratko, Pola Muzyka, Meg Moseley, Linda Clare, Jim Bell, Barbara Majchrzak, and my author friends in my writers' groups in Santa Cruz and San Jose.

I couldn't write without the support and encouragement of my husband, who works so hard to provide the time for me to write—I love you, Leebears! And thanks to my beautiful daughters, Megan and Amara, for so many great ideas, tough critiques, and bunches of love. Above all, my heart spills over in gratitude for my King and Savior, who has delivered us out of darkness into his marvelous light. To him be the glory forever and ever.

DISCUSSION OF
THE LAND OF DARKNESS

THE GATES of Heaven collection of fairy tales draws from Scripture, to help readers experience the power of God's Word and come to know our wonderful God of hope and integrity. *The Land of Darkness* is rich in allegory, some quite obvious and in other places, not so apparent. I started with the idea of a bridge, and of Jesus as that bridge, as the only way for humans to cross over from the curse of sin and death to immortal life. Other famous books like *Pilgrim's Progress* (John Bunyan—which, by the way, is *the* best selling novel in history!) and C. S. Lewis's response to that book, *Pilgrim's Regress*, use the allegory of a wide, uncrossable chasm to show how impossibly separated we are from God and his holiness.

Many scriptural themes grew from that idea. Most important were the ones regarding the need for faith. Callen represents the doubter in all of us, for it does take eyes of faith to believe, not only in God but in his means for salvation. We have to step out in faith, into thin air as it were, to let God reveal himself to us. Of course, this book is meant to be a fun, exciting adventure, so as Callen and Jadiel search for the bridge and the Eternal Tree, they have to solve many clues and work their way through the many contradictory stories and even outright lies to arrive at the truth and find what they seek.

So much wisdom spills from the pages of the Bible that I seek, in this fantasy series, to draw from verses that not only move powerfully within my own heart, but also from those that lend themselves to the story being told. Clearly, many of the Scriptures used in this tale are not closely following the actual contextual meanings as presented in the Bible. I have taken liberties to apply these Scriptures to a make-believe story, but my intention is not to corrupt or alter the divinely directed meaning of these verses but to use them with respect to the spirit and idea they represent. All Scripture ultimately points to God's purpose in his chosen one, the Messiah, Jesus Christ. That is also my intent. Here, then, are some of the Scriptures used in *The Land of Darkness*, and some questions for discussion:

1) Obviously, darkness is a big theme in this story as it is in the Bible. Jesus is spoken of as the "light of the world" that has come into the darkness (John 1:5) and Jesus, in turn, called his followers light of the world (Matt. 5:14). How does the Land of Darkness represent the darkness of our world in a spiritual sense, and what are some of the Scriptures used to compare it? What does Ebed tell Callen and Jadiel to do in order to see in the darkness?

2) What is the significance of the bridge, and why does the boar laugh when Callen asks if the bridge is made of wood from the terebinth tree? What are some of the falsehoods told about the bridge, and what do Callen and Jadiel learn to be the truth? (see 1 Peter 1:18–19). Why does Ebed say the bridge was built to be destroyed?

3) The boar tells Callen and Jadiel that the answer they seek is on a scroll in Ethryn—ten words, ten branches. Discuss how the ten words apply to the "bridge" as foretold in Isaiah chapters 52 and 53 of the suffering servant.

4) Why are there drawings of the terebinth tree on the bridge? Ebed recites the parable in Luke 13 of the tiny mustard seed that becomes a great tree with birds nesting in its branches. And the boar recites from Ezekiel 17 about the twig that the Most High will plant and that will grow into a lofty tree over all the other trees. Based on this symbolism, how are the bridge and the tree connected?

5) Jadiel is sent to seek the leaves of the Eternal Tree. How do the leaves foretell and show the fulfillment of Rev. 22:2? Why do they have to cross the bridge to receive the benefits of the leaves' healing properties, and why does Huldah die when she takes and chews them?

6) The king-priest of Antolae is an important figure in the book. He represents the foreshadowing person of Melchizedek in the Bible, the only king-priest mentioned, and who prefigures Christ (Gen. 14:17–20; Heb. 6:20–7:10; Psalm 110:4). In what ways is this king-priest similar to Christ?

7) Callen accidently releases the evil one from his imprisonment. Second Peter 2:4 speaks of the angels that sinned in Noah's day that are held in chains and reserved for judgment. How does this one's attitude parallel that of the rebel angels in the Bible, and how does Ebed deal with him?

8) The boar speaks of those who will receive a stone, a name, a pillar, and a star if they cross the bridge. Look in Revelation and see if you can find where Jesus speaks of these rewards given to his faithful ones.

9) Ebed means "servant" in Hebrew. How is he portrayed as a faithful servant, and why does he appear to Jadiel and Callen as a scarred and repulsive man? (Review Isaiah chapters 52 and 53.)

10) The theme of beauty is woven throughout the story. Huldah is obsessed with it, yet Jadiel, who is naturally beautiful, realizes that true beauty is within. How does this attitude help Jadiel see past Ebed's ugliness to his true beauty beneath? How are the elements from the classic fairy tale "Snow White" shown in the story of Jadiel, her wicked stepmother, and the use of mirrors in the novel?

11) As Callen is crossing the bridge, he starts to doubt and begins falling. How is this similar to Peter in Matt. 14:28–31? Ebed asks Callen, "Why did you doubt?" Why does Callen doubt?

12) At one point Ebed tells Jadiel and Callen, "Now you are ready to cross the bridge." He could have taken them straight across, but he allowed certain things to happen first in order for them to be ready. What experiences and problems did the two have to face before Ebed says those words?

13) Callen wonders what the people in the Land of Darkness did to deserve their punishment. He claims they are not unlike him; that they shouldn't have to live under the curse of darkness because they are good people. How does that compare with people today who say being a good person is all that's required to merit God's favor? Is being a good person good enough to be removed from the "curse" humanity is under? (See Genesis 3:17; Revelation 22:3.)

Some additional meanings of words in the *law'az,* the ancient language of the realm (from biblical Hebrew):

Ebed: servant
Huldah: weasel
Ramah: deceive, betray
Kinnah: jealous
Elon: oak
Za'ker: book
Azar: helper
Shamma: desolation
Araf'el: heavy, thick darkness
Jadiel: may God cause to rejoice
Law'az: ancient language

SCRIPTURAL REFERENCES
IN *THE LAND OF DARKNESS*:
(Taken from the New Revised Standard Version
unless otherwise noted)

Job 14:7–9 "For there is a hope for the tree, if it is cut down, that it will sprout again, and that its shoots will not cease. Though its root grows old in the earth, and its stump dies in the ground, yet, at the scent of water it will bud and put forth branches like a young plant."

Job 18:17–20 "Their memory perishes from the earth, and they have no name in the street. They are thrust from light into darkness, and driven out of the world. They have no offspring or descendent among their people, and no survivor where they used to live. They of the west are appalled at their fate, and horror seizes those of the east."

Psalm 2:1–2 "Why do the nations conspire, and the people plot in vain? The kings of the earth set themselves, and the rulers take counsel together, against the Lord and his anointed."

Psalm 78:2–3 "I will open my mouth in a parable; I will utter dark sayings from of old, things that we have heard and known, that our ancestors have told us."

Proverbs 4:19 "The way of the wicked is like deep darkness; they do not know what they stumble over."

Isaiah 5:20 (NKJV) "Woe to those who . . . put darkness for light."

Isaiah 6:10 "Make the mind of this people dull, and stop up their ears, and shut their eyes, so that they may not look with their eyes, and listen with their ears, and comprehend with their minds, and turn and be healed."

Isaiah 6:13 "The holy seed is its stump."

Isaiah 7:9 "If you do not stand firm in the faith, you shall not stand at all."

Isaiah 8:22 "They . . . will see only distress and darkness, the gloom of anguish; and they will be thrust into thick darkness."

Isaiah 9:2 "The people who walked in darkness have seen a great light; those who lived in a land of deep darkness—on them light has shined."

Isaiah 11:1–4, 10 "A shoot shall come out from the stump . . . and a branch shall grow out of his roots. The spirit of the Lord shall rest on him, the spirit of wisdom and understanding, the spirit of counsel and might . . . with righteousness he shall judge the poor, and decide with equity for the meek of the earth . . . and his dwelling shall be glorious."

Isaiah 32:8 "Those who are noble plan noble things, and by noble things they stand."

Isaiah 59:9–10 (NKJV) "We look for light, but there is darkness! For brightness, but we walk in blackness. We grope for the wall like the blind, And we grope as if we had no eyes; We stumble at noonday as at twilight; We are as dead men in desolate places."

Ezekiel 17:22–24 "Thus says the Lord God: I myself will take a sprig from the lofty top of a cedar; I will set it out. I will break off a tender one from the topmost of its young twigs; I myself will plant it on a high and lofty mountain. . . . Under it every kind of bird will live; in the shade of its branches will nest winged creatures of every kind. All the trees of the field shall know that I am the Lord. I bring low the high tree, I make high the low tree; I dry up the green tree and make the dry tree flourish."

Habakkuk 2:3 "There is still a vision for the appointed time; it speaks of the end and does not lie. If it seems to tarry, wait for it; it will surely come, it will not delay."

Matthew 6:22 "If your eye is healthy, your whole body will be full of light; but if your eye is unhealthy, your whole body will be full of darkness."

John 3:19–21 "People loved darkness rather than light because their deeds were evil. For all who do evil hate the light and do not come to the light, so that their deeds may not be exposed. But those who do what is true come to the light."

John 20:29 "Have you believed because you have seen me? Blessed are those who have not seen and yet have come to believe."

2 Corinthians 4:18 (NKJV) "The things which are seen are temporary, but the things which are not seen are eternal."

Revelation 22:2 "And the leaves of the tree are for the healing of the nations."

Parables told: The Parable of the Wicked Tenants: Mark 12:1–9
The Parable of the Mustard Seed: Luke 13:18–19